WORKBOOK PRESS LLC
187 E Warm Springs Rd,
Suite B285, Las Vegas, NV 89119, USA

Website: https://workbookpress.com/
Hotline: 1-888-818-4856
Email: admin@workbookpress.com

Ordering Information:
Quantity sales. Special discounts are available on quantity purchases by corporations, associations, and others.
For details, contact the publisher at the address above.

Library of Congress Control Number:
ISBN-13:   978-1-956876-45-1 (Paperback Version)
                    978-1-956876-46-8 (Digital Version)

REV. DATE: 23/03/2022

HARD-LUCK STORY

DEAN CHOLLETTE

authorHOUSE®

PROLOGUE

It was September 13 2004. The sea side districts were completely dislocated looking like a big beach sand and Rocks, Boulders was thrown miles in land. Concrete building were destroyed like paper not one was left untouched. Hurricane standard homes went down and on the other hand old lumber shacks 80 to 120 years old were left standing, at the mercy of god. Many took refuge in some of these old Caymanian homes and would live to tell the tale. Old wooden siding and zinc roof cottages stood. Some looking as only the paint was keeping them together. Some facing east others south and super structures all around them wobbled and fell. The Island was a hazard zone Ivan had turned Cayman upside down and into a sad situation. Light poles were down streets uprooted, grave yards were under ocean and the dead and buried afloat. Trees broke apart limb by limb and were brought down. Tops blew off animals and coffins were never found. Sea creatures were found in what was left of people living rooms. Dry land had become ocean, and blue water black. Cars homes storage containers had run aground. Yachts were found on house tops and inside buildings. God had sent this trumpet but it made little differences many still continued to do evil. They moved forward for material ways. There had been a national day of prayer and Rastafarians were allowed to burn herb freely as a symbol of peace and love and thanks given. Ivan had hit us from the southeast but destruction was pretty much the same all around. This thing had bust us in two Sam, with all this abomination going on in the island Sam trust me it was just a matter of time before god shown us who was in charged. This wasn't no 'pong pong' hurricane the island was under 75% salt water. Low laying areas saw as little as 25 feet of flood. Building that were left standing were saltwater contaminated and ruined somewhat. Hardware stores restaurants supermarkets suffered huge loss. Some water wells and cisterns survived, food was at shortage. Public water pipe lines were damage. The utility company lost two of their major generators not to mention the building was totally unusable. Likewise government buildings were in the same state, the air port was under water. Hurricane shelters were damage people terrified to death. Bank building dropped down volts and safe were discovered. Vegetation suffered and anything that was green a few days afterwards became brown or red. Couple breadfruit and mango trees made it all the same. Damages were in the billions, people drowned or was buried alive when building and home crumbled. Days after the rain stop there was a dengue outbreak in one area a barroom and a church were the only two building left standing. A preacher held the bible one hand and a bottle in the other. Ocean front property became just ocean. Cliff had sand and swamp had boulders. People were living in anything with four walls and fasten together some kind of habitat as temporary shelter. Hurricane experts had said Ivan was the worst hurricane of the century at the time. 208 miles per hour of fury had play with us, tornadoes title waves went through and over Grand Cayman. The Cayman island people would consider themselves lucky. Within days the runway dried out and was cleared, relief aid came promptly and two British warships were in the George Town harbor. Not only did Ivan bring out love but it also showed up the worst in people. The price of a small bottle

Coca Cola had reaches 5 dollars. There were more con artist and rip off experts than ever. All that was spoken in the early days became reality, not to my heart contentment. I left the wicked in his ways the more I looked at life I became depress, confused angry and loving. He that understands and carry on is the strongest of all. If tomorrow never comes so be it, Love as much as possible and complete as must as you can.

The more things change the more they stay the same. The circle keeps getting bigger and bigger wickedness had become contagious. And for those who wasn't affected yet hopefully it's not too late for them. By 2004 I had saw almost a decade of unemployment, No gainful or lawful or steady employment whatsoever I was cursed. I had been deprived but I had forgiven. I was proud of who I was and my accomplishments. The island the people was the way it was meant and intended to be. Everything was according to god, the birds were free.

As the morning sunlight began to shine its glory upon the earth and begin to devourer the dawn. There he sat on the front steps of his little cottage, if one can call it that. Another sleepless night. Who could sleep given the circumstance? Hurricane Ivan had just pass by only day ago the little place was still livable thank god but it had been wreck up. He moved away years ago to a piece of land up in the bush out of the city. There he sat looking out into the swamp and black mangrove trees that surrounded him. Even here there is an abundance of life, the parrots were in pairs the birds and ducks seemed happy as they went about their morning duties. Lizards and insects wondered in the bushes in survival mode. Some looking for pray others would become it. Yes even the sand flies and bullfrogs seemed to be contented as they took advantage of the damp mud, that the morning drizzle rain had soften and brought forth. Even Caymanian bush sake could be seen dodging in the rubble debris of hurricane Ivan. It was an attractive little house, He loved it there. Now it was only tarpaper to what was left of the walls they rest would be used as Ivan recycled materials. The east wind was picking up he noticed as he wiped his heavy eye sockets from lack of sleep and the burning tinkle of the morning sunlight on them. The place had served him well even the suffering if you can call it that. As he put together his thought he remember what had brought Cayman to this state. Dead bound with disease ignorant and lack of strength. As a cage for every bird that fly's high. Then he remember it the angel that had spoken these words and by no means did he forgot them. Looking back in time now one can only say Cayman was truly blessed.

By the 70's Caymanian sea men were home for good most of them any way for better or worst. Putting their hard made money to use. Some bought land for cattle and farming, to build homes apartment's supermarkets stores of all kinds etc. Trade work and labor in general was in demand. And heavy equipment operators, masons, mechanics, carpenters, plumbers and electricians along with many others would play a role in further developing the island. Second class jobs as these became number one priority for most able body men and helped power that train up that mountain of success. Consumer item became of a necessity with the men being at home now too. Cars for those who could afford them, 20 years later every house whole would have at least three or more per family. Some went abroad for an education others thought themselves. Tourism was beginning to boom taxi gift shops restaurants etc were needed; Night clubs bars hotels as well. Rental car business insurance companies were growing. Stay over tourism was happening; D C 7's were the air liners of the day. Decade's later people would come from all over to see this piece of rock known as the Cayman Islands. The sea men were no strangers to alcohol and drugs and this meant they did them at home now. And family abuse along with other ill's follow, divorce were forth coming. The environment may have played a role in some of these social challenges. Murders grievous body harm was still kinda in the back burner but an upcoming event.

There was one two murders a year max. Two people would get drunk and cut up one another every now and then. A prison would soon be needed. Some men knew nothing but the sea and continued to struggle to make a living there. By selling turtle, conchs, fish and other marine life. Men went to work at any available resource public works department, as police officers, at the hospital, the electrical provider gas stations telephone supplier at hotels and other hospitality jobs. Men made a good living as bar tenders and garbage collectors believe it or not. Construction was in its infancy but it a wasn't a problem securing a job, There was plenty to pick choose and refuse. Labor was cheap and so was food and clothing a day pay was about 25 dollars for a professional. With a week's salary you could get two Corduroy pants and feed a family of five for a week and do what you wanted with the rest. The population also grew with the men more at home now eating sea food three times a day. Women went to work too those who needed to and were considered modern women of the times. The children went to school and were though the white man philosophy. Rich kids went to school overseas and the poor went to work for the rich, for little and nothing. The rich became the upper class and slowly changed Cayman to their liking. Who knows maybe they had good intentions, Short term planning and self interest was why we fell I think. A number of banks promised tax free banking and once again these Islands became a hiding place for the pirate's stolen treasure. It was easy to borrow money back then. Cayman economy grew bigger so did the banks, Even more than the sea fearing days. Real estate development became a big business especially on west bay beach. Where now a day's one can hardly see the ocean. Small business also grew in time and it became a national pride to have your own business. Competition was friendly and welcomed. The island excelled in banking and telecommunication and up until March 17 2003 still held a grip as the world's fifth financial center, and every man woman and child within access of the Internet and a TV set. By the 70's or there abouts most of these sea men were a dying breed. The majority still poor the dignified money they made at sea was drying up fast and hardy enough to keep peace with a challenging world. The men continued with sea fearing ordeal, many bought small cargo boats to transport materials along with fruits vegetables. Some transported coconuts from central and South America, and other places in the Caribbean to contracted destinations around the world. It was a growing profitable business and many Caymanian entrepreneurs became rich. Many business and shops etc back in Cayman now depended on these shipments. Fishing boats went beyond too to sell lobsters conch and fish at overseas markets. Boats became ships and survived up till today.

By the 80's we were becoming like the rest of the world ate what they ate and worn what they worn. Hamburgers and fries instead of fish and bri-kind. Name brand clothes became a must, some we thought it was better to buy rather than to plant. We were second best even for ourselves. The rich and powerful bought the so call best and whoever wanted it paid an arm and leg for it. The cost of food began to go up due to world market conditions etc. The more one knows about history the more one knows about life. Christopher Columbus claim the new world for Spain and England but they were already owned. Natives were on these Islands which in years to come were killed off by old world colonials who took their gold, rape their women took their food and live stock and claim their land. Those who survived were to live like the roman's lived in sin and most of them in slavery.

Powerful so call mother countries corrupting these here promised lands, because they don't want to burn alone in hell. The cost of living in general was a little higher compared to other places in the Caribbean. Corporations and Associations begin to take out work permits, The Caymanians became lazy all of a sudden, And never wanted to work. Grass pieces where kids played ten years ago now had four stories building on them. Modern day Cayman was making Caymanians proud it was something to be happy about nothing to reckon with. Traffic jams unemployment high cost of living would soon be a way of life. BY change Cayman would become a cut throat dog eat dog catered society. What does it gain a man to profit the world but lose his soul? Those old people were rich in life sea food and crop, life is worth much more than gold. Yet in Cayman living without is a miracle, how wonderful it would have been for Cayman to remain isolated and forgotten and I mean that in a good way. All the same people slept with their doors unlocked. Yard fires were a thing of the past, you had to plastic bag your garbage now. And made sure the dogs never got to it the mugger dog act was law and dogs needed to be licensed. Begging on the streets was no more and bombs and hobos were being dealt with. Women had to be careful were they breastfed now. Cayman was developing a new standard, Becoming a more tourist friendly island. All littering and other violations had finds attached to them, Septic tanks waste drains were a must now. Urinating or any other bodily extraction on the streets was highly prohibited. Mosquitoes were being controlled and pesticide. The streets were kept clean of any miscellaneous junk by public works department. All government and statuary authority buildings likewise were maintained. Main highways were paved and black toped. One could not have hogs cows chickens or other live stocks in current areas of town. Nor could one walk about drunk with beer bottle etc in your hand.

Now corruption was no stranger to Cayman by now it was in deep and in high places. They had been a couple of unsolved murders by the 80's. Maybe even committed by big shot people and they got away with it, Because of who they were and who they knew. Look this kind of thing happens all over the world in any growing democracy. Were there money there's greed and corruption wickedness and confusion. Innocent people went to jail too were beaten and raped, someone had to do the time. Cover ups and thing took place, lock up the petty ganja man mentality. Some arrest were lawful and justified don't get me wrong. Over the decades the country continued to be developed, we had no choice be to move forward our future depended on it. And it would come with consequent.

BY the 90's Cayman was just starting to step up on the world scene.

A wide avenue of employment was available. The little gas station with one pump and a small tank with a shop inside was being up graded and digitalized. A local television station had been established. The community was still somewhat together family still had Sunday dinners and visited one another. Along with laws insurance had become institutionalized and pets house cars and family were insured. One could not get a job almost without an insurance policy. Paper work had to be in order and you were a trouble maker if it wasn't. Sky scrapers and plaza's etc were going up on dead people's property in the best areas of town. Old timers had passed away and families would have needed to sell or lease the parcel of land. Or people moved out and made some arrangement with the space. Old homes and building etc that had become eye scores were a must to be knocked down. Kids played ate ice cream and candy, sang at Sunday school and wandered if they would work in any of these new building. Know your customer laws were being established at the banks. There were around 500 banks so far operating on the island and over 200 churches of different dominations. The 90's in Cayman was known as the glory days.

Country music could still be heard crime was teenager the population was 25,000 people altogether, including those that had required citizenship. Capital projects were being put into place. Public water new roads etc, Planning department were establishing better building codes. Companies Business of any kind trade men etc needed to be licensed now. IT was becoming a little complicated to open a bank account. People stilled in hope and confidents any problems could have been worked out Caymanians still knew one another. Fishing was still a part of life and becoming a sport, men took their families on fishing trips around the island. People had parties and watched football and talked, went to church and community meetings. Unemployment was unheard of corruption was the size of a mustard seed, by comparing it to other places. Cruise ships were about two to three a week and stays over Tourist were happy. The cowboy mentality was disappearing and there all kinds of religious movements happening. The 90's were a time of prosperity those who left decades before had now returned many that had further their education were professionals in their respected field. They were Politicians Lawyers Doctors Engineers Bankers and Administrators etc. Some started their own business and others became executives in some of these world wide corporations. These people would lay the foundation in the early years. Both men and women that paved the way were known as the horsemen would carry the sword until the new breed of Caymanians took it over. Cayman still had a Caribbean flare and we were the front runners. A day for a laborer in the construction field was something like 50 to 60 dollars a day. A trade man left the job on Friday with 800 to 1000 dollars to his name, now a days that unheard of. People were still building their homes back then out of their own pockets. Ten thousand dollars was a good honk of change back in the 90's and you could have done something with that kind of money. The world was becoming smaller all the same a loft of bread was at a dollar twenty five and fish was two dollars a pound or less in some places. These were the 90's if you wasn't working back then you were lazy. And like every where you had some that could not be motivated for anything in this world, it takes all kinds to make the world go wrong. My grandmother would say she had ambition tablets for sale. Back then it was plenty for all big man small man expats and locals. Back when Cayman was Cayman 8 dollars an hour was top pay, for trade work and went far back then too. You could pay your bills and had extra to sport with everybody had something in his pocket on Friday back then and a piece of mind of some sort. Over the years it became more difficult to save a dollar the Caymanian way of life was to eat good sleep good and never odd money to no man if possible. Everyone had a set of wheels to get round with no matter how it looked you had to move with the time or be left behind, was the attitude. What went wrong were we sailing on a sinking ship, if we had known back then what we know now we would have been set today in life? Caymanians broaden their horizons and tried to make more money, the government rewarded scholarships to students with high academic achievements. Those with current amount of a level passes etc to attend universities overseas. And many whose parents had means by which to educate their child would qualified. One needed money to live the more the merrier the only thing that wasn't going up was wages. Caymanians worked side by side amount themselves and expatriates alike. Peace love respect was the name of the day. Back when Cayman was Cayman and people were striving to become what they are today.

Back when the rest of the world was busy searching for answers that they become not victims of their own doing. Back when the powerful were making laws and policies Cayman come in like they had no choice but to fall in line.

Back when Cayman was Cayman and you could still hear the birds sing back then it didn't matter how hard the wind blew it was always a cool breeze. Back when Cayman was Cayman and we still had maidens and wolves along with dry coconuts. Back when the tape never had the fractions written on it like they do today.

Even from those times people were saying how slow things were becoming. A lot of outsiders in the country both rich and poor hurting us. Back when Cayman was Cayman and we still had bush and trees life was good. Back when the realistic idea of a successful tomorrow was instilled in our minds heart and hands. Back when obtaining the Cayman dream was a possibility and not a fantasy far fetch, Many too many would have lost their chance. Back when hope was the fuel that drives our people into today. In the years to come people would come in the name of peace. They took our jobs, fishes, birds, ducks, beaches and our people and land. They stole in all kinds of ways and am not telling you Caymanians don't steal some of us were helping them. Professional killers and thieves pedophiles, Terrorist were in the country on work permits. Some working for little and nothing depending on who you was you were given more sometimes. Those coming from third world destinations work on there so call legitimate job for 3 dollars an hour and all the goods they could collect. They brought along their bad habits lifestyle and dreams, some were use to this dance hall many knew the party well. Coming from big time countries with small time morals some knew exactly what time it was others never bother to check. Prostitutes come in on work permits along with homosexuals, transvestites and church going people. They sent their money back home to care for their own and minimized their expense here as must as possible. Everyone wanted a piece of the pie money this time that is.

Cayman was a new upcoming country high in tourism and a tax free crime free island with growing banks and a rising consumer base. Foreigners came and invest bought high end real estate made big friend, built condos using contractors from elsewhere. Criminals put their money in the banks and paid the right person to get it wash. And the more educated one was it came in like he was more wicked and luckier. Even though the country made progress a minimum stride was exercise on the common bird. Expatriates underbid and won contracts and this was good for capitalism Cayman had a free enterprise market system everyone had rights even not to have rights. Something better than nothing work for little or stay home and starve became the saying. By the wind of change people became worst in all aspects, Pay masters started making excuses not to pay. Checks were given with special dates and could not be changed right away. No matter how good the work was done bad pay masters always find fault and you had to beg them for your own money. If you got heated and say the wrong words the law was on their side automatically. Caymanians stop working for in and everybody from then on we were learning the situation on land was dyer.

Where did the country on wrong, Love was becoming a stranger and deceit and hatred a close friend.

All kinds of people were coming into the country perverts, sat anis, rapes you name it they were here. The CI had attracted them not the Cayman people many were given better opportunity too Caymanians kept other Caymanians down. And the majority allowed them to, the corrupted put these islands where they are today.

The poor contributed too don't get me wrong they broke the laws of god and man just to survive. Some stole land from those who could not read or write. A good second hand pair of shoes would have gotten you a couple hundred acres back in the olden days. Immigration held the power to grant work permits and it got out of control. Greed and corruption once again got it way and the poor was left to pay or throw aside and used. Salve license were granted by government this went on for ever more Caymanians were starting to see what was going on still by now. Some of us had learn fast and when they were going to the party we were coming from it. Why did god put it this way we wander, Permits were granted without limits to help so call develop the island. Even Johnny come lately people who had no companies or business were taking out work permits to build homes etc or for establishments. Lawyer's doctor's politicians taxi driver's restaurant owners and the common crook had become big time merchants. Even banker's preachers and civil servants had companies to their name. It was like make money or die some people had three jobs others had none. And kisses went by favor a Caymanian working in the construction field would bear witness to a lot of stuff. Jah had put one man there for this cause and afterwards took him out of the race completely. Jah opened his eyes and many more peoples as well. Back in the boom of things the mid 90's it was normal to rent emigrant workers for 30 dollars a head. Some contractors paid them well all same and never treated them like no class citizens for other it was too must money to be paying those kinds of people. Years later after the expatriate person got set up on the island after years of taking hardship from permit boss, they would get married and only give employment to their people and slowly move the Caymanian out of the work force it was becoming more expats then natives, This was the strategy of war. Back in the early days of health and pension the employer would collect it in cash on Friday out of your salary and went straight to the bar room and drink it out, Paper work fix it up on Monday morning somehow or it wouldn't. The money never use to be on time if you got it at all Friday evening the boss would come around with some hard luck story. When you got the correct amount you were lucky or it was a mistake some time it would be 11 o clock at night or some other convenient time before you got what was your. Employers would pickup emigrant worker whose name was not on the list. From public places and around corners Immigration would make numerous raids in some of these areas. Visitors or tourist would be hanging out in certain spots for no apparent reason, And for someone to give them a day work or two. Even at night they were there same way and many contractors started working skeleton crew. Those emigrants who got lucky would be worked like animals. Buildings would almost be completed sometimes when the authorities would appear out of the blue and arrested all illegals. Someone had reported the matter maybe even the same employer in some cases, so he would not have to pay the emigrant workers. Or undercover operations would be going on too. The boss would be held responsible if he was bad lucked and slapped on the wrist with a find that he could have handle. For the illegal it was if you get catch you're on your own type condition. All kinds of things use to happen in those good old days. The employee would be paying the employers health and pension and that of his family directly in most cases. It was becoming a hot war and a fool's game out there with Caymanians and foreigners mixed together on the job site. Expatriate workers went above and beyond the call of duty and enjoyed kissing the bosses back side.

Caymanians remained passive and a minority in the war they were waiting on someone to help them. Associations and mega Companies continued to get their way through political influences and worldwide trends. An Honest day's works was taking on a whole new meaning.

In other situation women would engage in sexual activity to get a permit for herself or the spouse. It was a serious battle the fight of life. Don't use another man give him his fear shear, the rich the poor the bad the good all were fooled during these times, People were confused. What is to be will be the more one knows the better? By the mid 90's terrorism was on the rise suffering was talked about the world's population was growing faster than ever and technology was the wave of the future. The had been some slow time but the economy had bounced back.

By the 90's lottery was still illegal but it was played on the streets hard in Cayman. It was the most successful black market business ever. Started back in the 80's by whom no one knows for sure, most likely emigrant women started selling numbers to make a living. But by the 90's all kinds were hustling numbers, the market had been organized by then and turned into a multimillion dollar a year business. Sellers worked on commission and sold without limits backed by the mafia. It become a cat and mouse game with the cops and sellers. Money was confiscated and pocketed by police and put to use by law. The dirty cop scenario would unite the two and make them survive for decades. Over time sellers got bad name if you won them they would not pay up. Eventually they stepped on the wrong toes and paid the price. Contacts and contracts had slipped and sellers got bump off. Many were arrested with millions in there bank accounts. Which was just the tip of the iceberg, Citizens dreamed the winning number and became millionaires over night or they would pay someone to help them win. Sellers got robbed beaten and killed and lost money in the six digits.

PART ONE

T he wind blew steady across the flat, The Hurricane was dissipating in the gulf. The western tip of Cuba had experience Ivan's strength. It was September 13th a good day out to sea cam for the next few weeks according to the weather report there were some big swells all the same. Jah had made everything perfect with the Hurricane had came its rewards. Life is full of surprises he thought it time to go he say as he entered the house.

One year earlier. BY 2003 Cayman had finished it transient into a heathen nation a vampire state a Babylonian jewel from my point of view. We had become like the gentles at a higher sophisticated level. The homosexual law was reality which was attached to the white paper earlier. Laws were handed down by the king to be accepted or Cayman would have to walk the line and remove the union jack. The blind was starting to see and the cripple was running. And the uneducated in the ways of god's words became wonderers and you couldn't burn a yard fire in peace. It had been a while since the man had lifted a hammer and the chronic workaholic wasn't taking it too well, he was just living on the mercy of god to tell you the truth. He had done some small game fishing that morning in the bight then some hunting for whatever he could find. He was down to one square meal a day, how long would it last this time he thought. I have to find something another job to do soon. He was going crazy again, no woman wants a brake ass man I need money. Love is a different thing altogether, those old people would say put love on the table. He was a humble man all the same and thanked God daily for all things, but over the years he had changed. He didn't have a dollar to his name and barely a window to throw a piss pot through but he was still alive and kicking. It was unemployment that made him this way and it would make many countries fall, intelligent people became activist poor or criminals. My island Cayman what have you become he thought a soldier that takes no prisoners like the rest of the world were greed corruption and money takes over. A promise land but only for the chosen few. The man had seen unemployment years at a time and never gotten use to it. IT was hard to explain which he had stop doing and the criticizing didn't end. HE had ran up down the whole week all over the place looking for any little thing to do. IT wasn't no one's fault nobody was compelled to give you work there was either no work or too much workers on the job site the boss would say. Some of them wouldn't give you a job period or the man chose not to work for them because he had his reasons. There was the new player who would not hirer locals and the fly by nighters you worked with them only if you were on the merge of dying, and even then it was a gamble you could die quicker. I Na dropping down yet he said neither am I ready to. I got to make something happen for myself soon. If the devil wants me he said he ga come better than this. Even him a normal man took those long sad hard Cayman unemployment days in pain. He would cook porridge in the morning and if any was left he would eat the rest at sunset. He knew what they were saying about him round town but it didn't get to him after all these years. The people were confused and didn't know what was going on. BIG hard ass man doing nothing laying down home all day listening to the radio watching TV sleeping was the talk. As far as he was concern it was another day in paradise he had woken up to a fresh crisp clear Cayman morning, blue skies and green grass and the fresh smell of herbs blowing in the wind. IT would almost make anyone feel content that was in his situation. AS he lay there in his hammock hiding from the sun a small pot was boiling over a outside fire, Two concrete blocks and a grill on top balanced it. HE wasn't worried about the worries of his life god knew what he was doing. Laziness wasn't in his blood ambition was all he left more than ever. AS bad as it was he always accepted the problem was all his fault not god's or anyone else. JAH was telling him something by all this and I better learn the lesson he would often say.

BY 2003 there was a global warming crisis going on scientist and conspiracy theories all around the world were agreeing Ice was melting faster than ever oceans were rising and the UB ray of the sun was getting hotter. The ozone had a hole in it, Crops were getting harder to grow and genetic scientists were cloning meats and chicken directly which contained no blood. The rich were getting richer and the poor poorer, the poor man had no chance or say. IT's like that all over I guess we are the slaves of Babylon, Forced to warship their Idols and lifestyle and to live under modern colonialism believe it or not.

IT had been several years now since he had found any real employment. He had only done construction for most of his life this was all he did as a professional. HE had already made up his mind on a career change he wasn't going to sit around and wait on the great white hope. But for now it was the same happy life a lot of things still had to be done in his life, but he lived in hope and knew it was just a matter of time before god turned the page. HE become closer to god during these times. Crime was plaguing the island these days people had disappeared and bodies were found mutilated.

Just a few days ago a man was shot dead in his home word on the street someone had paid a hit man. Every man was holding his own corner friends and brethrens could be found in their yards sitting chilling under a mango tree in his case burning a yard fire. Mediating and absorbing the surroundings. Coming up with ways to deal with the devil's philosophy. TO have wisdom is to fear god, of course they were those out there in a rougher boat and they were not handling it as well as him. And instead of finding JAH some got closer to evil. Poverty can make people do things they never even dream of turn sensible people into fools and make some unreasonable. Some days he had no sugar for his porridge and could not buy a can of beans, many days he ate pain and became full. Nothing surprised him any more now a days; he was still at the bottom of the pit but on top of the muck. The war in Iraq was over for the time being. The weak was becoming stronger and the biggest losers were going to haven money could buy anything. IT was a sin to be poor and seemed to be a crime, if you had an open mind you kept it to yourself.

STATUSES were continuing to be issued by Cabinet and Immigration more and more people would be able to vote in the coming election. Slowly the Island that time forgot was disappearing IT had grown up and was becoming a metropolitan. Houses were being built in the most remote areas, Cliff land and on Iron shore in the swamps and ocean. The price of land sky rocked. WE were eating the food on the king's table, what happen in the night came to day. What happen to the big passed onto the small, and space was limited. The world was slowly becoming a living hell. Even paradise is another reflection of big city chaos greed and grudge-fullness. This one got more than me mentality, and I want his share one way or another. HE thought about the mindset of the wicked on a daily bases. Smoke came from his mouth as he rolled in his hammock trying to take a nap. HE knew the road all too well often he found himself in that same place riding that same old donkey. BE it willing or mistake faith by god or punishment one can't question 2003 and the months that followed. IN Cayman more and more eyes were starting to open up.

IT was a still afternoon a few days later. The man sat under a tree on a picnic table contemplating his situation. HE just finish building a boat shade in town, can you imagine that one week's work him and a friend of his. IT wasn't anything going on work wise and the four hundred dollars he made was already chopped up into sections, of everyday living in Cayman. HE had been living from hand to mouth for a while, way to long if you asked him. And things didn't look good on the horizon. They were a couple of jobs going on down on the bay all the same big hotels and condominium projects. First thing Monday morning I'LL find myself down there and ask for a job. Come cross round four and get your money he said to someone over the phone. Bring me something different if you got anything.

Kingdon found him outside in the same spot he had been all morning. The two men bounced fist together and greeted each other. You got papers kingdon asked as he took out a sandwich bag from his waist line. MR bill gave us fifty dollars extra says he more than happy with the work, he's a good hearted old man you see him the. If everybody were like the Patterson's everything would be alright Sam said the man to kingdon. IT getting harder and harder to make a honest living, Sam I would give it up myself but then what will I do replied kingdon. Yah a new career would be the same shit.

THE men spoke in the third person and called each other Sam, IT was just a figure of speech Sam and a habit and style in the way they talked. IT's the way of things, the nature of the world for people to take advantage of one another. Kingdon took a paper from the pack they men said nothing for a minute or two, then puffs of smoke blew in the air. I know what you mean old boy we got family wife and children to support. IT either living like this of crumbs or hit a bank or something, northward prison na that bad we can take a chance up there and the food pretty good too I hear. I'LL miss my gypsy girl but that's how it goes said Kindon. YAH and it Na no more buried treasure in Cayman to find so only JAH knows. They laugh Kingdon rested the lighter on the table the two men continued to talk all evening until sunset. I going cross the bar little bit said Kingdon see if I can get some sale or see somebody bout a job you never know. Yah man cool I'll check you out Monday we'll go long the bay see if we get lucky, plan our next move we can't go on like this king. Later Sam yah later Sam they said to each other.

Monday morning the man needed his 91 Toyota Corolla jump started she didn't looked too good but it was pretty reliable. IT only needed a battery and maybe an alternator to begin with, and the license coupon was expired years ago. There was no Insurance on the thing in fact every company on the island had refused to insure the thing. The car was a piece of junk frankly the tires were worn and the young man had repainted it himself with one can of spray paint. After getting a jump start from a passerby he was on his way. IT was 6.45 AM sharp when he stop and picked up his friend the two men set out on the highway headed west. They needed to beat the traffic because the stop and go would have impaired the mission. The car ran hot too it over heated while running along, he left the hood line open slightly too let the cool air past through the radiator when driving. The radiator was cracked open and the fan was busted and unrepairable. A half an hour later they had reached their destination safely. The car pulled into the beach club parking lot, a small hotel one of the oldest on the 7 mile beach strip. They would leave the car there for a few hours and go by foot to the various sites asking for a job. WE na going be picky they said one to the other we'll take anything that comes along. There were at least three major Construction projects going on hotels from fancy chains and world class franchised. There was a man standing at the gate of the first job site they came to. He had on a hard hat and a black support strap. THE man was smoking a cigarette and shouting at a man operating a lifter, HE asked them bluntly what is it, he spoke American. WE looking for a job said the driver of the car, can we please talk to the boss. The man had a tan and you could have smell the sun screen there was frothy saliva at the corner of his mouth. You got to talk to me and I say there's no job here so be along on your way. He was rude to the boys but they just walked off. The second site brought them no luck likewise so did the third. AT the second site they had manage to get cross the gate keeper a Cayman guy and spoke to someone in the office. A gentleman project manager who smiled a lot and gave them some double talk, I needed guys last week but we worked it out with the subcontractor. You can check us out again in about three month's time when we start the next phase of the hotel. I can't even take your resume at this point but to be honest I like what I see you guys Caymanians he asked. YES SIR. Umm well thank you for coming I know how it is being unemployed been there myself. The office was a 20 foot container of some sort with a window and a small AC unit attached to it was parted into various sections two office and a bathroom a storage area but only for office stuff. The man opened the door and told them good buy with a cold face as they left. That another foreigner sounds like an English man to me the taking over the place Sam.

THE third stop was more of the same kind of chat, run around beat around the bush thing. YOU boys did any prison time asked the Caymanian foreman who you all for. Get the police record and all that personal information together and drop it off at the main office in town. WE take random urine test here just so you know. Fill out an application we'll keep it on file. AS they left the site a Jamaican worker yelled go way Unna na fuh come ya we run things.

IT was 3.20 PM they had beaten the evening rush hour traffic. Further east out of town they stop to asked about work at the smaller sites on the way home. IT was a waste of time they knew the residential projects were worst and they were insulted by bosses workers and owners.

THE men sat underneath a tree in the yard talking and meditating into the late evening. They had not eaten breakfast, lunch, and there was no supper. Their all political jobs one of them said, YEAH this been going on for years. A piece of log wood was threw on the small fire they had made, smoke was all around. BY now a few more boys had joined them around the fire they were in session. IT was 12 AM when the small camp fire went out, the boys had been reasoning for hours. They were in their Trans like high said their good bye clashing fist together and holding two finger in the form of the peace sign then touching their chest with the hand. They were all red up. IT had been a long day see you later Samm Kingdon said to the Indian man yeah Samm later. INDIAN the driver of the Toyota didn't get much sleep he spent the night twisting and turning.

Time rod on time past and nothing changed for him he was haunted by something and he would soon have to soon comprehend it or die in confusion.

THERE he was a 30 year old man sitting under the mango tree all day burning yard fires people were starting to envy him. HE too was sick of the situation living on carrots cassava peanuts and dreams. But it was not his fault god had spoken or was it the devil that had him cursed. What had hit these shore of his beloved Cayman he wondered one thing for sure he had to survive one way or another. CAYMANIANS were smiling less these days they were isolated and forgotten democracy was helping itself. ALL hope had left him he was a failure and not afraid of dying any more a hard core original grass root Caymanian lion like him was eating straw. ONE thing for sure poverty wasn't no place to be happy about this ain't no place to want to die in. FOR REAL god had not forgotten Cayman yet he was just occupied right now. With all this stuff going on in the world today with bin laden and nuclear bombs and shit. The Indian man trusted few and those whom he trusted in he watched out for them.

The days and months went by slowly Cayman wasn't getting any better this was a failed democracy. WE had been listening to the wrong mouth and seeing incorrect visions you see the human race not really smart unless JAH guides us. WE are living in revelation times the Sunday law in affect and was instigated hundreds of years ago by the Roman Empire and Implemented by Columbus in the so call new world. The devil himself down here putting obstacles in the path of the righteous, the greatest thing is to know. Greed is an idol and corruption is a disease a slavish mentality is still in the land, the poor could be bought for a pair of shoe now a days. That great city that rules over the kings of the earth won't be so great any more. EVERY thing is linked to the anti - Christ. THE man burnt yard fires more than ever.

This was his deck of cards. Little work around the yard kept him going and odd jobs once and a while. HE built garbage pan holders from scrap lumber and sold them. HE did whatever he could to make do if you what I mean. HE sold fruits and vegetables that were grown right there on his place. INDIAN had even applied to work on a garbage truck but was turn down because he was over qualified.

A gentle south east breeze blew across the flat, the swamp was going asleep for the night. The last man-o-war before sunset glided in the sky it was around 7 PM the moon had not yet come up. A piece of dry mangrove stomp was just beginning to burn slowly on a fire mostly to keep way mosquitoes. A young lady was inside a house doing girl stuff reading a fashion magazine and doing something to her hair and talking on the cell phone, to one of her girlfriends. IT was a three way conversation. The couple was expecting company this evening the girls would be inside while the boys smoked drank and talked bullshit around the fire. INTO the wee hours of the morning when they fell asleep it would be round the campfire sometimes. The girls would pass out inside on the floor with their blankets or on the couch. AT times all the girls would crash in the queen size bed of the one bedroom flat. IT was a 1900's Cayman style cottage the zinc roof was painted red and the walls outside was a modern bright yellowish color. IT was an upgrade version of an old Caymanian wobble and Dobbs home. With hardy board siding and single haul colonial windows the porch had a railing around it with designer blisters. AN X shape would break the pattern from straight up and down. There was a board walk leading to the entrance stairwell. THE owner had an eco friendly idea and ran with it he planted trees and others crops all over the land. The little home was elevated above the swamp enough to get a hammock under the floor. IT sat upon iron wood posts and a huge black mangrove tree stood nearby. THERE were lots of coconuts palms banana and plantain stocks. The ackees and breadfruit trees were full grown and they were other trees coming up and being planted. IT wasn't terrible swamp land there were pockets of soil without salt and was good for bearing. Mosquitoes land all the same and there was jungle all around him. AN hour or so later they were more cars in the yard along with about one bicycle and a scooter. I know what going on Samm said one of them survival of the fittest, the rise of the anti-Christ Samm. That serious Samm said one with dread locks lulling on a tobacco pipe. Babylonian oppression and persecution of gods people Samm. THE last angel in revelation told us this would come about in the years 2000 said Kingdon. The last seal has been open and the angel has poured out the content of the vase upon the earth. FOR real said the Indian the owner of the place. These are the last days smoke blew all over, it was hard to tell if it was from the log wood burning or it was from something else. THEY boys drank Guinness stout and smoked into the night, going off into Trans like meditation talking philosophical crap, if you may.INVOLVING world history Religion, Science and Politics all base on common belief. THEIR were about four to five of them, some nights even more young men no more than 22 to 31 years of age. THE one they call the Indian started to tell a story. Remember Christopher Columbus to me god choose him to bring religion into the new world that's all. HE looked around with a serious face and pulled in on his spiff. HE was a mercenary the white man the Europe the human mankind, CAME to the CARIBBEAN to fulfill his role in history. THE Mayan civilization stretched from North America through central and south, along with some parts of the pacific and Caribbean. WHO knows for sure ASIA the Middle East from where did these people came.

COLUMBUS was a man with a dream a courageous man anyone who goes into the unknown is special in my book. HE was a man of God and saw the power of maker many time at sea am sure. ON his fourth and final voyage or there about he came up on these islands and called them Los Tortugas the name would change over time to the caimans because of its abundance of crocodiles. COLUMBUS recorded this in his log book there were also a great number of Indians here at the time. After a few days of complicated negotiations they gave him food and water, AND chocolate in its primitive form to drink. FOR their kindness Columbus returned to them hoes pickaxe shovels rope, neckties and thing whatever little alcohol he had left on the ship. THE Indians had their own tobacco and cannabis, for real said one of the boys around the camp fire. THESE places that were so called discovered by this Spaniard share similar history. After couple weeks of vacationing Columbus sailed and never returned again he had all the information he needed. OVER the years with more and more vessels patrolling the areas of the Caribbean trying to claim what wasn't theirs among the contenders were royal fleets pirates runaways outcasts deserters and animal slaves. These waters became a death wish with the worst of them making these Islands a home away from home or a Treasure Island. They would steal kill and lie in the name of the King and God, In the name of revenge fun and the church. Natives who did not run were being finish off for their women, Treasures, land and water. THE Island was rich in natural resources too jade, gold, silver, brass, copper, rubber, oil, cotton, silk, and even diamonds. Outsiders came in the name of both war and peace, and would make one sided bargains with natives. THE new comers the pirates offered gifts and so called valuables from the old world to secure their well being on the Island. GIFTS like rum, combs, mirror, guns, old world money and games of all kind. TREASURE went back sailing to the old now wealthy world. Then we became a worldwide idea, what deals truly excised behind the curtain who were the people the valuables and the countries for. Many fights broke out at the time between world powers with Mother England the successor. IN time to come pirates with their super weapons started to control the Island they brought slaves sold them to the elite who forced them to work on plantations and cotton fields and to do all things under the sun and whatever they wanted them to do under the moon. THE native Indians were rally up to do mandatory labor too many would have runoff and escape those who could. A lot never made it and only achieved freedom in death, Indians, Blacks, colors, and other natives along with slaves and capturers fled to where ever to try and secure a piece of life in general. IN a quest for betterment they ran but it was no place to hide everyway was the same more or less. MOST had jumped out of the pot and into the fire wars were justified and blood flow was the result. Many died in the name of peace and many lived in the name of hate. Today a small population of indigenous people still exist in secret paradises around the world. IN Jungles and other remote destinations. They lived like their ancestors did from the land and sea directly they are among the world's best divers and hunters and the smartest people there ever was. Today they fright to maintain their own way of life and godly belief, away from the orthodox churches. THEY are sky watchers and are all mixed together with other tribes now a days. THESE are truly the last people of god to be conquered in the world today. THEY are of an indigenous race and try to live in harmony as best as possible, Most of the time I must say. HOW ever drugs and alcohol is moving the world over and it pass through these Territories one way or the other. THE Indian man continued to talk the boys paid attention each one holding something in his hand. LIFE started in the four corners of the world and mankind was evolved around these and there from.

Back in the ancient days the people made images from stone, gold, jade, silver and other precious materials. THEIR art work is all over the world they made them to warship to praised the sun the moon the stars and ocean, Along with others gods of the land. RAIN was a good spirit and for others it was considered a bad one. THE first people came from AFRICA EYGPT ASIA INDIA AND CAYMAN the boys laughed I know what you saying brethren said a voice among them sounding high as a kite. OR the first people came from no were Samm, said the Indian man entertaining them. THE girls looked out the window at the men, they going smoke 10 pounds of weed for the night done you watch. IN about BC some time by some miracle and sea vessel found their way to the new world. About a thousand years before Columbus it was their destiny god lead them here. Ancient ships with Kings Valuables on board and men and women were left behind to start a population on their own, AND to gather and preserve life. EYGPT was a strong nation in her days and had the best sea men the world had ever seen at the time. PHARAOH sent ships into the unknown some found their way back home other did not, some died on the journey others would survive on whatever piece of ground they found. THE ships carried prisoners and respected men of difference occupations, Cast a ways people who brought shame to their families were put on a boat and sailed where ever the wind blew him and that was where he stayed. THEY were heathens and so were those who came after them who murdered them and left them for dead. FOR disease and maggots to take over and slowly extinct their civilization one wasn't better than the other. Every man was fighting for his own rights and life, FIRE with fire was the name of this serious game. FOR land and resources think about it we've come a long way but things haven't change that much. Treasure still infest the island of Cayman if you where to look. Millions of dollars in treasure have been discovered over the decades and up to this day are still being found and taken. KINGS and QUEENS were the heads of the colonial world and they had their disciples out there. THEY had royal ports and pirates and armies to do their dirty work which were the tails. SLAVES' eventuality got their freedom somehow by Emancipation of slavery. These foreigners would settle on the island and inter breed with natives. Most were without a country in terms of being disowned. OUR blood became one by the will of god many eyes had been opened which brought about emancipation. THESE islands were crowded with tears bloodshed outrage curses blessings and spirits, the remains of wars. Many war shipped the devil and his sons willingly and in innocents. THE experimented with the living and the dead and committed ungodly acts in witchcraft. THE ocean became as blood. EYGPT was a world power and they had ancient warriors in wooden ships pharaoh sent fleets of ships to broaden his Territories. HIS ships came with beans corn wheat live stock weapons gold etc. and other important Items. THEY might have needed them in the new world. Slaves came along with religion and culture. THE tower of Babel was being built and the people mocked god it was at this stage too that man went into the unknown God made them confuse and wonderers. AND unable to speak and communicate with each another. THEN again the world was joined together all land was connected before the great flood. THERE after the flood man and land got separated by sea and people remained where they were including those in Cayman. REMEMBER nova and his family were the seed bearers of the earth after that as far as the story goes. DON'T doubt it the ark made it and so did some of those ancient wooden ships god may have been with them. BY the time Christopher Columbus found these on the Island running about naked, the rest of the world had fashion clothes lived in brick homes the rest of the world was pretty much advanced. THERE was a time warp between the two.

BY 1503 the Mona Lisa was already painted the Roman Empire had already fallen or we thought and the great wall of chain was done conquered and England and Spain were number one contenders for world power. COLUMBUS was a sailor from the time he was 12 he knew of a kingdom that was not far away and that It was a part of the old world. SO he was not just lucky he knew what kind of odds he held he was not just going on a voyage. IT was more like the first steps engaging in war to conquer land and slave another race while making themselves rich. SPAIN and ENGLAND was on his side the ripe all that they could from this new world which was not really new. YOU remember when I told you he was a man of god I lied don't even argue. GREED over came and the powers to be embedded somehow in their thoughts they would never die or would never have to pay. THIS same gold would generate a revenue to this day to support and create a beast as big as today's stock market. COLUMBUS was basically another religious freak like many others who came before him and would come thereafter. HE was a star that hit the sea the message he brought was both change and fulfillment to this part of the old world, WHICH was new in the sense that it had not yet been conquered by the white man the civilized man. PERVERTED people moved up in high places over the centuries then became united in their satanic rituals and forced the rest of humanity to warship them and suffer. IT was this way even before Columbus but he opened the door in the Caribbean. THE whole era was an apocalyptic event and a seal was broken believe it or not. THE world is one corrupted place Samm those from so called great lands see us as inferior to them.

IT WAS AROUND 2 A.M when the discussion stop among the boys by that time they had made themselves comfortable underneath the house floor. THE two hammocks were occupied and the others slept in long wooden chair that the Indian had made. ONE young man lay out on the picnic table in the moon light. A bottle of white rum stood by him still full, He wasn't in any condition to touch it. KINGDON and the Indian man talked softly the rest of the pack was in dream land no one knew what they were talking about.

DAY light came and the boys burnt an eye opener said there good bye's and went their way. INDIAN had landed a temporary job filling in for someone driving a cab. THE guys would get together at least 5 times a week at the Indian man's place. THEY had grown up together somewhat and were school friends lived in the same neighborhood as kids they consider one another blood family to the max. THEY associated with known gang members them themselves all came from good families and Christian homes and back ground. THEY had been baptized what seemed like a century ago but they were only kids at the time. Tate E. Wood was the only one who done time in northward, for stamping a hitters brains into the pavement in a fight. OVER money that was owed to him the junky said something about his mother then his woman too big mistakes don't tell a Caymanian any such thing. TATE got baptized in prison during his first year in the slammer. OUT three years now after serving five he was pardon by the judge for behaving himself and as an example that northward was rehabilitating inmates. The prison was crowded anyway he was a change young man going to church. And studying to become a preacher but he was still unemployed and shacked up in his mother house. With a little baby girl and a young Christian wife she had accompanied at the sleep over, and now they were headed back to Bodden town where they stayed. JOHN the youngest lived just a few miles down the road.

AS a little boy the Indian lived in Georgetown where him and kingdon became friends, after that he lived in the country on a Reservation. THEN they were some trouble in the 90's that brought him here to this swamp.

NOW the talk show was the heart beat of Cayman since day one. IT was a pressure pot where people let off steam every now and then. OVER the years it became a political macunisim people would voice their opinion on the air and be subject to repercussion by and through unchained moves and stops. WHOLE families would be victimized government agencies were monitoring the show and on days when there was a hot issue on the island the talk show would have on guess talking about plants and pet food. BY this time nothing was a secret in Cayman and if you think too loud people would know, a lot of things were going on and happening. THE Cayman Island royal police Department had grew and expanded regular traffic cops carried guns now and criminals started to use them more. THE gun law had gotten slippery people were given license just because they had a gun. PEOPLE would be cooking or having sex with a gun on their side several accidental shootings had already taken place. ONLY certain people were allowed to get a gun license rich people business owners framers and civil servants. GANG war fear had become the music of the day gangsters shot at each other in bar rooms and hospitals had drive by shootings and car jacking's. THE island had became a chaotic place like any other major city in the twenty first century and growing fast. GANG violence continued or call it plain old crime execution style murders went on and became a plague. MURDER trials had hick up's and there was always something missing judges and lawyers were not good enough for some reason and jurors were hand pick. CRIMERIAL cooperated with police and got plea bargains and lived to kill another day. FEW cases were being solved there were more guns on the island than you could talk about. MACHINE guns assault rifles rocket launchers man had license to carry and use grenades and plastic explosives. THE situation on land was worst than ever taxation was forth coming there would be new roads and high ways throughout the island, WHICH was well needed in a rapidly developing island. SEVERAL new five star hotels were being built on the beach by private investors there were other projects plan to be constructed as well in undeveloped areas. LIKE swamps and other virgin plots in a go east initiative. THE 7 mile beach was saturated and others areas of the island were virtually untouched. JUNGLES ETC would be suburbanized and projects done in a way to blend in with natural surroundings, land would be striped even more. THESE were some of the topics being talked about on the radio show. IF you were living in Cayman during these times you were doing it in tears. HOTELS were buying up from the extra high water mark right back to the reef and rezoning everything. THE Cayman parrots and other birds had become a rear site. THIS massive development had left few spots for these creatures. LOCAL animals and house hold pets were inter breeding with foreign ones. QUIT frankly they were more criminals walking the streets every day. A homosexual man was seriously assaulted recently and injured he had been beaten with a nail club and then chopped up he was alive but in critical condition. POLICE said it was racially related and were calling it a hate crime. ANOTHER incident had lift a five year old boy dead from a stray bullet. OH my island Cayman what have you become these were the ingredients that turn activist into vigilantes and honest people into suspects make sound women and men confused. IT wasn't a free for all and everybody get away thing all the same. THE law was putting away killers' petty timers and the common everyday foot soldiers.

PYSCOS and mental cases were not uncommon now here in Cayman, ESPECIALY during these hard times. PHYCATRIST had pronounced about half the population as boarder line crazy. SOME people were manipulating the system to get free drugs and meals. THEY were roamers of money laundering and tax evasion racket. WHITE collar criminals were having a field day Instead of going to jail those guilty would do community service. THEY had been several more arm robberies and police came under gun fire. THE local talk show was being accused of promoting and drafting an anti government pledge of legions and an eye opening campaign and stirring up things. THE island was on the same track it had been on for years there was political turmoil all around, conflict of interest everywhere you look and no answers to the questions. THE Government seemed to be going through territorial unrest and was cracking from the inside out. ALL kinds things were taking place Business men and tourist alike would come into the island pick up cash lump sum and leave. THE Government felt sorry for nobody. CIVIL servants and no bodies started buying up prime time property and opening real estate companies. CRITICAL parcel of land would be bought or confiscated by Government and then individuals would be the new owners. THESE were some of the tricks being played and people spilled their guts on the talk show. THE Liquor license was another mess besides special groups of people owning one there were more liquor facilities than gas stations or native trees. BAR rooms were right next to churches and in some cases even closer. CORRUPTION had become a house hold word due to knowledge by families talking around kitchen tables and way of the talk show. CAYMANIANS were starting to wake up from the fairy tale world they were living in, People had finely come to the grips of reality. WE were becoming a social service state and status holders, permit workers along with tourists that were unemployed or by a good reason in need of something anything would be maintain and supported by the government. AND they were put on priority list before the natives it was an unfair situation. MILLIONAIRS regular Joe's and teenagers got in line at social service to receive unemployment checks and food vouchers. EVERYTHING was at a fast pace Government ministers would have unofficial cabinet meetings. MONEY would disappear from treasury without a trace or reason. POLITICIANS were taking unnecessary trips abroad with their secretaries. THE Cayman people money was used on prostitutes and invested in casinos, ON some of these worldwide tours that the leader of the Government of the day was taking with his members. THEY were also promoting independence for Cayman. A man had drop down dead yesterday from worriation and bathroom problems. THE social state of the island was in pieces people were having trouble coping with day to day life. BY the sound of the callers to the talk show one knew they were frustrated real people were behind those phone calls. PEOPLE were hungry and in need children were going to school without lunch or money to buy any. ELECTRICITY was being disconnected people were living in misery with no water and not enough food. BUT according to the Government it was only happening to the minority of the population among the poorest of the poorest broken homes etc. Government programs were only helping some.

SHOW him were to pick up the voucher, Right this way sir said the social worker to the alcoholic slash drug addict man. WHOSE next how may I help you ma am the woman ask the young lady. I still having find nothing yet miss. HAVE you check the news papers, there was a long list on Friday.

I seen them said the young lady it's like they just running a sham the add says they looking for Caymanians to employ but when you go down there and apply they already got somebody on permit working. WELL you will have to take that issue up with the Immigration department. I have more than once and they keep sending me down here. AM afraid we can't help you the department is operating on a low budget these days. WE are on the merge of bankruptcy it was no later than this morning that the premier sent out a statement in regards of the situation all benefits are very limited. WE just don't hand out checks to everybody that walks through those doors it doesn't work like that. WHY can't you borrow money from friends or someone? THINGS too hard miss for anyone to lend money out. I can't understand this you a educated young lady I've seen your qualifications why can't you get a job. ALL I can tell you is keep at it won't happen overnight that's for sure. MISS can I ask you way you from. NOT that it's any of your business but am Canadian. THE young girl smiled see what I mean maam, Your not even married here. NO am not am a widow my husband and I came here years ago way before all of this got started. WHAT happen you couldn't find a job back in Canada I can't go there and get work over a national from the country. THE girl walked out and left the woman on her own. THAT little tight ass bitch thinks she knows it all at that age. KEEP her out of here she said to the security guard she was rude and she insulted me am filing a complaint about her first thing in the morning. THE woman said from her office door. THE young lady went home broken hearted she cried that night. THE Indian man held her in his arms. AM not able to make a living in my own country why is this happening her eyes were wet with tears as she looked into his. I don't know what to say baby God will soon make it right. IT'S wrong they giving work to permit holders only because they work for less she said. WHEN it's a white foreigner or someone that speaks with a classy accent there some kind of other favor going on. EITHER they know someone or someone knows them to help them out. ALIZA that's how it works baby the white man makes money for the company by his connections and thing, White people like to do business with one another. THEY can't understand how we talk even if we speak good English that's how it is babes. THE only thing that will stop them is a militia. THERE stealing the Caymanians future I don't hate those poor people for trying to make a life here but what about us said the girl. SHE rested her head on the man's chest they were laying in bed there was a deep silent. A gentle breeze blew against the window the crickets could be heard outside Aliza slept in his arms. HE rested her head on a pillow softly cover her up with a sheet he stared at her for a good while thinking wondering a thousand things going through his mind. SHE had to bed hungry although he had driven a cab all week the money wasn't enough it had been evaporated on other neassary things. FOOD was in the house but the refrigerator looked poor. AM a man he said and I must provide with my blood we fight to the end. THERE may not be no honor in death, but to die trying is a sacrifice. HE wiped the eye water from his eyes and blew his nose into a paper towel. THEN begin to pray in an Indian tongue his native language, that of the Cayman Indian. WHEN he finished he went outside.

IT had been weeks now and the Indian man was still holding down the job. HE put in 15 to 16 hours a day on the road. THE woman he loved and soon to be future wife was taking care of things at home. AND dealing with the reality of what it was to be a poor man's spouse. SHE was suffering from poor woman syndrome.

HE took Aliza on several job searches and Interviews If the job wasn't already gone we'll call you was the echo, But he knew what was going on after all he'd been around. TAXI business was slow but he was making money on the side if you know what I mean. THERE was only a few days left before the fill in he was doing ended. HE was only a hired hand on a schedule for the owner of the operation. THE three weeks works had come in good something else going come up he told himself.

IT was woman galore on the streets of Cayman and they filled every crescent and air line crack of church towns and main street district. THE Caymanian man was voted all time sweetest in the world for the pass decades, AND every woman wanted to get one Caymanian men were spoiling the women in a good way. HE had it all class money power and they were number one pipe layers men would fight and kill up over a pair of legs sometimes. BAR maids become rich by late night work and putting in extra hours if you know what I mean. BOTH men and women paid good to get lubricated money was sex as many soon found out and would become short time gigolos if you may. AS you know in modern day Cayman no one gives you nothing especially money. FAMILY or love ones didn't always had it to give man was in need and found ways and means. THE were on line web sites that got you in on the action people meet with each other at night clubs supermarkets and other places. OLDER women mother and daughter teams, nuns, lawyers, doctors the girl at the candy store. THE man had pulled down more draws over the last month than most women had worn in their life time. THEY insisted he use protection some of them were just lonely and needed to talk and for someone to hold them. HE played the game cooked and messaged them he was living a play boy life and loving it, drinking alcohol and stimulators smoking to keep up. THINGS wasn't going well for him on the outside he made some money all the same before it was over. Wasn't proud of what he had done by any means he had stoop low this time, IT had gotten out of control he got carried away on the job. A righteous man will fall seven times and get back up but the wicked going drop once and that will be it, was what he told himself to feel better.

ALIZA was a young Christian woman and trying to live life according to god. SHE was one of the sweetest Caymanian girl you would eve meant after high school she continued her education in the states, and had work up there for some years following that. SHE had been home several years now and got lay off her accounting job, working part time here and there but couldn't find anything promising. She wanted to run her own company one of these days. ALIZA was in Church that Sunday morning. HOW things going with you girl said one of her girl friends. THANK God it ain't no worst said Aliza. THAT man of yours not in church today what he doing these days got a while I having seen him. HE working today still driving the taxi off and on you know he's been so tried lately. LAST night he came in 3 from the grave yard shift. UMMH said Babeth her friend. ATLEASE he putting food on the table said Aliza. LAST month I had to go to Government for help, One Canadian woman in charge down there now tell me bout if we were to give food stamps and pay the bills for everyone that walk through that door young lady the Government would have gone broke long ago. BIG eye thing like her. They na going help caymanians child said Babeth if you a foreigner you gone clear if any of them lost the job get layoff or going through marriage problem anything like that can't pay their rent social service will assist them happily.

YOU got to be a pregnant woman from another country so they can help you. THAT the problem some of these Caymanian man so dumb getting long with these foreign women boy I tell you.

THAT won't happen in no other country you know that though only in Cayman. THESE man got to learn to keep the carrot in the pant and stop chasing these old slats said Babeth. SPEAKING of carrots all may not be what it seems my dear girl. WHAT do you mean said Aliza? THE music from the church quire had stop playing. DON'T give me any of that gypsy talk Babeth. SHE put her hands up long side her mouth and whispered into Aliza ear.

IT was 8.30 Monday night and you could smell supper cooking all throughout the woods. Aliza was preparing a nice meal, a Turbot that her fiancé had caught just a day before was being steam, with stir fried vegetables and ackees cooked in olive oil and boiled green banana. THEY were poor but royalty would envy the way Caymanian people eat some times, the man's yard had provided it all between the ground and his little garden out back. Instead of going to church yesterday Indian and MR Patterson had went fishing. THAT hit the spot babes he said all I need now is some good loving up. AND way you get that from one of your bitches of the street said Aliza. The words hit him like a digger to the heart, what you talking bout sweetie. DON'T sweetie me you no good brut I done find out what you were doing all these weeks. YOU don't have any shame the whole Island knows how you been making money, you don't have to work for me you know Indian that's how you going support those children you got out there. I thought this situation was humbling you but look like you getting worst I thought the running up and down days were over. THIS it with me and you I don't want anything more to do with you. I was a fool thinking you would change. INDAIN remained cam only looking at her he was taking verbal blows. THREE weeks ago I was feeling dizzy and gray in my head Aliza said and I missed my time so I went to the clinic and found out that am pregnant, but now I don't what going happen might through them away since you don't love me you never did. BABES please Indian stretched his arms out as to comfort her with a hug. ALIZA double her small fist and strike him on the cheek she was aiming for his eyes. IT hurt but all he did was backed away and rubbed the spot with his hands. COME on Aliza you know how Caymanians like talk news and tell lies people just talk to talk and make trouble, I love you Aliza even more now that your having my child. OUT of wed lock we living in sin Indian that's why we are curse nothing we do prospering you don't see. FOR all I know one of those women or your sons mother could have obeya on us. Don't talk like that I don't believe in that crap Aliza. Indian where you getting this money from. I driving a taxi babes your girlfriends telling you foolishness, they watching too much days of our life's. INDIAN please just admit the truth you's a Rasta so be a man and speak the truth. I done tell you Aliza believe what you want. Indian you think am a fool taxi business ain't that good dam well not in the slow season, the biggest transport company out there not making that kind of money you making in one night. I look in your wallet last night you know so don't come telling me nothing. ALL the girls in church and down at the market laughing at me and I didn't know why, she had broke out crying by now Aliza raised her hand to claw him but the Indian pulled his face away quickly. DON'T you try putting your hands on me you know Indian cause I will call the police on you and tell them what you been doing dirty thing like you let them arrest you for prostitution. BABES you don't understand what is going on it not what you think nothing happen with the women. I know everything Indian my girlfriend see you with her own eyes. BABES I running a taxi all kind of people be in it, you over reacting sweet cake look at us this Na us. From the day I got long with you I Na see what another woman something look like. WELL I hope you took a last good look at this one cause you'll never see it again. I trying to make a honest living for us and they spreading lies on the I. HE spoke slowly and careful tears were in his eyes. I love you babes just believe in me I need you to trust me for us to make it through this, WE going make it out of these hard times. THAT's a wonder you never choked saying that I know who you is Indian I was right there is some kind of evil spirit cased over this place and it's destroying you and you're not the same Indian I fell in love with. AM moving out going to the Nightingale house until I decide what am going to do with my life, I've made a huge mistake getting involved with you. AND remember I own half of this place, I been living like an animal out here all these years with you wasting away my life. PLEASE baby don't do this we can work this out, IT's all lies honey we're beyond this. ALIZA took a deep breath I need a ride into town if it's not too much trouble. SHE had left behind some of her belongings and told him she would be back tomorrow for them. THEY drove into town not speaking another word. HE had let her down broken her heart he felt terrible and alone, It won't happen again he told himself she meant too much to him and he wasn't sure now if he'll ever get another chance maybe it was too late. HE never hesitated when it come to having sex with those other women and that was what scared him Aliza was right he was a dog. I should have just stick to the job and didn't involve myself physically. FOR give me father he said in his native tongue as he drove home that night.

EARLY the next morning Indian walked around the yard in his underwear with a marina on. HE hadn't sleep well, IT was 5 AM when he put a small joint the size of a cigarette in his mouth and lit it. ALIZA was gone don't know if she'll be back were his thoughts, everything is my fault still. I can't lose that woman he said it's time to fight back against my oppressors. HE pulled on the joint looking into a hole in the ground. HE was building a water well there but had a boarded the mission for the time being Now it was time to put the plan back in motion and claim what was rightfully his. GOD had brought him to this world for a reason, success was his destiny money was on the man mind and lots of it. ALL that they stole from my ancestors' god will give it back to me, he hauled in smoke into his lungs and look at the sun as it came up from behind the forest. AND the wicked will be compensated for all they do on the earth he told his self. HE had only gotten about two hours sleep last night and had dreamed that a river started to flow out of the hole in the yard.

INDIAN kept busy fishing and diving and hunting along with MR Patterson the two would go to the big key some days. THE Indian sold crabs Iguanas nothing was of limit nights was the same as day, he would sell a few pounds of fish to the market and keep the rest for his himself. OTHER stuff was going on with him still unimportant things he said that he really couldn't mention to anyone. HE made use of the time he worked at the landscaping at home it was sure to impress Aliza, Despite what she had said he knew she was happy there and loved the little place. SHE hadn't moved back in yet but at least they were they still engaged she was the best thing that had ever happen to him. HE kept up the phone calls and visited her every day at the Nightingale place he was trying hard.

THEY were out spearing sea food one day. IF I lose her MR Patterson I don't know what will happen. I know son you two really love each other, like all women treat her with respect and listen to her when she talks. ME and Marsha been married over 30 years now we argue but always work things out. DON'T tell them about all the troubles in life else they'll get worried and sad, AND they don't want you sleeping with every woman on the Island know what I mean.

I know how it is with unna young boys still but you got to hide wha you doing when it comes to those things, or better yet don't do it. ESPECIALLY on this island who you think na seeing is the one watching everything. DON'T ever carry home any sickness and remember your wife is always the queen, never make her look bad. ALIZA tells me you all going to church this Sunday. YES sir answer the Indian. NOW I told you a hundred times already Indian drop with the sir you making me feel too old, I going try myself and make it Marsha keep insisting.

ALIZA sat on the back steps of the Nightingale house, she was sad and depress confused and upset with the situation. SHE had been unemployed just as long as boyfriend almost. THE Pattersons had raised she they were both family and friends, she had known them all her life. THE Nightingale house was their home and she was always welcome there.

HER boyfriend was doing the best he could as a man, the little fish money kept her with her womanly things and needs and chased way duppie's sort of speak. THE Indian man and MR Patterson who was like a father to her would fishing at least three times a week. BUT it was nothing not enough she had other financial needs she wanted a better life to put it frankly and a career again after all she was well educated one of the top in her field. OTHERS with less credentials than her were living a more successful lifestyle, besides she was pregnant now and wanted a home and father for her babies. A foundation was started for a bigger home up on the land, but now with this problem between them she didn't know how it would turn out. SHE had told Indian she would get an abortion but that was definitely out of the question. IT was mare girl talk to frighten up her man he had hurt her bad and don't know if she could forgive him. EVENTHOUGH she was in love with the no good two timer he had other fine virtues about him, cute in a manly kind of way ambitious and he had a brain too. HE made her laugh and now cry she looked at the engagement ring he gave her some five years ago it was only intended for a short time before they were to be married. SHE squeezed a pendent that was on a gold chain around her neck a brown stone hung inches from her breast, also from her boyfriend one of his first gifts to her. INDIAN had found it one day while he was on the property they had up in the bush where he was building the little shack they now stay in. HE said it would bring them good luck for sure. But so far that wasn't the case.

ALIZA spent the days helping out at the Nightingale house and doing other church work with Mama Patterson. She had job applications out there and was signed up at the unemployment office right here in town nothing was happening. MARSHA Patterson came outside it was just about sunset. Don't you cry my child she said while giving Aliza a long hug all men are idiots dear? THEY talked a while until it was dark and then went inside and prepared supper.

ONE Friday morning four black boys packed there gears to go fishing, they were headed for the big key also known as Volcano Island. IT was a good ways of from Grand Cayman miles to the east. THEY would fish and hunt too the trip they made tons of times as boys with their fathers their people had done this for ages in times gone by. VOLCANO Island was mountainous about 10 square miles in size so it wasn't too small.

NO one lived there since the 32 hurricane fish and wild life flourished there. THE boys all came from the little village farthest east of Grand Cayman, loaded with Caymanian hospitality and customs. MANLY fiscal hard work was only seasonal and lacking for these simple people. FISHING was their lively hood and they respected the sea. THE ventured to volcano Island frequently more than normal over the last year the villagers could be seen there every day, different fishermen all the same from the east end community. A day's journey to go and return by motor dory, which involved pronging for fruits crabs wilks lobster iguanas wild bores any food kind was up for grabs. THE Island belonged to no one in particular same parts were zoned to be national park, but people were allowed to fish and hunt as they please in other areas. IT was loved by all families spent Easter weekend there and had picnics it was a place of harmony and relaxation, a dream come true for hunters and fishermen. Campers slept in caves and under the stars around a camp fire. THE grass was tech-na color and the trees same to hold the wind better there It was pollution free as secluded. The rain ran off the hills and into the valleys that formed a nice little gully. THE water was sweet and in abundance the spring produced sufficient during the dry season. LOCALS had even found two great water wells chiseled into the cliff at two separate parts of the Island made by old Indian settlers most likely. THE little Island was a paradise now and its dark history was no longer talked about.

THE Island had been unclaimed ever since the Indians almost a century ago, those who died there in 1932 had Indian blood and Creole genes in them. HUMAN sacrificial warship was made by the Indians to their Gods of prosperities and for rain. ALONG with other rituals associated with ancient religion, there was a small burial site on the Island. Where only the common Indian lay kings queens princes medicine men and other considered important ranking Indians in the tribe were put to rest in another location though their tombs were never found. NO one of any statue was buried there quite strange for their honorable. IMPORTANT Indians would have been buried with glory and their wealth and other symbols that would have identified them in the other world. ARCHAEOLOGIST had study the site and graves and didn't know what to make of it. THEY had uncover a few Images though to be pre –Mayan some even claimed it was a prison of a sort and that only a certain section of the population lived there. BUT there was no proof of nothing. For some reason trees were found here that could not be grown back in Grand Cayman or any of the other main Islands. THEY were paintings on the cave walls of Indians, nature, birds and animals of the wind fire and water. IN one of the cave ceiling high up in the mountains an illustration showed native Caymanian Indians drowning according to scientist it was related to the great flood. A tourist found a knife one time with a jade handle in the shape of a snake and some letters printed on it. OTHERS were lucky and discovered artifacts of pottery. THE Island was a volcano and it was impossible to see that it had not erupted maybe a thousand years ago. SCIENTIST had examined formations and analyzed rocks from inside a crater.

CHANGE had taken place all the same and the Island was now one valuable piece of real estate and a billionaire had secure himself with 30 plus acres he had built a mansion and a hotel resort on the best part of the Island in terms of scenery. HE owned oil wells all over the world and was a successful business man, who made political ties with chains that were unbreakable with Downing Street's permission he bought half of Volcano Island.

THEY had been several instances there so far with fishermen and hunters trespassing, people were disrespected by guards men called names and ran off the property. THE cliffs and mountain pecks area around the mansion were heavily guarded these days by arm guards. THE resort was a private world within itself and only the few could afford it a real city of Enoch where sadist fulfilled their deepest desert. NO one knew much about the place not even the law. THE site was operated by giant solar system and a few wind mills. SOME said it was a secret military training camp for Special Forces of the British army and counter terrorist groups involving information gathering and sophisticated torturing biological war fair and research etc.

SIGNS were posted all over the Island even in places where the Arab billionaire didn't own. KEEP off trespassers will be shot no hunters allowed.

THE wind started to come out from the north seas got bigger the boys decided to move around to the south side of the island. THAT Arab might own the land but no one owns the ocean. EARLIER while on land the boys had loaded up on mangoes which was in season all year round on Volcano Island. They found cashews nuts and other fruits and wild bri kind all secured in the boat head of the 20 foot panga. THEY were half dozen Iguanas two big birds and a small deer already skinned and protected from spoiling. AN old 22 rifle lay on top of the hunt, with couple sticks of cane, jack fruit and a bucket of red plums. THE panga reach the spot on the south on the outside of the reef there was a huge building on the hill off in the distant. THIS was their last stop for the day they would fish for an hour or two before heading home. THE boat was loaded with trolling fish the boys had caught earlier and now they were killing snappers. FISH biting said one of the boys ga make good of this can't go back gun bay empty handed. GIVE me one of those Benson he said to one of them. THE 3-0-clock sun had gone under a series of clouds, SO it wasn't that heavy down pour of sun light. THE fisher men ran joke and pulled in thigh hand they were pulling up some big boys out of the ocean. THE sound of gun fire broke the rhythm of silent the boys looked at each other in confusion as bullets flied over their heads. THEN came the racial slurs that were without boundary. TWO people were in a speed boat with camouflage uniform on holding machine guns pointing at the Panga. ONE man spoke into a speaker horn get the fuck out my ocean you bunch of niggers you're trespassing. IT was hard to tell how many shots were fired and if they were warning shots or not. ONE of the fisher men got hit in the throat he fell over a bunch of green plantains dying fast with his hands on the wound another one took two slugs in the chest and drop over board. BLOOD was all over the boat. THE speed boat flung across them producing big waves the remaining boys on the panga were hysterical one of them cut the anchor rope and tried finding the 22, a second later the super speed boat rammed them, breaking the panga in two. IT looked like a little toy long side the super 600 speed boat. AS the boys surfaced to the top in their half dying breaths the men took out their side arm a 45 automatic. A bullet went into the ear of one and to the head back of the next, KILLING both of them instantly. FUCKING niggers giving us all this work today, do sharks eat black meat said one of them then started to laugh.

THE 6am news reported four men missing at sea after heading to Volcano Island the day before had not been seen. SEARCH and Rescue team were dispatched late last night but have found nothing so far. MARINE unit along with cost guard and air search had been carried out. IN other news police arrested several members of a prostitutions ring, disguised as an on line dating service ten people were arrested in Cayman and over twenty in the U.S including the owners and CEO of the company. THE undercover operation was a success according to police more arrest will follow in the coming weeks.

THE Indian man turn off the radio the weather had gotten nasty over night all the seem but it wasn't nothing those boys couldn't handle he said to himself. NO one knew what to think of the whole matter they had been a candle light ceremony for the boys the following night.

THE boys gather at the usual place the Indian had been alone for the last week. THE little house seemed abandoned without her even the parrot were giving Indian a hard time. ALIZA wasn't pleased at all and was keeping him out to dry a little longer. HER clothes some of them were in the house so Indian felt there was still a change. HE didn't get back into the taxi driving too much temptation. I giving her some space he told the boys when they tested him I the man in this thing he said. THE boys would laugh you hiding your real feelings Indian towards that woman she got you wrap around her fingers dawg, said Tate. THEY meant a little earlier today the deal had when through they chipped up and bought a few pounds of high grade Jamaica marijuana, they weighed it off and shared it up. A small fire with light smoke blew to the west ward as they burned weed under the house floor. THIS some good SES Samm said one of them while inhaling and making a winding sound with his mouth his lips were in a roundish position. IT was a good while before he blew out any smoke which was clear and tin. A small battery radio rested at the bottom of a house post the evening talk show was on. YOU hear what happen to those boys said Indian openly. YAH that bad man who that was asked Kingdon. MCLEAN and them him and his brother and two other friends of his. THEY found some empty gasoline containers and couple bunches of green bananas floating but that's it nothing else. That Panga capsized with em man said Tate. THINK so. MOST likely. THOSE east Enders say they could had have trouble with that white man that owns Volcano Island. ALL kinds of things going on out there and the police and them know bout it too. ORGANIZED to the max said Kingdon puling in hard on his spliff. THAT Na going stay like that they McLean's this time Samm.

THEY were callers to the talk show voicing their sympathy for the missing boys. OTHERS talked about unemployment one guy called saying a tourist had walked out in front of his car, and a neighbor's cat had peed in some one porch an old lady had dreamt that the whole Island was on fire.

THE guys talked and hanged out into the late night, Indian made fish tea. THEY prophesied whaled sesimenya taking the bible out a few times to read Psalms and Proverbs. PHONES were ringing off the hook they made phone calls and home boys and respectable people check them for stuff. THE were outsiders there tonight and girls visited but Indian stayed clear from them.

COME morning the place was desired Johnny the youngest of the crew had lift his bicycle under the floor and left with a chic last night in her car. THE Indian watered the plants and began to rake the yard.

THE forces of Babylon continue to rise but people took it as the norm. Many carried on their good works by talking reality and talk wasn't only cheap it was dangerous. ALL the same when the wicked set a trap God made it known to his people, and they kicked it down. THE Island small you see so you had to watch out else they say you rebelling against the queen. MORE and more each day God was talking to Cayman and the fig tree leaves were shaking the signs of Jonah the prophet apparent. We will be ruled by women according to the prophets the queen owns half of the world today man bow down before her like people do before Sad am Hussein and many other so named leaders in history Haile Selassie for argument sake. MORE and more women are involved in politicks now a days remember every dog is born free.

BACK in Cayman in crime was becoming better organized even by the pettiest of criminals, aggravated assault and robberies home invasion wasn't nothing strange on the morning news. A bomb had already hit the Island it just hadn't exploded yet. THE days in Cayman discussing Cayman had forgotten God and his laws they sat and worked hand and hand with the wicked council. WE called good bad and bad good. THE forces of darkness were on the surface not by any one person or organization alone but by a joint effort of all sinners and evil combined. CAYMAN had gotten worse in the name of betterment and it was in fact showing up it's colors as a modern day vampire state. CAYMAN had become one of the fastest growing destinations in the Caribbean. LITTLE Church towns now had bar rooms and mega shopping plaza and large amount of budget homes and housing schemes, many by private developers. THE winds of change and the boom of the 90's had cleared the way for such programs. THE banks made interests and contractors made profits few native born Caymanians lived there mostly status holders and married permit workers who tied the knot with some venerable Caymanian occupied such homes. STEADY employment was necessary to maintain bank loans and real Caymanians were highly unemployed. WATCH no face call no names many were happy to be breathing still and in the place GOD wanted them to be. THE Indian man unable to find any kind of employment period continued to steal his little sea food from the ocean and make do, MARINE laws were in every good spot along the bay. HE was in pieces and hurting to see what was happening, The Island that time forgot had not really been forgotten and it had grown up to became Babylon the Great or one of it's mirrors. NO more was he believing the system of lies, THE devil and his disciples were teaching. HE was willing to defend this place the peace movement wasn't working he would have to do whatever it takes. AS an ordinary man he did not want to accept what god was telling him as a spiritual man and a soldier he was willing to die for his rights to life and his people. HE was failing JAH by not warning Caymanians about Babylonian oppression and wickedness. ME as a RASTAMAN and human being Na doing GOD's work he told he self one night rolling around in his bed sleepless. HE was still eating one meal a day and slapping of mosquitoes at nights.

CAYMAN seemed hopeless an honest living had become a lie success was to obtain no soul. THE whole labor market had been capitalized at every corner.

PHASE two of the Hotel down on seven mile beach was finish and the landscape people were planting Washingtonians. THE boys had kept in contact with the office but they wasn't ready to hire anybody yet the secretary insured. THE contractor started phase two a week later after the boys had checked there for employment.

PERMIT workers and Emigrants were the new work force in Cayman strings had been pulled and someone knew someone else down at Immigration and in parliament. WHO was taken out one night for couple drinks got drunk and Julia the bar maid slash working girl went down on him in the car out in the parking lot. THE old man almost had a heart attack and whatever the Developers wanted was granted. THE boys were going job hunting today to hell with seven mile beach they thought they would scout out the eastern part of the Island and see what gives. ONE two residential projects were going on up there besides they had nothing else to do today anyways if the weather is better tomorrow they'll go fishing. NONE were fishermen by trade but they could handle themselves at sea they were Caymanians it was just in their blood. FATHERS took their children fishing in days gone by, both boys and girls and they taught them to swim as soon as they could walk.

ALIZA and the rest of the girls didn't waste time with their boyfriends they had other constructive plans for the day too they were selling food from the back of Babeth's blazer.

THERE was no traffic to speak of on the east side so it was smooth rolling for the Toyota a net of marijuana smoke followed the car going fifty miles an hour. A radio was playing the same battery operated one that was underneath the house floor the car stereo hadn't worked in years. THEY had only past one police trouper so far about ten miles back watching for speeders. THE rookie cop noticed the busted tail light on the Toyota but was too occupied talking to woman on his cell at the time to even bother. A playboy magazine lay on the seat next to him, for Christ sake get that thing of the road he said shouting out of the car window. THE boys listened to the radio program they were numb up man had already burnt five spliff each and it was only 11 A.M. GOOD thing you never came in Babeth's ride king you would have never get that weed sent out of it said Indian. YEH she would have probably kill me and didn't give me anything for months. THEY each brought a fresh shirt to put on as they went to out to the site and ask around for work. A pack of cigarettes was in the glove compartment just incase of any emergency like being stop by police, they would light up quick and blow smoke to drown the weed sent. THE job site had no bosses nor foremen no one there spoke English and when they did you could not understand them. THIS kind of thing only throwing wood on the fire Samm said the Indian man.

BY 2003 there were some serious political activist in Cayman and these hard times were feeding them. IF the local Government and police couldn't handle it the mother country would be sending in the National Guard that was the feeling everybody had and when that happened marshal law would follow then it was all over for Cayman. A letter had been sent to the radio station and the talk show host read it over the air.

THE crew gathered that evening they would be pulling a all nighters involving small time juggling selling strictly grass. A few intellectuals came by looking marijuana but incase these guys were cops they didn't take any chances even though they had dealt before. JOHNNY and his friend lance pretended to get the stuff from someplace else you could never be too careful. THEY drove to a bar some miles down the road and Johnny went into the restroom took a bag out of his crouch and put it into his waist line lulling a big shirt over it. HE bought a beer and talked to a man that had nothing to do with the situation seven minutes later he when outside where Lance awaited him with the two computer geeks.

ALIZA babes I need you more than ever Indian said into the cell phone, I suffering without you here I don't know how long I can go on like this. That'll be OK if I come cross and look for you tomorrow Baby. YOU don't get any Ideas Indian replied Aliza.

THE following day they went to the supermarket after socializing with a few people they stop at a place in the water front and had cookie and smoothies. THE parking lot over looked the sea, IN the car they sat looking out onto the harbor. A small church was across the street all around were souvenir and gift shops it was the tourist part of town. A craft market and a hard rock café were just steps away. A little deli nearby that catered to tourist and locals made the best smoothies on the Island. KINGDON call asking where he was at but he told him he was with his woman and not coming home right now go head and burn that Kool nothing wrong with that Samm. THE cruise ship was leaving for the day it was late evening she was disappearing rapidly on the horizon. THE man held her hand and tried embracing her. I going sell the car we need the money he said. HOW much you will get for this thing Indian. SOMETHING enough to buy the electrical material for the house I want to try and get the floor poured, before bush start to grow in the foundation. I can get bout on foot for a while the house is more important right now. ONE Pilipino man wants to buy it he's a mechanic can do most of the work himself get parts easy from Asia. YOU don't have any work coming up then Indian what are we going to do. ALIZA honey this means am one step closer to getting the floor poured everything will be all right babes don't worry yourself. I want the best for this child too give him what I couldn't give the rest. IT'S two of them Indian. YOU mean we having twins he took her in his arms and kissed her she didn't move away or responded to it. THEY talked some more he wanted to ask her when she was coming home but decided not to push his luck.

HE carried Aliza to the Nightingale house then headed home. HE smoked a Bob Marley spliff that night outside his shack.

THE morning brought rain and flashes of lightening could be seen through the window and the down pour of the rain was heard upon the zinc, ALONG with soft thundering in the back ground. THE Indian man was on his knees praying he prayed every day actually at lease four times. HE kept no special day for warship and claimed no specific religious domination. HIS usual morning ritual also included smoking two to three joints. THIRTY minutes later he was looking out of the glass plains of the little bush house. HE wasn't drinking coffee this morning he was sipping yellow plum juice from a tree out back in big cup, and eating a piece of homemade bread Aliza had giving him last night Mango jam was spread all over it. THE rain had slowed down to a few light sticks. RAIN drops dripped from the overhang eaves of the little cottage. MR CHISHOM'S cows were of in the distance they seemed to be loving the weather a flock of sea gulls and Bobbies had gather around a puddle. SOME whistling ducks played of to the other end. THE mangrove forest was colorful this morning as the sun awaken the vegetation. YOU could almost see the blueness of the ocean through the trees which was only a couple hundred yards away. THEY owned it all right up to the ocean a good six acres. HE finished the juice and put the cup on the small wooden table and looked at the foundation out in the yard. HE had started it years ago with not much head ways it was 1995 he recalled.

HAD just finish a development for an American man he worked for at the time, a series of affordable homes in different locations on the Island. A young entrepreneur with his hair in a pony tail back then twenty pounds liter and making more money than what he thought could spend. HE went to the bank one morning to make his usual and final withdraw the project was over with but other jobs coming up. HE put money into a fixed deposit and savings account one of many at the time. HE finished up the transaction and headed back down stairs. STEPPING into the elevator he said good morning to the only other person there a nice looking Hispanic girl with long legs and a Coca-Cola bottle shape. SHE was tin but not skinny flesh over her bones hair was like silk and beautiful diamond shape eyes. A French nose small and neat with find lips, she was a knock out. SHE worn no makeup she looked amazing like a God sent angel. SHE looked like she was glowing thought I died and went to heaven he said to himself remembering. WHAT floor you going to he asked her. FIRST please said a sweet voice. THAT makes two of us said the man pushing a button. HE was quiet at first but kept looking at her like shy little school boy and she kept smiling back at him. THE elevator made a sudden jerked and came to a stop the lights went out everything was dark for a few seconds. YOU OK yes and you yah the elevator must be stuck. USING the light on his cell phone the Indian man found the emergency switch bells went off when he pulled it, but the elevator didn't move. WELL this a first for me, me too said the girl. Since we stuck together you mind if I ask you your name. ALIZA, nice to meet you Aliza and you are asked the girl he told her his name but everybody just call me Indian. I see said the girl with a curious expression in her eyes. YOU got a beautiful smile and a accent Aliza way part you from. GEORGE Town she answered. YOU mean you not Spanish, Good lord no she laughed softly. Sorry if I offended you, IT not like that just that no one ever told me that before. YOU got a nice name what that Creole, Jewish or something. SOME thing like that maybe even Indian I got a little of that in my blood too. THAT makes two of us then doesn't it your beautiful Aliza is it MISS or MRS. YOUR fast she said and it's MISS BLAKES by the way she extended her hand for a hand shake. THIS is a real coincident I couldn't asked to be stuck in an elevator with a better person it's a real pleasure she laughed again. THEY talked for about 15 minutes before the elevator started moving again. SHE invited him to church and he managed to get a number they went out on a few dates and the two of them hit it off. THEY started to see each other more often.

ALIZA BLAKES worked with an accounting firm at the time and was sent to Trinidad and Tobago, also Bermuda to work for a year he flied off to see her couple times and in contact every now and then she came home on holiday etc. INDIAN gave her the time she needed they both respected the relationship and the love between them grew. IT took me three years before I could reel her in he said to himself. WHEN she finely returned home for good from her work overseas one night out on a date at a little spot on the water front while eating cookies and natural ice cream for desire. ON the open terrors up stair on the parlor under the stars lit night a little table was of in one corner. DOWN on his knees was when he pop the question and ask her to marry him, she accepted and they kissed. HE placed a ring on her finger they were to be married in a few months time. BUT one thing lead to another and he got into some trouble with the bank and that complicated things. THEY paid cash for a piece of land and there were no lends against it the price of the property have triple since then. ALTHOUGH he had broken the fix deposit and their saving went they managed to build the one bed room cottage and started the foundation on for their home.

THEY were to take out a mortgage like regular folks do and have a normal life that is until they ran into this wall of problems that they never gotten over and had changed their existence. THE hard luck stories followed one after the next from there on, construction slowed down for him big time and he couldn't even get a lawn mooring job to save his life. THAN Caribbean accounting relocated to Johannesburg South Africa changed name and down size to just three Employees. THEY eventually went bankrupt nine months later. ALIZA doesn't even know I had something to do with it he said rolling a spliff I was only trying to do the right thing anyway. ALIZA got her employees benefit all the same and was paid off according to law but most of the money evaporated in the bureaucratic system of today's world on legal assistants, Insurance, Pension and other taxes. THE rest went on living expensive, not that they lived a glamorous life style but she too had fallen between the cracks and seemed to be forgotten by those that were meant to protect her. LIKE many other Caymanian born at the time due to political reasons and over site if you may. INDIAN stared out at the foundation it was a slab type construction about three feet up of the ground it had been closed in with concrete blocks and filled up with dirt or marl then compacted with a machine typical Cayman building style. HE installed the plumbing pipes himself, BY the help of God I'll get it pour soon he said.

HE put on his blue jean and went outside shirtless the rain had subsided and gone the morning was cool. HE took a shovel and pickaxe from under the floor and put them into a wheel barrow and pushed it over by some aggregate piled up in the yard. AND begin to fill back up a hole he had made the day before the same pit where he was digging a well at, but he realized the spring was poor.

LATER that day he was inside frying fish and breadfruit when kingdon came cross looking for him the cottage door was open and the sea breeze blew right through. WHA going on blood that fish smell good though. SAMM this taste good too replied the Indian man, you want some. WHY not can turn that down that fish this time Samm. BOY I Na eat nothing yet still me and Babeth at war too you know how that go. YAH tell me bout it must be the moon said Indian. SHE fined a strand of hair on the bed last night and said I bring woman up in the Apartment and screw her on the bed. THAT her own piece of hair now, bout that Na her hair she know her hair. Man ga go through plenty shit in this life boy especially with a sick in the head woman like wha I got they. YOU and Aliza Na ga no problems compare to me and Babeth, she the worst out of all them

Cayman woman whatever pops into that head of hers that's the holy truth. I love the gal all the same don't get me wrong just that I can't understand her you know what I mean.

THERE was plenty fish to go round and the two men ate and reasoned, when they were done they lay in the hammock underneath the shack. EACH one stuck together two rolling papers and twisted up a big one, coughing every now and then. AN hour or two had zip by when Kingdon said I ga go Samm and pick up that woman from work she in one of her gypsy spells over whatever she can find to or how bout if I get the late that's a perfect excuse for her to argue. SHE had already called him saying he was driving up and down all day in her car smoking weed when he should be looking a job and making money for her. YAH man I know how it is old boy said Indian. WHEN the spliff was finish king waited around for a ten minutes long enough for the marijuana scent to die down a little then got into the ride. SEE you tomorrow Rasta Kool Samm get that gate on the way out for me.

INDIAN talked to ALIZA on the cell for a while he hated phones period they were evil and a Babylonian creation they carried radiation to brains he stayed away from them as much as possible. THEN he lit up another one and meditated in the hammock a little longer rocking from side to side as his thoughts ran deep.

THE 2 o clock sun burst in the sky but wasn't until around 3 before he started to work at the hole again it was near filled to the top. HE continued into the late evening. Night was upon the swamp and the Indian was naked as he was born outside bathing. WATER splash off the concrete pad that was under the water tank it was high up enough to stand and shower. THERE was a bathroom inside but he felt like outside tonight not a light was on. ONE piece of solar panel was adequate to operate the electrical needs of the shack he had rigged it himself. THE little old Caymanian home was comfortable and functional, he was whistling under the water. LATE into the night he was on the phone with Aliza when the rain started back up. I love you ALIZA Blake's he said. YOU sure about that she said seriously. I positive bout that. TEN minutes after Aliza said good night see you in church tomorrow Indian I asking GOD to bless your sole. YAH sweetie good night he said. THE Indian wasn't much of a conversationalist and Aliza knew this but she just needed to hear his voice it comforted her.

BABETH was spending the night with Aliza her and Kingdon fought he was burning up gasoline and had no money to buy any, she took her car away from him. I claw him in his face after he insulted me he probably in some bar room now drunk as he could be I aint go let this man treat me like a piece of rug Aliza girl. THE Indian man cut up a whack of weed and packed his challis pipe. AFTER Church tomorrow I'll go and look for mama he said it had been a month since he saw her about two weeks had past and he didn't even pick up a phone to call her. AM a worthless son he confess to himself? POOR old dad he said and started thinking about his father.

THE year was 1984 his old man was a carpenter on a job site. AT Sparks and Dougely Construction Company. THEY were one of the biggest names back then when it came to construction they had been around for almost five decades. GORMAN Sparks never went to sea he made his money from real estate his family were among the first settlers from Scotland. MOST were carpenters by trade, and they built sail boats back in the olden days. BY the 60's they were well known in the furniture business and anything to do with lumber basically including home etc. MOST men went to sea but Gorman sparks stayed at home and invested in land along the way. THE sea men sent money home and the women bought land and built homes. EVENTHOUGH family and friends helped construct one another homes in some cases those who could afford it would hire the best. IN the 70's Real estate was flowing like a river and one had to ride or step aside? THE Cayman Island had seen the light the world had found them Democracy was becoming a phenomenon. MODERNIZATION was a part of life people needed habitat in the form of land and building.

ISSAC Dougely came from Jamaica with a career in Architecture was hired for a project on the seven mile beach one of the first of it's kind here in Cayman at the time. THE Construction of a two story hotel that was to be built on the sand by foreign Developers. IT was 1955 and Gorman Sparks and son Construction would also be a part of the project as general contractors. TWO years later the hotel was a success and Isaac Dougely and Gorman Sparks became partners and form Sparks and Dougely. BY the 90's they were the tycoons of the Construction industry.

A major five story building was being erected in the summer of 1984 the labor force was 50/50 with Caymanians and Expatriate alike.

MALACHI HOWVETT a middle age Indian man was up 50 feet in the air working on scaffolding. A sky lift had just eased some material into place to attach an iron beam to a wall. TWO other men worked with him wearing hard hats and harnesses along with other safety equipment. AS the lifter backed away it jumped a gear and launched forward into the scaffolding throwing two of the men onto a small plate form just of to the side. THE socket that the harness was fasten to, came loose and broke MR Howett fell forty feet breaking his spinal cord. HE was confine to a wheel chair and practically bed ridden for the rest of his life. INVESTIGATIONS follow and indicated that MR Howett had deliberately flung himself of the place barely missing a wooden storage and tool shade and inflated cushions boundary around the building down below. LANDING between two pieces of rebar's pointed up right. HE did it to sue the company but his plan had fail, said the report from the labor union and injure workers organization. THE Judge didn't buy it after witness testified in court the ruling was negligence at best, on MR HOWVETT'S behalf he was not paying attention to the operator of the lifter signal and miss the timing completely. THE two other work men got promoted and MR Howett life was a hear after. HIS wife spoke to lawyers but they were reluctant to take the case. SPARKS and Dougely was divided into several share holders by then couple politicians and other wealthy merchants along with judges and famous unknowns. WHO were not about to go down or pay out billions to some Indian that was drunk out on the job. MANY knew it to be corruption and the tree was too big to cut down. THE man lived on well fear and the Caymanian Government took care of his medical needs until they got tired of it and find legal ways to get round him. HE died seven years ago with a broken heart; the old man had grown up with some of these same people that turned their backs on him. HE knew most of the men that owned Sparks and Dougely they were good people he told his son until money happen to them. THEY were rich and white and dad was an Indian he said to himself holding in marijuana smoke in his lungs. THEY took away his life and that of his children and wife. THE kids grew up lacking and went to school hungry to bed same way sometimes father was unable to provide for them now God only knows how my dear mama managed it he said. 1996 came Indian was a young man and ruthless after learning the details of his father case for his self and understood what had happen. HE hired a team of overseas lawyers but it was too late by then the so call Statue of limitations had ran out. THE technical maneuver would protect SPARKS and DOUGELY no one could touch them.

TEARS were in the man's eyes as he remember what had happen to his father his eyes were glistening red he stack the challis pipe again, for another round. SOME days after he went to the office of Sparks and Dougely while they were having a board meeting and insulted and curse the bunch of them out. THEY called enforcement and had him removed from the establishment. THEY got a personal hatred for all us Malachi Howett people the Indian told himself, he punch his fist into the wall a few times. HE continued smoking the pipe it was raining outside hard now and lightning there was a big crack of thunder. HE stripped down nude can ran out of the house dancing and chanting words in the native tongue, looking like a mad man. HE was speaking to god in the Caymanneki language. DEAR creator forgive me and my enemies give me what is minds in this life rightfully and correct me went am wrong.

FULL my heart with love provide me with my needs and those of my family. ACCEPT my father's spirit into your kingdom. AND if I have anger you in this quest for betterment show me thy way dear protector smile upon your people o great one. AT that very same moment a piece of rotten limb fell from a tree nearby and frighten the hell out of the man. THAT'S a sign from JAH he said and got inside quickly and smoked his challis.

MORNING came and Indian did his usual ritual got dress and went to church. HE sat next to Aliza she knew he was high but would continue to pray for him. THE preacher had gotten use to seeing him in blue jeans and cowboy boots that were pointed. WEARING a yellow dress shirt with a collar that Aliza had bought for him he looked decent to be going to a night club. HE only worn cotton shirts other made his skin itch. ACROSS from him were the Patterson's and Kingdon and Babeth.

THE church was just on the out skirts of central George Town a small congregation with unions to bigger movements. From the Indian's point of view all Sunday churches were sister to the mother Harlot he had been raised in the Sabbath church considered himself to be a Jew, but he had conclude recently that all of them were the same these days and was cautious. THE world gone bazurk he said to himself looking around the room. THE Cayman Island Government had granted million dollar loans to churches and children went to school hungry and senior citizens were in need of medication and other care that could not be provided to them. THE Church was being renovated and expanded expats on work permits could be seen there through the week days, and poor natives had no jobs and were turn down. MILLIONS more were being donated to the churches by anonymous donators to build so say hurricane shelters and once it had the churches name on it there were no Audits or back ground checks by banks or other financial institutions. THE Priest drove a 2003 BMW and lived in a million dollar home how can the Government give way money in these hard times there had been official statements claiming the Government was Bankrupt.

SO tell me my son when are you two getting married said Indian's mother that after noon. AS soon as god opens the way mama. YOU been saying that a while son. I know Mama but hopefully soon now the situation hard to explain. TELL me my dear what's wrong. I was dreaming about papa last night. AND what did he say to you this time. Nothing I only saw him. YOU must have been provoking his spirit from the grave by how that happened. NO actually I was thinking about those demons that put him there mama. CAME on now son she called him from his full name there be no such talking in my house she was talking in the Caymanneki tongue revenge is in the heart of the wicked, and forgiveness is the ways of the righteous. ALIZA Indian and Mama sat at the kitchen table where Indian had eaten as a boy. A picture of his father hang on the wall of the dining room along with other paintings and ornaments that decorated the home. TWO little Indian girls appeared in front of them with their hair breaded in two pieces. UNCLE they said at the same time and a priestess they spoke Caymanian English. ALIZA said something to them in Caymanneki and they understood her and replied.

THE two of them took Aliza by the hand and wondered of in the direction of the bed room. Iomi still in the Brac chasing that man of hers said mama the children here with me for a couple days. AND junior asked Indian he still at the tenders. HE sure is not making anything much but he's there as long as they need him. WHERE your boys are. INDIAN shook his head not wanting to talk about it but finely said they all right I haven't seen them in weeks they call me sometimes. HE had two son by different women they were grown boys 18 and 14. THEY continued to talk in Caymanneki ALIZA is expecting twins' mama he said. SHE didn't seem surprise am glad for you it's a blessing son god is good, he will help you to provide for them. ALIZA returned with the girls they were still holding her hands one of them was playing with an Indian doll. I made pumpkin cake said mama especially for you Indian. I going enjoy that mama how you know we were coming. MAMA cut two big slice of cake and they ate heavy cake and drink fruit punch then talk some more. IT was some two hours later when Indian said good bye to his mother. SHE kissed the both of them on the fore head god be with you my children she said. DON'T let him scare you with that Apache talk of his Aliza mama said smiling as they walked outside.

THE old place brought back memories. THE Howett family home sat on one acre of land. I remember I shot my first agouti rabbit right over there pointing at some trees as they walked to the car. DAD made us practice for years before we master the art of killing the animal with one strike of the bow and arrow. HE thought us the right tree to make the bow and arrow with he showed us how to make a fire and clean and cook what we hunted. WE use to make sling shot to shoot birds. OH Indian that so cruel. WE were just kids Aliza didn't know what we doing. DAD learn us basic self defense and how to use a knife and other survival techniques of the Caymanneki people how to fish hunt fight he said bragging to Aliza. SEE that big Neeseberry tree out there we had a tree house in that man we we you to have fun. WE would get torn pickle for spikes wrap it with a leaf in the shape of a cone then tie it up with a vine that was peel tin like a tread. AND blow it through a bamboo pipe and kill lizards we would do it just for badness. ALIZA made up her face in discuss. IT'S was how our fore father hunted and fought wars. THEY would dip the dart into poison and shoot it into the brains or the eyes you will be amazed by how much dangerous plants in Cayman no poison frogs or anything like that but lots of other insects carry deadly toxins. THE car back away then turned exiting the yard he gave his mother a wave goodbye. AS he drove through the neighborhood he talked it wasn't always fun times and business for us we passed same hard days especially after dad got his accident I had to quit school and go to work after social service find out that I was skipping school I had to study and work too. WE use to caught the bus right there they would be some fights and thing on them girls too ripping off each other uniform. YEAH I remember some of those on our bus too sometimes the bus driver would go and part it and end up fighting he would get beat up too. THEY both laughed, George Town use to win all the school sports day every year said Aliza that's true Indian said agreeing but they never use to win the events that I was in. YEH right said Aliza. WE use to have break dance and rap off competition I was the best said the Indian bragging again. ALIZA laugh YEH right, I don't ever remember about Indians break dancing in school especially if they were fat the kids from school wouldn't have forget that a fat Indian boy dancing hip hop no way. YOU must have been the crowd controller. THE laugher went on a little longer this time. THEY had been through the school system together Indian a couple years ahead but didn't really know of one another.

THE little shack was off the main high way about 300 feet into a dirt road the only house in that particular area. IT was in a remote section of the island public works roads authority were too busy doing other important things in those soon to be high class subdivisions farther down the road, not even a sign posted the street name yet it had been this way for years. UP the road they were laying public water pipes and installing electrical over head lines. Other than that there wasn't a soul around for miles only wet lands patches of savannah, Button wood swamps and Mangrove Marsh Forest. IT was Monday morning and the man had just finished his usual morning mediation and was praying JAH protect us from all evil this day in any form that it might appear. From illness envy and accidents continue to guide me and show me your true way on this earth, he said some more words in silent BLESSED then open his eyes they were red as fire. HE was standing on his feet when kingdon drove down the long drive way. HE had on a Rastafarian wardrobe a loose fitting blue jeans camouflage long sleeve cloth Jacket unbutton and a white t shirt underneath. BLACK work boots came up a little above the ankles and an all color cotton fabric handmade Rasta belt was hanging two feet or so from his waist. IT protected him from evil spirit a haggler from the village made them. HE worn sunglasses and a black baseball cap with a Jaguar on it.

HOW much you said you want for the car again asked a gentleman. One thousand came the reply. I can only give you eight hundred. THERE was a pause, all right give me that for I change my mind said Indian bluffing. YOU still get good deal she needs lots of work done remember I pay back license Said the Philippino man. INDIAN ran some errands in town and met with his brother, JR worked on the tender boats that transported cruise ship passengers to from the docks. I sick of this shit now he told Indian five dollars an hour I can make more selling weed. HE had built on a section out back of his mother house where he lived with his wife and kids. The truth is they would have a hard time if they tried to remove him from the job it was easy going and he loved chatting foolishness to the tourist. AFTER going cross to see ALIZA then stopping at the hardware store Indian left the George Town headache behind. BY mid afternoon he saw his little shack again. HE and King did the usual smoke under the floor thing listening to talk radio a preacher was the guess on today's show. A man called asking about having more than one wife but the preacher had no comment. THE program finished early when the host read a poem that someone had sent in. THE two men blew smoke and reason, they both had pipe in their hands tell me something were the dinosaurs around during the great flood. No not in my knowledge said Indian or less they would have gotten save according to the bible. SO that means they were on the earth before Noah times. Yes and two world disaster by that time the destruction of the dinosaurs and the great flood are two different things, SCIENTIST got it all mix up. THAT like religion Indian said lumps of smoke clouded the air. THEIR brains were numb their heads heavy they found it difficult to lay down, they spoke slowly with a slurp. INDIAN's skin was the color of light brass his eyes were brown but the white area were mostly red and his eye brows join slightly. DOTTS of hair form a beard on his face he looked like he needed a shave but this was how he kept it. They grew naturally and there was no distinguish edges from a razor shaping them. HIS hair was good not straight and it was the same high as his beards he had a normal face and you could see he was a Caymanian. HE wasn't fat or small short or tall. KINGDON was a much darker man with RASTA hair and a thick beard.

Hours had passed the Indian man was now alone kingdon gone. HE walked into the bushes out back of the shack into the bite towards the

43

sea. Walking pass a boggy area of swamp the whole place opened up into something different, a small barricader. Continuing along a sandy foot path that had grass growing in the middle a good ways more he stop by a coconut tree and reached down. A few seconds later he brushed off a big glass jar. Sitting on a canoe that was turned upside down just a few feet from the water's edge, he removed some weed from the jar and rolled one up. There was a small waft close by that Aliza and he had built and a pair of her old slippers lay on it from the last time they were out there. HE took in the scenery as he lit the thing up and looked at the time on his cell phone he never did like watches. AT that same instance it rang, a foreign area code blinked on the cell screen with lots of numbers after it. THE man on the other end had a strange voice the young man seemed to be taking information the call lasted 30 minutes before the Indian hanged up then deleted the number.

THE following day another latter had been sent to the talk show, people were starting to pay attention to them they were socially political and seemed to strike at the heart of the Caymanian mind set. They expressed the public knowledge of what was happening on the Island from an anti colonial view. Apparently a computer wiz had broken into the radio station data base system and had broadcast a message of the latter by means of a computer automated voice. IT repeated itself three times over the air waves before it crash and burn. Technicians were unable to stop or do anything about it.

These were some serious times we were living in man, people would be molested and raped in the work place in church and night clubs. People were being murdered in dance halls and you couldn't look at anyone peacefully or smile at them some took it the wrong way. THE police continued to carry out law and order and there were new avenues along with territory to explore but strings were left dangling. CRIMINALS and the powerful continued to intimidate and if this was allowed to go on pretty soon the world would become ungovernable. There was more wickedness than good, minimum wage was justified and according to most cheap labor didn't exist. Other things were going on still that really couldn't be mention the law was the law. Caymanians were being blindsided all how I'll leave it at that, the Island was still in a compulsory situation we were yet to develop a mind of our own if you follow me.

AND radicals, politicians, gangs, and revolutionary seek to over throw imperialism CAYMAN was becoming all you could expect from a little gold mine. ALL bastard child were being named correctly and registered, heck politicians had even promise to legalize marijuana. CAYMAN had become the new land of opportunity in the Caribbean domestic helpers on work permit open there own companies etc. etc. The Island was operating by some strict rules and there was a section out there with this do for self mentality. SMALL fish were being eaten up by shark and the waters had become polluted and predatorily. Life on the rock seemed unreal and funny there were an overwhelming amount of traffic tickets be issued. Preachers began lying on national radio and claiming to be the Messiah. Years went by and you didn't hear of any major cocaine bust, but on the other hand container loads of ganja were found and decoys successful. Work permits continued to be granted and discourage the most ambitious. One dear to say anything about the situation if you did you were out of control or a trouble maker and would have to be dealt with.

You had to fall in line keep quiet and do what we tell you kind of mentality and attitude with the authority. All was well in paradise organizations were set up in the name of god and building were being named after living people. There was a mass migration happening around the world and most of the people were coming to Cayman. Old property was being confiscated by fraudulent means that would be later made into legal transaction by expensive lawyers, even grave yards were starting to disappear. Every now and then fresh knotty up grades marijuana would be on the street and you would be bless if you had a little some people would say. Now gangs they had grown deep and wide even in schools, and class rooms were crowded kids had sex more than you and me. Not only bad man carried tool but Christians got out gun license and youngsters walked to the play ground with them like toys. This was becoming the style all over the world I might add.

ON the labor front it wasn't much to report they were still only hiring foreigners and people they could use. THESE were truly the last days and everyone was being tested and religious movements were springing up all over, never before in the history of Cayman had so many people been converted bombs, street hobo's, Alcoholics, druggist,rapist the blind and deaf were falling down professing the works of god. None believers had no choice but to cling to my great god. A man had chopped off a woman's arm the other day for burning him and he said god had told him to do it. IN another incident an old man hack off the head of his roommate over cigarettes and alcohol. IN other news a catholic priest had molested a little boy but this went unreported by the media. Slowly our colors or strange colors were starting to show up and more and more people would be heard saying Cayman Na wha it use to be. Among the largest financial capitals in the world and what did Cayman have to show for it mistakes and clay institutions. Cayman wasn't no so so Island they were top notch in the Caribbean. BY the end of 2003 they had signed several new contracts with gay cruise liners to visit the Island other top liners made routine stops here. ONE main capital fed the Island's population of 30,000 and growing traffic had reach that of a small city people would walk into town and get there quicker during rush hours. THE aids academics was becoming a loosing battle there had been a number of disease outbreak around the world foot and mount for one and starvations in third world countries. IN Cayman people were occupied trying to get money to buy things they needed and didn't. There were some small back yard farming and agriculture program by government but imports of food and materials and labor was the facts of life.

THE 2004 elections was around the corner and candidates were pushing money buying appliances and building stuff for there constituents etc. Legs were opening up backsides being busted nuts were sore and being hang out to dry. People would be driving new cars without explanation etc. etc. BANK accounts increased over night, businesses would be sold without for sale signs going up. Homes were remodel and built for people without money and the work done by elves. ALL kinds of macaroni pudding was being handed out pork was being eaten up like rain in a dry weather. IT was the same no name game being played as always and all aces were protected. POLITICS had become like cooking up a pot of strew turtle no need to add water just put the fat on top and it cooks in its own self.

THE electrical rough out and plumbing on the main building was finish, Indian would save up fish money till he had enough to pour the floor.

HE was sweating profusely in the midday sun he was digging another hole in the ground nobody knew what he was doing to the place. A well or septic tank It looked like everything had to be in the right spot with him, then it would all come together. HE really wasn't listening to the show today he was too busy. BUT you could've hear the radio in the back ground all the same. HE knew what the people had on their minds they weren't skinning up. Mark my words said the caller to the show this going be a serious election hear wha I tell you the queen better pay attention to wha going on in the ILAND. THE small hand healed battery radio echo under the house floor. THIS place becoming like Bagdad said the stubborn caller the government has just issued a bunch of permits to a group of Muslims. You got any proof to that asked the host. MANN listen ya if I tell you it so it so, England even talking about bring back the gallows to hang some of these criminals as a form of capital punishment. INDIAN felt alone still his mind was all over the place, ALIZA hadn't completely forgiven him yet he wouldn't loose that girl so easy again. HE still needed to work on his attitude in general. THE TALK SHOW ended with another one of those anonymous letters the host seemed to be enjoying the resent excitement they brought. THE rating had been sky high over the last week.

AT exactly 3PM the news came on a weirdo had been arrested for exposing himself and a police man on duty had been shot and seriously injured after a drive by at a restaurant where he was having coffee. THREE men robbed a burger king in town with a machete and base ball bat.

THE boys had come together another night around the camp fire to un wine tell ghost story and smoke Sensamainya. THE Marshions was cold tonight Indian wore an all color wool beanie type hat to keep his head warm. HE pulled it down over his ears and began to tell a tale.

From the day that ancient slavery began kingdom rise up against kingdom and the defeated became captive slaves. The Hebrew were enslave to Egypt the Jews to the Romans the blacks to the whites the sick to the healthy. Following the day of discovery pirates infested these waters of the new world, and you know the story war far came about with no positive results first with the enemy then in making friends. Trading was established and with it came justifications, slavery, and organized labor. This made some rich or richer and others poor. IN 1500 AD Cayman was just a piece of dirt in the Caribbean Sea a little cay, with rocks sand and swamp. LOADED with Turtle Caymanas Crocodiles fishes and iguanas some birds and a variety of fresh water basins. CONWELL invaded Jamaica up on orders of queen Victoria of England and the Spanish army was defeated and retreated back to Cuba one of their strong holds in the Caribbean at the time. THE battle was drawn out and went as far as Cayman Brac and those bracers which was known as wild people mostly Indians slaughtered em like turtles that's where the name bloody bay came from in the area of the fighting. Governors from Jamaica there after made voyages to Little Cayman basically for recreational reasons and they were taking chance when they did so. THE Caymanas as it was later called was pretty much an untamed place and up in the air as to who the real owners was. IT was a no man's land and un-colonized especially Grand Cayman for about a century after Columbus set foot on it. THAT'S according to the history books said the Indian but we know better the indigenous was always here my people my people fought off Vikings, middle eastern armies even Chinese before we were so called discovered. BY the time the conquistadors came they wasn't enough of us left to fight.

EVERY NOW and then an old pirate would pop up looking for something or up to no good. RUNNER ways and passer by stop on the islands for food water and refuge and may have been killed off in certain situations. THE Island was flat manly accept for the Brac that had a high cliff or bluff with caves to protect against Hurricanes those who happen to be living there at the time. LITTLE CAYMAN and CAYMAN BRAC were settled first by all those living under the British flag meanly they were closer to Jamaica a day's journey by sail so getting supplies there was reasonable. WITH the vast majority living on the BRAC same framing could be done there too not like on GRAN CAYMAN were it would have been better in the earlier years, if any one lived in GRAND Cayman at time they did in hardship. NEVER the less scouts were sent there to teem and clear a way for those to come and the were encounters with pirates and scout and Indians. THE Indians were basically a lost tribe of the PAYA INDIANS who had reform and was now known as the KAYMANAKI people. THERE were some noble men who had made mistakes and out casts living there too who had took a chance at life on that rock. IT was pretty much an outlaw state and things would soon change but for now it was butter to die trying than to die out right. INDIANS segregated themselves the pirates seek economical doing and tried ruling the land at the time, if you wasn't a man on the run or had something that someone needed you were forgotten but everyone had something that the other wanted. SEA FOOD was abundant and water could be found along with log wood, thatch that was needed to repair ones ship. Treasure ships were perpetrated on or salvage after being sea wrecked pirate come here to recover or secure treasure this place was Isolated ungoverned on the count of no population and pirates had it their way. They took advantage of the un-expecting and double crossed and killed one another. THE Indian man stop speaking as he thorn off the sticking part of the Rizal rolling paper the glue on that thing will kill ya I don't care what the company say I don't thrush em Rasta he looked angry but he wasn't he lick and seal the paper and lit it. THE night skywas clear cloudless and blueness could be seen in it the few stars that was seen were scattered over space tonight. THE rest of the Caribbean was being developed bigger chunk's of land with more people were getting more attention. HE said his voice sounded harsh and brickly by now like as if he had a cold. SLAVES ran here and took a gamble on this cay until better days came if at all they did. DONN'T fool yourself still a lot of famous pirates were here they were entrepreneur engage in criminal activity of all kinds' theft, murders, and rapes. THE most famous of them and those that couldn't be killed or captured become buccaneers and went on to work for the royal powers like Henry Morgan. BLACK BEARD was an American force to join the British army and serve on their ship. AT the time England ruled North America and there was a shortage of sailors for the British navy. HE hated every day of it and despise the British after serving his time as a soldiers he went into pirating and rebelled against English ships and whatever else was up for the taking. EXCONVEXS escape Convicts and educated persons became pirates as well as those that had nothing to lose or no future in anything else some them may have even been ex slaves. THE same ingredients that makes up a criminal today can be compared to a pirates back ground right back to childhood, and purpose of life. ORDINARY folks from all over the globe came to this here promise land and started to settle in the name of freedom. THE wind of the wicked is but for a time and eventually this period would have come to an end, though they left their offspring behind pirates in this form was over. PIRATES were being hunted down executed but there was no real end to Piratism they got of the ships changed their clothes and work on land now. THERE was a chain of coughing then he clear his throat then he started talking again.

SEAMEN, Fishermen and those who were shipwreck here would be the second settlers and in centuries to come would become true natives like the Indians. THE Fishermen came from nearby Islands ship wreckers from all over as free people or running men. They came with animals and possessions same with nothing to live here. The Colonial powers had Gran Cayman under control by now the pirates were gone more or less and the resistant from the Indian abolished. THE Islands were upcoming with a small growing population. CAYMAN was the last remaining paradise on the face of the earth not only in beauty but the soil was still fertile if you know wha I saying still. WE were basically untouched we had pine trees in abundant white beaches and lime stone coast lines the swamps were mangrove havens I not even going mention the fish they were so plentiful in the shallow water they were long as my leg, there was a bunch of laughing. WILD LIFE was endless this was a jewel of an Island that even Robertson Crezso wouldn't have mind being stranded and deserted on, JAH made this place special. FISHING and Framing was a way of life throughout the Caymanas and would remain so for hundreds of years to come. EACH family had a little ground to plant or a grass piece to glaze cattle the children played gigs and marbles real horse power carried you about back then or sea vessel, from ya to town would take two days by foot and you packed food and water and you stop to sleep some way bout over night. THEY lived in a care free world mixed with worries like us today if one had food, water, strength, and a roof over his head you were bless. THE children played hide and seek jump rope and pirates and Indians and were teach the ways of life as much as possible. GROWN UP'S and older heads told tales of Treasures and ghost and of days gone by, nothing was taken for granted. SOME settlers came as special interest groups with land to live on and the right tools to work it, by land grants given to certain people from the crown and slaves to richen. THEY raised cattle, horses, and other live stock they lived a simple existence never the less they were living in the modern world at the time. WOMEN made heavy cakes and cheese salt came from the sea and sugar from cane cooking oil was from a palm dale berry or animal fat cooking was done outside or in a caboose. THEY found multiple uses for coconuts and other plants which became their medicine in most cases. FURNITURE was from the wood the forest provider limestone was melted to make wattle and Dobbs type habitats. BLACK MANGROVE was the proffered Mosquitoes repellent footwear and clothing were hard to come by the women sewed together what they could and these were kept and handed down. THEY may have obtain them from passing ships, wreck, or from people who had no more use for them. FABRIC was stretch and leather was ever lasting footwear was made from whatever was worth the time mostly slippers shoes were too expensive for the common and poor if you had to buy them most went barefoot. OVER the years populations growth some how made life's delicacies easier to come by ships called on the Caymans more often and brought along supplies. 95 PERCENT of the population was poor and I would say 100 percent of them was wise Life was life and you dealt with whatever it dished out for you. MAN did what he had to do to keep his family alive. With ships delivering cargo more and more frequently they also transported small among of goods from here some live stock for specific people overseas especially horses which were breed here and raised then sent to owners. THACTH rope, rare craft work made from turtle shells and black coral also small samples of sea food. IN decades and century to come the waters of the Caribbean would be teemed Caymanians continued to survive they built cat boats schooners and exported turtles and turtle shell to those who wanted them. THACTH ROPE would be eventually overcome by a new material called nylon.

THE voice was smokier than ever Indian paused for a minute his throat was filled with smoke, drinking from a water bottle he had beside him he looked around at everyone he seemed vex. HE carried on. THE civilized world at the time and its leaders were hard at work instigating plans to dash us to pieces. THE devil had surface you see and implemented immorality disguised as good while our people were fighting off mosquitoes and sand flies the superior race was busy studying and examine them. They seek to change laws and times. THE Indian man eyes were glassy as he talked he looked completely different. WHILE me and you fight now a days for simplicity the leaders of the organized world and their rich friends suck the blood out of the poor and needy. WE like gene pigs living in a life of bondage by the white man. HE was beginning to talk out off his head again the whole lot of them were charged up out off their minds. IN those good old days you had the rich and famous long with the poor and discriminated the rich ate flesh and the poor ate mangos and the remains of the riches vomit. ONLY the mercy of god saw them through it. CAYMANIANS died at sea during wars civil wars uprisings and personal feud in Hurricanes disease out breaks and life threaten injured got the rest of them. THE financial struggles we go through today back then was like a drought on the land or bad weather which would have prevented them from planting or fishing. ALL trouble makers were jailed or killed off one way or the other. BEFORE the Emancipation of slavery it is unclear how many people died slavery was an apocalyptical event even within the first years of the order tens of thousands were killed. WITH a massive population they became uncontrollable too much money and life's were being lost trying to do so and it was becoming more and more risky to manage the problem. VOILENCE was one reason like the Hebrews become in Egypt. THOSE who tried to over throw democracy were flogged hanged and even killed, and most of these wise men lived in famish. AND blood flow was the price we paid for freedom; they were hunted out and persecuted like those before them. THIS was a growing epidemic more and more inferior people were being hanged each year by up risings around the world slaves were starting to rebel many plantation owners were killed by slaves. THIS promoted awareness and courage among the slaves and the down fall of the one sided idea of in enslavement. DICTATERSHIP was insulted and inferiors were seeking and gathering their own power, each time it happened it was more costly and difficult to cam the unrest. HANGING and the lost of slaves was hampering the production of the goods being supplied to the Merchants. MANY of the best slaves were being killed or went into exile. ECONOMIC royals were being tripped up and this could not be allowed to happen they would have to come up with a solution. THEN by the late 1800's Emancipation of slavery was given or so it seemed to make a long story short it wasn't over yet. They were still rascal wars in some of these slave countries around the world, and groups of people who lived to enforce superiority. AMONG the Spaniards, Pirates offspring, Caribs, Ship wreckers, and Indians all would be mixed and boiled into one cup of tea to become a new breed of people. BY slaves being so call free now this added more of a work load to the loyalist rich man of the day in some cases like how it was here in Cayman ex slaves were allowed to take care of the animals for their ex slave masters. THEY also continued to farm and do other constructive labor for them at a rate of couple shillings a year, or in return would be given live stock and bri kind as pay. The value for cleaning one acre of land was a cow, even shoes and clothing was replaced in substitute for money. ALL the same they were still called niggers Monkeys foolish and stupid people they were still at the mercy of the white man who continued to held authority over them in terms of money land and animal stock, power in general.

NO change would come about without sacrifice and Blacks whites and other minority seem to make the best of it which was treating each other as equals. FOR those who had come from slavery it felt unreal after all they were less than animals for too long, remember slavery had occurred during the time of the civilize people it wasn't the so call dark ages most of the world had been conquered the gun was a 200 year old invention. IT wasn't uncommon for slave masters back then to breed the slave woman they owned them so with freedom ex slave children kept their masters name by rightful genetics or otherwise. AT the end of the 1800's mankind looked forward to the industrial age Democracy had been established in Cayman by then women were allowed to vote like in some other parts of the world. JUDGES Teachers and other educated men made up the parliament capital punishment was hanging and harden criminals were transported to Jamaica which was still under England and the capital of Cayman. MURDERS and crime in general was very low every now and then people would go missing or lost in the bushes or out to sea and never seen never heard from again. MOSTLY niggers and colored slave descendant, Indians unimportant people some found dead victims of drowning and accidental deaths. THE money only circulated among the higher class the gap between the rich and poor was a ocean rich men started dating and having closet or one sided relationships with poor, Black and minority women. BY the turn of the century unto the 1900 Cayman would be subjected to most of the world's new tools and inventions, it would soon become dependent on them. Until the late 1940's the first car could be seen in Gran Cayman when a plane flew over the simple folks though it was the lord god almighty coming to redeem them. SOON a sea plane would be landing in the north sound taken Passengers to and fro from Jamaica to Cayman. THE bicycle could be seen more than the horse now but for longer distances people still proffered the horse and boggy. AFTER world war two little dirt trails were widen by hand and they went as far as BODDEN TOWN, with the boggy stopping at designated areas and it made no more than two trips to town a day six days a week when it was at its best. IN those days every yard had at least a Nessaberry, a Breadfruit, and a lime tree in it. THE main diet was fish only on Christmas and other special holidays the people would eat a piece of fresh beef. SOME still raised cows though even right here in George Town. THE Thatch roof was replace with the eye con of the day which was Zinc tin roof. THE times were moving away from the wobble and Dobbs type to pleasant lumber homes with board siding and wood floor still on posts however. CEMENT floors or homes would have given you Cancer was the ideology of the day in Cayman besides that who could afford them. Couple Generators the size of a pickup truck powered the Towns in certain areas if you were lucky. THE may have not been too reliable but highly appreciated. MONEY was starting to have more meaning to the people now too. FAMILY entertainment was sitting on the porch talking luxury was white sugar for those who could afford it. LITTLE boys at the time cleaned fish for local fisher men and in return would get to carry home some for themselves. HAIR cuts were done under a tree, a pocket knife was as important as a car today and the smoke pan was as famous as our cell phone. THE biggest bunch of plantain recorded that year was a 21 hand by a framer up in North side. A WOMAN had collected a pound of mosquitoes as a joke to show the royal family. THE MEN could have husk and chip 200 coconuts a day back then. Caymanian fought in World War 1 and 2 and many wars after that and a Caymanian American pilot had drop the first Bomb over Hiroshima. Caymanians had family connections in other parts of the worlds and some moved away. THERE was only one doctor for the whole island for a population of around five thousand soles, A MIDWIVES rode on horseback to the rural parts of the island to deliver babies those who could afford it went to Jamaica for child birth or serious sickness.

BY this time Education was mandatory and the subjects were English and Arithmetic. MONETARY transactions were still being done via western union it was somewhere around the 1960's before the first bank came to Cayman, the sea men money contributed to this the cash flow was big it only made sense to open up a branch and the rest is history. AT sea was where the action was those who went there were admired and most men needed to go it wasn't nothing here on land for them. BY this time a bigger airport with runway we were moving away from the little sea plane. A new Hospital was built with state of the art equipment and foreign doctors. YOU could also see cement block homes with concrete floor and shingle roofs, glass windows and nice lawns. ROADS were improved on too barber green and what not and they reached the outer districts. CAR SALES MAN was a good business to get into everyone wanted one of those moving things. SOME fisher men had out board motors now and the price for fish negotiable and they would even trade you for bri kind, each district had it specialty weather it was Lobster you wanted conch or turtle. BY the end of the decade Jamaica would have gotten its independents and Caymanian parliamentarian succeeded in getting Cayman its own currency. LIFE still remained somewhat humble at home families were close nit their neighborhood were their friends. They helped to build one another home the women would cook food for the men as they labored; LITTLE boys raked the yard and enjoyed the outdoors. BREAD was 50 cent if you needed to buy it soda pop was about 15. This would have lead to the farther development and expansion of the Island in the 70's and up to the present day. THEIR were no dirt rich people here like in other places some was just better off than the next that all and by then respect and Caymanian hospitality came naturally it was considered a way of life. CAYMAN carried on the sea Fearers life style, life was still somewhat slow people were trying to deal with betterment and change. THE boys wasn't holding up they were burning hard not much alcohol was there tonight but the amount of ganja being burnt there it looked like the exhaust pipes from several Freight trains every insect and creature in the area was high. A white owl was perched on a limb above them he had forgotten how to flight. THEY were smoking the challis too man those boys wasn't easy at all, a spell had hit them and they started laughing for no reason. IT was just after ten PM the camp fire was still smuckering the Indian man started up talking again. WHEN you look at things good there's still slavery in the land instead of plantations and cotton fields we now have sky Scrapper's and job sites factories building complex. SOME still work under SLAVE like conditions he said with devilish eyes the slave drivers are those in authority and the loyalist are the owners, of the multinational corporations and one sided business. NOT all of them still don't get me wrong the young man spoke slower than ever the more we work they more those that own us gain we get little compare to what we lose. TIME share with love ones or even JAH if you worked on the Sabbath too busy making money to talk to him, they were all serious again listening to the Philosopher. WE forget about JAH and his laws and try to find our own ways and means even though we know he always provides yet we feel compel to live under this Babylonian system. WE buy food from their super markets and stores to kill ourselves we use useless consumer items and, tools to work with is necessary to do their organized labor. WE rent their buildings and support their holidays no other choice right I know we converse into this society.

ELECTRICITY was a god given gift to benefit mankind not only the selected some like kings and Merchants that control it and use it as a Economical tool, he said with a funny look we buy and glamorize cars which boils down to metal and pollution petroleum that leads to wars and destruction. WE cook with gas and electricity, their used to keep us warm and light up the darkness two edged swords I call em. MINIUM wage for all humanity was like no wage back in the days of slavery him who warship the master may have been favored uncle tom told the master what the slaves were up to he had a little place like mind's in the woods away from the rest of slaves or he lived near the master's home if he was good he would become a house slave. WHEN slaves were finely liberated he never change his ways and may have paid for it. LIKE the right hand man today of an employer who by making the boss happy and kissing ass get rewarded for killing, informing, and spying even whipping his co workers friends and piers. SLAVES who revolted were killed, flogged or separated from the rest for a time and in some cases all three. LIKE when you stand up for your rights today you get fired from the job if you go on bad they jail you and find you a sum of money and you get a bad record and name or the kill you one way or the other. THINGS haven't changed that much Rasta you Na see just a different elution. THE sophisticated crooks of Wall Street along with fortune five hundred companies dirty Merchants and Bosses are the children of the loyalist of yester years. They made the world what it is if the shoe fits put it on I might sound pathetic if I say this on the highest mountain top old boy but we ga see way we come from to know where we at. And to decide way we must go. HIM who have eyes let him hear and him with ears see so we can make a step forward to a better life free from slavery. GOD intended us to be free the devil and his angel want to keep you captive by ways of lust. IF all own is by a bank loan then you are doom then life becomes a hell instead of an Atlantis, man listen to me thank god for what you got and what you don't need and he will give it all to you and if you got nothing thank him for that too. REMEMBER you ga life old boy as bad as you think it is some other sole got it worst than you any day above ground is a good day for me cause when you dead you can fight the wicked no more in due time JAH will call you to rest so no man should wish he was dead. PENSION plan comfort to a fool health insurance mandatory by law organized governments once again come up with ways to ripe the poor. THE only true plan is a godly plan any system built on evil will fall money will value nothing at all in the days to come, when the company claims bankrupt we'll be screwed cause we were dumb, tomorrow is a promise to no man it might never come. GOD will sure my bread those old people use to say. NOW a days the people like hold up man money that's a sin and the wages of sin is death the Indian man was talking bluntly now standing with legs spread arms folded posing off a big one was between his fingers. LEVITICUS 19 13 he said the wages of him who is hired shall not remain with you all night until morning. THE world Economy not going to improve to make things worst it will take a down ward fall and the devil knows this the anti Christ will come forth he will be among the riches people in the world weather he was born into it or obtained it along the way. THE world was broke in a sense and he used his money to corrupt and lead as much people as he could in to hell to build a army big enough and try over throwing god. THEN there will be the last world war those who died at the time were the lucky ones Sam. THE water bubbled in the glass as Indian pulled in on the challis pipe that was being passed around he blew out but no smoke came most of it was in his lungs, mouth and brains. THOSE who remained were meant to suffer but given another chance to plant and to speak of that which had passed and revel the truth. OTHERS got sick from the contaminated water and never made it across, then came the Day of Judgment and the true god walked with man. LIKE slaves with the knowledge of trade are today working on a construction site in colonial times built the country up one piece at a time by mandatory fiscal labor who got little to eat and lived below human standard condition slaves of today's world can barely feed and shelter themselves. MOST of the money goes back to the loyalist one way or another the banks too are part of this monopoly of organized labor. THE stock market is where they put and gamble their money that was obtained from humanity. FROM us fools they get this money the government put tax on it and use it to support their regime. We borrow our own money from the loyalist through the banks and pay interests on top of it. ANOTHER trick to favor the rich it time for us to stop being money tools for our masters people you see this thing call need is a son of a bitch and you'll agree to anything once your insecurity is thought to be fixed, and the lack of knowledge is why we feel we need useless things don't matter how important they may seem we need nothing other than what JAH gives us don't bank up money for the anti-Christ seen…

HE stood in front of the mirror fixing his tie he had a meeting in a half an hour. HE ate two soft boiled eggs with the yoke running, smoke sausage and hast brown. IN the car on the way to work he took a shot of scotch and chased it down with more scotch. Throwing two peppermint candies in his mount treasured the burning sensation. Another day in paradise he said to the car, openly there was no one else there. IT was bumper to bumper traffic this morning a small fender bender was clogging up the high way he went right to left switching lanes circling too much round about in his opinion. AFTER what seemed like a life time the car pulled of the main road through a short cut in a rundown part of town. THE tires splashed water as they hit a pot hole filled with last night rain, he shook his head as a hitter crossed the street look at that Na. SHORTLY thereafter he was in a parking lot he enter the building. MORNING boss morning boss said two men in plain clothes good morning gentlemen he told them taking off his RAY BANDS and putting them in his jacket pocket. WHAT is the latest on those missing boys asked the reporter in his office, AS soon as he stepped in? Those guys were mixed up with the wrong people, drug deal gone badly. DON'T write that down. Crime is starting to stir up again on the street getting restless out there it comes in swells off and on you get use to the pattern when you do this kind of work. ANYTHING on the missing man. INVESTAGATIONS still ongoing that all I can tell you.

PATRICK BOWING was a veteran cop with 25 years on the force 20 of which as a detective half the service took orders from him. ON the Island over the years he had seen a lot of changes in his days on the streets drug dealers and other criminals feared him. IN the office now a days behind the desk he was slightly over weigh and had respiratory problems. HE worked out twice a week and was getting back into shape he had a long way to go all the same before that happen and he didn't care, he was only doing it because he had promise his wife. ENJOYING his lay back life style of a job retirement was still far away and it was harder than ever these days being a cop the salary could have been better. BUT he wasn't only into it for the money no he had grown with the job and had a passion to keep the Island under control. WITH his family home on a canal lot in an upscale neighborhood and a boat to take his family to the sand bar on Sundays he was quite contain. THEY had three cars and he had his motorcycles his pride and joy. EVERY now and then him and some buddies would ride around the Island from east to west. PATRICK BOWING was no show off or kick around he had raised up in the ghetto himself of central George town dogs had died where he lived Bowing knew what time it was.

THE white ford ranger pickup turned into the Indian reservation in lower valley the agriculture part of the Island. IT jointed with the district of savannah over all good farm land.

THE surrounding had changed a lot since his childhood days everything had been ruin by putting that thing up the road. THE whole area now smelt like smoke and a light sent of garbage was in the air. Political procss had located the Dump six miles east of the reservation. THE old Garbage Dump site in George Town had expired according to official reports. BUT the people knew better.

HEARTFORT Corporation and world wild Development owned land in the area adjoining the old land fill at the time it was purchase the dump was fully active. JUST three quarters of a mile away HEARTFORT built a small town a semi charted city several mega corporations had head offices there. BANKS law firms Insurance companies, Cinemas, Restaurants, Shopping centers, condominiums if you thought of it they had it there. OVER the half century the George Town dump had become the highest point on the Island. CRUISE SHIP passengers could see it way out at sea. THE stink from mount trash more could be smelted on the high way nearby and along famous seven mile beach. IT was a national disgrace to put it frankly. THE dump was connected to north sound a major part of the Island's eco system especially marine life which was starting to affected. Seepage was polluting the sea for miles out and along the shore line. THE situation had gotten away on them for some reason decades of poor planning and low or no maintenance. GOVERNMENT after Government kept pushing the problem under the rug. THE Government of the day eventually sold the property to Heartfort Development the sale price and overall deal brought questions from the opposition and public. HEARTFORT Corporation would even give the good people of the Island an alternative dump site in the eastern district. THE Heartfort group would remove billions of dollars in scrap metal and other recyclable materials dangerous gases etc. were extracted the site recap and turned into a golf court. WHERE club houses and yacht clubs with bars Restaurants and fancy recreation areas were built. A corrupted deal by crooked politicians and his friends felt many in the community. THE dump didn't need to be moved just some tender loving care struck back opposition and activist. Along with implementing a new idea to Cayman recycling programs Island wild. IT was the no one wanted it in their back yard sing drum IT was better off where it was most of the garbage was accumulated from the hotel and other business along 7 mile beach and the capital of George Town. BY it being on the eastern side now meant Dump Trucks would have to travel farther and the Government would have to spend more money on gasoline and this would be coming out of the people's purse traffic is insane as it now, not to mention putting it in a residential Agriculture zoning area. POINTED out one power hungry politician while on the local talk show it should remain in the industrial area where it is now. THEY were two large furnaces burning garbage all day on the present site which would be turned into reusable energy that ran the compound. AND people would get a few bucks for carrying in plastic bottles cans and other metals. ALL of which could have been done at the George Town site. BUT trade winds blew most of the time and the cinch could be smiled from Bodden Town to west ward throughout most of the Island really making the situation worst off.

INDIAN had lead the protests that follow when it was declared that the site would be located just above the Indian Reservation he became the most out spoken. OTHER passionate Bodden Towner and Caymanian in general stood next to and behind him holding up banners on TV and news clips. Interviews and television talk shows and face to face confrontational debates with dump supporter and even politician made him a public figure somewhat. BUT all of this would have been done in vein and the night would become true. SOMEONE got a suite at the Ritz Carlton and a Swiss bank account out of the deal he told a reporter at prime time at six news live.

THE Indian man pulled into his mother's yard she sat in the rocking chair in the small porch. SHE was expecting him even though he didn't tell her he would visit today. HE greeted her in the native tongue and kiss mama on the cheek. Hello son she reply go head put the fish in the fridge. THEY already clean mama just ready to cook. INDIAN said his goodbyes after talking for nearly an hour mama kissed him on the fore head and he left.

A few hours later that same night the moon was full and up high in the night sky. All right do what we say and nobody gets hurts empty the register? A woman screamed but was quickly silence with a gun in the mouth. PUT your belonging in the bag people we be out of ya for you know it. THERE was a tumbling sound out in one direction. MINUTES later a car skids away from a restaurant.

A POLICEMAN sat inside an Ambulance the back door was open he had an ice bag on his head. I saw the car parked on the yellow line went inside to ask questions when I felt the lick out of nowhere. YOU remember anything else I saw two guys with guns half their face cover with handkerchief Black clothes black hat long sleeve shirt last thing I recall as I hit the floor was seeing black military type booths. I'VE seen that car some way about before though with a busted tail light. DIDN'T happen to get a license plate number by any chance. AFRAID not sir I was going to write it up on the way out 8 1 that all I can remember at first glance before I went inside. THAT means little to us as far as the plate's concern thank you officer me or one of my men will contact you if we have any more questions.

IT was 9 AM when the man walked into the police station in George Town. GOOD morning he said to the police woman sitting at the front desk. MORNING how can I help you. AM MR Sanchez I will like to report a stolen vehicle another officer took the report then escorted him to an office on the second floor? MR SANCHEZ waited there for a good 15 minutes he was getting impatient the door made noise and a large figure in a suit and tie appeared. MR SANCHEZ Patrick Bowing here he said extending his hands sorry to keep you waiting please sit. The man had risen for the hand shank. Ten minutes later the interview was still being conducted. AND you say you lost the paper work for the car yes I told you all the paper work was in the center consul of the car. Right right and you don't know the name of the person you bought the car from either. I tell you already said the Filipino man I never ask name why should I it suppose to be on the log book. Which you didn't look at. THAT'S right I open it to check if it was correct papers and fold it back and put away in the car. THE guy wore darker and a hat with a thing on it like a tiger light beards they were two of them one waited out in the van. THAT Information means little to us what kind of van green looked like a bronco. What color they were. Black skin came back the reply. YOU see anyone acting suspicious around your Garage last couple of days or anything, Sanchez shook his head. They steal from me because I Filipino I know I ask you that you treat this case as equal as any other and that justice be serve I have right too.

Mr. Bill and Indian man were fishing this morning. They were both shirtless. Bill Patterson wore a straw hat and the Indian man had a bandana tied on his head. The brown skin men kept quiet as they fished, they would have enjoyed a beer in the heat but only two gallons of water and some cheese sandwich were in the small icebox. Alcohol brought bad luck when fishing. "WA you done last night?" asked Mr. Bill. "I went home. Got a nice nights rest." Said the Indian man.

"When that low tied come in and the fish stop biting we might as well go do some searching out on the volcano. Might get lucky and find something."

"Yeah, that sounds good."

A piece of tarp polling provided the shade over the fiber glass south seas sixteen footer all the same. The water was clear and you could see good ways down into the ocean. The Indian man was burning another marijuana cigarette. Bill had blew smoke earlier and was still high, actually. Just after sunset that evening they were at the launching ramp, loading gear and fish into the back of the truck. The boat was on the trailer hooked up on being towed.

He was a middle aged man, skinny and tall with hair on his forehead. He had a moustache with no beard and a pair of bright cheerful bluish eyes. His wife Marisha, was attractive with a good shape for a woman her age. Her brown and blonde hair mixed together. Her eyes were a bit lighter than her husband's. Her skin smooth and she always had a smile. The Patterson's saw the need for Nightingale orphanage; a lot of homeless children were suffering. Even those who were parentless and abused or the people were too poor to give them basic needs could be helped now, the children came from all around. They themselves has a pair of twin girls and two grown sons. The Patterson's has been married for twenty seven year now. Mr. Bill was a professional fisher and seaman and had been all over the world in his days from the age of twelve in which he went to sea. Coming from a poor family the sea was life. He was a tall boy for his age and could pass for someone older. He had falsified his birth papers somehow. In those days people gave you a chance once you were willing and prove yourself seaworthy. He spent twenty years a sea with National Bulk Carriers and was one of the best captains and navigators from Cayman that the company had came across at that time. He was a man with a past. He got into a fight one time aboard the ship in his seafaring days with some rednecks. He threw three of them over the side of the ship on a dark night. The man over board alert was sounded by the captain. Bill Paterson and other deck hands and crew noticed they were missing, the ship was stopped and the ocean was searched with spotlights and people in life rafts but no one was ever found. They had died on the line of duty and their families were taken care of for life. He forgave himself and found peace with God. It could have been him thrown over board by them. Lonely nights at sea were spent researching old pirate tales and maps, and reading the Holy Bible. Cayman had changed since his boyhood days and had made him sad. At nights he would sit out on the veranda of the little orphan house and shed tears often, as a grown man in silence when his wife and the whole orphanage were asleep. He was unsatisfied with the failure of this life. Despite his success he knew God was good to him. He would preach every now and then at the community church been asked by the congregation. He needed one more chance to secure his golden years with him and his wife. He was doing God's work with the orphanage but still wanted a home away from the orphanage some day. When he died he wanted that piece of mind that the twins and Marisha would be taken care of. His older boys were men now. One was a missionary working in some part of Africa. The other was in Alabama working for a heavy equipment company. Bill kept pretty much to himself and had few friends. The Patterson's took care for about twenty kids from ages six to seventeen with no outside help. The Nightingale football club had won the football cup two years ago. Schools and other sponsored teams competed with each other in a yearly tournament. The orphanage had received awards for community service all the same over the years. Bill had been baptized and was a practicing Christian and church people had considered him a "backslider". But bill knew that such things didn't exist in Gods world. He had been in the rat race all his life and had his own views, ideas and beliefs about things. God and religion. He kept them to himself. By forty he was already married with two kids and the National Bulk Carrier Fleet had been bought out by competition and most of the ships were turned in for scrap metal in dry docks around the world. Mr. Bill was retied and replaced. Younger captains and highly computerized ships became the new way. Even with more training it would have impossible to keep up. He continued to live from a reasonable pensions but he puts it all into the Nightingale house.

It was 1966 when he met Marisha in Mobile, Alabama. Ships from all over the world tied up in the United States to unload and reload cargo. She was working at a children's hospital as a nurse and love happened between them. Amongst many other things Bill had been a gun runner when he came back home. He was offered a job as a lobster boat captain. He mainly worked the coast of Nicaragua the boat had been shot at by the Nicaraguan coast guards and military and captured. Negotiations kept him and the crew from dying in a third world prison. The lobster boat was taken away by the communist government from Nicaragua. But Bill quickly found another one to work. Another deal kept him alive by running guns and ammo from Venezuela to the Sandinista Rebels to overthrow the Nicaraguan government. It was a stupid mistake he told himself, every time he thought of it. The boat flew on Nicaraguan flag from a wealthy opposition party member of Nicaragua. The boat also carried the white lady from Venezuelan guerrilla leader. At the time a man by the name Hugo Chavez arms went along as well to raise power for a new regime. All throughout south and Central America. This had bought the man little satisfaction if any but he was a changed man now. He was obligated somewhat. They would have killed him if he backed out from the deal. And he had a loving wife and young boys to care for at the time and not enough money for them to live from. He made a couple big runs with no hiccups then it was over. He returned back to Cayman and with his cut from the Sandinistas, Bill started the orphanage with his wife.

The Nightingale house was on Shadow lane. Just off the congested highway on Schoolhouse Road. In an old housing neighborhood in George Town. It was modest size house. Built from concrete blocks in the late seventies. A four bedroom, two baths family house with an open floor plan. Jalousies windows and the shingling on the top had done their time. The soffits were of one texture one eleven plywood. Old and rotten but painted quite nicely. The veranda had a three foot high in closure also from cement which formed a railing. Some kids were sitting on it. The house had a fresh coat of paint to it. The fence around the yard was only plastered on the outside after all these years. A Labrador named Ciao, played with kids outback. A handmade swing set, sandbox and some toys laid next to the drive way. Just enough out of harm's way in the front yard. Supper was on the stove, kids watched TV in the living room. Mr. Patterson sat at the table in the dining room helping two children with homework.

"Why my mama don' love me?" said a voice of a thirteen year old girl to Mrs. Patterson.

"Cuz you mama on crack" said Brad, a fifteen year old orphan boy.

"Yeh? Well yo mama don' wan noting do wid you too cuz you ugly"

"The two of you behave yourself!"

"Well he start being rude to me first. Poking his mouth into tings dat don' even concern him."

"That's true Nanny? That my real mama fool fool? Our teachers in school tell us crack means wen you fool in the head?"

Mrs. Patterson loved children. Her boys were grown now. One married and Jackie and Tracy were just four years old. Marisha Betty Patterson was forty-seven but carried her age well. She was African-American and Creole. Spoke with a southern accent she had lived in Cayman over thirty years. She and her husband had built the Nightingale when he had came home for good. The little orphanage housed 9 kids besides their twins. The Cayman government had only provide 20% of the operational cost and supplied lunch for the kids at school. Medical care was free for all children of Cayman until the age of sixteen by way of public hospital. The Patterson's wanted to expand but they were living on the small pension that her husband were receiving and his health wasn't what it used to be. Her nursing days on a mainstream would be hard to fulfill with the day-to-day operations of the orphanage. She only did volunteer and charity work nowadays for the church. She felt fulfilled, happy and didn't waste her time sitting down worrying about money. That night after they had put the kids to sleep, her and Bill sat on the veranda looking at the stars, talking and watching the traffic go by. One car passed toot its horn and yelled "BILLY!" Marisha had her feet up on his lap as Billy massaged them. Aliza had did her yoga and was in bed. It was around ten thirty that night before the lights went out in the Nightingale house. The next morning Aliza helped Marisha with the kids. There were four boys and five girls. Two of the girls were six. Aliza shared rooms with them. The ten, thirteen and fourteen year olds were in another. The twins slept on a bunk bed in the master bedroom with their parents. Aliza told Nanny that she was expecting twins too.

"You going to' have your work cut out for you girl when those two are born." Marisha said jokingly.

The morning rush hour was over in the house, Aliza was alone. Her boyfriend ha called to tell her that he loved her and to sweet talk for the morning. He and Mr. Bill were going fishing or something today. Mrs. Patterson had loaded the minivan up to carry the kids to school. She would be busy for the rest of day doing church stuff.

Aliza herself had been raised in the Nightingale Orphanage. It was 1982, Aliza was eight years old. Her mother had died, her father was an American killed by the Klu Klux Klan in Mississippi. When she had been given to the orphan house by Social care.Child care budget was low in those days and the government found it difficult to give these such children proper health and care, not to mention tender love and affection. Cayman was still ruled by loyalists and segregationist of colors was still a harsh reality even back then. And white children were treated more important than others by the upper class and communist government of the day. A social worker had taken it on her shoulders and gave the little Indian girl to Ms. Marisha. Her Christian friend who ran the new orphanage in George Town. The little girl with long hair, braided into a ponytail was welcomed with open arms at Nightingale House. She was the light that the orphanage needed. She remained there until obtaining a government fund scholarship partly. By working part time while still studying, she finished put herself through college. She became an American citizen and was employed as an accountant for a leading firm. The company eventually opened a branch in Grand Cayman and she was sent here to fill a spot. She didn't forget her past however or her island all throughout the years. Abroad she kept in contact with the Patterson's and what was going on in Cayman.

SHE showered change and went to run errands locking the door and closing the small entry gate at the walk way in front of the house as she step out onto the busy George town street. ALIZA was a roots gal her complexion was the lightest tone of brown. THE tattoo on the back of her neck of a spider's web was from her University days. TODAY she wore an all color tam that all of her hair was packed into, a set of Cayman IKE ear rings that didn't hang down too far and sun glasses. HER checks didn't had too much fat on them and they were separated from her chin line beautifully. HER breast were medium but looked larger with her figure and she seemed taller than she really was. HER hips were small the buttock tight and didn't shake legs slender and flexible. THE hips moved as she walked and her feet went slightly to the sides. SHE had on an angle braw and the pink strap cotton blouse went great with the brown corduroy skirt that past the knees. HER foot wear was a pair of burgundy women's loafers that she worn with white ankle socks. SOME guys that were working on the light pole whistled as she pasted. I'LL pay your rent said the driver of a bus hanging himself out of the window. Nearly getting in accident. THE girl was put together don't fool yourself. SHE walk the somewhat hectic street ten minutes later she came to a place on Cardinal Avenue. THE sign on the building said JEM Stones international.

I would like to get an appraisal on a Jem stone she said to an elderly gentle man, with square glasses on. ARE you sure they're gem stones he reply. I don't know she said. RIGHT this way Mam. THEY stepped into a room at the back of the place the girl removed the stone out of the bright all color fabric hand bag. SHE placed the stone on the jewelry table in front of her. THE stone was one and half inches long by about three quarter's wide brownness more or less. THE jeweler placed a magnifying glass over his spectacles closing one eye and looking through the other he examined it. YOU won't mind if I take a few pictures he asked. NOT at all said Aliza. IT'S standard procedure now a days you know for my records and such. THE man spoke slowly with a European accent. HE took out a digital camera from the top drawer of the wooden desk and snap a few shots. Then he looked up at Aliza. Where did you get this from am temped to ask." Oh it's been in my family for years my mother gave it to me her mother gave it to her been handed down over the years you know. I see, wait here I'll be back in a minute here's your stone. ALIZA wasn't no fool not with an answer like that. BUT had no way of knowing as to the depts. OF what she was doing. ABOUT five minutes had past and Aliza was beginning to get nervous in the spooky old place. WHA he doing calling the law on me or something these white people always suspicious of we Islanders. There was a window in the room and she looked out at the busy street. THE man returned "ok my dear" he said. I can give you five thousand dollars for it. WHAT said Aliza in disbelief? "OK seven CI he said. "TO be honest you maybe able to get more maybe nine in the states but you have to flight up there yourself and cover expenses". "THANK you sir but I was only looking to get it valued". THE truth she was thinking about it now, they could used the cash but she would have to speak to her boy friend first. "I see" said the jeweler "if you change your mind let me know. ALIZA walked in the morning sun she was surprise the stone was worth that much. IT wasn't that far to the Hospital she had a 10.45 appointment to check up on the twins.

BACK at gem stones international the Jeweler was on an internet web site that was the first time he had seen this kind of rock he study the photos on site for all most an hour then he sent an E mail to a dealer in European. AN hour later he was on the phone talking to a man name Adolfo. "The dealer in Paris referred to it as sugar babies" he said. "I'll send you a picture over the computer it's worth 20 gran on the current market". "HOW much will you take for it".

AFTER finishing up her chore' for the day Aliza was in a local down town restaurant after a long wait in line she sat with girlfriends at a table with a big plate of stew conch white rice, sweet potato, Cole slaw and corn bread. Babeth ate oxtail and rice and bean with one of the same side orders. "SO what did the doctor say" "AM doing alright the twins are too". The stone around her neck dangled on a gold chain. The radio play low in the Restaurant. SOME one in the Restaurant said "all right everybody hash please the talk show man going read out another one of those letters". PEOPLE laugh but then the place went silent. THE whole Restaurant and Island was listening. TRAFFIC came to a Holt the sun went into a could people stop doing whatever they were doing.

A car drives up to a mansion in south south and a man got out with a brief case. THERE are only one hundred of these sugar babies in the entire world. Only ten have ever been registered as accounted for, said the chec Republican man from gem stones International. HOW much of them do you say you have ask Adolfo? ONLY one I think and am afraid she doesn't want to sell we'll have to persuade her a little. OF course my friend who is she." SOME Indian girl, who doesn't know what she got," "WHERE their one always a chance there's more". "WHAT'S the history behind it, you know." "ONLY what I down loaded of the web". Apparently it's a stone from an ancient civilization from South America. THEY warship the stone of gambola the stone God. ABOUT three thousand years ago the continent of South America was all one people and one tribe. THE premagans or the English translation the beginners or the first people. A rock grew up out of the Amazon River with a face on it. AND the ancient people called it the rock of god or gambola. THE amazing thing is that it's one of a kind that's what makes it so bloody valuables. THERE'S never been another rock specimen equal to it found nowhere on earth, not even on meteorites. THOUGH some scientist believe it came from another solar system tied somehow with the city of El Dorado the ancient city of gold in the South American Amazon BUT the city was never found.

ABOUT a thousand years ago an earthquake destroyed the Gum bola monument, crumbled in pieces and lost in the Amazon River and most of the Premagan people perished along with it. Centuries later civilizations came and found bits and pieces of the precious stone and made craft work. By time the conquistadors came it was even rarer. They took it to the best craftsman of the day, reshaped it into nuggets and it would be worn by royalty. The queen of Spain wore one and it is said it brought her bad luck. It supposed to glow at night and can't be destroyed by fire. That's remarkable, even gold can be melted but this stone cannot. The stones were shipped to Europe aboard royal fleets. No one really knows what happened to them, thereafter as far as the legend is concerned. At the beginning of the 19th century, all but ninety of the stone showed up in Venice, Italy. The ten that surfaced are owned by four different people today. All together they're only worth about three million dollars but whoever owns them can ask for more. They are rare and few of a kind. So that with its self is special. "I want that stone."

He didn't went fishing today he took the day off and went into town. Aliza and he spent the day together. She told him the details on the stone and the twins. She was thinking of moving back home soon since Indian was sorry for what he had done to her. And he won't do it again. "The doctors said I don't need any stress Indian. I need you he said she needed him too be they would have to wait. "Everything is how you left it Indian" she said. They kissed goodbye and Indian rode the bus home. The talk show played on the radio of the public bus and everyone was listening to it like Sunday morning in church. It was the usual redbrick and complaining. An anonymous person had mailed a letter to the talk show. People on board the bus began to mumble. A gentleman replied "Those letters are gang related". A woman in a janitor's uniform said "England probably sending them letters themselves. You never know. Or one of those candidates for this coming election. "Those letters are talking about the whole world at large. Not only Cayman." Said a young girl dressed as an emo.

THE Indian man was at home now pitching a big knife into a stump about fifty feet away. Tonight wasn't a ritual night with the boys they had came cross about an hour ago but had already left. HE had other plans for later on that night. HE thought of the lady he saw in town today with two kids begging they were dressed in rags hadn't beaded in a week properly. AND the man that took food out of the garbage cans. POVERTY in Cayman was getting worst and he was complaining about his situation others needed more help then him." IF I ever become rich by some miracle

I'll do my part he said in his mind". ALL these billionaire right here on the Island not to mention round the world and yet children are in so much need. AM just as bad with my two boys he was only six teen when he became a father I wish I was able to help them even with the basics. I can't look them in the face and say any thing am a worthless father myself. IT's hard for a rich man to enter the kingdom of god but if I had money he thought, I would give the devil a hard time by helping gods people. A little boy was reading a book of Robin Hood on the bus he recalled. HE walk over and pried the knife out of the log then noticed something in the bushes. "Wha going on ya he said to himself these look like crocodile eggs ""mother ga be close by". THAT evening he went jogging an advert runner but he hadn't jogged in months. ALIZA teased him he was getting a pot belly. HE threw on short jeans that he had made with the scissor it reached just above the knees, it wasn't hemmed and the cloth strand out at the bottom. With no shirt and lace up booths to the ankle they were soft and comfortable for running. HE put the base ball cap on backwards on his head and worn a set of shades. THE Indian man ran along the road crossing a school and then into a seclude dirt road the same Ruth he usually jogged. THE dirt road went on for miles it would eventually become a new high way one day in the future. THE existing high way was on the sea front side it was only wise for the Government to relocate another one in land. Connecting to George Town and boosting development but on the political scene other things were on the menu now. And these such roads were postponed and somewhat abandoned until national elections were over the someone would be made a hero or villain THEY had started with that same reason in mind with little concern of the countries budget just before Election Day. After an hour of jogging none stop he was urinating off to the side of the road, into a ditch. AND as luck would have it a police car on patrol approached. "Well that's bigger than average "said the lady police to her partner. THE squad car came to a stop in front of the man who had folded it into his pants and sipped up quickly, he'd turn around and was facing them already. IT's Illegal to piss on the street said the cop what you doing in this area. "I was jogging and stopped for a minute on my way home now officer". WHERE you from ask the cop. NORTH SIDE came the reply. What you name. THE man gave them his name. ALRIGHT be on your way and don't do that kind of thing again have some respect suppose a civilian car was passing and kids were in the car. THE Indian man started jogging again and didn't stop until he was home. THE road went through wet land and black swampy water formed a ditch on one side deep enough to sink a car. CONTINUING with their patrol of the area the cops notice it off in the swamp, Indian was out of site and long gone.

PULL it out men and run the plates said Detective Bowing to the staff of police men. WE stop this guy couple minutes before we found it. DIDN'T have any ID on him said he was jogging, told us his name was Norman Cox from right here in North Side. THESE roads aren't exactly off limits a lot of people use them to run, walk their dog and biking. HE looked Indian to me sir spoke Caymanian said the police woman. Had a black cap on with a puma logo on it work booths, short cut jeans no shirt. THAT isn't proper jogging outfit now is it said Bowing. A puma on the cap you say. Yes sir. THAT's like a black tiger or something. THAT's right sir, it was turn back ways but I notice it went he took off running again. BOWING took out a small note book from his shirt pocket and started writing make me guess black booths right he said to the cops. THAT's correct sir. WHAT else. HE was brown complexion medium built prickly beards like he hadn't shave in a week or so around five ten in height. THAT's all we got sir. ALRIGHT good we'll find him. BOWING spoke to the press officer, make sure you keep the media in the dark about the car for now.

LATER that night at the Indian's little shack bill and Indian were in med conversation. THAT sugar baby is worth more than that the last time I checked it was nearly 25 gees. YOU know those Jewelers always want to pocket a big profit for them self. I never know she was going to get it value said Indian she don't know anything else still. Best thing to do is to hang on to it for a while longer see how things go with us before you sell it, you read me said bill. I'LL keep praying Sam said Indian. WE stay on track and I guarantee you we won't be sorry. IT Na looking good we can't continue to do this under cover for too much longer someone ga soon find out said the Indian man. No one knows what will happen we just have to see this thing right up to the end said Bill, we'll know when the time comes to stop. WHEN that moon rises tonight we start doing what we have to do. YOU lock that gate so no one will know if we here or not. Yah Sam reply the Indian boy, INDIAN mention nothing about the main event of the day to Bill. IT was no big deal he'd been stopped, questioned, shake down, draped up and harassed by cop all before. I had that dream again last night Sam he said to Bill.

THERE had been another robbery last night the police never had a clue as to who was doing what. THEY were not giving out much information nether making any commits no chances were being taken by the Department.THE word on the street take every threat seriously because man Na take no check, any problem can be popped away with the right contact. CRIME, hardship was becoming the norm and the small man was feeling it the most. WORK permits were still being issued left right and center cowboys were still coming into the country along with drifters, losters and no bodies, and people that you were better of not knowing. IT was getting worst and worster by the day and it didn't look like any end was on the horizon. THE powers to be knew what was going on but you had to wait until they fix it their way, if it could be fixed. THE Cayman people over the centuries had fought to become all that they could be, man had became millionaire from pumping shit and digging deep wells. Making concrete blocks or selling meat patties men built big time home from selling fish. BUSINESSMEN turned mom and Paps store and small lumber yards into chain companies and became billionaires. MANY of them were good people down to earth but this was the last hand being shuffle the final battle. HE who had was the enemy in many eyes and he who never had didn't need to worry again. CHURCHES to the least had million dollar accounts and billion dollar cathedrals they made loans among themselves and put donations and collection money to their use. PEOPLE lost confidents and was beginning to question the Churches to find out what was really going on. MARKETING strategies were going the wrong way if you what I mean. THEY had been UFO sighting hovering over Government buildings that went unreporte. Politicans had companies with 100 percent work permit holders and these were in the cases that we knew about. TWENTY FIVE dollars couldn't lift up legs those days were long gone the unless monkey was making money on her back, and big men were making a living on this knees. EVEN cheap labor was costing you, one way or another man would give you an unbelievable price to do a job then turn round and rip you off all how sometimes you would have to re do the work. TEENAGE pregnancy and single mothers where more than ever. In these now times witches became bitches and the average Creole man was hitting the challis. MAN with dread locks started hitting the rock; all the same the true Rasta man knew what time it was. CRIMIALS became christians and outstanding citizens became crooks, more and more people started saying Caymanians not righted. IT was the same song the same team all around. THE war in Iraq was improving Saddam Hussein would be hang, Fidel Castro was dying and Hugo Chavez was public enemy number one.

NOW the drug business had gotten more sophisticated than ever, man would deliver it like the pizza guy they were drive through and walk inn's quick phone calls so it could not be trace. E MAILS text they were head shops all over the place. LIKE everywhere else the drug trade was operated by old school pro's and new comers alike. BY white collar people and the little old lady around the corner all kinds of people were mix up in the trade right down to the common guy. PEOPLE were high 24 / 7 hear what I telling you they were stress out over life and three quarters of the time the Rasta man would get the blame and be arrested. BUT everybody had it if they wanted it red, yellow, black, Spaniard all had a sample. THE butcher the candle stick maker Carpenters Masons Mechanics the framers the fisherman, high class people and the peace makers the little school boy was saying things. MILLIONS of dollars were still being spent on the war against drugs. POLICES were still under paid and money being used to buy fancy vehicles SUV's etc., along with sophisticated instruments and gadgets for surveillance purposes. ON cameras that could see through walls and shit and nice little toys to kill you with.

THIS wasn't no joke thing still what was happening on the Island, even though it seemed funny. IT was at a time when the country was socially run down its people last nature and according to politicians broke. THERE was joblessness and the place was lowly criminalized people were eating grass, nails and screws Insects and pets. UNKNOWN animals were seen for the first time in the bushes, birds and fishes were acting peculiar according to simple local folks. PEOPLE warn about revolution or some kind of down rising would take place soon.

IT was November 10th 2003 they had been an Island wide black out a bolt of lightning stuck a major utility transformer. A freak thunder storm came in suddenly over the last hour, the funny thing is it was just after another one of those letter poem things had been read. THE morning talk show had been bombarded with them actually by E MAIL from an unknown source. ALL the hear after wasn't heard yet, the police information gathering branch had set up hot phone lines and was reviewing all calls and mails that went into the show. The letters seemed to promote violent and discord and some of the langue that was used offensive to the crown. ANYTIME one of those letters came in within twenty four hours a criminal act would take place. THE whole letter ordeal had taken of like fire in a dry grass piece, bandits and punks support and endorse them. WORD on the street it was a science man behind these letters, he's a Satanist who wear black underwear a woman said to the old man from the shoe shop to a bunch of ladies who were asking questions. EVERY time one of those letters were read people acted strangely, pictures fell from the wall TV's malfunctioned, plates, glasses, china drop to the ground and broke into pieces people's car wouldn't startup and thing. THE letter had became more famous than the zodiac letters they stepped beyond the MR meaner barrier who ever the writer was is guilty of a felony,said a business man over lunch with some colleagues. This can be looked at as a crime against the state said another. This wasn't no mediocre thing even though they were only nursery rimes in the letters. Everyone was talking and the police were investigating. They had searched the homes of well known activist and animal heaters anti abortion critics ex social workers and alcoholics. They were questioning atheists' skinhead and special interests groups a talk show host was being interrogated.

The two lovers spent the day together on their six acres Indian showed her the latest happenings. The parrots had young ones and he had found a dead crocodile and some eggs. He'd also made a little place for the ducks by in closing a pond with some rock around it. Finished the electrical rough in to the big house. Planted more of her favorite plants and flowers, in the garden out back because it was bigger now. "I ga start grow carrots, peppers and tomatoes". HE said to her. "I sold a bag of limes the other day, the lady never seen limes big as that before". The sweet potato were coming along nicely "In a month's time or so the cassava going be ready". Indian chopped a stick of cane and they were eating as they paddle out a few hundred yards in the canoe. ALIZA threw over a line and sometime later pull in a descent size fish, but afterwards felt sorry for it then let the creature go. INDIAN rocked the canoe and they both went over into the sea with a splash. LATER they claim a three to watch birds through binoculars. BY late afternoon they were exhausted and laying out on the little waft where the canoe was tied. The man rolled a joint and Aliza took couple puffs Indian made a joke and she giggled rolled over on top of him and began to French kiss. HE moved his hands along her back and under her T shirt he pulled it off there was no bra his mouth found her breast. SHE arched her back one hand was on the floor board of the dock with the other she had a choke hold around his neck and was squeezing. There was a sound of an engine he looked off to the side and saw that a boat had driven up onto the small beach. ALIZA dived to the side and shield herself as she quickly slipped back on her shirt.

THE grayness of the late evening was upon the swamps it would be dark in a few minutes. TWO men in blue over all's jumped from the bow of the boat and into the sand the one that was behind the stirring wheel came over the side. INDIAN was about to curse bad word when he notice police written on the boat side. ONE of them held a shot gun and the other had an automatic on a gun belt around his waist. WHAT you doing up in here this time of night said the tall skinny dark man. RELAXING replied the Indian. TAKE a look around fellor see what you can find, he order the other two. YOU look frighten son tell me who up in here for. THIS is for some Americans sir we got permission to use the place, they off the Island right now said Indian. AM captain Sullivan from the marine unit we got a call saying somone was fishing in the replenishment zone, in a green canoe. That thing yours he said pointing at the canoe with his chin. IT's for the owner of the place sir. YOU were out there earlier right. YEAH but I thought it was on the outside of the marine park. IS that right I'll give you the benefit of the doubt this time said the officer. YOU see we were thinking it may have been one of those Jamaica canoe, Sullivan watched the expression on the young Indian's face but there were mix signals. THAT girl she your friend or what. AMM yes sir reply the Indian not sure if he was to answer him or not. SWEET little thing isn't she what she is Spanish. Yes sir don't speak much English. The two officers returned and stood one on each side of Sullivan. The Indian stood faceing them the girl was out on the wharf. She could not hear what was being said. "WHAT's your name boy?" Danford "What your last name is." POWERY ". THE Indian man had stop with the sirs. What you know about that old wreck out in harbor that been there for so long. THE Indian was getting tier of the way the officer was questioning him. "I don't know anything about it, just an old boat far as I can see. SO what kind of work you do ask Sullivan. I the maintenance man for these people, I keeping an eye on the place in the mean while. WHO they is. THE McIntyre said Indian good people. Sullivan looked up at Aliza I saw you out on the wharf just now when we were coming in, that whore got a find piece of ass on her he grind. Indian remained calm the two officers wink their eyes and threw kisses at him. "Bunch of fucking perverts" said the indian.He ducked as Sullivan swung the **shaft** at him. But on the way back up one of the other officers hit him on the shoulder with the butt of the riffle. He went down hard. The officer stood over him ready to do him a second time.

"That's enough" said Sullivan. "It's getting dark and the sand flies and mosquitoes soon be out. You better learn some manners boy" was the last thing he said to the Indian.

Spotlight came on in the boat. The captain pulled down the lever as the boat backed away from the shore. The stern turned the toddle went forwards all the way. The bow lifted slightly, the Indian man was on the ground. He could hear the sound of the engine moving further away. Aliza ran up to him and hugged him while he was still on the ground. She was crying.

"Why the done that for?"

"Cause they assholes." He said.

"We are going to have to report them" said Aliza.

"Don't worry about that. That na going do any good."

Elroy Sullivan was as black as they come. A mouthful of gold teeth, red lips and spoke with a twang. Skinny but he had a big 'beer' belly and a bigger ego. He was in command of the marine unit and ran the whole operation. He made his money the easy way. For weeks they had been reports of sightings of a Jamaican canoe. They were bored today all the same. Wanted to have some fun playing cops.

"You want me to write up this one" said an officer drinking a beer and handing one to Sullivan.

"Na he just a little punk. Na worth the ink on the paper."

7:30 pm at an apartment complex in Crew Road, George Town. The nightly news had finished and a rookie cop switch of the television. A man was still missing after three months. He had disappeared from his home. So were the fishermen. The cop picked up a landline telephone and dialed Mr. Bowing, RCIPS in George Town.

"Yes, serge, Chadwick here. I remember where I saw that car from the robbery the other night. It was on Queens's high way last week.

"You sure it was the same car?"

"Definitely two maybe three men in the car. It had a busted taillight. It was daytime so I didn't really pursue them. Maybe I should have."

"Anything else?"

"Yah, one of the guys had on a black hat."

The next day two men sat at a plastic table with an umbrella over it at a small outdoor type eatery on the waterfront in town. Talaya fast food stall served the best barbeque meat in town, baked potatoes and garlic bread came along with it. "I need you to find someone for me a girl, locate her where abouts ". Said Aldolfo "keep an eye on her for a couple of days I want to know who she talks to and where she goes she has something that belongs to me, this is half". He said putting a white envelope on the unoccupied seat next to the private eye.

SUNDAY afternoon Bill went outside of his home "I Na buying no more of this shit I give up". HE said and thorn up a piece of number paper. HE spent two hundred dollars on the local lottery 98 played and he had bought 89. Indian told him he dream about a river in the dream book it played 88 he add one but didn't turn the number around. HE had won five thousand dollars three years ago from a contracted number but nothing since then.

LATER that night a number woman was robbed at gun point a witness saw a white truck in the area.

"THE stolen car that was found in a ditch outside of town was registered to Malachi Howett of George town courts. WE'VE checked with the owner of the duplex and he can remember him. THE address is from ten years ago". "AND the license coupon" said Bowing. "IT'S under the same name sir". Said the woman police officer. "WHAT about Insurance". "Apparently it hasn't been Insured or licensed in at least two years. ALL the Insurance Companies upgrade their files annually". "WE ran the name through the national data base but as you know half of the Island is Howett's" said another police officer. "A thousand Malachi alone in George Town". "IT doesn't make sense why would I sell a car then turn around and seal it". Said a Detective. "Commit a crime with it and leave the plates on it for police to track me down". "I'VE thought of the same scenario" said Bowing "but maybe he's building a defense at the same time". AND that's smart whoever he is we're going to have to catch him red handed". "LET'S look at this from a face value the Filipino man said he bought the car from two big niggers with sun glasses and black caps". A patrol unit saw someone in the area where the car was found fitting that same description, black military booths and all properly just before he pushed it into the swamp". "ANOTHER RCIP officer identified the car on queens high way a day or so before the robbery three guys in the car". BOWING'S cell phone rang but he paid it no mind he knew who it was. "Check out some of these Howett's see what happens" he order his staff. "OH and another thing we to put together a list of suspects we believe to be writing these letters to the radio show". THE briefing room laugh, "don't take these letters lightly" said a detective looking at a copy of the letters in front of him. "DON'T let those nursery rimes fool you he's musically incline this guy got a personal thing against the system" "EVERY other person out there got something against the system if you ask me sir" "WE'RE going to have and bring these snakes out of the bush we not leaving any stones unturned with any of these cases. I don't know if any of you saw the police report yet but a number woman was robbed last night too reminds me of a series of similar robberies from way back, where some lottery winners and seller got mugged no one was ever caught".

"Me na know no body name so" said a Jamaica national at a shanky town apartment which only rented small rooms and a bath and kitchen that you had to share with ten other people.

"MY lawyer tell me I mustn't talk to the police by myself" said another man. "I name Malachi Howett yeah but I knows nothing bout no car" he was high on weed and alcohol speaking from his house window. AT another residence at dog city a ghetto in George Town police shown the picture of a white 1990 Toyota corolla. "That Malachi car yah I remember it but he sold that long ago though". WHAT'S his middle name you know ask one of the Detectives? "THOSE old people only use to put two name on thy children less confusion they say. Mali must have never got it transfer from his name when he sell it". "CAN we speak to him just need to ask him a few questions" "YOU going have go grave yard see him ma dear". "IS that where he works ask the woman detective". "NO that way part he buried been gone now for the butter part of 12 years". ANSWERED the elderly man walking into the house shaking his head never did get that car transfer you see that. We wasting time said one detective to the other, yeah lets go by Talaya's and get some lunch said the lady detective.

Patrick Bowing was in his car going east in the passenger seat was his right hand, and second in command by the name of Harry Phillips. They were both eating hamburgers and sodas "Burgers taste better every time that woman can cook" "Which woman Miss Talaya she doesn't run the Business anymore which world you living in she died about a year ago" said Bowing. "What I didn't know that". "Yeah man her people sold the whole Business out to some Richman he bought the name and the franchise the secret recipe". "I'LL bet lots of people don't know that". Bowing cell phone rang "HELLO" he talked while driving he was on it for five minutes. "THAT was the commissioner he said to Phillip wanted to know about the progress on the case especially about the missing people another letter was sent to the media too". "WHAT in the hell it is with these letters" said Phillip. "THERE up heaving the people and provoking the justice department is what they're doing". THEY drove in silent for a while the phone sounded again it was his wife this time he spoke briefly then hang up.

THEY drove the east coast Patrick Bowing had a hunch he looked at his watch then turn on the radio. IT was ten minutes of news then the talk show came on.

TWENTY minutes later the two Detectives were in North Side talking to a group of boys gather around a tree. SOME of them wearing black caps but none with a tiger on it. "LOOKING for Cox you seen him today". No one seem to know him. IN East End they spoke to some fisher men went inside a Bar and asked more questions but people shook their heads and said no sir. THEY were back in the car by the time that the letter was about to be read Bowing turned up the volume and the A/C as the car moved off.

THE lips of the righteous feeds many but fool die for want of wisdom. TO live in Babylon means to be oppress some are blind others couldn't care less, the beast lives in Babylon, Babylon belong to the beast his tail is the false Prophet which could be scientist teachers and even priest. Babylon is the place were merchants are base, the seven heads are seven kings but who they are that might be the mysterious thing some smoke pot when they were in college others were members of satanic faturities.

Destruction of the poor is a rich man's poverty, we have no right's In a land of communism but you can go to the store and buy a dildo in a place call freedom. ONE world order that's the three six if you Na reading the last part of the book you'll get it. What kind of world and in what order will it be Christopher Columbus was a star to hit the sea. Every green thing will be avoid live within your means but the laws want make us Israel will rise but the wicked will rust. POISON shall hit his words for those who having heard. Confidents in an unfaithful man in times of trouble is like a broken tooth and a foot out of joint. The more things change the more they stay the same, the righteous falling down before the wicked is as a trouble fountain and a corrupted spring. HE that keepeth his month keepeth his life and he that openeth wide his lips shall be removed from his wife. The simple believeth every word but the prudent man looketh well his going. HE that is slow to wrath is of great understanding but he that is hasty of spirit exalted folly.

AS soon as the radio show was over Patrick Bowing was on the cell talking to the program host. "THIS is senor Detective Bowing of the RCIP I'll like to know the author of that letter you just read". "IT didn't have a signature" reply the host. "WE over at the department been listening to them for the last couple week and would prefer that you decline from reading any more of them the appear to be offensive by nature". "well thank you for listening to the program didn't know I had such a wide audience but at the same time the last time I checked this was a free country boss man and still a Democracy and if anybody wants to write as much as a poem to this program I think we o them that much respect to read it sitting here where I do in the chair. And it aren't nobody out there going tell me how to run my show star. There's no profanity or name calling, the citizen of this country got the freedom of speech amendment and I know my rights. So with all due respect sir am going to continue to read those letters and any more that comes in here to me". The man was no other than the smooth talking Carl kneels he'd been a disc jockey for years slash free lance reporter, now running an independent talk show by the name of speak your feelings. Sponsors advertisers and audience basically paid for his air time, on national air waves. Over the last three year it became one of the most popular kneels had become as famous as bob Marley here in Cayman. "NOW if there's anything else I can help you with you just give me a call ya hear". Carl slam the phone down and the line went dead. BOWING looked at his partner and "said that's a feisty West Bayer". "You want me to go teach him a lesson boss" "No I na ready for him yet let him sit a little while" said Bowing.

A Honda Civic parked under a burnt out street light next to a chain link fence outside the play ground of a school. A soccer match was being played there tonight. The classy car blend in among the rest and was hardly noticed. The tinted windows of the car was just a few inches down from the top. A white man with a square face, small eyes and straight black hair sat low down in the driver's seat. THE man had obtain Aliza's picture from the surveillance camera in the Jewelry store, ran it through the department of motor vehicle data base. HE got a hit on her driver's license learnt she was born 1974 and that she lived on school house road number 127.

ALIZA sat out on the veranda of the orphanage house, talking to Indian on the cell phone she had went to a job interview today "things look promising" she told him. They talked for about ten minutes then she turned in for the night.

THE Indian man dialed an overseas number on the phone talked to a man with a strange voice after a short while he hanged up and deleted the number. HE rolled his last spliff for the night. Around the little night table with the night lamp they were some writing paper he jotted down some of the things he needed to do. HE rest the phone down on top of the papers when he was finish. Lying out on the bed he reached over and switch of the light he light up in the darkness. He didn't dream that night his sleep was sweet his mind blank.

IT was a dark night in the North Sound a speed boat could be seen pulling into the mangroves.

"Mission accomplished" said a man on the boat. Nice and easy said another with uniform on standing on the small dock, what going on tonight. He held a flashlight that had been used to signal them with.

"Making money captain another drop off the usual amount of that Columbian flour, you right on time too we running this show men no worries. We control this harbor. Help them with that boys". TWO men in uniform took hard case suitcases from someone with a bandanna on his head and threw them into an SUV. The black speed boat had three out boards with two hundred and fifty horse power each. "This one going to B A W cargo wear house then off to England someone will take care of it once it reaches there". "This is yours Sullivan no need to count it". The man on the boat handed him a red looking back pack. "SEE you next week" he said then they were off again.

Snow man smoked a cigar as they went through the channel with no running lights on. He was white but his skin was sun tan. HE wore a dark blue base ball cap and his long hair came down the sides he had a wide face. "The weather like glass sake" he said to the other man on board." We'll be back on the island in no time". Each of them carried an automatic pistol sucked in waist and there were a couple of mock 10 machine guns on the floor of the boat up in front. THERE were a few scattered stars in the night sky. The shape of Volcano Island could be made out in the glare of the night. Snow man follows a red blinking red light from a beckon antenna that was located on a mountain of the Island it was only fifteen miles away. THEY were from south Florida and had connections all over. Snow man worked for a godfather in the Florida mafia. Now he work for the sheik who provided a protected shell and means of client base in Europe and the Middle East, the Arabs had poppy flowers the mean ingredient to make heroine and they traded back and forth with each other. Three or four times a year the sheik traveled to the Middle East on his private jet a CRJ 200. Snow man and snake went along and they brought back cargo. There was a private runway on the Island. IMMAGRATION, customs, Aviation control were all paid to arrange none stop flight and quick check through points in places like Canada LasVegas and Miami international airport. POWDER on the other hand went out on commercial air line by means of air cargo or mules depending on the buyer. Around the Caribbean snow man and snake did the run themselves in a Donzi 500 super speed boat, that was capable of going 300 knots on open water on a good night. They dealt with strictly 80 proof Cocaine and Heroin it was manufactured in one of their labs. Every now and then a big order of couple thousand tons of high grade marijuana would come in. and they would point her south and pack the 38 footer Donzi with Columbian gold buds and resell it to the North American Mafia.

Snow man was trying to monopolize the Marijuana market in the Caribbean he wanted this business for his self, but he was having a hard time against the Jamaicans. THE sheik owned hundreds of acres in JAM and was beginning to farm it growing Ganja Plant, Hemp and Hashy along with other honest to goodness crops. He employed local Jamaican farmers who had no idea who they were working for. Political and Judicial payoff around the world made things happen.

The two men were silent as the boat went into a cave in the bottom of a mountain cliff that was on the sea shore. Only the sound of the water against the boat could be heard as it slowed down from cutting the waves and finally stop at a dock the engine went dead. A guard's man stood at one end of the concrete dock with a machine gun. He was wearing a security uniform "welcome back boss" he said.

IT was 6 AM Indian had finish usual morning thing, he had even read a few psalms this morning before going into George Town. Three straw baskets were strapped around his shoulders and chest. Two hours later he was in the water front selling coconut water to thirsty tourist on a cruise ship day, he already had sold ackees and bread fruits to the market earlier. A few of his produces were spread out on the table, so tourist when passing by could see what they looked like. It was the first time most had ever seen such things and they would stop and ask questions. What are those said the white woman with a bathing suit on. "We call them Ackees cook them with vegetables and fish good source of iron". "How do you spell it" she asked. "How much for the coconut water" asked a man. "Tree U.S sweet Cayman coconut water I'll chop it in two if you want the jelly". "Jesus what you kidding m the other islands sell them for one dollar". "This Cayman sir nothing cost a dollar here". The Tourist laughed then said "give us four it's getting hot. The Indian took four coconuts from the pile alongside the table a big umbrella over head provided shade. A local woman cooked and sold turtle meat with breadfruit white rice and cornbread under a tree and a Talia's food shack was just down the road. Later on A 20 year old tourist with red hair came by "yow dude you know way I can get some pot from". The Indian said something to him and the young man put a fifty dollar U S bill on the table. A bag of Guavas from the basket was handed to him "Is there a liquor store nearby he ask ".

"Right out thy" Indian said pointing. THE tourist put the Guavas in his back pack and was off. BY noon there were only a few coconuts left it wasn't a bad day after all tourist had even bought Ackees and breadfruits as Souvenirs, some would even ask the ship's chef to cook it for them." Can I please see your permit sir" said the port authority officer to the Indian man." I didn't bring it today, didn't think I needed to". "Well which is it you didn't bring it because you don't have one is more like it". "WHAT you think you above the law can do anything you want". THE Indian hesitated but he realized that the port officer had just as much power as the police. "YOU don't hear what I say O what". INDIAN gave him his ID, "I know you had to be from George Town. I got a good mind to arrest you and lock you up for illegal selling. I know there isn't any more coconuts in town so you had to steal them from somewhere else". HE spoke in a local dialect to the Indian man the officer seemed unconcern with the tourist looking at them. "MAN I Na in the mood today pick up ya things and get out of here and don't come back. The Indian gathered his things and left.

At the nightingale house Aliza was in her room staring out the window when she saw her boyfriend. He had sent a text saying he was five minutes away. She met him outside and gave him a kiss. I have some good news she said. I start work on Monday.

"I happy for you babes"

"I know that means a lot to you"

I made over a hundred dollars today but port authority came down on me.

I really Na worried bout them still. I got to do for my family they do wha the they have to and I going do what I need to do. Way Mr. Bill and Marisha they gone on the beach. Wasn't any school today? Two vehicles loaded with children. So when you coming home sugar plum asked Indian. Next couples of weeks after I get settle in on the job that is if you behave. I will stay here for a few more weeks with mamma and the kids. They have exams coming up and mama wants all of them to pass I'm going to help them study cause if they don't do good. First thing education department will say the orphanage isn't doing a good job and they might want to take away that little funding they giving. They can do that said Indian, they have to put more unto it, they might do that all the same but we want them to pas, we got netball competition coming up too the boys won the football cup once but we girls have never won nothing yet. Mr. Bill asked me too to practice with the boys. And help out any way I can this season said indian. Get out of the way you drunkard shouted a man passing in a car to an old drunk sitting under a tree, across the street. There was a bottle of rum resting on the ground and he held a radio to his ear. Every now and then he seemed to be holding up a coin in front of his face looking at it in the direction of the orphanage house. The bum was bare footed had on a tear up pants and a dirty t-shirt wrapped around his waist. He had a long beard and rusty nappy hair. He was a dark brown skin man he looked like a regular bum. It wasn't strange to see these kind of people in this area of central near rock hole. But they had not really see this one before that a new one said Indian. A lawyer or something lost his job and family over money, drugs or alcohol. I feel sorry for those people still he said. That could have been me or someone I know. He crazy too see how keep looking at that 25 cent in his hand. He was just beyond the fence of the orphanage house. Aliza and Indian talked some more, and they saw the old drunk get up and walk down street mumbling to himself. I need couples boxes Indian to pack my things in plus mama is giving me some more things to carry home for the babies when they're born. I'll pick some up tonight for you, how much more money we need honey to finish the floor on the big house said Aliza. 3,000 dollars or so worth of concrete. I should have that in two months in my savings said Aliza. With this new job. Yah baby I'm working on something too myself. The house important but we going to need some serious money when those twins comes along. You just take it easy let me worry about the house. In a couple of days I going buy the concrete god spears. Way you get money from Indian. I been saving it sweet cake. Just don't stress yourself out. Concentrate on the job now that you have and the pregnancy. You been outside too long. You want to go inside and put your feet up and relax. Exercise is the best thing for the unborn children those old people used to say Indian. Aliza told him. I Na see you getting any fatter babes, you need eat plenty now for three of Unna. Oh Indian everything alright with the twins. There only six weeks now remember. You worrying more than me.

Everything will be fine. I told my employers according to law they will give me maturity leave, that a wonder said Indian. Things getting better out their in the job world. The talked and Indian gave her some longer kisses they coated up until the Patterson's arrived with a bunch of energetic kids. They were excited to see Indian. They were kicked around a plastic ball together out in the yard. And after that Indian gave them a short lesson in martial arts showing them basic moves. By supper Aliza and Mrs. Patterson were in the kitchen while Bill and Indian talked out back in the late evening. I'll call you one night this week to let you know said Bill. They said grace around the table those who couldn't fit sat at the breakfast counter. They ate fish rundown with bread kind and white rice.

That was delicious said Indian when he got through, would you like seconds said mama. That would be nice. She came back with two plates one for him and the other for Bill. Aliza couldn't finish hers. She had been nibbling on fruits and vegetables all day and her stomach was bulged. And she felt like she was getting too fat too soon. So Indian finished her plate of as well. You embarrassing me said Aliza humorously. He Na got no problem with food Aliza said. They all laughed after that it wasn't over Indian bought ice cream for everybody when they had finish dinner. From the ice cream van that drove by every night. But as for him he pass on it. He never ate ice cream he had his own reason.

It was getting late Indian called king. "Yah I ready now" he said over the cell phone. "You say you could give me a ride home. Right." "Yah blood

I coming across they now. You by Aliza right" .> "yah". Ten minutes later Kingdon arrived. Babet was with him she would stay by Aliza until King came back from dropping Indian home. Indian kissed Aliza goodbye. She held a little girl half asleep in her arms, with big eyes the child looked at the Indian and said "would you be my daddy". "Sure" he said and she kissed him on the cheek. "Tell king take time on the road Indian" said Aliza you know it Na like how it was before police all over now "." Don't worry Babes I na smoking much or nothing now since you moved out I trying do better, I'll call you when I reach home so you know I made it up OK ". Indian said his good nights to the Patterson. HE bounced fist with King as he got into the car and drove away." Don't let man fool you up girl said Babet we love em but they going burn at least two spliff each before they reach frank sound, and couple more when they reach there ". I know said Aliza we know our men they sound so sweet when they're trying to be sincere ". "Make a quick stop by the auto shop I ga pick up some boxes for that woman" said Indian. "Yow you ga anything burn on you" ask kingdon. "Yah I ga a little thing" came the reply from Indian which he was referring to about a half ounce. THE Explorer pulled into a 24 hour auto parts store. The men sat in the vehicle talking and rolling marijuana cigarettes. "I told Aliza I was getting some money this week she wanted to know from way part I had to lie to her if I don't do this it will be years till I get that floor pour." Indian put saliva on the paper and seal it.

"I need to get serious and finish off the house I got kids on the way you know what I mean". "YAH Babeth told me congratulation dug" "Tha thing supposed to be coming in any day now we should have a good draw". The Indian man got out and went over to the garbage container where off to one side next to it lied stacks of card board boxes he throw three or so in back of the vehicle. THERE wasn't much traffic leaving out of town on a Sunday night and it was smooth sailing. AS they got out of George Town they put fire to their joints. Indian held a cigarette out the window and a spliff in the other. "I na work in a long time I had to take a chance". "I didn't know ship was coming in today". "ME neither I saw her coming in early this morning when I was running on the beach" THEY took tin halls from the spliffs and listen to Bob Marley on the sound system. There was often silent as the men drop off into highness and mellows then they reached the dirt road where the little shack was. TATE and the rest of the gang was already there, in the pitch of the darkness the Indian man went into the bushes five minutes later coming out with a bottle weed. AROUND the small camp fire they talked through the night. INDIAN talked to his one and only on the cell likewise so did kingdon, only Babeth had call him. "Come and pick me up now she demanded I can't be round people house this time of night wha happen to you". KINGDON left mad the woman was driving his patience the SUV spin tires as he pulled out almost hitting another car in the process.

BY mid night the place was quite once more the small camp fire was going out and the Indian man was alone showering outside. HE was back inside when the cell phone rang it was the number with the funny area code and the man with the strange voice, he erase the number when the conversation was over. HE had a daze look on his face.

DAYS later at the Bodden Town police station. "Good morning officer" said a Canadian woman. She was the same one who worked at the social service Department down town and usually in a bad mood. "I've come to report a matter" "Right this way"

"And so officer this big van pulled out in front of me going about a 100 miles an hour with no lights on" Actually it was the other way around the old lady had forgotten to switch on her head lights she didn't realize it until a driver cursed her about it. "I live in one of those new neighborhoods up in frank sound and a little ways down the road from me is this little house by where the car pulls out from every night there's like a some kind of hippy convention going on". What do you mean asked the officer? Well that isn't a proper resident you know there's cars parked everywhere from the balcony of my home all I can see is smoke traveling through the air the bush and trees hide everything. I thought at first someone was clearing land you know smoking out mosquito and what have you. But then I hear music playing into the wee hours of the morning, I was among the few Canadians that was at wood stock she lean forward and whisper probably naked girls dancing too officer. NO one knows what happening at night up those swamps if you following me". Thank you for your concern ma'am said the police man.

IT was 3.30 AM a man sat around his desk top computer at his home a table lamp was on and the hum of the air conditioner could be heard along with the sound of the key board on the computer as his type away. HE sipped coffee and looked into the screen it was a spacious two bed room studio in the suburbs of tropical gardens only six minutes drive outside of town. The space in the loft was converted into a small office.

WHERE a gold color name plate on the desk said Matt O Bryon private eye.

HE touched a key with his index finger and a picture of Indian came up on the screen, finely after hours of searching. The Indian's license had been expired years now and his photo was automatically removed from the system he had click on a link which only posted the names of those whose license was suspended or expired and the web site was out dated all the same. WHICH he wasn't surprise at that,he had a picture on the computer table of a man but no name. HE play around with different sites for hours matt was a computer engineer an expert in the field of technology he also work for the South African Embassy. MOST of his work was done at home, "am going to have to hack into the national Registry data base". HIS Company had designed the system two years ago he disarmed the two security walls punch in the three pass words in the space provided. THERE was only three minutes before the alarm went off down at the station where he was in charge, but he didn't want his two employers to spend the rest of their shift calling him and scratching their heads.

HE rather leave them and let them sleep two minutes and 45 seconds was plenty of time to go through fifty thousand names. HE entre the Indian's photo into the program the computer would scan through the web site at 18,000 names a minute. TWO and a half minutes later it stop at a face it looked a little different perhaps younger the computer had a positive match. Ezekiel Howett matt scramble down the address and exited the site.

A man in a telephone company van did some work at a pole at the Indian Reservation, he had on kaki clothes with the logo of a local company there was a small instrument in his hand. Wire stuck out from a metal box that was mounted to the light pole. "Wha you do here" said an Indian native. That had been eye balling the van since the time it set foot in the Reservation. "Am installing a phone line".

"Why" asked the Indian "we don't use those things". "Its standard regulation these days they sent me from down town". "What and cable TV next week" claimed the Indian, then the internet after that".

"Am not going to argue with you or justify reasons am only doing my job you people are my friends" said the telephone man. "I have a lot of Indian amigos from when I went to school most of them stay in town you know Ezekiel Howett I having seen him in years". "Which one I know about a hundred of them personally" said the Indian. "I think it would be butter if you go" he pulled out a big knife from the chafe that was in his waste. "I don't want any trouble" said the man adjusting the glasses on his face while looking at the knife. "Then you better get out of here" said the wrinkle face Indian with long black hair. "I don't feel like killing any white man today but if I see you around here again trust me I won't be so nice".

THE man hopped into the van and drove off quickly forgetting an Aluminum ladder that was against the pole. "Dumb Indian" he said out loud inside the van as he made the corner out of the site and away from the Reservation. "NO wonder they live on a plantation away from normal people" HE pulled of the beard and fake mouth stash and eye brows. THEN he took of the rest of it a silicone rubber pad from his head that made him look bald likewise the big nose and spectacles. HE rested them on the front seat next to him and shook his hair loose with his fingers. "AM going to have and follow him see where he nest at".

ADULFO held a picture of Indian "so this is the boyfriend how charming". MATT had took the picture with his newest toy, a digital camera that he made himself and placed in a microscopic camera chip between two Cayman quarters then sealed them together heads and tail. IN the queen's eye of the coin a tiny hole almost invisible were the lends that allowed him to take pictures. IT was the latest in Chinese espionage equipment he learn about on a Chinese web site. FED EX had hand deliver it right to his front door a month ago direct from Tokyo. "I'll have something solid for you soon" said matt.

LATER that evening in George Town an Ice Cream van was robbed and the driver assaulted by two men with bandannas across the bottom half of their faces.

EVERTHING was what it was up to this point and the world was moving forward.

CHIRSTMAS had come and gone the New Year had settle in and it was the same old story.

THERE was a new push for Independence, but the scare had pass the smoke clear.

People were still figuring out the we's from the we wee's.

BY 2004 time had catch up with us and was passing us by.

THEY were still blowing themselves up in the Middle East, they had been a worldwide virus.

That had affected millions of computers.

CAYMANIANS were still taking licks.

THE world was bigger than ever.

ALL kinds of wares insects and flying roaches were seen about the place, Cayman never had them before.

A new type of worm was appearing in school children hair the school was like ant nest with all these New Year's babies' bastard kids, Status Children, exchange student, and cabbage patch kids. Space was running out in the city, the streets were crazy, people becoming facetier.

IT was like the Devil himself had came out of the ground and was ripping havoc in Cayman.

ON the business seen executives in sky Scrapers had view looking into people out houses.

People had sold out land and was worster of. THE middle man went beyond the valuators and Bankers.

MONEY people were buying out money man and the rich and powerful purchasing towns and neighbor hoods.

ONE person was buying up thousands of acres of swamp land.

MOVIE stars and famous people were secretly doing things. BUILDING a house was so expensive it was like making a bomb shelter.

THERE was a reorganizations going on and the chosen some would be left behind the Jews and Arabs were walking a fine caulk line and the way out was all in the mind.

SCIENCETIFIC brake through had put ice in the desire and man living under the sea.

NEWS papers continue to show only one point of view and tell their own side of the story.

ELITE person were in charge of the whole media organizations. RADIO TV news papers even marl road talks etc.

CAYMAN still had a low crime rate and the 6 o clock news was loaded with commercials.

NOW witch craft wasn't something to make fun of people buried live fish with needles stuck in it in a friend's or enemy yard at mid night or when the moon was right.

THERE was a lot of praying going on too.

THERE were more accidents and road rage than ever before, Traffic had become terrifying with these new kinds of people in the country.

SOME of them were dying to come here latterly selling their souls and shit.

MONEY people were dropping down dead like flies and on the other hand man like Rudy the local bomb was better than ever. Employers would cancel the work permit of anyone who asked for raise in pay or better working conditions if it was a Caymanian he would be fired or permeantly lay off.

STUMBLEING blocks had become death cards and black roses.

PEOPLE did whatever to get a bank loan or steady work.

THE banks continue to stereo type people with particular last names or back ground.

THOSE with certain skin color got preference along with those from special groups, Religion, and clubs.

All this would determine if you got a loan or not.

EVEN who you employer was and how much power and influent they posted on the community.

PEOPLE would be injured by poorly built and Maintain building, and it wasn't no one's fault.

THEY were truckloads of mal practice cases and a couple of world class action law sues that would be settle out of court some way or the other.

DEPENDING on who you was dead or alive.

MORE and more people started calling Cayman a wicked place.

PEOPLE were beginning to ask who was really running the Island us or them.

BY 2004 we become the mother of all harlots and the Government fourth cast growth and stability for the Island economy. According to the press release Cayman had nothing to worry about, a new airport along with other projects would spark the construction boom. There was a cruise ship berthing facility plan and another Hospital.

CAYMAN would set the new standards for the financial industry we would become a five Diamond Island in time to come.

FINANCIAL growth Tourism and Development would continue to fuel this rapid elusion.

STRONGER Infrastructure for international Companies to house their off shore head offices.

AS in every Government money was approved collected and the work not done on the project.

OVER the last four years they had been no audits carried out on the Government.

BUT money was being used without fear or care.

THE Island had been one hot potato for years and the November Election promised to make it right.

WE had come to the end of the rope the higher ups were getting their feet wet now.

ON the world news there was talk about a global warming and a worldwide recession.

IT was 6.02 PM a small South Seas fiber glass boat was in the north sound. A man pulled a rope with a eight inch block attach to the end of it out of the water it was an anchor. A boy no older than 12 sat on an ice box in the middle of the skiff. Both were bear back and wore hats. The man pulled the cord twice before the engine started. The two had been fishing all day and had gotten fisher man's luck. The boy didn't go to school today they needed food, but all day at sea they only had three grunts and two skobs. Earlier that day they chatted with a charter boat captain loaded with tourist out by the sand bar bathing with sting grays. But was hours ago by now there wasn't any more boats in the sound, they had it all for themselves. Boats with tourist dollars had gone in for the day. The currents had died down the water was clear as Cristal. The silk from out boards and other Commercial vessel was east of them this time of evening. This will be the last time I coming out here in day time tell you that. The men said to the boy. We black enough as it is now we don't need to get sun burn for nothing. The boy smiled he was too tired to laugh. Pap we going in now. No we can go in empty handed son. It Na nothing home to eat. We going stop up here right below the reef. We still got 20 minutes before she go down, let us try get some conchs at least. A minute later he killed the motor and the skiff glided on the water and came to a grassy bottom over the sea floor. The boy took off his hat and dove unto the cool water. The man pitched in seconds later. With just the ropes tied around his waist. He swam and pulled the boat along. The water was deep all around. But the little area where they were at formed an underwater buffer that elevated it. At the inside of the reef. It was a small mud bar hill with grassy and sandy bottom. Running for about 150 feet along the reef edge, and around 30 feet wild. The boy brought up conchs two three at a time then took a deep breath and dove down again at a distance of nearly 18 feet. Using the pointed end of the conch shell to another the cracked open. He cracked open a small horizontal break across the crown of the shell. Pushed a knife into the opening while turning his wrist and the conch meat popped out, from the shell. The man listened for boat engines and looked around as he popped the conch. Throwing the empty shells into the deep sections of the ocean. He kicked his legs to stay afloat every now and then holding up on the side of the boat as he threw the conchs inside. He followed his son as he dove. Ten minutes later they had 50 broad leaf conchs, gutted and horns off patched away in the bottom of the ice chest. They laid fish and other gears on top of them, the ice had already melted but it was still cool enough to keep them fresh until they reached land. They were on board getting ready to leave seconds before the sun disappeared. When a huge green turtle passed a foot under the boat. Aint he a beauty said the man. The boy put on his t-shirt and laid down in the bow of the South Seas. The engine started up and they headed for shore. Seas were a little choppy and the skiff skipped over the waves. The small engine blared. Only a few early stars were scattered in the night sky, the moon was nowhere to be seen. It was no talking the boy was half sleep, he had exams the next day. The knotty hair man drank the last of a small bottle of Appleton rum that he was sipping on all day. With no chaser and an empty stomach. He began to sing an old Andy Martin tune. I'm in the Yellow Pages listed under fool. He looked at the finished bottle and tossed it over the side. He repeated the chorus several times over and over again. Because he didn't know the rest of the words to the song. A while later the engine slowed down and came to a steady hum. The shape of the mangrove buffer could be seen, in the bight. It was pitch black but the landscape was a few shades darker than the night itself. The fiberglass skiff slipped in behind some mangroves and out of eyes sight of the main harbor. This Na the dock said the boy lifting his head. Keep it quite we inside Little Sound. Daddy wha we doing up in ya? Catch couple of bugs' boy they always good to have. It had been a long day the boy thought the old man was talking out of his head and had one too many to drink. Up in here ga plenty mosquitoes Pap wha you going do with bugs? They nuff of them on land. It was the first time the boy had been there with his father, the place looked creepy. Lobsters son bugs are lobsters in fishermen talk. The skiff moved along the mangroves. The paddle went into the water down to the handle pushing the small boat in and out of the curves. The bottom was only four feet deep. The Yamaha engine was tilled up and out of the water. The skiff slid on the black water of the night it made absolutely no sound. A propane lantern burned dim on board of the boat. The man cleaned the conch and threw the hide at the foot of the mangrove. Where lobsters gather and fed on tiny fish and other marine life and sea carcass. He launched the hook into them. A thin iron rod about five feet long with a big fish hook bind with wire at the end of it. The other end of it was sharpened to a point. It was easy pickings sometimes hooking two at a time. We stealing these daddy? The boy whispered. No son we just taking our share God put them here for all of us. We getting a nuff for today and tomorrow and the days after that.

Soon thereafter ice box and buckets were filled with burgundy reddish looking Caribbean lobsters. We na going starve this week son God has provided I got enough to sell too even though it out of season the restaurant will still take them off my hand along with the conchs. They going want pay nothing but we got plenty. The man smiled at how much bottles of black label rum he would be getting, from this catch. Daddy I hear a boat coming. Before the man realized what was happening the boat was long side them. A spot light shined into the men's face. I should have known that was you Bucko. Looks like we catch ya red handed. This go round and you teaching the boy too the ropes on how to steal. Only one reason why you up in here. The season closed Bucko you know that. I just have some grunts and couple conchs Sullivan, that I got out by the sand bar. Come up in here clean em and going home. I was fishing for mutton snapper with the conch bate something big run off with my line just now and cut it off up inside those mangrove roots. The boy kept quiet as the man talked. He had his hand over the four head shielding himself from the blinding light. Get that light out of my face screamed Bucko but Sullivan paid him no attention. What you got inside the cooler. I done tell you already what I ga. Wha you think I some kind of idiot? Sullivan motioned at his men and they jumped aboard the skiff almost sinking it. One man opened the icebox and whistled "Jackpot Captain" he said. Sullivan grinned and showed his gold teeth. You do five years for them easy. Don't make sense to waste the judge time with this minor instance. Begged the man. The last couple months been hard cap, I only trying provide food for my family. I begging you cap from one countryman to another, go with your heart and give me a chance. I sick of giving Unna chances all the time I get let down. You ga have some respect for the law. I don't WA to hear no more. Tell me something. Tha alcohol I smell on you? Probably was smoking ganja too in front of the boy. You should be ashamed of yourself. The marine officer lift the top of the second icebox and under the fish, bait and other stuff over three dozen conchs were stashed away. You killing um tonight Buckling. Now that's what I talking bout said Sullivan. Look at the pleasant white meat said the others. That's tempting. The officer close back the cover of the ice box "Cuff these criminals" Go to hell you dirty bastard. You think you big shit now cause you got on that uniform? You Na no better than the rest of us poor people out here fighting for a living. One officer reached to put the handcuffs on Buck but the man picked up the hook stick off the floor of the skiff. He moved with a speed not even a young man could match. Seconds later he jerked the hook into the officer's wrist. The officer screamed as the blood spout from his hand. The other officer fired a shot in the air and then brought the barrel of the gun to the man's face touching his forehead. The steel was cold on Bucko's head. Pa don't give him reason to shoot ya cried a little frightened voice. Now Unna have something to carry my ass to jail for.

Sullivan slowly removed the hook stick from the officer's wrist. It was painful. He threw some peroxide over it and wrapped it with gauze and bandage from his first aid kit on the boat. Blood pools were on both boats and the new bandage was already soaked around the officer's hand. The two criminals laid face down in the stern. The back deck was opened up. Their hands were cuffed to their backs. The skiff was tied to the police boat and towed behind. The officers kicked Bucko in the rib cage and swore at him. Sullivan radioed in the situation. Five minutes later they were tying up at a dock in North Sound.

At that same time, that same night at a car parts store on Eastern Avenue, "Put the Bumboclaut money in the bag quick time fore I blow your fucking brains out!" said someone in the ski mask to a store attendant holding a gun to her face. Another man stood by the door. It was over as quick as it had happened.

Tires skid, rubber burned as the vehicle left the scene in a hurry.

"It was the same MO as the waterfront boss" said Detective Harry Philips.

Twenty minutes later after arriving on the scene. One guy wore a cap, black clothing throughout, and ski mask. Gun to the head demanded money, they exited through the back door where the getaway car was parked. What happened to the security guard? He wasn't supposed to come in till eight. The place closes at eleven. I know what you're thinking. We're checking him out now. What nationality said Detective Bowing to Phillips? He's Jamaican sir. Married here, kids etc. Been working with Top Notch Security four and a half years. People say they saw a big vehicle speeding away. SUV-ish. Judging by the size of the tire marks, that's about correct. It headed West Bay road direction. Bowing shook his head. This doesn't look good. The year just started.

There was a draft coming out of the South West that late evening in January. Indian and Bill walked the cliff land of North Side. They're supposed to be some Caymanite around here said Bill. They walked deeper into the bushes where there was a hole in the cliff forming a big a contour of the rock. There was some brown and grey colored stones point upwards like cones on an ice cream. The two men smiled. Na much of that left here on island.

I tell you that said Bill.

The Brac have plenty, not as good as the one from up here. There's got a lot of salt particles in the rocks it ain't as hard as this one either.

The craft man can cut it however they want cause it soft but two of them have advantages and disadvantages. You got to have the right one to fit it to gold or the Caymanite will turn blackish.

The gold on the salt particles mixed together forms discoloration of the rock. Jewelers prefer the ones from up here. We have to go back and get the things out of the truck. By the time they came back the sun had already set. They put the small generator and a jackhammer with a long cord on the ground near to where they would remove the Caymanite. The Indian man chopped leaves and shrubs from the area and covered the generator to drown out the noise from it. He left the exhaust clear then he wrapped the cloth around the jackhammer to likewise muffle the sound. They were miles away from civilization all the same and the wind blew the sound of the equipment into the sea. The two men worked briskly, not missing a beat. One held the flashlight while the other handled the jackhammer. Taking turns every ten minutes or so, big chunks of rock with Caymanite came from the cliff. Some were solid, others had mixtures of cores and cliff rock. They threw them into the bucket and an hour later the bushes were silent everything was back in the truck, they carried equipment and several buckets all in one trip. Going over an under sharp cliff land with slippers. The market was low on Caymanite this time of year.

The next day they were at a craft shop in George Town. "I can't give you that kind of money for it" said a man in the shop. "There's a lot of work involved in this" said Bill "But I'm not going to get greedy and kill you with big price. Give us ten and you got a deal and you can take all of it." The man looked at the Indian who was walking around admiring craft work. Then he scratched his beard and extended his hand, you got a deal. I could do that. A cheque will be alright with you this time? Bill was reluctant, if that's the best you can do then I guess I'll have to take it.

Tellers at the Bank gave Bill a funny look. How would you like it back Sir?

"Hundreds and fifties."

The split went half and half and each man got five grand. The merchant at the craft store picked up the phone and called Stones International, spoke to the manager "Hello this Mikey down at the Craft Shop. Want to find out if you need any more Caymanite to buy?"

"Sure" said the manager. "I'll take it off your hands."

"It's about two wheelbarrow load this time" said Mikey.

"I'm asking fifteen. This the good one."

"We could do that" said the Czech Republican man.

It was more like thirteen when it was all said and done. Stones International, likewise made a profit. They would double their money. Caymanite was unique to Cayman, Stones International resold most of it to buyers from Europe and North America and would keep some for themselves in the storage room until there was a high demand. They also cut and made jewelry to sell retail. Over the years Caymanite was becoming more limited and craftsman and jewelers could hardly find the precious stone. People paid thousands of dollars for a tiny piece of Caymanite, after it had been made into a piece of artwork.

IT was 9.27 AM when Aliza walked into the building on fort-Street, it was her first day on the job. SHE spoke to the receptionist then took the Elevator to the fifth floor she was well put together.

"THERE you are" said an elderly lady with a British tone to Aliza "you look lovely darling, your desk is over there in the corner the one next to the computer. HERE you go my dear" she said handing Aliza some paper.

"THE CEO doesn't get in tell around ten-nish or so and the Accountant is away for the week. Andrew is a good boy, you may have to serve them coffee every now and then when the secretary is busy. EVENTHOUGH it's not part of your job description". "I understand that'll be fine miss Abegale" reply Aliza.

AT her desk she went to work she type something on the key board and entre the accounting package software.

THE small office in the Accounting section consisted of seven employers including Aliza the CEO and the Accountant. SHE had meant most of them the day of her interview. THE company had down size but had still hire Aliza, she would have to pick up the slack for less pay if she wanted to keep the job.

IT had been almost two years of unemployment for her. SHE was only being paid half of what the job was worth but she had little choice other than to take it, after all they were waring in the Middle East. AND the world Economy was hurting, nothing much had change in the labor market. THE time lost would never be recuperated she was convince of this fact. THE Philosophy behind the whole labor system was worst this time. THE office still had the same smell she'd remember as the rest, and maybe even the same people with different faces. SHE told herself she would stick it out until the end, some day she would be in her own office running her Company. SHE directed her thoughts to postiveness. IT was a full time position but not as a qualified Accountant she would assist the CPA on a mediocre level run errands and deliver paper work on time, down load info etc. provide copies and type outs.

STILL she was happy to be there, the good lord had open a door for her and who knows where it would lead to.

THE money went as fast as it came. That'll be 35 hundred said the man at the pre- mix Concrete office. HE would share the good news with Aliza when they meant up later Indian didn't want to risk calling her on the job, some of those employers can be a real pain when it comes to private phone calls on the job.

A week or so had zipped by on the street things were still busy. PATRICK BOWING was having breakfast that morning when he got a call. IT was the station he made a few jesters then hang up.

"THERE was a robbery last night, Liquor store and a craft market got hit" he said to his wife.

A short chubby woman who hadn't heard a word he said she was too occupied thinking about something else. SHE worn diamond ear rings and house coat over her silk night gown. Curlers were in her hair and lip stick and make up to the face.

SHE stepped out from behind the kitchen and came to the Dining room table. "Honey have you seen my necklace". "Which one" ask Patrick. "The Diamond and Safire one, you bought me for my Birthday. That year in the Turks and Caicos, THE twenty Thousand dollars one Patrick".

"NO I having scene it I don't touch your stuff".

"THAT strange I only keep it in the Jewelry box locked away Marie only comes twice a week she don't have access to my things". "WHEN was the last time you saw it". "I remember wearing it the last time we went to diner a few weeks ago, and I put it back in the box that same night. Hope I never misplace it in those clothes I donated to the Red Cross my God honey".

"NOW Norma just take it easy don't get stir-up sit down for a minute. AM sure it going to show up go through your things again, don't worry we'll find it".

HE kissed her "Right now I have to get to work and catch some bad guys. I'll help you look when I get home love you sweetie".

SHE made herself a glass of protein shake, BY early afternoon Norma Bowing had particularly turned the house upside down, and inside out.

SHE had drilled poor old Marie the maid to the point of confessing to something she didn't do, SHE was about to quit and go back to Honduras.

NORMA had even drove down to the RED CROSS and search through her donated wardrobe with no luck.

SHE shade tears then for her necklace then realized it was insured, and Patrick would buy her another worth twice as much because he loved her.

SHE picture the look on some poor suffers face when they found a 20,000 dollar necklace in an old coat that was donated to Charity.

Indian and Bill were on the highway headed east that night, the financial situation was improving a little at a time for them. Indian would be putting down concrete the day after tomorrow. He was on his way home to the swamps. Traffic wasn't too bad and the cars were flowing. They past three round about on the four lane freeway and the road out of the town switched back to a two lane system. About five or six cars behind them was a Honda Accord. They crossed homes in Savannah with front porches and white picket fence. In one of them a little girl sat on a horse, a cowboy held the bridle rope. Miles more down the road they passed the Indian reservations. They drove some more then came to the sea side village of Bodden Town. They were a number of houses along the beach. The evening was going dim, the early moon was just coming up out of the edge of the horizon. Its light could be seen on the ocean and it exposed the reef which was out of the water. Ain't that a beauty said Bill. The truck stopped at a gas station that was only a few yards from the sea. A nice beach was off to the side where a little hut with a coconut limp roof was at, a man and a lady sold food out of it. Calypso music played low from a tape deck that was on a table outside. People stood around eating fish and drinking. Full her up said Bill to the pump attendant as he went into the gas station. Indian's cell phone rang it was the person with the funny accent and strange area code on the line. The call lasted three minutes, "be on your guard and be careful" was the last words the voice said. Indian deleted the number. A few hundred yards up ahead a Honda Accord was pulled off the road side next to a laundry mat,. The person inside stared through the rear view mirror. The truck passed him headed east once again, both men drank Heineken in the bottle from the gas station. There were four left in the pack. That money wha we made will keep the duppy away for a few weeks the men joked. Ten minutes later Bill made a left turn onto Frank Sound went down the road a little ways then turned off to the right into a dirt road with no name. Home sweet home said Indian. The Accord passed the dirt road circled back and parked hidden in some bushes.

Bill Patterson placed a clear glass of water on the ground nearby. Next to it was a linen cloth the size of a towel and an open Bible on top of it. He moved a metal detector slowly from side to side as he walked the premises. "this Na going bip for the sugar babies we know that. Only if it happens to be in an iron chest with gold". They had played treasure hunting in that area at least twenty times so far, I dig this spot a 100 times already said the Indian. Yah I know said Bill we keep getting a signal.

Matt O'Bryan watched quietly in the bushes from a set of night vision binoculars. A small satellite looking antenna was jammed between a branchy bush tree, he could hear every word they spoke. Matt wasn't dressed for the weather. All the same he hadn't figured for the misquotes and sand flies he had underestimated things and was in the heart of the nesting grounds. Swamp flies and bugs of all kinds were biting right through his clothes and baseball cap. The thin longs sleeves shirt offered no protection. Insects sang round his head and ears. His white skin was becoming red and bumps were coming out all over his body and face. Only after fifteen minute. Every now and then he would wipe the blood from off his cheek and forehead with his bare hands, the blood smelled like rusted iron, he cursed to himself. The insects seemed to like white people blood more than the locals, he had heard a black man say one time at a burn fire out in East End. But he would stick it out cause he had a job to do tonight.

Bill held a bottle of beer in his hand Indian had a spliff, they walked around the yard and stopped by the same place as always. Indian Bill said. look referring to the metal detector.The two men picked and shoveled. the moon was perfectly round in the sky, the night was still nothing moved nothing was heard except for the occasional owl and the sound of the pick axe as it drove into the ground and made an echoing thumping sound. After a while they began to speak "this is further down than we went the last time" Indian said. Yah I know said Bill holding the machine over the hole as it made a bipping sound, for some reason I lost the signal the last time after we had reached six feet. We probably was digging the hole a little off. The ground has water in it too, that could have kill the signal. Well tonight we going go to the bitter end with this I got a good feeling said the Indian. You say that every time we dig Indian. It good to be optimistic. They were about eight feet down Indian filled his shovel with dirt and shift through it with his finger. The worked in and one out in the 4 x 4 pit. And they took turns using the tools. Bill finished picking and Indian climbed down into the hole with the shovel. Bill pulled the ladder up out of the hole. Both of them wore slippers and the damp black soil made their feet wetish. A small Hickory fire chased away the blood suckers. An hour and a half went by. Indian filled a bucket with dirt and lifted it up over his head passing it to bill who grabbed it and emptied it onto a pile of dirt about three feet high now. It was four feet away from the hole. They had done this about seventy times so far. Bill noticed something is that beach sand. You hitting there now you see those white rocks they were used to mark a spot. Indian continued removing the sand and soon it was clean of loose stuff. Bill climbed down the again and started with the pick axe driving it into the dirt. Loosening up hard ground. See what I tell ya he said to Indian a while after he had started. This ground muddy again no sand or beach rock. Yah I thought it was the beach level we had reached. hundred of years back this whole land was a beach. You have to go about 15 feet from way part we is now Bill said before you get to the beach height. The two men worked briskly and talked about what they would do with their share of the treasure.

I'll tour Europe for a couple years said Indian. Then around the world. But I Na going forget my little islands nor the people. I going help the poor, the sick, build orphanages all over the island. Along with homes for the homeless. Buy up a whole heap of land for farming. Just keep enough for myself and the family I Na going have no load of money sitting in the bank. No way that's a sin. Jah bless ya so you going and have to help. His people. Wha you going do with yours Mr. Bill? when we find the big one that chest of gold. It would help with a lot of pain tell you that answer Bill. Probably do the same as you more or less. Me and Marisha seen some tough times together. I've missed a lot of birthdays and present for her and the children. When they were young and a lot of time had been lost between us when I was roaming at sea, chasing a dollar to have same kind of existents. Lonely nights for us both many broken hearts and tears. Time that we'll never get back. My pension is barely enough to keep us much less our two small girls. The orphanage house just fills a void Marisha loves the children I don't know how she does it. Yah Indian my boy if I find anything I'll be so excited I probably have a heart attack. The two men laugh. They had been digging two hours nonstop. Let's take a break said Bill.

They sat on the foundation wall of the house that was being constructed. I was away at sea when my two boys were born. I never seen Shawn the oldest one till a year or so after. When Billy Jr. came along I was stationed in the Middle East at an oil refinery for Shell petroleum. That was in 1968 I was making $500 dollars a month. I wasn't around for many of the boys birthday Mariyah raised the boys on her own. I was gone most of the time. They were going through childhood they became teenagers and men without me around. I mean they understood the reason why I wasn't there. But that doesn't make much difference in my heart. I never seen them learning to ride that bicycle or comfort them when they got their knees scrape up. Man got to go through a lot of things in this life. I read the girls a story every night before they go to sleep and play with them on Sunday at the beach. I try and give the kids a better life I wouldn't have it no other way. I wasn't there to beat my boys when they had done wrong. But I spanked the twins the other night for being rude. That hurt me more than it did them. The men drank their last beers in the icebox. They talked some, then smoked a rifer each. I lost a lot in 2000. Indian I had some retirement money tucked away in one of those American banks. As a result of a shrinking market between Wall Street and the US Stock market nearly seven trillion dollars evaporated from people personal wealth. Bank went down with it so did my life savings. Bank claimed bankruptcy and never reimbursed a cent back to nobody. They drank some water and went back to work. The pit was about nine feet deep by now and the seven feet ladder was short. Bill tied a rope around the tree nearby and the Indian man lowered himself down reaching the ladder then climbing on and eased into the hole. Bill handed Indian the metal detector. We still got a strong buzzing signal said Indian. They shoveled and they dug they dug and they shoveled.It was some tlme later when the shovel hit something that sounded metalic Yes said the Indian man. We got something now. He remove the soil from around the thing and saw it was an old metal tin can, shit he said. They diged more and came across other stuff. Bottles, sardine cans, old kitchen utensils, which are useless in value. An old fan and a car rim was just a few things amongst the garbage. Look like we found a garbage pit. Yeh don't make this discourage you we ga dig some more,. How deep did they bury the gold ask Indian. Six seven feet or so answered Bill. According to the stories I heard were the true stories ask Indian who knows said Bill I never knew anyone that found gold yet. They cleared the hole out, tying the buckets to the rope and the man on top pulled it up and dumped it on the hemp*. Matt O'Bryan was still in the bushes, he was numb from the mosquito bites. He watched every move and heard every word they said. That is to say when he did not get too fatigued to pay attention. He kept looking over his shoulder because he been hearing sounds all night. Noise like what a crocodile would make and saw two little red dots some ways off he thought. He had a gun on him just in case but it would blow his cover. Back in the pit they had gotten back to dirt. It was more like mud now and two shovel full of this made the bucket heavy. They were down about ten feet, the shovel made a cut into an old Crocker sack at the bottom of the hole. A stink smell came out of the pit and fumigate the place. The Indian pulled himself up out of the pit. The signal gone light again Bill explained. After removing the instrument from over the hole in the ground. Yah cause we were picking up that garbage thinking it was gold. Probably but we don't know for sure as long as we get a signal we keep digging best bet. Bill tied a handkerchief around his nose and mouth and eased himself down the hole using the rope. The pit was hot and smelly and sweat drip from Bill's forehead. His shirt was soaked. He fastened the rope around the sack something had rotten away in it.

The Indian man up on top pulled the load up carefully. He sat it down away from the hole. He ripped it open and saw crab, conch and wilk shell.

containing swamp water from over the years made up the smell. Matt was killing himself laughing at the two clowns digging up garbage. He too had smell the scent coming from the hole. He had spent two and a half hours so far up in this bush and was sick of it and about to get out of there when he heard I got it. Everything stopped it seemed Bill came out from the hole quickly his back was to the bushes. Matt could not see anything. Bill's arms went to the side, stretched out something was in his hands.

Matt put the night binoculars to his face. Inside them was infrared and he saw small brown round objects in Bill's hands. They seemed to shine. A big mosquito sucked on Matt's neck back and he slapped at it missing the sound of that seemed to echo through the night that was the last straw all he needed besides he had gotten what he came to find out. Matt left that God forsaken bush in a hurry forgetting to remove the antenna that was in the tree. Found something exactly what don't know until we get it clean up. It look like an old coin. You hear something his head went towards Indian who was pale yellow he was pointing with this mouth open. The Indian was hollering but nothing came out of his mouth. Bill spin around and saw something glowing over the hole. It looked like a Chief Indian ghost. He had his arms folded and his eyes were florescent green. His hair went beyond the shoulders and he wore a chief on his head with many feathers. His gray hair seemed bright white. The thing was floating in midair. Bill's heart was pumping the spirit turned into a ball and sprang toward Bill in a half second. Bill found himself on the ground a second later Indian was in the air but came face down on the dirt pile. The ball of light made a circle around the yard then vanished into the night skies. After catching his breath Bill got up and ran over to Indian. You alright no,said indian. Me neither replied bill. What the hell was that? We lucky we Na dead son. Thank GOD it was a good spirit. Otherwise we wouldn't be here. My shoulder killing me the thing lifted me up and threw me face first into the mud. Bill saw that the glass of water was empty but it was still standing upright. The Bible was closed.

They washed up under the pipe Indian wet his head while Bill put a water down handkerchief to the back of his neck. They were still shaking. Indian screwed the cap off a bottle of rum he kept under the house floor between the floor joist and the column. The young man took it to Bill. It dissolved in his mouth this whole area here is Caymanakis territory long ago white men ran the Indians off it and owned it for a while til the government gave it back to the native people. Look like we disturbed something. The moon na full yet until a couple more days. When the moon was full Caymanakis feasted smoked peace pipe and danced late into the morning as a form of worship. That spirit was killed or buried there.

That spirit licked me down. It knew who you was and that you got Caymanaki blood in you. That's why you only got pushed over. Aliza people were Caymanaki Indians too. This land been in her family for more than a hundred years. I know said Indian. That why it was important that we got it back. And keep it in the blake family. We going. Keep what happen tonight between us. I don't even know if we should continue digging in that spot at this point tell you the truth. That signal could have been some kind of energy malfunctioning the detector. Their hearts were beating normal speed again and they looked around for any signs of the thing. See what I found said Bill staring at the coin,. It was a miracle he didn't lose it in all the commotion. After he washed the dirt off,it was silver. They went into the shack. I can't make the date out too clearly Bill said holding it under a light. There was a head on it with other symbols that he did not recognize. The Indian handed him a cup of strong coffee and he added rum to it. Back at the nightingale house everyone slept contently. Marisha and Aliza knew the men were out looking Caymanite or something.

Bill had told the women they would set a few fish pot so he would be late tonight. It was 2:35 AM when the men finished placing planks over the hole. They laid them in both direction, then sat a ply board on top of them, then covered it back with dirt, hiding the opening. They wheel burrowed the remaining soil away spreading it around plants and vegetation. The signal on the metal detector was faded but none the least still there as soon as possible they would resume digging. They would have to be careful at this depth the ground around it that made up the walls of the hole would soften if it rain or by dew. The whole shebang could collapse on them.

Adolfo smoked a Cuban cigar and drank a glass of red label whisky. He talked with Matt out on the second floor of his Terries. His legs stretched out across the leg rest. Matt was speaking "Her boyfriend's name is Ezekiel Howett, hangs out with an old man Bill Patterson, who runs an orphanage in town. I track them down followed them couple nights ago, the boy lives in a little shack out in frank sound. HE and the old man started shoveling away some dirt, near a three I wasn't sure what the hell they were doing at first". MATT took a sip of whisky it burned his throat when he swallowed.

"AND the girl where was she" ask Adolfo. "BACK at the Orphanage the Indian stays alone. THE dig and dig for what seemed like an eternity removing garbage and stuff from the hole they were making.

THEN the old man came up from the hole with a pouch in his hand. HE took something out of it and showed it to the Indian I could've seen the object clearly with the night vision Binoculars it was brown Oval looking obviously a sugar baby stone".

HEY hey smiled Adolfo relighting the cigar and putting his feet on the ground. "WHAT do you think will be their next move"?

"AS far as I can tell the old man is the head piece".

MATT mention nothing about metal Detectors, or the fact that they maybe Gold involved if there was any Gold to get it didn't make any sense to shear any with Adolfo.

BESIDES it was just a myth so far he needed to investigate some more.

"THEY sold some Caymanite the other day to a local Merchant, but I don't think they'll play that seem card it's too risky with the stones. I'll have to continue and watch them and see what they do.

THEY could always jump ship and sell the stones abroad.

THAT would make more sense that way they wouldn't bring suspicion on themselves".

"I hear what your saying there's people right there in Miami that would take those sugar babies off their hands, for a good price no questions ask". Reply Adolfo.

THE ointment to suede rashes and mosquitoes bites matt applied to his face and arms earlier that morning was starting wear off.

HIS face was Balch up and he was red all over, he looked a mess and was beginning to itch again. MATT rested the empty glass on the Marble top table. HE started scratching the blisters were becoming infected.

Adolfo looked at him but said nothing for a while. "THEN he ask how's the relationship with him and the girl".

A few seconds when by before matt answer "he's just screwing her Creole men are the worst kinds of dogs. She's a hot little thing all the same, I didn't notice any ring on her. Heard them talking the other day she's knock up for him."

"Charming just charming" smiled Adolfo. "I'll be a gentle man and make an offer on the stones.

Good work Mr O'Bryan my money was well spent, I need you to do something else for me".

HE said handing Matt a stack of bills.

"BUT of course sir".

"Let them know am willing to pay 16,000 dollars for each sugar baby in cash".

Accounting International Group was a small yet compact company. IT handled Hedge and Mutual funds they were a broad base company they also set up trust and Insurance did a little of everything Investment and Real Estate Management Audits and Wills. Mostly for overseas clients they were also a service base holding company that only rutted money off to other Destinations, and charged a fee on vehicle Accounts.

Money would be wire from high net individual or Businesses to and fro South and Latin America set up in fix trust and hedge funds Investments even to purchase Real Estate etc.

A.I.G was divide into two main parts also a small retail bank with around Approximately 300 customers.

Two hundred of which were overseas clients.

A.I.G was a chain company sister to the Cayman Islands Bank linked to HSBC and UBS and the royal Cayman bank along with one of the biggest shareholders South America International bank.

ALIZA sat at the computer she had did some research before starting to work there and had discovered A.I.G main headquarters was Sao Pablo Brazil.

IT was 3.25 and the afternoon was winning down Andrew the head accountant was back and there was plenty to do the office was hectic.

For a new Employer Aliza was handling it well although she had been out of it a few year she had work in major banks and trust companies before.

She could practically do the work in her sleep, after completing the demands on the order paper for the day she was looking over tomorrow's works.

Andrew lean against his desk with his back to her looking out the window, he was on the phone talking softly to someone from the monitory authority in codes.

"I hear there's a new band coming in from England in the next couple of weeks their pretty good according to the reports, let make sure there's a nice stage set up for them to perform on".

As standard requirement all employers were provided health and life insured by the company. Aliza had filled out the from upon being hire she punch in her personal info into the computer and access the A.I.G web site she click on the mouse did some more typing and her name came up. IT was a 250,000 dollar life Insurance policy in circumstances of death a cash lump sum in full was paid to the beneficiary.

SHE strolled down the page and read some more after five years with the company A.I.G paid a full 80 percent of the health insurance. IT wasn't a bad arrangement she though. Maturity leave was a full four months with pay after giving birth. SHE wrote down the policies numbers quickly, right before Miss Abagail drop a ton of paper work on her desk. "I need done before five honey or we might have to work a little late".

THE Concrete trucks would be there at 6 AM tomorrow morning, and Indian was busy taking care of last minute stuff. He was up early this morning did his regular eye opening thing then water the crops and had fallen back sleep until a little before noon which was uncommon for him.

HE read a few psalms to keep the bad spirit away walking around the outside of the shack now he felt uneasy. "BE care full" the voice on the cell phone had said the night before.

He search the bushes and found a small Seattleite antenna laying in the mud it was strange he hadn't come across it before it looked new but it was damage and useless. Something was up "these swamps holds many secrets". What him and bill had witness the other night with the spirit of the Indian chief was still heavy on his mind.

Bill sat around the table at home eating a tuna fish sandwitch he was also thinking about the Indian spirit.

"Was this a death pit they were digging and was the whole place hounded the metal detector could have been throwing them off it was ten years old and the 12 volt batterers was over a year old gone now.

The signal could have been a number of things more junk if it was a burial site coffins had metal decorations on them especially those that were recent as 50 years ago.

Even magnetic energy from the bed rock would give off a signal". Bill thought to himself.

"They were only a few feet from sea leave and the salt water could also be a factor for a bad reading". All these things ran through his mind.

He had a metal sea detector but that only work when submerge under the ocean.

"Treasures were not normally buried that deep" then he realized 12 feet into the ground today was only 6 feet or so a few hundred ago.

BILL had done his homework on the whole area frank sound was a big bight he had read up on the history long ago.

An Irish man by the name of Frank McCoy died there while fighting for the native Caymanian Indian and their land.

Bill wiped his mouth with the napkin and took the plate to the sink to wash it.

He then put it away in the drainer and then walk towards the living room shaking his head in disappointment.

HE had thrown away 300 dollars on lottery tickets over the last two nights he was salt bad.

To make things worst Marsha had found the tickets in his drawer.

He was obsessed with the gambling and treasure hunting thing.

Not every night he played but when he did, serious money went to hell. He just need to break even and he would be rich he thought.

Bill look through a dream book to see what number to buy when you see a spirit it was a good spirit and he had a good feeling.

He came across the number under Ghost and figured out some more digits. Then called the number woman over the phone "I want $200 dollars on 89".

I'll pay you later on when I see you. He took the crumble up hundred dollar bill from his pants pocket in the dresser, he felt lucky tonight. He was dealing with a new lottery seller now. The old one he could not win. She was some kind of witch he thought that's why. Bill cut 3 limes into four pieces and throw them into a bucket of water. They floated on the surface, he poured coconut water into the bucket along with a purple flower and a white one. Then carried it to the bathroom after showering he said a pray.

He dipped up water from the bucket with a plastic container and poured it over his head it ran down his whole body. He didn't dry it off it absorb on his skin.

The coin was in a glass bowl filled with liquid that it had been soaking in all night.

It was becoming bright bronze bill threw more chemical into the bowl he shook it up, then remove it and started scrubbing it some more with a tooth brush.

Bill made out the words georgius II DEI gratia that was written on the edge shaping the coin, there was a harp the British court of arms, Lions and a few more symbols that he did not recognize.

Bill had become somewhat of a scholar and historian in Caymanian and world history in general.

He had became committed by finding and extracting a number of small gain art fax over the years from sites around Cayman's three islands.

PLACES he believed to be Indian and Pirate spots or Treasure holes, walking the beaches many hours with his metal detector.

Life was simple for him now these days the orphanage, church, and in his spear time he hunted for gold.

Nowhere was off limit if he had an idea or gut feeling very grave yards sometimes were search.

Any digging and shoveling that needed to be done was at night.

FULL Moon or Moon less depended on the folk tale around it, this wasn't the first time bill had come across ghost. But it was the first of its kind for the Indian.

He didn't take his job lightly treasure hunting that is. He took spiritual baths rubed himself down with ointments and read particular psalms when going on one of his expeditions, he'd gain a respect for those in the other world.

Bill search and dig caves, and swamp lands with pick and shovel all night sometimes with nothing to show for it but a buss ass and sleep deprive.

Even having dreams of pirates, old timers and fisher men telling him exact spots where Treasure was buried.

One time in one of his dreams a pirate had told him the biggest treasure in the world was right here in Cayman there was enough gold for him and fifty generations of his family to spend and throw way and live out the rest of their life with Said the one eye pirate.

"All yas gat to do mate is a give my living off spring thy a share".

He had broken age old rum and burnt ganja and other incents in the cave at the spot the pirate had told him in the dream. But it had been in vain most times.

Mr Patterson looked at the electrical bill for the month it was outrageous he thought some more about long lost treasure.

"Never trust a one eye pirate" he told himself "those old drunks had a sense of humor they fuck you up by leading you on a wild goose chase which bare no fruit.

But always some kind of trick, mystery or even a bobby trap surrounding it.

Over time land scape would have change and sometimes cliff would be growing out of swamps wet land would become savannah etc. A mango three in the middle of a button wood forest could have been a marker for a buried treasure. It was uncommon to see a fruit three in the swamp or a particular three growing in cliff land.

Most treasures were stolen and hot some got the better of it and it got the better of some.

And all those who lost gold or wanted to find it never stop looking for it.

Bill Patterson heard it all read almost everything old folk tales, firsthand information that was pasted along over the centuries from real pirate maps. From family members who were honest to goodness pirates even letters indicating where a bouts of treasures chest.

But taking things into consideration now a days navigations may have been off a little or other people own the land today of course treasure hunting was also illegal.

All treasures were considered state's since the 70's so it was a dangerous and strategic game.

Bill mostly work alone with the acceptation of the Indian.

He felt like he was wasting his time discourage and disappointed, when he got drunk he would convince his self all the treasure in Cayman had been recouperated long ago and ship back to Europe.

4:45 PM an SUV speeds away from the Caribbean utility company office. Just before closing two men with fire arms asked a cashier at the bill paying section politely to put the money in a bright color nap sack.

A black wool cap with cut out at the eye was pulled down over the face of one of them a red handkerchief covered three quarters of the face of the other perpetrator with a black baseball cap on.

Later miles away up in a bush in frank sound some boys were burning weed when the news came on over the radio.

The gathering had started late tonight Indian and kingdon were running up and down with their woman at lease that was what they told the boys.

The usual talk of politics religion and history had been damped somewhat with the concrete pour tomorrow they talked about aliens and wishing they could snap their fingers and the floor would magically be finish this when on late into the night.

Indian made his good night call to Aliza "how come you didn't come by the orphanage this evening like you said you would" "I was tried out babes preparing for the pour tomorrow". "That never stopped you before only when you want some you come cross".

"Now baby you know that na true".

"Dad been gone all afternoon he just getting back him and mama quarreling. Mama tell him he been acting strange lately. YOU acting warred too Indian what going on with you hope you Na fool in round on me".

"Hear way this woman gone, na no way just life you know".

"MIND me you Indian any way I hear the preacher down at my church got arrested today".

"Really what for".

"You know how news is you never get the story right news on the street said he was money laundering through the mission".

"You joking". "I wish so I got baptized in that church Indian it makes us look bad the pastor's wife and the whole church is praying for him".

"Bunch of demons that good for him I know something illegal was going on".

"NO man Indian don't say that".

IT was 1:30 AM when Indian put his head down on the pillow.

AROUND that same time in George Town off Main Street in the central, behind bar rooms and next to project housing in a ghetto. A man walk away from an old refrigerator outside in a yard.

THE scent of burnt cocaine linger in the night and around the user.

8:30 AM three concrete trucks pull out from a road that leads to the little shack in frank sound.

THE pour was a success Indian had a spliff in his mouth as usual and was sprinkling water from a hose over the quailing slab. EVERYONE had something in his mouth actually, waterbooths and other concrete tools were clean up and neatly of to one side.

The girls had brought lunch cross but the pot of last night's fish tea had been relit and it tasted better than it did last night.

AS life would have it, so happen the trucks pulled out in front of a police car.

DAYS earlier the officer had gotten a call from the bodden town station stating that drugs were being used at an address in frank sound.

THE police officer pushed down on the breakes and stopped to let the truck out.

HE looked over his left shoulder and saw an explorer parked off to the side, he memerized the plate number and color.

A couple men sat under a tree off in the distance the small house blocked the view from anything else.

Exhaust smoke from the concrete trucks went up in the air in a puff, it was noisy as they Speed away, in first gear. Headed back to the compound to reload for the next job site. As they got on to the highway they played with the stick shaft and came to the proper speed limit and stayed seven miles an hour above it. The officer followed behind for a few seconds then overtook them farther down the highway. At the Bodden Town station the officer spoke to inspector Miles, who was in charge of the B.T. precinct. It's the same address we'll set up a surveillance team to watch them close before we move in. I agree we don't need any surprises. If they're using drugs like we suspect they might have weapons too and won't hesitate to use them.

We don't need any of our men hurt by some little Getty head punk I don't want to overreact they may be just having fun good old boy you know what I mean. Yes that's true. Those areas aren't hot or anything like that. I just need to check them out. Don't want wild dogs in my neighborhood. This is mid-town country for Chris' sake. Hope things haven't got that bad yet. The phone rang and inspector Miles picked up, yes, uhmm... that's right. He wrote something down on a pad on his desk. "Good work, the explorer 2001 is registered in the name of Kingston Seymour of George Town. And a woman Babeth I presume she is his girlfriend and on the insurance." "He from town, what he doing all the way up here. We don't know if he is the owner of the property or he's just working there." "But that's the car the old lady say she saw coming out of there like a mad man the other night." Miles pulled his file up on the desktop computer. Some traffic offenses and a couple of misdemeanors, nothing serious. He's a fast driver, outran a police car once. Miles turned the computer screen so the officer could take a look at the photo. He's a dreadlocks, that says a lot. "Find out if he's on anything else other than weed. If we arrest him for that alone it would look like an infringement of his religious rights." "Even though it's against the law the Judge will only slap him on the wrist and get real angry at us. Only if we could find him with any powder or soliciting five pounds of weed or more, we close them down, otherwise it isn't worth it." "We'll just watch them for a while until we can find out if he owns the place that'll take a while." "What kind of work does he do, he know any trade. There isn't anything on file," said Miles "What you getting at. I saw around 3 or 4 of those concrete trucks leaving his place just now. One of those concrete trucks filled cost $1,500 or so. Where he get that kind of money from." "That got to be a big project he doing with that amount of concrete. The bank don't loan those kinds of people money." Miles typed some more on the computer. "And said his woman is a beautician, not even a professional. There's a void in the whole picture if you ask me." "We had a robbery up to last night and today 6-8 thousand dollars' worth of concrete is dumped at his place. Not to mention the labor, probably got it done for nothing almost," Said Miles "Get couple druggie, give them some rocks and alcohol, they don't even worry about food." They laughed. "We got to be careful with this thing. Might be some kind of syndicate group. There were gangs of them under the tree. Let's keep this to ourselves for right now." "I don't want central to know this just yet. If we got these kind of criminals brewing in my backyard it's going to look bad on me and you." "All like how this is an election year coming up and this gets out of hand we can kiss the force good-bye forever," "but if we handle it right we can come out as heroes."

Officer Sullivan filed the report at the George Town police station. He swore that the accused man Mr. Buckwell Scott was drunk and disorderly. He was found in a marine park area in north sound, a place known for suspicious activity. The man was approached by the marine officer and questioned. After being found in possession of two lobsters and two conches, the other marine officers and I attempted to let him go with a serious warning. But before it could be materialized the alleged Mr. Buckwell and his son both attacked the marine officer, swearing and in a rage, Mr. Buckwell grabbed the hook stick, a utensil which was against the law and inflicted an injury to the officer's hand, so serious accounting to the doctor's report puncturing a vein and rendering him unable to work for a month. A small amount of marijuana was found on Mr. Buckwell's son, the report concluded.

The marine officer was back at work the next day. He would still receive his months' pay of sick leave while being paid for his regular hours on the job. Sullivan divided up the seafood between them and sold off what they didn't want. The couple hundred dollars got them beer money. That wasn't the first time he had done that. There was a new game of capitalization being played and only the strong would survive. Cayman had become a shit taking and an ass kissing state. Wasn't tired of being made fools of. All the same dead bolts were selling more than ever. People were confused as to who was who. Cayman was now a modern democracy a constitution would be voted on as well in the upcoming election. They would have to adapt the fundamental rights of the mother countries if we were to keep flying the union jack. Homosexual rights would have to be accepted. They were not a secret society anymore all the same and other human rights issues would have to be acknowledged. We had become a nation of scoffers spell casters and dream seekers. On the world front the Chinese had invented a new pill that killed people during an orgasm described as a sex prudent to help control the population growth. Along with kamikaze prostitutes. In Cayman things were unraveling like a fishing line that had been tangled. Confidential information would become commercial knowledge official speeches and interviews began to be broadcasted without being censored and in its entire length. Signs were taken down and new ones being put back up, things and places got new names all of a sudden. Old roads were being repaired and called new roads. Election was near. They had been some cults and they were some churches out there having all day church every day if you know what I mean. Things were still up in the air, pieces were yet to be connected. The weak had a hard time in these days worriation and stupidity was contagious.

A Cayman scientist had invented an engine that could run with salt water. There was a new drug going around that made women have their period only once a year. A local fisherman had patten a vitamin made of fruit found only in Cayman that gave women the capabilities to spit out three suffers a year without having sex. On the local news a body was found diced to pieces, they had been several reports of grieves and actual body harm cases to homosexuals, Trans genders looking toms and expats in general. Also racially motivated cases were a couple of Asian people had been hand beating in a public parking lot outside a Chinese restaurant, on a moon lite night. All eight of them were in critical condition at the hospital. A forty foot container had also fallen on a Filipino that was due to testify as a witness in court the next day against a drug lord. Police detective Patrick bowing said in a press meeting it was the first of its kind, a freak accident, no foul play was suspected. They had been another series of robberies to small shopping plaza local neighborhood shops. The moon was full once again. It was the last cycle of the Capricorn. In other news the prison director was found dead at his home, apparent suicide he had blown his brains out with a 357 automatic gun And Cuba had also asked the US to end the trade embargo. There was still a witch-hunt going on to apprehend the enemies whoever they were. A hide and seek game was continuing to be played and Cayman was suffering from battered wife syndrome. Besides that, cayman was a billion dollars in debt. It was the same old lie down and take it every now and then you were put in a new position to be used. On the rock in Cayman in these times not only hitters were stealing or begging or ranking yard. While Foreign labor was at 95%. employment. All the borrowed time had been used up and tomorrow had become a myth. The strong was nowhere to be found or already dead. There was a smell of corruption in the air and all throughout the rock there was a smell of fear. A lot of serious subjects were still coming into the country. The community was like a ticking clock attached to a bomb. People were more touches than ever. Most of these overseas territories around the world were falling apart. The citizen were rebelling and uprising. Territories were running out of money, and there was political turmoil. Making these places nasty in these situations. This made them on the merge of becoming a third world or communize country. The only thing that kept them stick together was the mother land. And how long that would last was the question. It got worst round election time independence or remain a part of the union jack. The people couldn't seem to make up their minds. Could Cayman stand on its own? This was the kind of thing lurking over Cayman these were reality tumbling around out there. We were like a cat boat in a bad hurricane a miracle needed situation. Crime had risen in general all over the world sexual assault, rape, kidnapping, drug trafficking was the highest in the world right here in the Caribbean. Malpractice extortion had risen likewise worldwide. The shockwave had added to the pile. Corruption organized, crime, racketeering, prostitution ring, embezzlement wasn't hard to find anymore. The island seemed to be in a semi-revolutionary mood. Politically speaking, the people with screw them all mentally, no threats were funny enough. The Cayman workforce had been long ago eliminated during the changes and it was now a small Passy across the board. We were outnumbered and only few pockets of battered and wounded soldiers were still surviving in the cornfield. Convicts were being rehabilitated along with free child molesters, for the job market. There were a number of community programs being run by the challenge disabled, convicts and master criminals.

By now Cayman was a financial capital. And with it came laws hypocrisy and death. Things like tax foundation a neutral research organization were given authoritative information on taxation. They were intrude to obtain information on amounts of money collected by various types of taxes and distribution of tax burdens. The foundation was used by those all across the political spectrum. People would illegally not report offshore income. And there was also those who formed organizations to lobby for highest tax, especially on capital. Mostly committed specialists. As in regimes of this short people on top get the most benefits. They obtain money but it's not called income. Others find that they could make a good living by pushing for higher taxes. Some of those same organizations that do this were using coerced taxpayer funds to lobby for these increase. It had become an innovative way for them to use laundered money, by funding themselves and other groups to battle tax evasion many member of employee unions would become board members. Also they were tax justice organizations supported by politicians therefore they did not legally have to report where they got their money, even though they themselves demanded transparency from others. In some case public unions would get sweet heart contracts from politicians who feared retaliation from some of these unions at the expense of the Poor taxpayers. Money would be deducted by the government and paid directly to the unions. Union bosses then the coerced taxpayer money and lobbied for higher taxes. And more public employees to help support and fund these so-called tax justice foundation. The President of the National Treasury of employees union sit on the board of these tax justice organization. People who were involved in enforcing and administrating the federal income tax around the world are part of these unions. This was the practice in many countries like Europe. At least in part these hire tax organizations were are funded by the unwritten taxpayer.

It was another day at the office everyone was busy at accounting International group, banking and trust. There were some paperwork at Aliza's desk that morning. And a note from Abigail, she read it and got to work. There were two new overnight account and one huge withdrawal. By transaction via wire to a bank in the Bogotá, Columbia, the account had been sleeping for six years. And now the only son of the deceased and beneficiary was $300,000 richer. They were about 2,000 dormant accounts in Cayman banks value in the billions of dollars. According to the dormant account law of Cayman. An account was considered dormant when it was open for at least seven years with no financial activity occurring in that time. The bank would make an effort to contact holders, when none was made or no other claims was achieved even after thorough financial reports and gazettes around the world. It was then transferred to the Cayman Islands government. There was a complicated process whereby legitimate account holders would be able to receive their money back. By Long court trail, and excruciating audits. Drug dealers, the Mafia, tax evaders, third World dictators, presidents etc. all had money buried in some of these banks.

The FBI had recently confiscated half billion dollars of Saddam Hussein blood money. Accounts went back as far as the 1970s. The governor had made a statement saying he planned to sage 200 million dollars from these dormant accounts this year alone. And another 500 million next year. I am sending a clear message, he said at a press conference to the nation. To these corrupted institutions which have long held multiple millions of dollars in the accounts that are dormant and whose ownership is mostly class A banks insurers license trust companies etc. Credit unions, building societies all were being heavily scrutinized by lawmakers from the US and Europe. Financial regulators were becoming more sophisticated wealth providers and their clients more creative. This money went all over throughout these institutions. Class B and C Banks as well. It was in this web of deception and darkness that A.I.G was wrapped up in. And Aliza poor girl worked there amongst it. There were also calls for closer regulations by the Cayman Islands monetary authority and need for director disqualification regimen in Cayman. By then the conduct of hedge funds Directors was governed by a combination of common-law duties and specific regulations in the mutual funds Law that extended to governance but there was no codified directors' duties on the island, company's law as it was done in the UK. Hedge fund directorship was being put under scrutiny as well. In recent court cases the fund directors were found guilty of willful neglect, some directors were paid by mega corporations to make their rivals fail. OR Directors weren't acting to protect their clients in some cases. Companies and firms had as much as 70 directors and there was no one to determine whether individual Directors were able to discharge their duties in an effective way. There were no independent perspective. The Cayman Islands monetary authority or the CIMA for short needed to be empowered to make capacity decisions. Overnight investment banks would be set up as subsidiary and affiliates to better US banks to facilitate commercial customers with sweep accounts. A.I.G. held one of these class B banking license. Basically they would pool groups reserves for US customers in an offshore deposit account. In these set up accounts balances exceeding a predefined amount would be transferred automatically to an investment account for an overnight investment on things like the stock market and loansharking. Before the depository account balances are read back into their country. They kept it to a required level to in some ways avoid taxes. Around 25% of these kinds of banks in Cayman made up over $2 trillion in deposit. And lending was the core of their operations, which they did to other banks. And insurance companies locally and around the world, especially the Third World countries where the money was hard to keep track of by tax watchdog groups. When changed into other currency it made it almost impossible. Angel organization would be set up in the blink of an eye with billions to their names. Philanthropist would develop countries and continue to hold valuable stakes. From some of these accounts these Banks paid large fees to CIMA to operate on the island, with the approval of the United States taxpayer's organization.

Aliza sat at her desk in front on the computer typing away. Indian had sent a Photo text of the Finnish slab with him posing in front of it. She giggled the progress was slow but at least they were moving. If only he had a steady job life would be kind of normal with this man. She looked at the babies in her stomach and rubbed it. But then things went south his career became his enemy. It was about five years ago now, that life dealt them this blow. Shortly after Indian father died, she remembered sadly the day Indian told her. His friend and boss Thomas had gone back to the States suddenly with no explanation. She had a funny feeling about the whole story but never did question the man she loved. Indian had been to court several times with Sparks and Dougley over his fathers' death and lost every time. Indian had went to their office on Village Street threatening to blow them up. He was arrested and found guilty of bomb threat without even having a bomb. The fancy lawyer was a smooth talker with lots of pull.

The money from Sparks and Dougley bought anything they wanted and they got only the best. On the judges pardon he didn't go to jail but got a criminal record. After that whole ordeal Indian drifted into his own world, and she had allowed him to carry her there as well. She placed both hands on the desk and pushed herself up off the chair and walked over to the water fountain. She could feel herself ten pounds heavier. In a few months she'll be as big as a hippopotamus she thought, then what she would have to stop working, Maternity pay would only be enough to care for the twins. Her belly wasn't bulged yet, the extra weight made her look solid in a sexy kind of way. Only Abby and HR knew she was expecting. She stood next to the cooler drinking water from a cone shaped paper cup. The time on the computer screen was 11:15 AM. Other girls stood around a work station nearby. The CEO and Andrew the accountant had gone to an anti-money laundering seminar. Abigail had a new boyfriend and he was driving her crazy. She had gone shopping and wouldn't be in until late afternoon. They had the place pretty much for themselves. After the usual soap opera chatter the conversation went to politics. "One thing for sure," said a blonde, "the democratic team getting out the election. They doing a lot of dirt, you see them there. And not being honest with the people, if you Na supporting them you aren't going get nothing girl." "They for the white people and the rich," said a black woman. "The Premier like kissing those rich people ass too much, we need a more pro Caymanian government in there." "But if the poor don't work the rich can't make any money neither," said Aliza. These were the feeling all around the island. Most poor people and ground grown Caymanians had made up their minds November 2004 would be the year we went independent ready or not. Or make a start by voting for single-member constituents and to hell with that party politics. The girls talked another five minutes on the subject and then went on and started pointing out the problems at work and what they hated about men.

Benson Wilcox, the CEO of A.I.G Bank and trust sat with Andrew, his head CpA. Around a table with two other men at an expensive restaurant on the 7 mile stretch. The A/C was cold and a light smell of smoke made its way from the smoking section into the non-smoking area, as the waiter passed in and out opening the door. The two bankers attended an anti-money-laundering seminar earlier that day, so they knew how to counteract any situation that may have arrived. They drank liquor from a glass. The leftovers of the fancy Greek food they were eating was still in the plate on the table for the Waitress to take away. "We stick to the plan Timeline everything will go smoothly," said one of the unknown men. "Some of it is in Euro pounds and Canadian dollars." "That's no trouble only makes it easier." "We get 40% as usual," said Benson. One of the unknown men nodded his head. "in agreement. It's settled then, let me know if there's any changes." "Will do." "Give the Sheik my regards, let him know it's always a pleasure doing business with him." "Will do." "Good day gentlemen and good luck." They shook hands. The CEO placed folded money into the bill folder, it did not include the tip. The two unknown men drank down the last drop from their glasses. And walked out behind the other two. Each pair went their separate ways. One pair to the office complex, the other back to Volcano Island.

It was another hot day in the Swamp. By late evening the Breeze was still warm. The Indians sat on the whaft overlooking the bight. The landscape formed into a sound, with mangrove buffers at the edge, of the waterline. The sea lead right out to the ocean. An old schooner anchored off in the middle hidden by a patch of mangrove coming out of water that made up a little island. The schooner was an insurance right off. It belonged to Bill. He had bought it 10 years ago at an auction. The whole place look like on authentic smugglers cove. Indian found himself down there every now and then meditating. The law was watching these areas hard still. Couple of days ago, they had caught a fishing boat with illegal turtles from Central America just a few Miles from here. The police were not taking any chances. Old ladies, middle aged women, laca boys, little schoolgirls, the handicap, were being watched. The police were throwing wild blows to see whatever they could hit, a lot was going on and they needed answers. Guns and ganja had been found along the bay among some shrubs. All those old back roads, lovers Lane secret spot, under the grape tree had become private property or was too hot to chill out at now. The public would report unsuspicious activities sometimes. You will be mashing a piece of ass and the boys would arrest you.

The land was unique and had quadruple in Price. Tourists would take photos of plants and wildlife in their natural habitats. By sundown Indian was around the campfire with the rest of his homeboys. "The wicked running and ruling this world right now." "God have left us in the hands of the enemy." Said the Indian pulling in on a spliff. Weed was on the island again but only Indian and the boys had this grade.

"The mark of the beast has long ago been implemented for those who are awaiting on it. All forms of wickedness that you are doing with your hands and heart and minds, what you think what you do for Satan." The Indian continued. It seems like one cannot survive without it in today's world. A fast paced world which puts God on the back burner. Some forget him completely in the vibe which they unknowingly find themselves in. Too busy trying to make money to remember God. Time and half and double Time at work whatever that meant. It's time to wake up or we will be asleepforever. As there was a beginning so will it be an end. Why are we here we must ask ourselves. From the day we are born we get fed, educated and go to work for the rest of our lives. Raise children, pay material bills, and Support the economy. This money is invested and used to maintain whatever and control the people. 25% of a countries revenue is used to fund their armies and other public and private interest groups or organizations of the state or country. Multimillion dollar corporations work hand in hand with the government to keep us wanting and needing. They keep us under control by manipulation and power of intimidation. In some cases politicians and government employers own the organization or are shareholders. Instead of Ganja, cigarettes should be outlawed by world government for good. The same way be battling the war on drugs by enforcement. It Na matter if it right or wrong, Good or bad, the process is illegal. According to the system, why should education and pension be mandatory? Forget health care for now that's another story. Sin taxes alone should be able to pay for that. It's just a way to control the world at large. The day coming when the good people will be slaughtered and denied food and water because they don't have this mark of the beast on them. The real war should be over morality but in time the good going lost that Battle. The righteous in time to come will sin for a glass of water. The apples won't be shared out equally. We buy an education to obtain the rights to buy and sell or we get a license for those things directly. Unfair business practice may have to be justified by men in those days or they may lose their job or life, forget the soul. We are basically useless until we start making money. And we can't make any without this mark. Scientists tell us lies sometimes even the preachers are confused with laws and rules of power. When we sick we go to the doctor who give us drugs and Medicine, deny us from seeing the herbalist or old bush doctor medicine man who didn't went to school or universities. But they steal their remedy. All you hearing nowadays is about natural medicine in some cases that be pure lies," said Indian. "They got all kinds of things out there now for back pain, sex benefits, depression, and some of them with side effects that would kill ya." "This miracle herb right here helps me with all that," he claimed, holding a whack of sensamenya in the palm of his open hand moving it about showing his fellow companions. "This na got no side effect, blood, millions of dollars could be better spent by governments." "Why can't they help the ghettos of the world?" "Don't tell me they can't change things, pure excuse and lies, mind games." "They use money to buy guns, equipment, fancy clothes, and shoes from their loyalist friends for their armies that protect us and them." "They buy vehicles of all sorts, pay for experts' advice on ways to make money and keep it, by ways of justifiable means and by making things easier for every human being on the planet." "Manmade Disease are abundant and plagues walk the earth. If you eat the words of God we will live forever. Ignorance is as bad as cancer and Aids. The best thing for cold and flu is herb and some of the grandmother's vegetable soup. Baal is the economy instead of asking God for answers we depend on the almighty dollar to solve them and set us free. Millions suffer from greed in the process by working for minimum wage oppress on them. If I tell you a lie it would be in good faith and when you don't believe me I might be telling the truth." Everybody laughed.

Lo and behold another letter surface at the radio station the following day. Fret not thyself because of the evil doers neither be thou envious against the workers of iniquity. For they shall soon be cut down like the grass and withered as the green herb. The more one knows the sadder he becomes, but the one who refuse knowledge death shall be his inheritance… the smarter mankind becomes the weaker we will be. Instead of sweet smell there will be stink… the common man will be brought down and the great man humbleth, Wise men went into famish and prophets will be afraid to speak.… Brothers' fight against brothers, nations rise up against nations and the righteous bowing down for the wicked… instead of well-set hair, baldness, every man shall turn to his own people. And flee everyone into his own land. Their children will be dashed to pieces before their eyes, their house shall be spoiled and their wives ravished. For it is a day of trouble and treading down and of perplexity… The people will be oppressed, everyone by another, everyone by his neighbor. The Land will be full of idols. They worship the work of their own hands. A woman will rule over them and in that day seven women shall take hold of one man... The rich will rule over the poor and the borrower enslaved to the lender... In those times it will be a crime to speak the truth is utterly. Prejudice will be given on to the poor and the wealthy, and whosoever reason with a ruling Head was considered the enemy. He who whispered Independence was a song to the drunkards and had come too late! Was at thought to be a socialize Oh city of confusion don't be partakers of her sins. What one chooses to do with knowledge remains up to him? What will be is to be we are who we are Apollyon will sit in high places and the merchants made wax rich. Some will know better others will not. We will worship idols of stone, wood, gold and want kingdoms will fall. But what's in the heart and against ignorance is the real war...

Cops sat around a long table, at Central police station. The conference room was on the second floor. Head detective Patrick Bowing stood in front of a whiteboard with a marker in his hand. A series of rectangular lights were in the ceiling with fluorescent tubes inside. A ceiling fan spanned slowly and there was a low sound of the air conditioning unit. The tray ceiling was white square panel Made of composite particle material. It have small dots on it. The vinyl tiles on the floor were shining even though it had wear and stain. There was a picture of the royal family and past police commissioners on the crimson colored walls. "These are the men we are looking for" said Bowing. "They are the ones doing all this damage." Pointing at the marker board, where two photos were taped against. "CCTV outside the parts store picked up these two men casing the joint, just three days ago. Here another photo of the SUV they were driving. It was late at night but you can make out someone with a baseball cap on, pretending to be looking for an empty boxes." "This one fits the description officers saw running away from the scene up in Northside, after he drove the stolen car from the waterfront job into a ditch. Their faces can't be seen clearly." "The technician did all he could. The other one sitting in the car is a Rasta dreadlocks is noticed. The camera from the other night shows two guys running away with guns in their hands, the getaway vehicle is out of sight of the camera." "Eyewitness said they saw a SUV type explorer skidding away from the shop." "The electrical company robbery was in broad daylight they changed up their MO little bit, but the gunmen were seen getting into a reddish SUV. The vehicle displayed no license plate. Three people were noticed inside it." "An Explorer 2001 is what we are looking for gentlemen, with tinted windows and classy chrome rims." "They're wearing black outfits in all the jobs. That means they are part of a Gothic or emo movement. Doom and terror said one officer. They're thugs but very organized. ""What was the take boss?" "On the CUC Job several thousand from the cashiers. Not bad for a couple of minutes the part store have their paper work all screwed up but they saying it was around five grand and change, more or less is the ball park number." "The manager only makes cash deposit once a week. The next one was due the following day of the robbery." "Any chance these could be inside job, boss? For insurance reasons especially with the private business the economy going through some tough times." "There's always a possibility but I don't want us going off on a wild goose chase we watching the security guard at the parts store and the managers of some of these businesses along with the owners for right now." "Any other questions?" no one raised their hands. "Good, that'll be all for now, men." A minute later, the room was empty and Bowing checked his messages on the cell phone. The wife had called four times. He erased the voice message. She had not yet found her necklace. He wasn't the least worried, there were other things going on to occupy his mind. Besides the damn necklace was insured and the appraiser a good friend of his up the value by $10000 more. "I know its insured honey," said Mrs. Bowing over the phone "but it had sentimental meaning behind it..." "Promise I'll help you look for it some more this evening after work. If it's in the house we'll find it, sweet cake, ok?" "Oh all right honey, what time you coming home?" "Round 6-ish," "bye-bye, honey" Bowing closed the face off the cell and slipped it into his pants pocket and took the stairwell down. It was noon in Cayman five-o-clock in downtown London. It was like a beehive, people were going to work, people were coming from work. Many wearing trench coats and hats and carrying briefcase, umbrellas and some har roll up news in their hands. Scott land yard surrounded an office building were a man had been shot dead from one bullet between the eyes. No one heard a sound or seen a thing. Nothing out of the ordinary. A gentleman in a long coat spoked to police. am the owner of the pet day care on the 8th floor. I was on my way to the bloody John when I saw the cat standing in the half open doorway. Poor feller was shaking and frighten to death. I went over and picked the little critter up. When I noticed there was a dead man lying on the floor. Totally freaked me out I must say never seen a dead man, before. I don't do funerals unless the box is closed. He held the cat in one hand and stroked its head with the other. He wore a Rolex watch and there were rings on all ten fingers.

A chef squeezed lime over a slab of pork. It was a slow day at Talia's food stool. It had been raining off and on the better part of the morning. The cook also the owner had just ordered his only worker to dry off the table and readjust the umbrellas over them. The little food shack was right in the heart of the water front. Right next to five story building and corporations where people made a living innocently, and vipers, business men and con artists lingered. He could see the fish market on the iron shore. Where fishermen sold their daily catch. And anchored their small boats. The rocks formed a little cove and in the middle a beach about ten or so feet long, with more pebbles than sand. The men cleaned their fish some over a 2x4 wooden table. A low concrete wall divided the busy downtown sea view drive traffic from the iron shore. And the sea in a bad north wester from the road. Grape trees provided a shade for bums, vagabonds and ordinary people who sat on the wall talking, looking at traffic, smoking cigarettes and dealing with the fishermen. Two cruise ships were in the harbor today, the chef noticed. But these cheap tourists were only walking up and down and looking around, with backpacks, slippers and shorts on. He had sold one soda pop all day. Hopefully when the tour buses are done for the day and come back into the town the tourists will be hungry, he thought to himself. He bought a share of the famous franchise name of Talia's and leased the spot of land next to the sea front and iron shore about six years now. He sold cook meats mostly as part of the contract he bought from his supplier, Talia's meat market whole sale. Occasional fish from the locals. Last week was the worst. The meat and pork was piled up in the fridge at home and in the small freezer under the counter at the food stall. He was a cook and butcher by trade. Entrepreneur some what and a professional in more ways than one. He would have to give the place up if business doesn't pick back up, he considered. I was just starting to break-even, then that stupid American president go and declare a war with

Iraq. He hated all Americans personally. I wouldn't be in this mess in the first place if that no good North American hadn't swindled me out of my money on that housing project. Him and his barnacle loving red shank fesses Caymanian friend of his. I should be in Milan right now living it up, said the Italian Chef. I owe him one anyhow, I should pay him a visit, like how I done old Thomas boy. It felt good when he begged for his life. I should have taken care of the Cayman conch at the same time. And pointed her back to Italy but no I decided to make bygones be bygones and let the kid live. But now today I reconsider it's not right for me to suffer any longer. My business is failing, I am old man. It's not right that he buy big real estate with my money and live happily. Now I collect interest and get the hell out of this hell hole of Cayman Island. My luck here has run out. And I have no money. I kill him and his whole family too. The butcher looked at the stack of monthly bills on the counter of the small kitchen where only a grill and sink fitted. Off to the sides the top half was opened a string held the wooden windows, which open out and upwards. There was no breeze. He became more frustrated and angry. I could have been a rich man today if only he said quietly. Seconds past of course he said in his mind. I will seduce my new girlfriend Abigail into giving me the money for this month's bills. She's more understanding than those little teenage girls I usually have. She's more mature and my age. It would be easy, women loved Italian men you know, I'll ask her over for dinner at my place tonight and cook something nice. And that will be it. No need to spend the money I have stashed away. After that they would have stress relieving intercourse. Life would be so wonderful, if only, he though.

Nightingale house was more fessty than normal tonight. It was ten to six. The Patterson's were throwing a birthday party for one of their kids. They considered all of the orphans their kids. There was about a hundred children of all ages round and about the premises. There was a bouncing castle in the yards, two clowns acted funny played with balloons and told jokes to the crowd. Kids played with noisy blowing toys and threaten to fight one another for possessions. The swing set and slides were well occupied. Light children music played from a speaker out in the yard Aliza and Mrs. Patterson served sandwiches and refreshment from a hand held platter. Babeth and the others played brown girl in the ring with the younger girls. Indian refreed the football game. One of the 12 year boys was turning 13 today and becoming a man. Some of his family members were there. Bill flipped on the TV to watch the 6 o clock news. The screen was black for a second or two then an anchor woman came on. "Good evening am Barbra Bars and this is news 28 at six. Tonight police say they are looking for two men who robbed a car parts store on eastern avenue just a day ago and the most recent robbery of Caribbean utility company." On the television screen was a police sketch of two faces. The rendering from the police artist showed a pirate with braids and ribbons and beads on them, and the other man was a drawing of Mr. Clean. They resembled no one bill knew. Look at those criminals and killer bill said to a room of children and grown-ups. That happen right out there round the corner, they don't look like Caymanians neither. The men are only wanted for questioning at this time said the reporter. Yeah right said a woman's voice in the room. The TV showed an explorer 2001 with some fancy automation police also said this is the vehicle they were driving. If you have any information on this or other crime please call the tipster hot-line on your screen. All call will remain anonymous. "There's plenty of those rides bout the place" bill said aloud. "thats the same kind of car like aunt Babeth" said one of the orphan boys only different color. Bill walked over and pushed the power button and the TV went off. It was an old set and he didn't worry about replacing the remote that had long ago been ruined. From a 30 minute broadcast there was only 7 minutes of news it was loaded with commercials and entertainment news. The broadcast only scraped the surface as to what was happening. There would be sport then weather and you only needed to watch that during hurricane season which still a good was six weeks away. People ate mountains of food from a plastic plate. Two hours later the party was almost over. Except for a handful of stubborn children who didn't care about school tomorrow. Indian and kingdon walked around with a garbage bag picking up party litter. Them boys thick on the road, yah looking for them thefts. Cayman gone. They looking for your explorer Indian said jokingly. Kingdon looked frighten but managed to grin. They'll arrest me too, he said. These little police around here don't know what they doing we need some CSI down here or two of those super cop like how you see on TV. There some serious criminals here on this island that the people don't know bout I know wha I telling you Sam!

kingdon said to Indian. People Na ga no work permit holders neither. Tis is an economic crisis we in. Rather than go back to their country where it Na nothing to get them men take the chance ya. You know what I mean. Them men Na going kneel down and pray like you and me Sam. Or sit down with their hands fold, bout the government ga help us. We know this would happen still said the Indian man we see it coming long ago. Man playing this game for keep Sam. Life they call it. Said Indian to King. The gates of Babylon open up this supposed to happen this is the beginning of a new world money is life preached the men one to the other. For real, for real they said at the same time. Changing the subject up a little bit. Tomorrow we suppose to get that thing. The Indian talked to his fiancé for a while kiss her good night and headed home.

That same night 8:27pm two masked men with gun entre an unlocked door of a resident in north sound estates. They wore gloves and long military boots, the pants leg was wrapped tight around the calves. A middle aged woman and a little girl were the only people inside. The home sat on a half acre canal lot. The screams of a woman could be heard as she ran into the bedroom with her daughter and locked the door frantically. One of the men kicked it open, and back hand slapped the woman down. As he pushed his way into the room. She sprawl out on the bed. The little girl cried in the corner of the bedroom, on the floor in her eyes was a terrified look. Two Doberman pinschers barked horrifically and jumped about madly in the backyard. Detective Bowing was five minutes away from his house when the call came over his radio. He put the siren on the dash board he swerve in and out of traffic and broke the speed limit. Inside the house his wife laid stomach down on the bed duct tape to the mouth hands and feet her hand were to the back. His daughter was locked up in the closet, a key was in the door, he turned it until it clicked and the lock opened. He opened the door and the little girl hugged him she was still crying, and trembling definitely traumatized. Quickly he untied his wife and comforted her. Three police rushed into the room. "You alright, boss?" Bowing looked at his family. A police woman went over to them. She picked the girl up and put her arm around Mrs. Bowing's shoulder to embrace her, and the three of them went outside. Those bastards going paid for this Bowing screamed. They beat my wife up and my little girl going be trouble by this for the rest of her life. Look what they done to my place. A landline telephone on the night stand was off the hook and the hand held part laid on the carpet with the cord dangling. The 911 call came from this phone sir. It was a man's voice, sounded Jamaican no good sons of B's playing with us now, replied Bowing. You better come take a look at this sir called an officer. Two dead dogs laid out on the grass of the night due. The rank smell of animal carnage was already strong and getting worst. The cops had their nose and mouth covered with white handkerchief as they stood over the dead animals. They were good dogs, said Bowing if they had gotten here ten minutes later when the dogs were loose for the night those scumbags wouldn't stand a chance. They must have been watching the place for a few days, boss. Timing your routine. Seen anybody suspicious lately around the neighborhood, noticed anyone following you maybe? Of course not. The place is ram sack sir. I'm thinking robbery gone bad. It went according to plan, said Bowing. Why risk it when they knew your family would be at home, that doesn't make any sense. It makes perfect sense if they wanted to give me a warning. They could have killed them easily if they wanted. Further investigation revealed the perpetrators had stolen a Boston whaler belonging to Patrick Bowing and had escaped by way of the canal. Small amount of cash was also stolen along with some jewelry. A 30,000 dollar necklace was also missing in the ordeal. It was determined a silenter was used on the dogs because no gunshots were heard. No fingerprints were found anywhere at the crime scene. A criminal profiler concluded it was a professional hit gone wrong mostly hit men use silenter and hand gloves. Detective Bowing was usually at home around that time but the day of the home invasion he was working late. This may have saved his life and that of his family. There have been a lot of publicity recently on a number of unsolved crimes. And Bowing was in the spotlight and all over the news. The profiler warned that the suspects are dangerous to themselves and those around them. And display psychopathic behavior and dellusions and even split personality with manic depression. Will forget a crime after it happens, probably goes to church. The Boston whaler was found some hours later in an abandoned area of frank sound swamp. An emergency meeting had been called by detective Bowing. The pressure was on, the foreign press was starting to notice. How can we be sure it's the same guys said Detective Philipps. Hell, this might be a band instead of a gang said Patrick. Continue to squeeze the streets and something will pop out, check the YMCA for Chris' sake. According to the profiler this unsub is highly intelligent he won't make any mistakes. May get off on beating women, he's some kinds of sadist or sexual predator. He's neat, a perfectionist, takes care of himself maybe a vegetarian and a carnivore sexually. Talk to the Rastafarian society but do it carefully, we don't need them starting any riots. We tying these guys to the rest of crimes. The missing man from couple months ago the letter writer is just them bragging and provoking us.

PART TWO

*A*n hour or so after the home invasion Indian sat under the night sky not a leaf was shaking it was good weather out to sea. This made him feel relieved that tomorrow would be a good day. The little one room bungalow was in darkness. The man sat upon a wooden bench he had made with his own hands just days before. Looking it over he thought, I ga make some of these to sell, put them out by the road on display. See what happen, the last spliff for the night was between his fingers. It had been a long day, he didn't recall every detail but who cares just the highlights were good enough. He had poured the floor and was ready to start the second phase. He had went to the party earlier remembered eating chocolate cake with white icing after the kid had blown out the candles. He had kissed the love of his life Aliza after that he was home. I was exhausted. He thought my brain must have shut down on me and I had fallen asleep. I must have burnt about 20 spliff today he said to himself humorly, and blacked out again. I don't even know how I got home. He woke up a little while ago showered and came outside. His eyes had a glare in them as he pulled on his cigar sized joint. And looked out into the night in the direction of the swamp. He had loving up with his girl on his mind. It had been god knows how long since they made out. She would be home soon he said in his mind. I just need to keep her away long enough till I find the buried treasure. He saw the Indian spirit in his head at that same time. Then there was a crackle in the swamps. But it was just the night just the trees expanding in the woods. By some miracle it wasn't a sand-fly or mosquito out tonight, not a bug or a creeper to disturb his charge or to interfere as he got his groove on. The night was chilly all the same. The humidity of the day had been evaporated into the ground and the swamp had condensed it into moisture it raised and mixed with the night climate. In fact it was becoming colder. He worn his T-shirt and boxer shorts, his feet were long out across the bench and a pair of flip flops rested at the base. A small handheld radio on his lap played a soul song by Percy Slage. Just minutes away from the midnight news. Indian smoked under the stars, the full moon was high up by now. He loved it there in that bush and was glad to be alive. There was a repeat of the 6 o clock news another cry for information was uttered by royal Cayman island police. And now the BBC world news said the radio. The Indian man made a loud cough nothing to worry about no one could hear him in this swamp. He hawked a wad of cold and spit it was brown, he had cancer he thought then laughed to himself. Afterwards clearing his chest he haul on the spliff again blowing tin smoke into the sky. A man has been found dead earlier today in an office building in down town London. The Scott land yard metropolitan police said, the man name was Lord Nelson Hopkins the 4th. The head of the complaint's commissioner office and Anti-corruption bureau for the British Empire. He was killed from a single bullet to the head. Police are saying no more on the matter while investigations continue but they are calling it an assassination. And in other news around the world today in Africa, the Indian man eyes open wide and his eye browse lifted. He meditated on the news and a hundred things entered his mind. All at once He shook his head while he finish up his spliff. He thought and planned into the wee hours of the morning. He got up and fetched a note pad out of the house and wrote stuff down then tore out the page putting it into a shirt pocket that was in the closet.

It was 6:35 am. in Cayman, 12 noon in London. Passengers aboard a jet, hours later Cross the Atlantic and two time zone British airways touch down at owning Roberts airport. It was a five hour flight with a quick stop in the Bahamas but the pilots manage to take 30 minutes of the time. A man in a long back trench coat and rings on every finger including his thumbs step of the 777 jumbo Jet with nothing more than a duffle bag and briefcase. There was a two man band playing calypso music for the people arriving. Over by the wider section of the covered walkway. The Airport personnel said welcome to the Cayman Islands. To people as they passed. The man cleared immigration then walked through customs. An automatic glass door open as he stepped outside. A gentle Cayman breeze corest his face. It was 1:00 p.m. Cayman time and 94 degree out. He walked over to a stand showed his past port the lady gave him a key. He made his way to the parking lot. Taxi sir shouted a man with a Hawaii shirt on. Am find thank you said the person in the black long trench coat and gold on all ten fingers. A minute or so later a shiny rent a car pulled out on the main road and headed east. The lunch time rush brought no hold up's. He had a good rest on the plane so he would do some scouting around before heading to the hotel. A map of Cayman was opened up on the passenger seat. It'll be like afternoon tea he thought to himself refreshing, god I love my job he said looking into the rearview mirror.

Reggae music mixed with dance hall played as a big motor canoe came into the channel and out from the bottomless ocean. It was1:45am the 28 footer had four men on board. All had dreadlocks of different variety. Kill the music my boy said the one at the engine. A we time this. Point her straight west with this load rude boy. Yah man. The canoe cut through the water in calm seas. The vessel turned right then left to avoid pan shovels, and sand bars. The captain knew the water well. Years of experience had rewarded him this gift. Na everybody know how to get round up in this sound Rasta said the only clear skin man on board. It was the first trip for the Caymanian but the crew had done this hundreds of times before. The Caymanian was basically a security piece came along with the package purchase, to make sure no one played any games with the merchandize and that it landed safely. He had stolen out of the country a week ago. A canoe came in from Jamaica with a load dropped it off and he had hoped it. Went to jam down, and with some contacts bought couple sacks. And was back home now no one would miss him he told his girl to keep it down and gave her strict order to say she didn't know where the hell he was if anything say am in jail. If I find out you talk my business right you a dead woman. Only a few of his trusted gang members knew what time it was. That's the way it had to be. Anyhow he left the country by legal means red flags would be all around and his ass would be watched like hawk. By the boys {Police} when he step foot in Jamaica. This reggae muffin style was better right under the Cops noses to rass cloth he said laughing, with the other as he told his story. They could see the mangroves getting closer in the darkness. Three of the men stood up over the nylon flour sacks as the canoe slowed two notches. The one with all the mouth the Caymanian rested his foot on his personal sack. He had made the deal and was involved in the run. I the one taking the risk and will do hard time northward if things go wrong. He told the big boss back in Cayman so he had gotten couple pounds over for himself. The guys in jam gave him extra as a sigh of good spirit. He brought a long some guns and ammo. The captain a true roots man never transported guns or coke. It was against his religion. There were guns and a few kilos of powder, That One of the rude boys back in jam had slipped them into the knapsack the young boy carried. Without the captain's knowledge the coke and guns brought bad luck the roots man always said. The Caymanian was starting to brag again when one of the crew said yow shut up. all of a sudden someone yelled Babylon Babylon to Bombo!The canoe made a sharp u turn to starburst side flinging two men off. The captain gave the engine everything but the bow didn't even rise. It was a big engine but there was no amount of horse power written on it. "Babylon! Babylon!," echo the Captain. The police boat came out of no wear and gave chase. Sacks and packages were tossed into the sea as the police boat maneuvered around them hitting some and cutting open other sacks with the boat bow and engine. The canoe got liter and she jump across the ocean and was almost out of the channel. The two men on board crouched and laid down as the canoe rocked and vibrated rapidly. A helicopter approached as the canoe got into open water. Gun shoots could be heard in the quite sound Harbour. Smoke came from the engine of the canoe. It slowed and came to a stop. It moved side to side in the gentle waves. One man cry out him catch me Babylon wicked. Blood dripped from his torsil.

Marine police Commander Sullivan posed in the front of a drug canoe in the headline photo of the Caymanian compass the next day. Ganja, guns and cocaine were found said the Head lines. After a massive shoot-out with police 3 Jamaican national are in custody there was a big article written up on the whole matter etc etc. This is the year for the Jamaica canoe said Sullivan. I feel good to know that the good guys won this one. These drugs won't be on our streets.

The same day of the incident within hours, before the news broke undeclared sensamenya from blue mountain. Some of the same stuff from last night seizure that was not logged in and recorded were on the streets. Instead of 1500 pounds of weed only 500 was logged in and recorded at the station warehouse data file. It was circle lating right left and centre and the market was flooded again.

An unmarked car drove out of a ghetto in George Town. No one noticed the movement no one cared but it was too early to tell. A man took pictures but they would be useless. He needed more than facts he wanted Justice. Three boats from Jamaica came in that night early in the morning only one was intercepted. One went south and the other landed east. Police could not be every way at once. Resources and money as always was short. Indian and the crew had gotten through. Before day light broke they were at the meeting spot to receive there poundage with no heck up's. They were at the Indian man yard now the bunch of them burning hard talking about the captured drug canoe. When the talk show came on and a letter was read. Listen to this said one of them, I like these letter they got some serious shit in em. They listened and laughed and smoked some more.

The 25 years old Caymanian had his socks on he was still shaking from being cold and frighten he was shivering and had a slight dose of hyperthermia. I was lucky blood he said to another gang member. When I fell in the water I dived and swam in by the mangroves and hide. I felt sorry for the yardy brethren he couldn't swim that good. A hand full of dry wet weed laid on the small metal table next to the window trying to become good enough again under the sun to smoke. The curtain was open just a crack. "One bucket floated in and got catch up in between the mangrove roots the cover was off it." "That how I got this I was there about five hours before the boys left." "Task force, dogs, C.I.D, everything was down there that way I see guns." "They shine the spot light on me couple times I thought they had see me." "I was lucky blood". He took some crispy blackish brown weed in his palm and rubbed it together with the other fingers and thumb. "This was some good herb too blood I feel like crying". "I could see that was good" said the other gangster in the room. They sprinkled some fine smelling tobacco over it. Using more tobacco than weed and rolled their spliff. He stood behind the window curtain and looked throu the tin opening. "One white rental car keep pasting" he said then he sat back down. They both smoked the shit. "I Na 0 them anything still" "Them yardy Na going say nothing homie" said his friend. "Boy I don't trust no man they lock down so you don't know" "They got everything up front from time we pull out of Spanish Harbour". "They family safe they know wha this kind of life involves" "Six months or so in northward hotel and then they send them home they still got two year salary by jam down standard". "Muscle's going be bad" said the other gangster. "F--k him that how this thing goes" said the one that was on the canoe while smoking the bitter weed, with a lump of smoke in his throat. He's a fool he can't come in my face bout give him his money back.

He only had a hundred little pounds. What about the boss how much he down he nah really lost anything if he play his cards right know wha I saying. The other man in the room shook his head and said yeh but he didn't know what the other one meant. I going sell off this salt contaminated shit to those hitters. Smoke too much of this and you turn crazy. You think someone inform on us blood. All that in it star I got plenty enemies who want to see me buried especially here up in west.

C.I.D Harry Philipps rested a cup of coffee on the desk at the interview room in central police station. He took out a cigarette from the pack and lite it then offered one to roots man. You want one of these. Na man me Na smoke them things. Given the situation I thought you might consider. This was the third round of questioning they couldn't get nothing out of him. Philipp stared him eye to eye. Look this doesn't look good for you. They coming down hard on the ganja man now a day you the captain of the canoe you going do the most time. You looking at five years easy. If you make it that long. They don't like black Jamaicans in northward. I can cut you a deal tell us who you were being it in for and you walk free. We'll send you home tomorrow on air Jamaica. You can see your family again you a family man. No answer came from roots man. You don't owe nobody nothing when it comes to this shit just remember that,Philipps went across the other side of the table and removed the handcuffs from behind the man's back. No one will know you rat them out. We'll make a press statement saying you were uncooperative with police and your still in jail awaiting trial. Couple of months after that we'll said you were sentence to five yards in prison. We don't want to know about yard we only concerned with our jurisdiction. You think if they shoe was on another foot and they whoever they is was sitting there where you are. Don't think for a minute they wouldn't give you up to save their own ass. Detective Philips throw some name out as to who the ganja belonged to local known drug dealers. But to none of them roots man reacted. Jamaica police said the canoe left with four man on board. Way the Caymanian onna kill him owha, you got murder on your hand now. This hit a nerve and the man said nothing Na go so Babylon. Yah tell me then wha going on. There was silent again. I getting sick of this. That the game you going play, Find by me. Joe grind going be happy sleeping with your wife and staying in your home. He may even do your daughter every now and then too. Philips closed the yellow paper writing pad and got up to leave wait thy Babylon said roots man, thy whole of we go home tomorrow right. Tell me what I need to know said Philipps.

Police surrounded a Residents in a suburban neighborhood in west bay. They had warrants to search and arrest the occupant in one of the duplex. The assailant fled on foot out the back door task force officer gave chase after him into some bushes. Minutes later he was apprehended throw into the back of the swat car. Cuff him said Bowing. The butt of a semi-automatic rifle government issued came through the car window and busted his nose. Down town in the interrogation room the young criminal screamed police brutality but no one paid him any mind or couldn't care less. The C.I.D (cayman island detective) would try and flip him and see what gives. Who you working for said Bowing.

The clouds went into the mountain top white cups could be seen on the ocean. And the wind made a whistling sound as it passed through the palm tree leaves. They blew in the same direction of the wind. The sheik mansion was actully a castle and it sat on a mountain top on level ground. The hill underneath it sloped gentle and there was a panoramic view. Below it guest sunned and swam nude. Beyond the beach the iron shore became a limestone bluff with caves, coves and yachts. Fancy speed boats were tied up at a long wooden whaft, with stainless steel pylons. Grand Cayman was a dark green object on the horizon 15 miles away. Projecting in the air skyscrapers in the capital could be seen on a clear day. Guest at the hotel on volcano island jet-skied sailed and fooled around in kayaks went hiking looking at iguanas and other wild life. The sheik was a man in his mid 30s he wore a turbine around his head. His first and second in command accompanied him. They sat near the watch tower that look like doom with a round top. And real Spanish tiles from Monte Carlo, to the entire roof. The court yard was cool today. The branch from a big ponsianna tree hanged over a railing to provide the shade. Giant porcelain tiles beautified the concrete floor which was the roof to the underground secret cave that lead to the sea. Three neatly cut lines of cocaine was on the glass table. With a curvy bronze flame. And a moderate amount was lumped in a pile next to it. Snow man held one finger to his nostrils bent his head down and took a snort. The sheik talked on the telephone. He had a long face and a tin line of bared. You could see the bones in his cheek and Jaw. His eyes were round and small. Yes, your Excellency governor that's right. In a few months we will break ground on the 6 star hotel on 7 miles beach it the only one of a kind in the world. All the other hotels around will become empty buildings by the time we are finish. If it was not for condemning that main highway on west bay road making more space for me to purchase the piece of crown beach would have been useless. It is the best spot on 7 mile beach. Next year I want you to allow me to buy the public beach. Why not said the voice on the other side of the phone. I will have helicopter pick up my guess fom the air port and bring them right to the hotel. I spoked to the Russian space projects directors the other day. They are planning to carry people to the moon. I have plenty of room to park a space ship. If tourist would like to go to the moon. They can go to space right from my hotel. The sheik left the table and strolled over to one corner of the court yard. Continuing to talk on the phone. It was a mobile with a long antenna. They gone forever said snowman to his compadre while taking out a picture from his wallet and looking at it. Of an attractive woman and a small boy. She took the kid with her four years ago when she found out what I was doing for a living. Nose heard the story many times before but he still asked. They still in North Carolina. That's the sad part I don't know where the hell they are now haven't talked to them in over a year. In union they took there brown bottles of beer and slog them down. Snow took his half stub cigar from the ashtray and lite it in his mouth. Am sick of this life and only me got to change it. Had a dream last night pal. Bout what. Remember that little house in what's it's name frank sound we saw weeks ago. You mean that little one up in the swamps. Yah we seen it when we were driving about. On that big piece of land call it whatever you want to call it divine intervention or what. But am going to get out of this once and for all I can feel it. Time to settle down watch my son grow start a new family or reestablish what I got to see if it can work this time between me and Gina. Maybe the guy will even sell who knows if I offer him a good price. Yah maybe Crist am 45 now I better quit while am ahead. Guys like us don't live too long in this kind of work. I mean your still young nose. You've done good son. You learn the ropes and caught on fast. Your old man would be proud of you. Snow had worked with the man's father back in the states. That is until he was killed by a mistaken identity. They were pros back in south Florida and did specialized jobs for wealthy client's crime syndicates and the mafia. When this one over I going tell the sheik it was a good run. I'll recommend you as number one around here. I'll only take on an advisory role for him if necessary other than that am hands off. Sooner or later some punk kid or bad guy or some heroic cop who's looking a metal will take a shot at me and that'll be it no more snowman am getting too old for this line of work I move too slow nowadays. I still have trouble sleeping and nightmares over those black kids we killed the other day. Cold blooded. We were only taking order snow. Ah tell that to my conscious. That wouldn't have bother me back in the days. Snow reached down and took out the big black automatic pistol that was rubbing against his hip bone and ribs. And rested it flat on the table. The police are doing a good job taking down those Jamaican dories soon they'll stop them all together and I'll be the only man when they think of marijuana the people will think of me like they think of Bob Marley. I'll get a few more soldiers and control things from this Job it will be plenty enough for my sons university education. And for my little house on the prairie. I'll go to church and live an honest life just like normal folks do. The men were cutting up more lines with a credit card as the sheik come back to the table and sat down. Now that business is over it's time to have some fun. A man servant with a silver color mini ice bucket placed it on the table carefully next to the sheik.A bottle of Arabian wine stick out of the top. Another servant placed a small plate of ordurbs infront of each of them. Any thing else sir asked the servant in good English with a Middle Eastern accent. The sheik waved his hand and they walked away, bowing their heads. The sheik talked and the two men listened hours past, by time the third bottle was put on the table the sun had went down in this part of the world and was rising in another. Clouds were pinkish gray in the dark blue sky. The sheik carried on talking he liked to hear himself speaking. George Bush thinks all Arabs and Muslims and Middle Eastern people in general are terrorist not so am Jew I love all people I will not hurt another human being. Half of the people in guontoamo bay are innocent victims themselves. United States is most corrupted place in the world. I no say this to be mean, they kicked me out of that country long time ago, and I forgive them. Mohamed Abraham both have told us this would past upon the city of the ungodly. The sheik took a drink from his crystal glass. I went to school with ben-latten, really no shit said snowman. Yes of course I will not tell you lie. In Southey Arabia all the rich children go to same school. I wasn't royal like Osama but my family very rich. My ancestors traded merchandise of all kinds. Cattle, slaves, food, valuables etc. So they become very wealthy people. It bad how kill he kill all those inocent people I agree they should hunt him down and cut his head off slowly with a hack saw. Ben-latten is in Pakistan today he communicates with sad am Hussain that serpent. My country not apart of this war, my friends' south Arabia good people. Another mad man is that dictator in Libya. I prefer capitalism over terorrisium any day, my good friends. It a bit more how you say humane. But we must be careful the last stage of capitalism could lead to communism if it get out of control, like in the United States. The little crime spree going on here is nothing compared to other places. No matter how bad Cayman get the rest of the world is worst off than here.

As long as it went on the sheik would keep buying up property the people were scare for their life and wanted out of the business or some owed mortgages on the establishment and couldn't take the loss. So the sheik would move in and buy the distress. It was the slum chum game of capitalism being played but no one had any control over it. It was legal. Business owners got money from loan sharks to pay off debts. Only they could never pay it off in most cases. The loan sharks would get a high profit on it all and own the business keeping same original owner employed for him. It was done through the banks in some cases or associated companies and organizations that didn't really existed. Only on paper. All that matter was tax and once they were paid authorities never checked the legitimacy of the company. Business never had an idea as to who really owned them. Or who they were making money for. After a while crime would stop and things would be back to normal with a new owner of the business and the net worth of the company or business quadrupled.

The sheik took a drink to wet his throat. Pretty soon I will own the whole island and these ignorant Caymanians will all work for me or they die. He slammed his fist down on the table, with his knuckles in an up and down direction. His eyes were dark and said nothing. He was drunk good night gentlemen I see you tomorrow if it Allah's wish and Jehovah blessing. He walked away with his two wives at each side. They wore long reddish garments. They had small pointed faces and a purple dot was on there foreheads. Snowman said something to the two guards in the watch tower, it was probably goodnight. Snowman and his number two in command made there way out of the 30,000sqft mansion through a number of doors and hallways. They made their rounds including at the hotel. John nose worn a suit with no tie and dress shoes sported a military haircut. Snowman's hair was to the back but not in a pony tail. His hair was tinning in front but he wasn't bald yet. He had on a bright colourful silk island style shirt it was unbutton half way down and tucked into his jeans. He sported a black leather belt. The 45 automatic couldn't be seen under his small beer belly. He wore cowboy booths his pants legs covered them as they ran up his ankle. A small gun was hidden somewhere in there. He walk across the laboratory where a scientist still worked cooking cocine and making other drugs. 20 minutes later they said goodbye and went to their rooms in the mansion. Snowman stood out on the small balcony with the sliding glass door open. He stared at the horizon the half moon light reflected onto the ocean. A fishing boat steamed across the seas with a dim light on in the wheel house. The sheik been good to me. But I don't know who he is. He'd had only work for him five year now. I respect him but he doesn't care about anything except his pocket. It's time to go.

The land belongs to an American citizen. That's all we know there's no name at the land registry. Everything was done up there in the states, we going to have to knock on there door if we want anymore information. Said Miles to Bowing We need more than what we got before we bring the FBI in on this. If we got Americans pushing this crime spree there going to have to handle things on there side. Right now all we got is a couple of petty criminals smoking ganja. You did a good job bringing this to our attention Miles. We setting up a surveillance team as we speak. I know Kingdon he's a sly one. I know the Bodden towner too he killed before about 10 years back. Can't take chances with any of em. Tate supposed to be some kind of Christian now they say. But he still burning weed. The other are northsiders said Miles. Wait a minute said Sullivan looking at a picture. I recognize this one there was a repot that came in about several week ago. Someone in a green canoe was fishing in Marine Park. Sounded suspicious so I went and checked it out. Far as I remember he told me his name was Danford Powdery. We'll run that see what happens. Show the pictures around see if we can identify the rest. This could be the bunch we looking for detective, said Sullivan. I got a strange feeling. Seem like they running some kind of camp sir said Miles they gather every night. This fits the profile of a Rastafarian group, or a creole supremacist group or something. Let arrest them all and beat them into a confession, said Sullivan. This is an election year Bowing said Miles I don't want this in my area. Little late for that it's already here said Bowing. He picked the photos up off the brown phonemical table top and placed them between the file folders and closed it. Kingdon owns a sport utility van just like the one seen leaving the crime scene. And he's dreadlocks. All the evidence point to them Miles but we got to grab these suckers in actions. These the same ones writing the letters Bowing. "Maybe "came the reply. What's the plan asked miles. I'll put one man to watch them. But this gang don't even trust that swamp. We'll be lucky to get anywhere near them. They not going let there mouth slip and jeopardize their cover. Only one man said Miles. That's right I know it dangerous. One man will be on location and another nearby in constant communication with each other. If anything happens he can call for back up that way the whole team isn't at risk of being ambush. They could have dogs down the back there not to mention guns. One of them get jumpy or trigger happy after hearing or seeing something and start tearing apart that forest with bullets.

The crime spree continued at a rate of about 14 robbery a week, last night two gas stations and a hotel was robbed and a safe broken into at gun point. The good new no one was being killed in any of these crime yet. Fish shops department stores. A Chinese maid had been robbed after leaving work that Friday evening. One man with a stocking over his face held a hunting knife at her throat. Police are now saying some of these crimes were copy cats and random acts. The sheik now owned two more hotels a gas station some liquor stores. The biggest car parts store on the island, five well established restaurants in the water front and couple garages all victims of burglary and robbery. Neighbourhood had been burglarized due to th resent crime wave. And the Arabian sheik had bought up a whole town over night at a good deal. He had thousands of acres scatter over the three islands. He owned government buildings and controlled the weather.

Sections of the police department work of him, they had been financial problems and he had loan the Cayman island government millions of dollars. Politicians, lawyers, judges, legitimate business people and all the rest worked for him if they knew it or not.

George Town had become more hectic then ever and if you were going into town you needed a shot of something for your nerves. Even out of town was getting congested now. Cayman was like a gold rush boom town. Everybody trying to find gold and to hell with the rest. It was everybody for himself and God for us all kind of mentality. The common man on the street was realizing the truth working girls were making house calls more often. People noticed the low tide was below normal and a large mass of red shanks crabs were crawling all over the island. Mango season was short this year and you could not give away a breadfruit they were so plentiful. You couldn't read your bible openly in those days you had to do it in hiding. People would say you were working witch craft especially with all these satanic letters going round. They had sent one of those mysterious letters directly to the church. Undercover police were watching the post offices and checking the mail service for anyone or thing that seem peculiar. Patrick Bowing had raid some of these gang houses and several organized gang members were being questioned along with dozen others that the net dragged in. Gang members were extorting business owner etc. There was no one to run to people got way with things other couldn't because they had power and the law to back them up. Politician and prime ministers were on there side and their speed dial. Others had links that went beyond the justice system if you know what I mean. On the marl road CID were also looking for a manuscript. A book was being written about this place, and the authorities wanted it. A professor at oxford university had exam some of the letters. And the psychology behind them was a book. It could be espionage for all they knew or psychological warfare on a revolutionary level. The book would be worth millions on the back market according to the professor. This book could backfire and show the island in a negative light. It was a national security issue. Books couldn't be written without the law knowing what it was about. Writers needed to be registered by law and preferably to be civil servant material would need to be censored if they the government felt it was too offensive, whether it was true or not. The book could even be used as a propaganda piece in this up coming election.The police would stop at nothing to catch this traitor. I don't know nothing about no book said one local want to be writer when integrated by police at the special investigation room. These people got my name mix up in all kinds of thing detective sir.

It was the middle of June the hurricane season was two weeks old. Thing were good for the Indian man he had came across some money God had provided it seafood was lucrative business every body bought seafood everybody. And Indian fish spear fished and worked the sea with Bill. The man had managed to get the walls up to the belting height. He smoked weed and laid blocks even at night the sand came from the beach and the gravel and cement from an old girl friend who gave him a deal she worked at the supplier. Weeks had went by however this wasn't the 70s or 80s anymore. Everything had to be done by the book now poor man or not. You had to pay tax and give the government their share for your success and you need blue prints to go along with it. Or no certificate of occupancy would be given, and no utility power would be connected to the house. The new home being constructed in frank sound had capture the eyes of building inspectors patrolling the area. It was beautifully designed around trees and other landscape. The little cottage was located just right to enhance the site. Central planning department sent in the building unit it was being built without a red card or even house plans. This was illegal. And police had arrested a man on the site for disorderly conduct. He spent the night behind bars and was released. you couldn't drive a nail in a fowl coupe now a days unless you had a building permit. I need a good 10000 dollars to get the law off my back said Indian to Aliza. They were both naked laying in bed. mostly bureaucracy bullshit. House plans planning fees, insurance, the inspector from planning ask me way I get that kind of money from to build this big time house. Bout they got the rights to knock it down if I continue without a plan. They don't know who the dealing with. O Indian don't talk like that said aliza. I going try put the roof on when the pressure ease off and I get my hands on some more money. You fixed the documents like I asked you to baby. Yes but it's a little too early for that don't you think. You never know Alize. Honey why can't you get a job. Said Aliza. Don't you start worrying your brains over that again? That building inspector was asking all them question like where you work and all that. He was thinking like you, I know what he was thinking but I got news for him. Even church money got blood stains on it nowadays stated indian. Don't let them get in your head baby and complicate it let you think bad things. Just believe in me honey and we'll make it. There's a curtain line I don't cross Aliza I'm praying for all those who judge me for God to remove the spell that they under. Depression still had it hands on his neck. These people trying push us over the edge. Am an innocent man Aliza who loves you. Yah baby but how come you haven't had a steady job in years. Am an entrepreneur honey they killing us off. But everybody got to work for a living. Indian kissed her on the forehead and got up to go burn a joint. You can't understand all this babes he told her. Because you're a drug addict no one wants you to work for them said aliza.You think that's what it is. He shouted from across the room it's a lot deeper than that. He walked out naked onto the screen porch A barbeque grill with the cover on it burned quietly there. The truth was only the black market would hire such a man but that was a different story. He had a couple conversations with the Russian mafia but once you become partners with those guys that forever. Maybe even end up in prison if the cops found you involved in any crime. A friend of his had been locked up for burning one little roach. Inmate raped him in prison he killed one of them and got life for it. They found him one morning swinging with a sheet around his neck, he hanged himself. Don't care what kind of person you was you would be worst than ever when you come out. One night was a nuff for me he said to aliza. Even drug free people would come out addicted to something. This roast fish ready you know babes. Don't touch that with you hands ! Said the girl. I have a fork Thank you said Indian and I don't mean the one in the middle of my body. Aliza wasn't home for good but the visit made him feel like a man again.

so went the kids get out of school for summer you'll be home right. If you behave yourself said Aliza. Am buying a car Indian then you wont have to drive me up and down every way? Aliza ate the grilled vegetables but left most of the fish, fish Na ga go to waste way part I is said indian. An hour or so later they were back under the sheets.

A politician sat in the restroom toilet of the legislative assembly building with the cell phone glued to his ear. He had gotten an important call this morning. He hated loose ends but soon it would be all looped together. The 25 year old youth that was involved with the contraband walked about wondering in his cell at the down town lock up. The walls were dirty and graffiti. He had been there a month so far. He had five minutes ago asked the police guard to let him take a crap in the bathroom down the hall But now he felt like he needed to take a piss. If they weren't in a good mood they'll make him do it on the floor or in his pant. They guards turned the A/c up high at nights freezing inmates balls off and by day they cut it off completely slowly melting them from the heat. It was noisy and smelled two or three men shared one cell of the six room jail house. But lucky for him he was alone today. The jail keeper pushed a tray under the opening in the bars. Eat all the eggs he said to the youth. Cut up pork sausages were scramble with the eggs and it had no taste the toast was burnt and cold. The coffee was water mixed. In the food was a note folded into a dozen pieces.

After he read it he put it into his mouth and chewed it up and swallowed. 30 minutes later. You ready to talk now said the CID officer,who you work for.?

I don't need some freaking building inspector playing cop. If planning messes this whole thing up so help me God. Said detective Bowing.

His real name is Ezekiel Howitt Malicah, our team missed it the first time around due to Howett being in the middle and it was spelled different. He's a damn Indian said Philipps apparently he was born in England by emigrant parents from Indian isn't family to any of the other caymanika Indians here. Told the planning officer he moved up there a year ago. Around the same time all this crime started said bowing. He bought the place from an American gentleman by the name of Tomas Springs. It didn't had any house plans and the foundation and floor were already down. And most of the blocks up. Philipps read from a piece of paper. He graduated with honours from the top trade school in England and majored in construction engineer and philosophy according to the file. Worked for several companies in England and here on the island. isn't that a coincidence said Bowing.

He's an educated crimeral probably hates white people and all that too. Surveillance managed to get a picture of him with the others smoking a rifer. They were talking but he couldn't make out what they were saying over the earphone. Bob Marley music was playing the whole night long. He say he heard something up in that bush sir. What you mean a noise asked Bowing. Yes sir. He didn't see any dogs but it sounded like something big crawling. He got out of there as quick as he could give me a break said Bowing to Philipps. Well he didn't wanted to take any chances sir. Said it might be black magic no telling what kind of spirit that Indian and Rasta be calling round the fire when they be burning weed. Your guy seeing ghost now detective Philipps no it was a caiman's crocodile if you ask me. He said the thing had a head like godliza. Oh fro Christ sake Bowing said laughing you sure it wasn't a colony of swamp crabs under the moonlight Miles too started to laugh. That'll be the first crocodile seen in Cayman in over a hundred years I tell you that. Look this guy could be some kind of international criminal Bowing said on a serious note. The west Bayer confessed little while ago to one of my men that he was bring it in for this guy the call the Indian Malicah lives up in frank sound. He's the king pin on the island responsible for all these robberies and drug canoes He the big one down here no doubt about it. He bring it in from Jamaica and unload right up in that swamp way part he is. Some of the guns and drugs stay here the rest shipped off to who know where. Europe, the states midwest or estern United States is one of the biggest route by flying from the island. A lot of people are caught carrying drugs into Minneapolis and other connecting cities. Old men little babies are found with the shit taped to the bodies. A lot of them get through with it. From the middle of the country it's easy to distribute all over the continent. We don't know who else is involved in this ring. The brits are running their names through international data poles search. Their intelligent agent working for MI6 who sits around a computer all day verifying identities. If Tomas Springs or Ezekiel Malicah are fugitives at large there information will pop up on the computer. It might take him couple day he told me over the phone he will have to do some hacking. Everything points to the Indian and his men. They from my speed boat in that swamp remember close to his place. The officers saw him sinking the stolen car from the water front job in the dirt road. He didn't count on bucking into no one up in there. We got some guy's lockdown now for some of these robberies Bowing, Said Miles. They just the small time run of the mill spontaneous jobs. Hitter looking cocaine money petty criminals. These guys do there thing clean, religious like they're well disciplined. I think I figured out a pattern they only do a crime on full moon once or twice a month. Philipps breathed heavy Miles looked at him and then at Bowing.

. Philipps was behind the steering wheel of a big grey Buick. When they balled out tyres from the Bodden Town station parking lot and headed town. Bowing punched in numbers on his cell phone. Mr. Orange this is patrick bowing here sir just wanted you to know we're closing in on our suspect. Over the next weeks we'll have him. And he'll be locked away for the rest of his life. I just spoke with Miles he's convince, even the commissioner says there's no mistake about it. We don't expect a confession he's a compulsive and pathological liar. We're going to have and catch him red handed. But things could always get complicated if you know what I mean we may not be able to bring him in alive.

Indian owed the I.R.S a good hunk of change he had gotten himself in that mess years ago. By being involved with the wrong crowd. The 90s were the golden years of Cayman construction entrepreneurs came down to the island and invested. In construction they built homes and commercial buildings. Indian was a young motivated contractor at the time. Operating his own company solid build construction. He did some homes for a developer from California a man by the name of Thomas Springs. It was a good run until the CIA came about along with the IRS. The IRS Eventually arresting springs for lying on his tax return he was chanced with tax evasion. The CIA got him for narcotics trafficking he had contacts with Noriega the Mexicans and even Escobar, med yen cartel up in South America. He was expedited back to the United States. Even though the narcotics agreement had long been signed the local authorities stayed away from high level crimes like cocaine smuggling by big shot people. Laws like know your customer banking laws had not yet been established by the financial crime departments. Laws were not that tight in the 80s and 90s. Banks never asked too many questions. Especially if you were a white man. And bribes were not too expensive. Tom opened a developing company under a false name and got someone to front for him. It was the old fashion way of cleaning money back then. But by the late 90s laws allowed these such authorities to look at tax crimes committed by US citizens in cayman. The CIA and FBI got friendly agreement to visit these so called tax heaven. Paperwork was done in favour of the owner of solid build company. He was the fall guy unknowingly. Tom and his people had fixed things According to the IRS accounting documents showed Mr. Springs reported his income to the internal revenue service of the united States. But the checks were cancle for the construction work that was to be carried out. Then somehow change into cash and money deposited into the contractor account for some reason. It looked like the contractor had out rightly stolen from Thomas. It was an open and shut case. Nobody was going to take the opposing side over the IRS. The caymanian contractor maintained he was an innocent man. He wasn't obligated to pay the IRS but they charged him with theft. When all was said and done he was lucky to get out of it alive. And from doing any hard time. The lawyer down played the situation and the contractor ezekiel howett cry on the witness stand but was found guilty and would have to pay the IRS back some 350,000 dollars over long term interest, slowly but surely. He had checked a death consolidator and a couple of those IRS guys on TV but this went beyond their reach. It was three years now since the man had made any payments to the IRS and his unemployment crisis was not helping. The last letter from the IRS basically said he had until next tax day to pay up or he will go to prison and his possessions sold off to pay the debt.

Indian never slept that night. He and Bill had done some more digging no treasure yet. They were down almost 20 feet. Still getting a signal in the ground water it wasn't salt it was brackish. They had secured the inside walls with planks bracing them from wall to wall and used them as a ladder. It could be anything down there at this point a land mine or missile from world war two. They could be digging to there deaths. Bill had already left for the night. Indian was under the house floor in his favourite hammock. I can't make them take my place not for Aliza's sake. I might as well be buried then, he said talking to himself. I need to finish this house up quickly and secretly sell it on the black market, before the IRS knows what's going on, get what I can get for it. Its worth two hundred gees easily with the land not even that is enough to pay those bastards off. Who ever buy it can double their money in a few years time. With that money Aliza could live comfortable start over her and my two children. The land papers in her name now so they won't be able to touch her. I never had anything for them to hold in the first place. I don't want her mix up in this what so ever, I can't tell her. Indian had a little pension money deadlock in the system from the days he did work. But he couldn't reach it until he was 60. He had made Aliza fixed the paperwork that she would be the beneficiary, in case anything happen to him. It was only 70 thousand dollars and she would give it to different charities. Worst case scenario. The Patterson's and Mama would be next in line as beneficiaries and would distribute the funds to charities worth wild. The Patterson were good people it's the best thing to do the orphanage can use some of it. Indian told himself. To hell with the IRS I have to get my life in order the day God calls me I want to be ready spiritually and money-wise, he pulled in on the ganja cigarette and a heavy low sounding cough exploded in his chest. There was nothing to spit out this time. He was burning hisself to death man.

In his will he had told Aliza that he wanted his body donated to science. She had laughed but he said it didn't make sense to let a good body rotten away in the ground, if it can help mankind as a whole. Even though I don't like science, doctors are useful. I smoke he told her but the rest of my organs are in good shape.

The sun came up and found the man in the same place under the house floor. Indian spent the day with his mother and two sons. He hadn't seen them in a long time. He visited his father's grave.

Bill Patterson thorn up a lottery ticket money down the drain again. Just let me win one good hunk of money dear God and I'll stop for good I promise. He had been checking some things out. Spoke to some old Indian but no one had ever heard about any gold up in frank sound. Indians didn't worry about gold the were more concern with corn, the spirit and the soul. Gold or treasure was bad luck it had too much curses around it. Water, wind and fire etc. things of nature were the true treasures for them. Many Indian had been killed and tortured during the conquestadores period right up until the small rebellion about 70 years ago. More Indian died during this time then the age of pirates. Some were buried in shallow grave others placed upside down in deep holes or wells in some cases to reveal where treasure was buried most never knew anything. Indians were treated like black and if you were a dark colour Indian then it was even worst, the whites ran them of their land for one reason said an old Indian to bill. Because of gold. As far as the coin that he had found went it was just a coin someone had lost long time ago. It was only worth couple hundred dollars.

It was 11:45 Tuesday morning a conflicting letter had been send the court house it was a part of the chain of letter that had been circulating the island for months. There was no way to track it. It came from outside the country and it had over a dozen posting stamps attached to it. They had been three armed robberies so far that morning. A pond shop got jewellery and cash stolen at gun point from a man with a skeleton mask on. Three gun men robbed a cable TV bill paying department of the company. And the men faces were covered with black ski mask. In another incident a man with a red cloth over his head robbed a bargain store with a machete. No shots were fired and no one was reported injured.

He smart, must have smell the rat and know we watching him. Doing he thing now in broad day light, we'll have to make the team watch him around the clock now not only at night said Detective Bowing to a small stuff.

Thomas Springs died back in 98 according to the FBI data. His murder has remain unsolved ever since. The IRS got him first then the CIA. He was in the business down here with a Caymanian name Louis Mood a contractor supposedly. The day before his trial he was executed at a Howard Johnson hotel under protected custody along with two special agent from the FBI. Louis was questioned and released, apparently he couldn't be in two places at the same time. Louis is fifty old years now he lives in George town owns a small paint company walks with a limp that all the MI6 agent got. He isn't a suspect in Thomas murder or the current case.

Malicah bought the place from Thomas seven year back in 97 he was telling lies to throw us off. Didn't think we would have check his story out. Or he could be the mysterious hit man that killed springs and the two FBI said Philipps. Could always be someone higher up giving the Indian orders. I don't want us talking to anyone else about this all the information comes directly to me we got to be extra careful this thing might be bigger than we think. Someone could be leaking information to our guy dirty cops can be in on this. Half the force is foreign nationals if you know what I mean. Can't be trusted. One more thing continue to work with informants of the street see if you can find out any more about someone who may be writing this book.

There was another letter said bowing. There so many ways to send information now it may be hard to find who ever is sending these damn things. The briefing was over Bowing look at his cell phone that was on the desk. His wife had called him six times.

Nightingale house had won there first match and there was an up beat spirit around the orphanage. Indian and Aliza was out back. The kids were scattered about some in their rooms others watching television in the family area. Mr. Bill and Marisah codled up in a love seat out on the veranda. A Lincoln town car pulled up next to the low concrete block fence out in front. A woman got out of it and walked over to the entrance gate. Mr bill went over to meet her, the woman said hello and then good evening. She spoke intelligently her hair was curly and brown it reached shoulder length. Extending her hand in a hand shake she said. I represent the Jewellers association of the Cayman Islands. There was thick make up to the face like a prostitute but she was a business woman. Bill noticed she had strong hands. I would like to talk to you about some brown rubies you may be in possession of, known as sugar babies. Bill kept a straight face. Sorry you've come to the wrong place, you're Bill Patterson am I correct. Yes I am. Then am at the right house said the woman's voice. Mr. Bill I got reasonable knowledge that you may have such valuables. A young little visited one of stores a few months back and got an appraisal on one of these stones she's your daughter I believe said it was in the family for centuries. Bill who is it shouted Marisah from the porch. It ok wave bill to his wife. She pretty isn't she, you really love her don't you. Aliza looks just like her the woman said. The commits were out of the way bill thought but he overlooked it. I didn't get your name. Ms. Baker am sorry she said handing him a business card. We do business with a number of high net individuals. We will be willing to give you 30 thousand a stone Mr. Bill. I don't have any more stones that's the only one and it's not for sale. You're making this difficult, how about we give you 35 CI not even in the states they'll offer you that. Take the family to Disney land. I don't have any stones I told you you're wasting your time. Bill was becoming irritated. Look it's been nice meeting you and all that but am going to have and ask you to leave. Sorry I can't help you. Perhaps I should be more direct Mr. Bill we are sure you have the rest of the sugar babies so it would be wise not to deny it. We are professional people its best not to refuse this offer you'll be sorry if you do. What that supposed to mean you threating me now over nothing. Look before I lose my temper you better get out of here I told you it a big mistake lady. I'll be expecting your call she said, don't keep us waiting too long. My clients will get upset. She got into the car and drove way. Who was that said Marisah. Some government Lady doing a survey of the living conditions in town but she was at the wrong address. I told her the place she was looking for further down the road. Honey get me some water please said bill.

Minutes later. Aliza said she never gave no one at international stones the address, much less told them she was your daughter said Indian. That means they been watching her from the first day she went in with the stones said Bill. If that lady was sure you had the rest of stones, then they must know a lot more too said Indian.

Yah it makes sense now yesterday. I notice some footprints in the swamps boot prints. And some tree twigs broken. The animals and the caimans is acting strangely.

No hits came back on the name Ezekiel Malicah. The cops wasn't only looking for one man or had eyes on one person. There was a long list of possibilities. Birds were singing on the streets none the less. Was it the columbians doing this reign of terror on the island, or the Nicaraguans even. Cayman was a melting pot and all kinds of ingredients was mixed up in it. This could be the work of the Germans, the Albanians, and the Chinese, the japs or Koreans. They could have all well and join up to take down Cayman. They were a lot of suspects if you asked the average Joe on the street.

The underground banking association could be involved. With all these banks here bankers could be in this thing for different reasons. This could be the Australians or even the Swiss themselves. The police were checking out terrorist group like the Caribbean Islamic army. And the Caymanian Muslims, along with other rude boy gangsters. The Jamaican passé. Ordinary people were being popped and red flagged. Doctor, realtors, contractors, fishermen, punks with little connections.

In a ghetto in George Town a rat stuck his head up over some garbage that was piled up in the yard, a man screwed a silencer onto a gun barrel and took aim at the rodent. There was a tump from the gun as he squeezed the trigger. Holding the gun with both hands. And blowing the creature apart. Blood splashed everywhere. He made an awful sounding laugh then spit on the ground. That should have been the governor's brain he said to the other two men around a make shift table, out in the back of the yard. Injecting heroin into their veins. Roof zinc formed a fence about eight feet high. Have no pitty when it comes to war men. Have no fear the only way for us to free ourselves from captivity is by destroying the crown. He was shirtless and wore a navy style trouser. His hair was braided into four pieces and the locks were at his neck level. He took a slog of night train liquor with the other hand he pushed the automatic in his waist line. Then pulled a small cell phone out from his back pocket and dialled the toll free number. And put the thing to his head. The noon talk show was on hello your on the air said the host of the program. Yeh good day to you and the whole Cayman Islands. Good day to you too said the host. Am going to keep this short today. That was a good optimistic speech last night by the governor on TV. But what he should have done was come right out and tell the people the truth why he don't want to do that. What do you mean caller. I tell you wha I mean the fact things Na getting any better, is cause the people of these islands powerless and we the natives don't have any control of our destiny. Politicians bought out and then they sell us out. Look at the labour situations in this country why can't the immigration board stop giving out some much permits and work with the labour department to employed those thousands of people without work. I am sick of this the Caymanian need to speak out about this matter. We ga have marches and protest like blow up cars and thing they way they do in other countries. Caller I hear ya man but you ga watch your language. The people Na ga no say. Continued the caller. We ga go independent this year vote for candidates that want this for the country. Expats got the whole island take over let's get rid of the British rule government ok that's all I got to say for now thank you. Well thank you for your call and expressing your true feeling. The phone line light up. We have a full house callers let see if any one else agrees with you. Yes you're on the air, hello, hello caller. I just want to say a few words myself. If that caller thinks we better off with out England he make a sad mistake. Don't fool yourself he nah see hardship yet, have it ever occur to him that England is the only thing we got going for us. I thought you would have cut that caller off the air talking foolishness like that. Why would I want to do that replied the veteran talk host isn't it good for the powers to be to know what's on the minds of the citizens of these islands for better or for worst till death us part kind of thing. The host was cracking up inside He does speaks for all of us. Am aware of that. In fact I think he's a lone wolf on that one well we going to have to wait and see want we. They were a few more callers who changed the conversation up a little. Then the was a commercial break. Three minutes later, the talk show host began to read another one of those insulting philosophical letter. After the letter the dreadlocks man cut off the radio. Time to hit the street boys he said to the two men make some dope money. He handed them a small bag filled with ecstasy cocaine rocks and heroin. Collect wha you soppose to man na gat no friends when it comes to these things. The men left. The natty dread man went inside the ran down apartment his feet hit some beer cans that were laying on the floor. He put a big stone in a pipe and begin to smoke it. He lit a black candle that was next to a human skull on a small platform, suspended on the wall. A boat would be leaving in a couple of days. He needed more money to get more guns. His friend didn't really know what was in his mind. He was a terrorist in the making. He flexed with homie all over the island vowed deep down inside to take cayman into independence but he knew the democratic process wouldn't work. It would have to be done with guns and by a revolution. Some of us might have to die but this was the price for freedom. The people that oppress us will pay he said to the skull.

He had passed through numerous reform schools, but had avoided prison miraculously. Hiding and deceasing his personality and criminal activity had become a gift to him. And the forces of darkness and the spirit of the skull protected him. Once as a kid he Carried cow-itch to school and that morning in assembly he throw a bag into a ceiling fan spilling the bag and blowing the content all over the room. As he ran out the building closing the door with key. Hundreds of kids along with teachers were affected with severe rashes and blisters, one child was permanently blinded. Skin had fallen off children faces. On the way out of the assembly hall he hit the fire alarm switched and had lit some books. Starting a small fire and setting off the sprinkler. The water made the cow-itch even more unbearable. In all the commotion no one remember or saw anyone doing anything. The kid himself had been hospitalized with minor cow-itch burns that he had a flexed on himself with no one's knowledge. By age 12 him and his gang planned to murder the premier of the country. By setting a bomb at one of his speeches. The 20 pound home made pipe bomb would explode sending nails glass and other pieces of sharp metals into the air most liking injuring and killing people, also that was in the audience. The plan failed when a young police name Sullivan found the youth drunk and acting suspicious around a waste basket in the town hall with a school bag on his back. He was the youngest person to g to juvenile prison. Four years later he was out burglarizing people's homes. And by then the leader of a gang controlling two blocks. And a number of street corners. By his mid 20s he was a career criminal without a rap sheet driving fancy cars and living not the high life that brought too much heat but a lay back style of life. He only operated from the ghettos in the central of town. He had a decent apartment he owned with a mean squeeze girlfriend in the classier part of the city. But he got around and had sex with which girl he wanted. Nowadays he trafficked contraband period things like gun drugs and human being and ganja was placed into 40 feet containers and transported via fishing boats and cargo fates to Texas for the Cripps gang. He sold arms to an undercover ATF agent one time, but had manage to slip out of the loop and someone else went down and did prison time for his crime. He laced a ganja spliff with cocine rocks and was smoking when a teenage girl came out from behind the curtain, which parted the room. The man with locks on his head gave her the rich up (coccine) joint. The baby she held on her hip was crying. It was a mistake the voices in his head had told him many times. Shut him up nah he said. I don't know wha wrong with him today said the young girl. He been crying all day. We need to take him to the doctor he Na get a check up since he was born. Living in this pig pen that a wonder he Na dead yet. I thought God would have taken it out of his misery by now said the man. Don't say that bout my baby you piece of shit for a man. Then carry him to the hospital Na you dumb bitch. Children get free check up and medication. You don't need to talk to me like that. I talk to you any how I want I own your ass girl remember that. I tell you done next month when everything set up we getting out of this place. You been saying that for years. You planning on three of us living together at the other apartment with your other woman. Don't provoke me Tita that I have to put my hands on you. The baby started to cry louder. The man put both his hands on his head in rage. I Na fraid of you any how you hit me I going call the police. He doubled his fist and stuck her on the side of the face. Her tiny body curled up on the floor. The baby laid flat out face down. Crying the baby sounded out of breath see wha you went make me done. The man picked up the child and put him in the kitchen sink. Then he forcefully spread the girls legs open, slapping her a few times and raped her on the floor.

It was 7pm in the hood a rental car was parked in the yard Two men talked. Fifteen minutes later the man with braids in his head got out of the car with a black plastic bag. And the rental drove away. He stuffed the bag in an old stove hiding it inside the house. The girl with black and blue eyes and swollen face and lips watched him from the corner of the room where she sat on a torn to pieces sofa. The child layed there asleep and swateing. Midnight the SUV that the man drove pulls out of the drug house in the ghetto. Heading to another address and life. The teenager was locked up and sleeping with the baby all alone in the house.

The last hours had been busy for snowman. He delivered another 100 keys to the man in the sound. The glider plane had landed on the bluff at the sheiks property on volcano island. Things went smoothly. By mid morning he was in Tampa. He preferred to drive up to Miami. He came through Tampa because the immigration at Miami international asked too many questions even to the citizens. They wanted to know your whole life story. And the customs profilers looked at everyone like they were drug dealers and criminals. Tampa airport was less hassle. There wasn't that much wet backs employed there or roaming the streets. He wouldn't be too long up in the city. He wanted to spend a day or two at his home in Tampa were he owned a 1000 square feet in a good neighbourhood. Nose had stayed back to get a feel of things on his own. Snowman made a couple deposit that day one into a small credit union in his son name. The ex wife was ok she didn't need anything he had treated her good during the divorce. He made another monthly instalment at the workers bank of Tampa Florida. Snow had a bad feeling about this one. It had been ten years since he pulled off a job like this. At lunch he talked to two hippies friends of his that he had worked with before. In a restaurant and bar at a marina yacht club in one corner in the VIP section. This is the rondavoo point said Snowman with his finger on the spot of a George Town map. When you get off the ship your tell the taxi to take you to this beach. I'll pick you up from there. Were going to have to break in to the security system and disable it. Then in and out as fast as possible on this one.

The butcher, and cook and also Italian mobster sat in the kitchen at his Taliyah food stand. Using a news paper he cut out letters big enough to make up words he needed. The stall was pack this day. People were in a midday feeding frenzy. I'll slip this under the door while he sleeps. I'm not afraid of the little punk. He'll be surprise someone got that close to him and could have killed him. The butcher was a big dude short but wide and hairy. Big head and arms. He bragged a lot about being part of the Italian mafia. But he was really an independence with very small and limited contacts. Had won a heap load of money from gambling in Vegas. Back when he was a mare want to be mafia fresh from Milan. He was living in California at the time working a 9 to 5 at queens burger. He drove over to Vegas every now and then, and had gotten lucky in the casino one weekend. He had killed before Once back in Italy. Another time in south america. After becoming a wealthy man he took a vacation to Honduras where he murdered a prostitute after a sex game gone wrong. No body would ever miss that whore he often told himself when the gruesome after thought flashed into his mind every now and then. He butchered her and paid two military men to throw their bodies in a river. He came down to the islands met a fellow Californian. One night at a bar. And paid him money up front for a home he never recieved.

He was paid back his money in bits at a time, from the developer. But got a lot of heat and scrutiny from the FBI himself that he didn't need. Other bad deals along with whoring, drinking, and smoking out the money broke him over time. He had a serious anger problem. And owed money to various sources also. He paid money to track down Thomas springs and got himself a room at the hotel where he was being kept under lock and key and protected around the clock by FBI agents. He watch the door and when they opened it for the pizza delivery guy he rushed in shooting one agent in the middle of the chest he had catch them off guard for a spit second even though the FBI had his hand on the gun handle in his holster. The other agent got one side of his head blow off but not before firing one round into the butchers shoulder right over his heart. It went clean through not hitting any vital organs only breaking a small bone. Tom springs got it to the back o the head execution style. Even the pizza man stomach was blow apart by the gun man he died days later at the hospital. The gun man disappeared and was never found. The cook had blood on his hands. He eventually cough up enough money to relocate to Cayman for good and to run a legitimate business tom is dead now you pay his bill, the note said he folded it and placed it in the enveloped and licked it seal. He whipped it clean with a table towel. This is chomp change am making in this place compared to what I could be making. He looked out from behind the kitchen towards the tables,they were all full. I had it all but then bad luck hit the kid will pay up if he knows whats good for him. He'll have to find the money from some where, sell a piece of land or two from his 6 acres or mortgage it off. Or I cut his throat with my butcher knife. It'll disappear into the Italian countryside forever not even my mama will know where I am. I want even worry about paying off the balance of money I owe on the lease for this place. Two large pork yelled the waiter. Coming up he answered. I get sick of this shit now he said to himself. He put the pale whitish meat on the grill and watched the juices evaporate into smoke. It looked delicious. I will chop him up and cook him over an open fire, even when he gives me my money. That theft for all the misery he caused me.

The man with dreadlocks counted money that afternoon. Next couple of jobs and everything will be set. I spoke to the boat captain little while ago. He already left pickcle bank will be in Swan Island early in the morning. To pick up the merchandize, then of to the gulf, Texas here we come. Everything safe like getting pompom from a prostitute as long as you got the cash in hand. Keep onna ears open so we know when any canoes coming in so we could make the boys (police) know keep them on our good side. Or I might have to put a lead in Sullivan head. Pitbull got his boys on the street asking about a book somebody writing. Yah Sullivan mentioned something the other day. If pit-bull or Sullivan gets a hold of it first they going sell it. That worth thousands on the underground market.

That's 80,000 said one of the crew plus 65,000 in drug money so far. We get 25 percent. We got couple more robberies then we chill out for a while. Let the money work for a while,

, they bounced fist together gang style.We can't let them tell us how much is enough men said the dreadlocks we going to have and hit his thing hard.

This week and do a job or two for we self you Na see. He rolled the cash up in a black garbage bag and put it under his armpit. Then shared out two rocks each for his men. They vanished into the darkness, of the night. He clicked the padlock shut on the zinc and lumber frame standing gate. And loosen the chain free from two lion looking dogs. He hid the money in the usual place in the stove left up top interior. He closed the cover down on the old stove and put weights blocks and junk on and around the old thing. Then went inside for the night. Tita saw everything, heard everything.

His woman driving a band new car said detective. Philipps to detective Bowing in his office at George Town police station. She works at AIG bank on forth street. We tracked the financial records a small loan was approved in her name by the bank, where she works. Smart now she can used the boyfriend's dirty money to pay it off. Tiny monthly payments so no one would notice Said Sullivan. It hard to tell at this point if she knows anything said Philipps. What about her father the old man he got anything to do with this. Him and the Indians fishing together sometimes and he helps him do work on the building. The other evening two of them were digging a hole most likely a septic tank or a cistern said Sullivan. Couple hours later he left with some bi-kind in the back of his truck he clean. The pattersons runs the orphanage on school road. The kid from north side is the youngest and a small fry in this if anything. We still watching the rest of the crew. The George Towner Seymour is notorious with the Rastafarian movement here on the island. Sell weeds at the bars some times. But he can't be trusted up to any to make a dollar. How can you be so sure about that? You sound like your protecting him now Sullivan. Said Philipps him and his woman. Owns an apartment in town. One of those rent to own. He's on the road all hours of the night in that explorer. Gets around with the girls if you know what I mean. When he Na with the Indian he hangs out monkey town down the back known drug area. How long before we take them down asked miles the quiet one in the room. We're bringing the commissioner up to speed first. We'll let Sullivan continue to watch them to see if anyone else is involved they may well be on there own but you never know. And we also looking to see if there crimes go beyond robbery. What you saying Bowing. Responded Miles that missing man Na been found yet, he was an investigative reporter may have stumble on to something big. If he knew somehow that they were committing these robberies they could have killed him and buried him in those swamps. Where nobody will ever find him again. Or they my have feed him to the alligators, said Miles laughing. You never know this story doesn't look like it will have a happy ending. Said Bowing.

This morning she carried coffee into the CEO office. Here you go sir your coffee. That's wonderful my dear rest it on the table would you please and could you take a seat and close the door behind you. I'll like to have a few words with you. I been noticing the hell of a job you been doing around here am impress. Thank you sir said aliza. A girl like you can go far in this business with the right man behind you. Excuse me sir. I find you very attractive Aliza I would like to get to know you a lot better, help you along with your career if you follow what am saying. Am engage sir I'm not that kind of girl. Aliza said with a strong voice. Oh come on Aliza don't reject me for that Indian of yours he's a real buggy night I hear a little boy if you ask me. A lady like you needs a real man he said with a cute smile. You and I could make a good team. Think of the life in front of you, your career Aliza. He was on his feet walking over to her chair. She got up to leave. He clocked her at the door standing in front of it facing her. You're so plum and sexy you Cayman women like the man to chase after it a little I understand. You like to play hard to get that's ok, he slipped one hand along the back but before Aliza could move he squeezed her on the butt cheek. She made him have it one strike in the face he went blank for a second or so then he saw stars literally. Aliza ran out of the office got her hand bag and quickly exited the building. Tearfully. Abigail rush into the CEO office what did you do to her she damaned. Apparently not enough he said with a sly look she refused me little bitch. She should have hit you harder you damn pig slime. Ahh let her go for the day she'll be all right tomorrow. Abigail went down stair to catch up and talk to Aliza in the parking lot. Later that evening Aliza sat in her room at the nightingale. I na going tell Indian nothing about what happen today cause Lord I know he will go and kill that CEO she was on her knees praying for answers.

It was another night around the camp fire, and the problems and hardships of the times didn't seem to worry them Indian wore his favourite hat tonight a cap with a jaguar in the centre of it. Kingdon was sporting a new hair style. Babeth had braided it into four parts it was the latest trend. Every man had a Ziploc sandwich bag with a portion of grades. The conversation had already started. The Indian man was the mouth piece as usual and they all listened when he talked, he had a way with words. This system called democracy a lie, a system that can never be for filled correctly suppose the majority is corrupted and wrong. To me it's mainly a one sided system. History show many example where the majority was not always right. Basically a government by the people, it should be a system absent from hereditary arbitrary class distinction or privileges. And communism a power which holds one race more superior than another, a force of out right oppression of the inferior, by the ruling majority or a powerful minority regime. An idea of social like behaver and a minimun of so called human rights and freedom. A combination of leadership and dictatorship by a ruling party or majority by oppression or free elections. No different between the two or should I said theres a find line. One man laughs while the other one cries. The beast of revelations will rise up from these political systems or another system that is against the ways of the almighty God. Man rule the world nowadays and scientist tell us we were created by a rock exploding in the universe millions of years ago. The boys laugh Indian went on speaking. Governments and multinational corporations put their heads together and came up with an ideal system that works for them. Rather than just take away and slave. The decided to trick you with lies and oppress you in financial bondage. With things like the cost of living and wages, which has not risen from the time we were babies. There are one two godly people in the banks and in other Babylonian organization, but they are limited. Money is wasted on war and technology and other foolishness, by governments we are oppress by financial control and the idols we worship. The more one has the more one wants. Then having none will become unbearable we'll do anything to obtain and keep these idols. That makes us feel secure. Too much weed is bad for us. And if I ga kill to get this or anything else, then I worshiping the devil. Control your mind. Don't let it control you. Emancipate yourself from economic slavery. The root of all evil is money. Indian stop for a while and Kingdon began to speak, the boys burnt and listened in silence. Ten minutes later it was Indian's turn again. The industrial revolution has contributed to mankind's destruction just as much as wars and disease. The era was an apocalyptic event, some many said one of the epidemics from revelations. By the turn of the 19th century the industrial revolution would help shape the world somehow. Brilliant minds and ideas along with money making solutions. Some by God other by modern day prophets of the time. Many of these dreams profited the world other were just fancy quick money making schemes, grown up games and toys. That did us more harm than good, in centuries to come. Automobiles were invented locomotives, electricity, telephone, motion pictures, industrial equipment was being developed. New uses for steel and iron had been discovered. Oil wells were daged and cotton was reinvented. Technology would be here tomorrow. The used their friends and supported their athletes. A new class of work force was being formed. But the ways of the wicked is as darkness they know not at what they stumble. Men went to work and standardized salaries were re-establish or labour right and zero unemployment would by here at dawn. Scientist went to work for governments and private people. They made bombs planes guns toys appliances. They wrote books and made equipment buildings homes roads bridges tunnels ships, and underwater vessels. They improved on and capitalized made new materials and social tools toothpaste, toothbrush and tooth aches were becoming an every day an every day something. The electric razor was already thought of and shaving cream was getting better. They came up with a new music to say the least the ability was endless and the door was open to the future. The air conditioner and cold water would become a reality in later years. The Indian stuffed high grade into the chalist pipe he looked terrible his eyes couldn't stay open. The whole bunch of them was in a mess.

Off in the distance near the seaside. Marine police Sullivan watch them the sound of his jet-ski went unheard. Several corns were on the grill those would be munchies treat for the night. After taking two big tokes from the chalist the Indian past it to kingdon, and began again with his lessons. His voice sounded Smokey and watery. He never exhaled but visions of fine smoke: could be seen leaving his mouth as he spoked yes Jah he said, thank you. It seems as mankind's journey towards his destiny has involved threats to his surroundings even how we look and smell plays a role in this life. We destroy trees plants flowers to make things like soap, shampoo deodorant, perfumes, toilet paper and other house hole cleaning products. Books for our children's education and other useless official uses. How bout the packaging and containers we get our food in. Cardboard products plastic and glass even the lead pencil we use to write with, like many other unnecessary items has become a multinational business. The world would have soon learn better or they would have not. The very sunglasses and cellophane has become a money making gemek. we must ask ourselves how important some of these things are or how important do we allow them to be. As the chalist came back round the Indian paused for a while looking around at the circle. They were a couple of new faces there again tonight girls and guys just hanging out and whaling up. The crowd was getting bigger and bigger. He took two puffs from the chalist again. Recycling plays a small role that boils down to money again. Humanity gone so far now we don't have a choose but to do it. The making of some of these item affect what I call global boiling. It na warming no more. Still God got everything to last for an appointed time. A civilization which thrives on the economy cheap labour and mas' production has taken the world by storm. Man smart but out of focus instead of making homes for the homeless we build buildings to house office equipment and furniture. The clothes on your back the shoes on your feet the food we eat the very car we drive around in and many others are all made or produced by poorer countries in some cases who get little and nothing compared to what they are sold for.

Wages are an agreement between world wide government and labour establishments and merchants. Now a days we don't only compete with others but with the opposite sex as well. More and more women are being employed in the workforce each day. More than men. On the merit of need or out of greed. Weather to satisfy ones ego, to attack customers or to talk ones business the book will be fulfilled. Jah said, we have gone astray. If men were paid decent wages then women could stay home. And lady don't get offended, but think of it. You could give more family support, cook lunch instead of buying all the time for those who know now to cook. We should be able to work five hours a day and make all ends meet. Work for six dollars an hours and it was valued something here on this island. The employer should pay pension and health plan from his own pocket and give you money for gas and for getting up early and sitting in traffic. What if we could become rich working overtime? And stress was wroth it. Instead of minimum wage maximum pay for all-companies and business wouldn't be short-handed they would be over staffed. Those that are free will be the prisoners and we will overlook the criminals that how it is in this life today. Said Indian.

The robberies continued at gun point the latest one last night was at a lounge restaurant establishment a tourist spot. Jacket and tie premises for the high class. Two mask men enter the place just before mid-night with fire arms demanded cash jewellery or anything with a value from the people in the place. They even took expensive pens and cigarette cases from customers. According to police they were no leads. The radio only broadcasted the light basics of the crime. These robberies in particular were about year old or on going. Who were they people on the street were starting to ask. Cayman had robberies before but these were different. There were bold thought out planed. Who were these guys' career criminals visiting the island taking the opportunity to make some bucks? Or people on work permits and status holders. Etc. this could even be police men on a rampage said the average Jack on the street. They don't make much money in the department. This could even be external inters or people with power and ability to make thing happen. Be it for a number of reasons. Hurt and make the justice department look bad or for the decline or weaken of the financial confidents on the island. Witness said the gunmen robbers spoke Caymanian and in other situations had an accent. I wouldn't put my head or neck on a chopping block and say they Na local Caymanian said an old lady to a group in church. Our boys hungry and dispirit, in need but the good boy they Na killing no body. You ever had a gun pointed in your face miss Jackson said another elderly woman. The streets, or informants didn't reveal anything, so far they could have been pros and made the laws work for them, unless this was the case it would have been very hard to conceal these robberies. Movements Would have had to be noticed by people. After all the island of Grand Cayman was only 72 square miles. Business owners got on TV and radio and started to complain and wrote pieces in the newspaper saying the cops were slacking off on the job by not catching these criminals. For some they were becoming like heroes. Caymanians getting back out of the system that held them down and oppressed and ruined their dreams of a better tomorrow May god be with them said some on the streets. watch dog groups became more involved and blogs were formed on the internet and neighbourhood watches were set up. Another one of those letter came to surface it was found in between the door space inside of the legislative building. Security camera picked up someone with a hood over their head slipping something under the door at 2:45AM the previous day.

It was July 23 2004.seven weeks before hurricane Ivan. Bill woke up in a cold sweat. He had an awful dream of a woman dressed in rags he could have actually smell her scent was like a dead corpse. It was 3 in the afternoon as he looked at the watch on his hand. He had taken a nap after lunch. What the hell was that all about bill said to himself out loud sitting up in bed? He didn't remember much detail, it wasn't a sound sleep. He was in and out of his subconscious. Bill switched on the radio to listen to the 3-0-clock news. There was a knock at the door. Bill looked through the half-moon in the door. Opened it and stepped onto the entry way. It was an old friend of his. How she going bill long time. Am not too bad how things going with you James. Can we go inside sure? I'll get right to the point bill said the man sitting at the kitchen nook. While bill fixed two cups of coffee. I got a good led something might be underwater near the castle. I was flying over that area two days ago and saw it. This aren't no bull shit bill, it was calm and clear. I was supposed to go on a charter that day so I checked the weather report, it was the clearest day in a decade. Visibility was looking like here to that front door from above. Crosby went out the following night after I pin pointed the area on the chart as close as possible. He got a visual of something on the sonar monitor. How far of shore bill asked. 3 miles of more or less, Bill whistled that near the Cayman wall, around the same dept. any way. No bottom down there. You can't get an accurate reading down there. It mighting be right into the abuses, the wall slopes gently. It may be laying on the ridge of the sea floor. You sure this thing down there I know what I saw bill. James places two aerial view photos on the counter top see there, what you make of that. Bill looked them over. There's a possibility but it's still hard to tell. I willing to check this thing out bill. Where do I come in on this James? You got the equipment. The knowledge, and experience bill more than anyone on the island. Alright said bill I'll make you know what going on in a couple of days, let's keep this down you know how it is James yah man sure. Get back to me as quick as you can. The next day bill was at the library.

The man with a long black trench coat sat in a beach chair outside his condominium on the 7 mile beach. He looked strange with it on. It was 90 degrees. A beach hut on concrete columns with artificial coconut leaves protected him from being incinerated. It was a classy place with a pool right next to the beach. A woman with a string up her butt dove into the deep area of the Olympic size swimming pool. He eye balled her while lifting the tall glass of long island ice tea, with a mini rainbow colour umbrella sicking out of it. The straw filled with liquid as he suck in on the beverage. The sand was powdery white as he looked across it. The sun shined bright around the corners of his darkers. Where is that over there he said to the young man a lining beach chairs, with no shirt on. North west point west bay he replied to the strange man who also had toes rings on.

It was his first trip to the island. He had done his homework made the necessary phone calls. He had found out where the subject lived.

Bucking ham had already given the ok to terminate use your own discretion they told him. An exact date and time line will follow. Come back the message on the advance smart cell phone. Everything was set his guns were upstairs waiting to be used. He would enjoy a couple weeks of vacation time before trending to business. After all he just bought a new condo from the money of the last job. From a couple a days ago. And He intented to break the place in right get him some Caymanian hookers and have a ball. He would make this execution different. He would use a small gun to the back of the brain, keeping the subject alive long enough for him to see his 55 custom made magnum, jammed down his mouth breaking his teeth's. Then jaw and pull the trigger. The bullet will travel up his nerves system blowing his brains to smatters the top of his head will have a big hole. It will be a clean job but the crime scene would be a messy one. Isn't life great he wondered and was feeling tipsy? His eyes crossed behind the sunglasses. He wanted something to eat. He sucked away from his glass as another half-naked woman walked the beach with her dog.

Can I see the menu please he said to a waiter.

The news the next morning reported six gang members though to be the leaders, were found dead. The deaths were wide spread amount six districts. Police attended multiple crime scenes. Word had hit the streets about informant talking to police concerning drug canoes. A 25 year old west Bayer was amongst the dead. Police said rival gangs were at war and its tic for tack on the streets as gangs fight for territory. Robberies continue also. Last night a supermarket and clothing store were robbed at gun point and an unknown amount of cash taken. A tour bus doing a night life tour stopped at a red light. When three mask men entered it by force opening the door. The occupants were robbed at gun point. The resent crime spree is bound to hurt us. On an international front said detective bowing in charge of the serious crime unit.

In a ghetto in George Town an area known as the east. An unmarked car was parked in the area of the dreadlocks man yard. The engine kept running as two men talked in the car with tinted windows. What happen to it you said. I don't know someone must have snatched it. I want to know how they got cross my dogs. So you lost the f---ing money is what you saying. I guess so none of my boys took it only I knew where it was. Those animals would have eaten them if they come in my yard, when that gate shut. Then who on the rass did it said Sullivan. What about that bitch of yours think she could have stolen it? She's the only next one. I already beat her half to death since morning she don't know anything you walking on tin line now, am the only reason your alive this long. After that screw up last night. That bus was out of the freaking box you ass hole no one told you to hit that. That was the sheik's very tour bus business. In this business you don't make eras like that. You can't keep your men under control you had to mess the whole thing up for a lousy couple of hundred bucks. Those dam tourist don't have any money on them like that. What if one of those had decided to retaliate and the thing got ugly and you ended up firing a shot and killed someone. That Na going happen again. Dam right it with that. One more full moon and it over, you hear me, then that it. The sheik is a powerful man. Someone going to have pay for this one. The dread locks man started to bicker and curse. Nah, it's my ass in the fire here this time, and I Na going let three naggers destroy my life and all that I work for. I Na going make my career go down the drain by Unna. Get out of my car and you got till tomorrow to find my money or the party over. The dread locks man felt like killing him right then and there, but Sullivan had his 357 resting on his lap with his hand on the handle. I don't believe that shit hole story of yours for one minute. The car drove off powder of dust behind it. The dread locks grabbed tita from her hair and pelted her across the room into a wall blood came from her mouth and nose instantly. Way the money you little whore. I know you move the bag way it is. I Na telling you nothing I going tell the police wha you doing. He kicked her in the chest close to the heart her tiny body was helplessly motionless. Stop she said her voice could barely be heard. Then tell me way it is. It gone I sorry she said, the man went into a fits the baby began to cry he jerk it up out of the crib went to the bathroom holding it upside down he dropped it on the head into the empty cast iron tub. The crying stopped right away. There was little blood but death was from a broken neck. He took the short square machete leaning up next to the room door in his right hand Tita skinny body was starched out on the floor. Where the money and jewellery Tita he yelled, she pointed towards a hole in the wall. But a voice in the man's head said kill her. He took two swings and it was over. Tita he said it was too late. A demonic force control him now. He searched around some more, pushed over a drawer and other furniture. Then he found the jewellery some rings chain bracelets with small bills wraped up in a cloth but the bulk of the money was still missing. He took tita's body and throw on a pile of garbage heap to burn. That was when he noticed the black plastic bag. But it was empty A few burn up bills scattered, the rest of it all was in ashes.

Chas orange laid in bed with his eyes wide open his wife next to him was sound asleep. The bedroom was dark but a dim light shined in the hall way and could be seen at the bottom of the master bed room door. It would all be over soon. That Indian will get what he deserves. And in the same place where his father was in hell. If only he had stayed out of the communist party business he could live. But now it was too late for that. He had bloody well ruined their opportunity back in 96. It took the party four years to bounce back and reestablished their good names. But it had meant a substantial amount of revenue lost for them. With only a few seats in Cayman and none in Europe. Arrests came from all directions, followed by sanctions and more arrests. And unsolved murders of politicians' lawyers bankers and informants. The Democratic Party won the elections and the majority of the seats that year and chewed the communize party apart piece by piece and spited then out. Men who were supposed to be honest spent time behind bars and political and personal lives were destroyed. Some of the best private eyes from around the world were paid top dollar to investigate. But everything was sealed tight and well protected. Until now that is. Premier Orange had gotten the report just recently. The enemy in London was history and now it was the Indian's turn. After the nice agent was finish with him, he would dispose of the dirty cop too. Scott land yard was questioning the integrity of the department. The corruption could not hide. England couldn't have it, compare to the outside world they looked like hypocrites. It'll will be over with soon he said in his mind as he rolled on his side pushing his head comfortable into the fluffy polow his dreams were sweet that night.

The Indian man sat under his house floor sharpening several knifes, he had them hidden here and there and around and about the property. They were still in their places safe and sound no one had touch them whoever it was snooping around his yard hadn't found them. His woman Aliza was having some problem at work but it was not nothing that she could not handle she told him. He cleaned a black revolver and loaded it with hollow point bullets Indian had two visitors that day a real estate person yelled from the road and asked if he ever wanted to sell he would pay top dollar for the place. The Indian man was stink of weed and red eyed behind the shades on his face. But a bush fire was burning so there was no way of telling what was what. The realtor Left a Remax business card with his smiling face on it. In the late afternoon the India fellow was still in his yard with a machete in his hand. A bunch of Plantain hanged on every (sucker) tree. He would sell at the market tomorrow He had already picked avocados. And papayas and they gathered under the floor next to him. Later in the evening when the sun cooled he would dig up the sweet potatoes. He notice a parrot he never seen before around the place this one wasn't eating the ackees or mangoes only following him around. This one was bigger than the other and would land on the ground, over the hole that bill and him had dig the top of it was covered up all the same. They don't usually pitch on the ground thought indian. He had reserved a note from the butcher one of Tom Spings old friend, that bastard had killed some ducks and a load of birds and dump them on my door steps. He was lucky he never came cross when. I was here especially with my woman. I never had nothing to with him and Thomas business, he said but I will settle up with him all the same. The date had been set. Indian talk to the other woman in his life that day. I'll come to see you in a few days he told his mother over the phone. He would meet with Aliza later at the nightingale. There was another ball game tomorrow nightingale vs east end football club under 16. He remember suddenly. Because he needed to be there.

The next visitor of the day came in a rent-a car drove half way down the dirt road and stopped some distance before the wooden gate The person stayed in the car and asked the Indian man who walked over for direction to the botanic park. Down the highway about 3 miles of to the right you should see a big sign. Indian noticed the man wore a black trench coat and rings were on all ten of his fingers. He had a diamond dot nose ring and there were two ear-rings to his left ear. He had on a hat but he was bald completely. His eye brows were thick and blond. He spoke with a deep hollow out voice. Indian gut feeling told him something but he kept it to himself. Be careful was the last thing the voice said over the phone to him. A.C.A. rule number one never let your guard down not even in church.

The water front George Town would be Jingling in a while. Bad weather and no tourist made it look like a gosh town earlier on that week. But today they were four cruise ships in the Harbour. And those in the tourism sector would be able to feed their family this week, regardless.

A man had just finish dry wiping his taxi with a rag. He was the first one in line at the cruise ship embarkation port terminal. The driver lend on his taxi smoking a cigarette. He had been in line from 5AM and so far not even gotten one lousy fare. The government ga do better than this, we taxi pay dearly for a license and can't make any money. There too many taxi on the road. There's too many foreigners driving taxi he said to other cab driver. I ga call Mr. Premier Orange later and make him know what happening out here. The taxi dispatcher came over with a crowd of enthusiastic tourist/ one man was in a wheel chair and the woman push him. They got inside and the sliding door of the van closed. Where to ask the driver as he was buckling up behind the wheel. We'll like to go to the Smith's cover. Said one of them. Way you from asked the driver being nice and conversationally. We're all new Yorkers actually. Yan I wasn't expecting this day said the driver not saying another word. He had a problem one time with one of those new Yorkers a few years back. They almost came to blows and kicks he nearly lost his taxi license. New Yorkers according to him didn't act like regular tourist, they knew and talked too much and were better than anyone else they felt. High class or low class he didn't want anything to do with them. It come in like they had become worst after the terrorist attack. He had already made a promise that no more new Yorkers was setting foot in his taxi, and this morning he had a bus load of them. I Na getting out and opening no door for them when we stop, handicap or not he said to himself. The taxi pulled into a nice beach. How much is it said a tourist by the driver side window. That 30 US for the five of you. 30 us asked the tourist? look here star I Na trying over charge you that how much it is. I could show you the taxi fear book if you want. We don't used meters here. That won't be necessary I believe you, he handed the taxi the bills. The car drove off cheap new Yorkers and some of them were Christians too, he counted the money no tips from them he got on radio and told the other taxis about the whole ordeal.

It was 10.07 mask gunmen entered the bank of America in the village down town George Town. Al right everybody get on the ground this is a hold-up A minute later a car mingles into the mid-morning commuters. There was no traffic to talk about. Almost 15 minutes later police and medics moved around in the bank talking and tending to victims or witness. A fat woman with heart trouble was still laying on the floor. Detectives were at the crime scene.

They were in and out in less than a minute sir said Philipps to bowing they clean out the safe and the five tellers. The manager saw them coming in and hit the silent alarm but it didn't went off down at the station. They disabled it said bowing, how did they get into the safe. So fast it a computerized locking system I spoke to one of the technical team boy. They still working out the exact details. It happen fast the security guard said, the car drove up on the side walk three men jumped out with what looked like white shirts covering their faces. Pushed the door open before he could react. One hit him in the head with the hand gun, after he refused to go down on the floor. The guys wore gloves so no prints will be find I suspect. Any make on the vehicle. Station wagon dark blue that all everybody was on the ground all the peps looked alike to them, no one saw much. Scared to death half of them. The cops continued to evaluate the crime scene. You think it our guys. Of course it is them. Sullivan said he was at the location until lights out last night. He was just going on duty when he heard about this. He knows we watching him, must have gave Sullivan the double, faked it till he figure Sullivan went then, they met up somewhere. Then pulled of this Job they spent the night at"the dreadlocks man yard, getting high shit we should have saw this coming they been working there way up to a bigger Job. They got smarter and more ambitious. Across town another bank robbery reported said the police radio, where said bowing into the mouth piece. Bank of Butterfield north sound road came the reply. What the hell said bowing? The two detectives ran to their cars. 3 minutes later the robbers were long gone. It's the same MO, same car, and same three guys. Make that four when you included the get away driver. They fired a shot this time into the wall. I'll have ballistics take a look at it, said bowing. They hit the safe and the tellers same as other bank. Two in one day said bowing to Philipps.

At a busy intersection three men with back packs stepped out of a car. A man in a wheel chair rolls out of an internet café. That was just 200 feet away from the bank of America that had just been robbed in the village. They had been over a dozen phone calls from people reporting robbery in process but only two had finally gotten through.

Most went to his computer and he had delayed the Cayman Islands royal police response time. And hatch a safe combination on the computer. It took the cops 7 minutes after the fact to arrive on the scene. He had even diverted patrol cars with in the one mile block. And a busy tourist day as it was didn't make it any easier for the police to get about. The computer master had temperedly blinded the security cameras during the robbery. In another part of the city a dark blue car pulls into an underground garage licensed plate were taken off to be returned and sold to tourist at a souvenir shop. And a new paint job was given to the car.

A rabbi a nun and a perfectly able man in a wheel chair, along with a common looking tourist waited in line at the terminal to go back on the cruise ship. Each one wore a back pack so did many others? Sir can you please help us onto the ferry said the nun pushing the wheel chair. To the port authority officer our father needs to take his medication the same time every day the prescription is on board the ship and am afraid he can't stay in line much longer, no problem you're all together. Yes sir. Right this way. They were on the ferry headed for the carnival cruise liner. The island getting a bit smaller behind them. When a Simon tenuous text came over there cell phones. Mission accomplished. It said.

A small airplane took off from owing Roberts airport with 3 men Inside it. James Harlot Bill Patterson and a man from west bay by the name Corby ebanks. It was 5am on the clock in the cock pit seconds later they were air born. The plane made a sharp dip to the south pasted through some clouds minutes later they over the south east coast. There's Pedro St. James castle, said Crosby who sat opposite the pilot, it was in this area I saw my baby harlot said sipping a cup of coffee. She Na a gosh she's a sleeping beauty. It will be clear for a few more days. Erectly when the sun rises we should get a good view. The plane flied towards the east, we'll circle back in a little while James said. James Harlot was a Caymanian American white man. He had been a commercial pilot for Cayman airways for donkey years before he retired. He was a seasoned pilot. Sprayed pesticides from a mosquito plane in his spear time. Also an ex air force pilot fought on missions but had been honorably discharged after an air raid carried out by him. Killed innocent vetetanize citizen in a town in the mountains. He had gotten orders but the connection was mixed up. He was a little shell shock and had a plastic leg. Back in the 70's he was shot down by the mafia while doing surveillance work for the C.I.A. now a days he owned and operated a small airline charter company with two sesna 200 he trained pilots. The plane circle the island once, below they could see fishermen in a boat. The left wing went down and the right one came up. The plane turned and headed back south east. The sun was just starting to show its tip on the horizon. The execution plan would have to be in the day under the sun said James still speaking. I agree with that answered bill. It will be less suspicion and great whites are more vicious at night, anyway he sounded a serious laugh. They talked some more on the details of the plan. The morning was clear and becoming from a quarter mile up in the air they could see the ocean floor. The plane dipped to the side once against as they headed south directly. And come upon Purple Ocean they passed over couple white holes we only going make two more circles. We don't want to risk someone seeing and started wondering why we circling the area. James said. The plane took a 180 and came back to the same vicinity. I know it was in this area said the pilot. Ahh there she is see that down there what looks like a cave. All eyes were out the windows. It was the mare image of a pirate ship, covered with sea grass and erosion it was black from the air, and mossy green. It was almost hidden to the naked eye, only someone who knew what they were looking for or at would know the different. Bill said how come no one seen her all these centuries only god knows, said Crosby. She was just meant for us it could have moved from her original grave site, by hurricanes remember that earth quake we had out at see a couple days ago it was small but it could have been enough to move her out of the ocean floor. The plane dove down until it was about 20 feet more or less above the ocean. Bill slide open a small window in the cabin of the plane. And dropped a yellow device that was attached to a marine bouy, it was a high tee gps system. Hope that's enough rope for the weigh to find the bottom. James pulled the sesna 200 up from her glide. Now on to the other business three ways equal share and everybody split the cost of overheads including me going overseas and turning it into paper, if we find anything. I'll put money up front for the voyage. I got a military friend with connections who knows how to do his thing. James fixed his bad leg into another position. What's his cut asked Bill. Ten maybe twenty percent he got to pay people on that end. Shit said Crosby we do all the hard work, and they do the walk. We like drug dealers cleaning money said Bill only we're treasure hunters. How will we know the worth of the take? Asked Crosby, gold coins we can research and figure out the value on them ourselves. Gold bars test the carrots and weigh and multiple that by market price, even little less what said Crosby to James. Investors got to make a profit that right explained bill that how this shit works. Bear in mind it may be a big loom sum all the same. We have to get rid of it fast. Remember this treasure hunting thing prohibited in Cayman and most places in the world now only big time glorified corporations etc. get permits to search for gold and other precious treasures with about 80 percent of the take going back to the state. And the fees attached to these license are far beyond what the regular Joe treasure hunter can pay. It maybe three miles out to sea but it's still in Cayman waters and for the state, even if we don't fund any treasure it's.

Consider and agrological find and they can prohibit us from diving there. We'll take the credit for locating the thing all the same. I can't feed my family on praises said Crosby. Remember what happen to the Johnson brothers point out Bill. They Na get out of jail yet. They dived the wreck of the ten sails for years and two years ago they found a medallion worth nearly 100,000.

By the time the media got wind of it, government soldiers came and confiscated the coin boat dive equipment and all. According to Law, any finding of an agrological nature on land or sea is crown procession. But the Johnsons good boys I know said Bill. They serving five years up in northward you think the Judge worried bout anybody. We can't make that mistake I not even dealing with those jewelers or gold people around here said James. They just middle men and scalpers for the bigger ones up north or where ever. Now if we find any rubies diamonds or Jem stone it will be difficult to price them so we'll just how to work out a price that makes us happy with the dealer.

Bear in mind this could but billions of dollars we're talking about so we will still need the cleaners. Stone are less complicated, they can always claim there getting them Africa. And the Jeweler can cut them up himself without going through the federal exchange. He can sell them right in his shop. It's even easier in places like Holland, London, Switzerland, to sell gold and thing. You could have sold it to Cuba up until the 70's. But you can't take any chance over there now. The CIA still cobert down there believe it or not ever since the Bay of Pigs affairs. What about after it clean said bill. In that case it's put into a bank account legitimately as money you inherited from your rich dead uncle or grandfather, nice and sweet. No one would question the transaction even if you don't have a rich dead uncle.

The paper work will stick, in some cases the same people your in business with owns the banks one way or another or share holders.

By mid afternoon the doctor was bored, the only excitement he had all day was pushing a camera scope the size of a finger up into some old guy testing for prostate cancer. Last night he paid a thousand dollar to a man for a heart and kidney of a teenage girl. The child's body was useless to him. He had taped it up and card board boxed it, put a fragile sticker on it and sent it to fellow doctors and scientist at the lavatory on Volcano Island. Human organs were big money and he had become wealthy from it. He had already found a buyer not on the black market but in Tokyo legally where there was a high demand. He would make fifty times more profit on it. The secutary was gone for the day. At 4pm the small doctor's office had a closed sign in the glass door. The doctor walked to his car with a small ice box sealed and packaged off.

What's the latest with suspects asked bowing to Sullivan at a Talaya fast food stand. They got into the car with his Styrofoam box of food. They clean their tracks but I still see some funny movements. Like what said bowing. After everybody left last night the Indian kept walking over by the hole he diged some time back and I notice he got it cover back up now. That's way part he got the bank money buried and stash away. I overheard him talking on the phone to some guy. Telling him in a next couple of weeks he can come by and get his money. That would be good if we can tap his phone but no judge will allow that. I getting a search warrant though for the property. By them gathering there every night and smoking weed and doing other drugs. The legal team has advised me already this warrant could fall under the public Newson's law. We go in shake em up arrest them see what we find. I think this may have been there last job for a while. Said bowing continuing to speak. That's 20 million they got away with this far in the bank jobs alone. Most of it Cayman dollars and u.s. The banks not even going to claim on their insurance. They just right it off on the dormant accounts. So it no lost to them. No insurance investigators and police department isn't pushing it. It there money according to the attorney general. But then again it really wasn't. Bowing continued to eat his food it was 10a.m. I need another coffee he said. His cell phone rang and he looked at the number but didn't answer it. Another thing boss they keep referring to one another by Sam this and sam that, you mean like coding or something said Philipps. Yah it the wariest thing man. Sam like son of Sam the serial killer, holy sit said bowing this a damn cult we dealing with. He bite down into his hamburger. The phone rang again, the same number as before it was his wife. Mmm this woman starting to become a pain in ass now. He made it rung out. He needed a drink before he choked. These hamburgers good said Philipps that Italian cooking like Cayman style. Bowing took a bottle from under his seat and put it in his mouth. Philipps and Sullivan looked at bowing as he took another drink what said bowing the day almost gone.

3. Am. Two day later a schooner sails out of the frank sound bight on the north sound side of the island. Captain bill took the gun from his pant waste and pit into the cabinet drawer under the wheel and locked it. James Harlot wasn't a boat man and they needed him on land. As part of the plan Crosby and the Indian man came along. They had just cleared the channel and was on open water. Bill had checked the forecast weather was good for the next 72 hours. Crosby enter the wheel house with a spliff in his mouth and a hot Heineken in his hand. Sweet weather cap he said. I see that Indian don't talk much, who he is bill. He with me he cool that all you need to know. I don't trust him said Crosby. You Na ga worry about it. Na that you need to know but my share, splits with him. Crosby said nothing else he continued to pull on his ganja cigarette looking out into the horizon. He broke out in a dog cuff that went on for a while. When it was over he said with a daze in his eyes and a big smile on his face I ga give this shit up. He slogged down the hot beer in four swallows. Breakfast will be ready in a hours cap he said and left the wheel room. The Indian stood on the stern with a hand line and a feather hook on it tow fishing. Around 5:45am the sun came up over the Caribbean Sea. The energy had drop anchor and the three men sat around the table in the galley eating fried Jacks and flatters, with strong coffee. I bought her from a police option inthe 80's. A Canadian man stole it from some rich guy in Nova Scotia sailed around the world and ended up in Cayman bill said. He was on the most wanted list for five years. Got a job at one of the newspapers as an editor. Worked there for two years before the Canadian police caught up

with him. He had the boat anchored off and hidden up in one of those swamp between some red mangroves. He was living board her with two Doberman pitchers ride a bicycle to work every day.

The hull was damage and something was wrong with the engine it would cost too much to tow it back to Canada.so it was given to the Cayman customs. After the trial it was option off. She cost me some money but I fixed her up and gave her the name. When they were done eating captain bill laid down the orders for the day. He didn't paid much attention to the dream he had, it was the same one as the night before that James had come to his door. According to the depth definer it was over three thousand feet of water under them. The schooner was anchored several hundred feet away from the site of the actual wreck. The captain was playing it safe. An hour later all three men were in the ocean in wet suits. They geared with two oxygen tanks, knives, and high-tech under water pistols. A mesh dive sack floated with them on the water top as they checked their dive gear. Indian broke the tension and said, everything seem too easy on this one bill and I don't trust that spandard over there one bit referring to Crosby. Don't worry I worked with these guys before everything good, sleeping beauty is just waiting for us to be salvage and we are the chosen one to do it replied bill with a light smile. Hope your right buddy, watch your back bill said Indian as he pulled his mask over his face and dived down. A few seconds later they were looking at the four corners of the ocean. The sea bed was nowhere to be seen no bottom in site. Bill carried the underwater gold detector and a small camera was fixed to his side along with a small device to monitor body conditions and sea depth. All three men had this instrument that could keep them from getting the bends. It read heart rate and lung functions under water. It was clear as crystal under neat the men dove quarternated for about 25 minutes then they came upon the image of the wreck. This was a sir valance dive more than anything at this point. Only half way down the depth of the ocean and bill could see the terrain and contour of the sea floor where the ship slept and died hundreds of years earlier. The wreck was sitting on an angle slope with the bow facing up hill. She was less than a hundred feet in length as far as bill could tell at first glance. He could barely make out the image of a canon covered in moss the wreck was split in two from bow to stern. Bill moved the camera around that was at his side snapping pictures.

Let's go a little deeper down bill said talking in his mask, it was the latest in underwater dive gear they could each hear one another speaking. They dived horizontal across the underwater mountain slope. Passing giant sea fans and small fishes, over an edge rocks and caves could be seen and patches of coral. As they got closer to the wreck the sea bed change into a sandy white muddy bottom. But two hours had went by quickly and they were running low on air they headed back to the energy. The boat had moved some 300 feet and was drifting slowly eastward. Seas had become choppy and there was a crazy wind blowing from all direction. Holly shit said bill as he saw what had happen. Indian removed the tanks and tied a floatation device unto them he swam hard towards the energy bill and Corby followed behind him. Ten minutes later after none stop swimming the Indian was on the bow of energy waving to the others. That anchor was well hooked said Corby that's right we both checked it said Indian before we left. That's a mystery they said that after noon as they recuperated on the back deck of the schooner. As far as logic is concern she broke away when this weather came in. these little seas couldn't make that anchor slip the rope would have had to pop first. Bill claimed besides it supposed to be good weather for the next three days. Yah this Mother Nature this time added Corby with the other two shaking their head in agreement.-the marijuana cigarette would not be far away and each of them held a spiff in their hand. Laying back on the deck listening to some music on the radio. Later that evening Indian was preparing the supper, fried barracuda and fried green plantains he would steam the barracudas head just in case for a night cap if they felt like eating something. He was also talking to Aliza on the phone. The nightingale football team had won their fourth game in a row only couple more wins to the semifinals Aliza bragged to Indian. The energy had moved closer to shore and away from the wreck this was a part of the plan. The conversation between captain bill and James harlot wasn't hidden the door to the wheel house was open. The men ate and drank beer, we only got one anchor left said the captain as they talked about the dive tomorrow. The weather looks like its back to normal now. Maps and other papers were spread out on the galley table. Bill was pointing at a picture in a book in front of him. That her right there the American princess. Indian and Corby looked at the image. Bill got a bottle of whiskey from the lockers and began to tell the story from across the room. It was 1860 the American civil war was on its way things were looking good for the confederate army. General Tucker was in charge of the battles near the coast line of the southern states. The confederates had just finish building the ship for their army that would eventually go on to win the war. Blacks and freed slaves fought for the Yankees but the southerners refused to let slaves fight in the war. However with the table turning and they might end up losing the war general tucker convince the states under the confederates to import blacks from Haiti and Jamaica who were mostly free men leaving southern slaves under their masters. General Tucker soon cut a deal with the governors of Haiti and Jamaica to buy freed black and slaves from Jamaica. For every two slaves bought the British governor gave the confederates army one slave as a good will jester to help the south win the war they supported their regime. And in return the south would give back one North American state to England, then together the two counties would monopolize the slave system around the world. Those free men from Haiti were simply gather up and tricked some of them coming from prison preparing to go to hell. In the mid-1800s Cayman was the leaders in ship building in the Caribbean. Even though materials like iron mahogany was limited schooners of all sizes were made right there in hocks sty bay. Whatever materials they couldn't find here it was imported. And that baby you see down there the American princess was built in George Town Grand Cayman. She was a sailing vessel but a steam engine was install for back up this gave her an edge over the other ships of the time. She was captain by an American admiral general tuckers nephew. Now to cut out the in-betweens said bill basically what happen she made one trip successfully with a 1,000 slaves from Jamaica and 500 men from Haiti. On her second trip she was to do the same thing and return back to Mississippi only she sank just of the shores of Jamaica. What made her sink asked Corby. There was a fire on board a rebellion and slaves brought her down according to the history books bill replied. The slaves who could not swim found something to float on and got away, with some of those who managed to swim. Dead bodies were in the sea for weeks. So wha the real story is said Indian. Well said bill according to myth there was a replica made of the American princess. Instead of one there was two that one was built in NEW Orleans. She was a lighter faster ship made from light weight iron of the time period bigger sails, engine more durable.

If that was a wooden ship down there it wouldn't be anything left of her by now. One made her maidenvoyage to the Caribbean and the other was loaded with gold from the Alamo destined to Italy. You see if the south lost the war they wouldn't lose their wealth. Six months later the replica returned with a ship load of swords and guns, ammunition. And 300 gypsy women prostitutes for the southern army or anyone who wanted to buy them. Over forty percent of the Alamos gold was missing the same amount the confederates had spent on the war so far. They could have taken it all said Corby. True but they were dignified soldiers not mercenaries it was the American people gold not theirs the leaders still had patronisum love for the south and all that. It was not really a civil war more like a political reform both sides had money and poverty only they didn't see eye to eye when it came to governing the states.

American was the freest place on the planet at the time the rest of the world was on unstable. If you had to choose where to live back then between Europe, Asia, and the Caribbean or central and South American you would have chosen North American. So the gold was an insurance for their children was how they justified it. Now this is where she gets tricky said bill on her second voyage back to Italy she never makes it. That is where the myth ends. No one knows what happen to her. Well if that is the American princess wha she doing down there. Said Indian. And which one is it the replica or the original. Am coming to that said bill. The original American princess lays on the sea floor of the coast of Negril Jamaica that has been proven bill continued. A book was written years later by an old gypsy about the American princess. Documented history states it was only one ship, but I'll get back to that in a little bit. Here's what I think happen I can now agree with the mythical tale giving this new discovery. The admiral be traded the south then eventually the yanks. A deal was cut with the Yankees on his second venture to Italy he carried extra gold bars that the confederates knew nothing about. He made to Italy but landed at a secret location he also made it back with arms and ammo that would have gone to the south went to the union army. Why did he switch bill asking himself the obvious question. For protection in hopes that the union would defeat his now enemies. The sono bitch was stealing gold from the first trip. The southern army realized what he was doing they were going to hang him after he completed the final mission, but the admiral heard of their plan. Even if he ran he would be a hunted man with his enemies still living. When he pulled out of the Harbour that faithful night never to be seen again by the confederates. The two sides would become his enemy before the war was over. Even president Lincoln would have him shot for committing treason on the united states of American and for stealing gold. The admiral and his crew of ten men disappeared along with four gypsy whores that lived on the ship. But not before stealing back the gold from the union army that was kept in a ware house at a port in Boston guarded only by three soldiers. Some say the American princess sank off Cuba's south wall some of the deepest water in the world a month later. The admiral loaded the gold unto another ship tied up the gypsies and shot several holes into the bottom of the princess letting her sink gracefully. The impact cracked her from bow to stern as she hit the ocean floor the mask broke sending her farther down the drop off. Bill put an empty glass of whiskey on the galley table. Then started eating barracuda the flesh from the barra head separated from the bones and the texture of the meat was almost jello like. The conversation paused for a few seconds as there mouth became full. After I was finish at the library the other day, bill continued I visited a gentlemen from south sound whose great great great grandfather was a settler from the American princess. The coverts family French Americans he showed me a picture, painting actually of the American princess with one of his ancestor's and Admiral Johnson. He even had a confederate sword mounted to his living room wall. Said it belonged to his ancient grandfather who was a solider in the southern army. It had handed down from generation to generation over the years and the history told along with it. Admiral Johnson believed the gypsy women brought him bad luck so he killed them to clear himself from the spell. Three of them freed themselves from the knots and swam ashore according to the soldiers who saw them from the other ship. The other one died on the American princess with a baby said to be for Johnson himself. When the reach their destination the men parted ways each with their share of gold. But by now it was only to be split five ways the rest of the soldiers were shot and throwed over board for the sharks. This was the story that the man heard over the years. As for Admiral Johnson he died decades later in the neither lands a very rich man. His family was one of the wealthiest in the whole of Holland. His daughters married into royalty.

I believe the old man's story said bill even though he's a drunk. The old girl might be hunted said bill if you believe in that crap. Bill pour more whiskey into his glass he drank it straight on the rocks. Now there's no record of the replica ever existing and the only image I know bout the painting in the old man's cottage. It was part of the south strategy while the yanks were watching number one number two was long gone. On one mission 300 soldiers were drop off on a beach in North Carolina when it was sopose to be dock up in Texas. The civil war was a dark time in American history and neither side admitted of any knowledge of the replica of the American princess. So no books or anything were ever written, there's only the myth told by folk tales. The two ships were identical to look at only the replica was iron and had a southern code of arms with two swords forming an x in the middle of the southern flag it was engraved onto a steel plate made by some of the best black smiths in the business back then. Right under the ships names. I took some pictures of the wreck when I was down there and after looking them over I saw it on the bow of the wreck. I could hardly make it out at first with all that sea moss over it but the code of arm is there. When you put the story together she didn't sink of Cuba, but right out here instead right where she lays now. Ship wreck hunters search for her for years around Cuba with no avail. Legends only tell you half the story sometimes we have to be careful down there tomorrow bill told the men. If anything happens to any of us it would be complacated to explain to the authorities what we were doing out here. The finished eating Barra heads and salt-tines crackers then turn in for the night.

Tita mcfield and her baby was reported missing by her family her boyfriend say she went for a walk last evening and never returned home. A man's headless body was also found in a swamp in the George Town area by public works department workers excavating a road. Was the high light of the six o clock news? A man had also been shot in the stomach during a robbery of an ice cream van. In a separate incident a man is in critical condition at the hospital after being shot in the head coworkers said the employer refuse to hand over cash to a lone gun man with a ski mask who robbed his jerk food stand. This thing getting away on us we have to get this under control they starting to kill people now. Said bowing in the coffee room at central police headquarters. This one makes it 13 in total said a woman detective throwing a letter down on the table. Where did this come from asked bowing? An old lady said some guy with a hood gave it to her yesterday ask her to bring it in to the station. Shit he's sending letters directly to us now said bowing he began to read it.

It shall come to pass in that day prophets shall became framers. The heads there of judge for reward and priests divine for money. Every man shall sit under his vine and under his fig tree. And none shall make him afraid. No more will they support war. For all people shall walk in the name of his god. Night shall be on him who make my people err. There will be no more smooth Sayers etc. etc. etc..

Who does this guy think he is Jesus or something said bowing? He is calling us everything accept monkeys this time I don't know what to make of it cry or laugh. 13 is satanic number said an officer in uniform from across the hall. Oh please said bowing passing the letter around it just comes before 14. Bowing walked into his office where Sullivan awaited him. Everything up in the swamp dead haven't seen the Indian the last couple days. Said Sullivan, Remember that old schooner in the bight it gone. It belongs to bill Patterson it come in like they had it diseased made it look a peace of shit they up to something boss.

A donzi speed boat speeds out of the Chinese yacht club headed to Volcano Island. Three days had passed since the bank robberies. Snow man smoked a cigar john nose his second stood next to him at the wheel conceal. Three silver hard case suit cases fill with cash was down in the sleeping area below. It would be deposited into the sheik a.i.g bank account then clean by them. The tourist had carried some in nap sacks back to the states the rest of their share would be wire and put into personal accounts. The money would bounce around from bank to bank then disappear in the jungle of monetary finance. Snow man had been the driver and the master mind behind the job.

The British customs found 300 kilos on British airways flight last night coming from Cayman said snow man. Even though they can't tie us to anything, after they test it and it comes back 70 percent pure most likely they'll figure out that it's a big operation and send in Scott land yard. The rest got through but Sullivan and his guys mess up. Their guy for some reason didn't work his normal shift at customs that night. It isn't easy getting stuff through Heathrow international. I know all about it said nose the sheik filled me in this morning. Really said snow man this morning ahh, I only knew about it 30 minutes ago. Yeah a lot of things been going wrong lately first his tour bus now this people leaving his organization. Nose pulled out his pistol and jammed it into snow man's side chest sorry it's got to end like this. What are you talking about nose what you doing? The sheik says no body leaves him he told me to get rid of you. You don't have to follow his orders said snow man, both of us can walk out of this. Nose took snow man's gun from his waist and throw it into the sea. Then he took his hand and push the trolled up stopping the boat. Not a soul to see anything only mangroves could be seen towards land. You can jump over board and I'll tell the sheik I killed you that's the best I can do snow. What about my money snow man asked? Now if your dead you would need it now will you came the reply. And my guys in Miami what about them. Nothing for them neither snow they'll remember how you double cross them on this deal. I use to think the sheik was and honorable man this doesn't have to end this way nose.

Nose walked him to the edge of the boat at gun point the gun was next to snow man temple. At least let me take my booths of so I can have a fighting chance to swim. Snow man took of one booth slowly and reach for the other pulling out quickly a short nozzle 38. John nose never saw it coming never stood a chance seconds later two slugs was in head. He fell overboard with his eyes still open soon to become shark bait. Snow man put back on his booth then grab a small brief case with money that was deck and pelted it into the ocean. Share that the sheik you ungrateful son of a bitch tell him to kiss my ass I quit. The donzi bow raised at full trolled and it speeded away, off to an unknown destination.

Hours later bucks' boy was in the right place at the right time he had lean his lesson not to take lobster or conch from Marine Park. His poor father was still in prison doing time. Jr was fishing in the mangroves all that day without luck of catching any fish. Then he notice the medium size brief case floating nearby. He had an idea of what it may have been but it was even better than that to his amazement it was full of cash.

The bible was open on the bed in the small cabin to a page in the book of psalms the Indian was reading that morning. Before breakfast he stood on deck listening to the ocean. He spoke back to it saying something in the caymanaki langue. The weather was as smooth as glass the captain had moved the ship closer to the wreck once more. He called for Corby to drop the anchor as they were over the blue hole. The plan was for Indian to stay aboard the energy today while bill and Corby made the dive. Ten minutes after they were overboard Corby spit into his mask cleaning it before putting the strap on his head he kiss the gold cross that was on the chain around his neck. He wore it for luck and protection. How you know they didn't take all the gold with them corby asked bill. I don't but am checking this gosh out any way, they were in a hurry to get off the ship may have been a chaotic situation left our share behind am hoping. Corby body disappeared into the clear blue water then only bubbles could be seen from the two men. At least it wasn't 6000 feet of the drop off bill thought to himself as he descended. Corby was already some distance below him bill looked at the instrument on his side it read 2800 feet when he was almost at the bottom. Corby moved like a fish under the water he turned on the flash light put the spear gun in front of him as he dove into an open hatch on the bow of the wreck.

Bill searched around the wreck with the underwater gold detector he followed his instinct and moved away from the wreck a little ways off. He had gotten a reading the day before but didn't bother to mention it to the fellers. He dived slowly up the gentle slope the old wreck of the American princess laid perpendicular to the under ground mountain. On the up slope the bow pointed towards land and the stern downhill to the drop off, it was dark down in the abyss and no end could be seen.

Bill was about a 100 feet up the hill when the detector light up he took something from sack that looked like a hand held blow dryer and began to clean away the muddy sand.

Corby came out of hatch looked around for bill saw him and dived over to where he was. Bill said I have a signal here that sounds good said Corby I want to check out one part of the ship I'll be back soon he told bill who shown him a thumbs up. Bill continued to blow away the sand Corby entered a large hole in the side of the ship.

It wasn't too long after that bill come across what he was looking for, a couple of stray gold coins. It was unbelievable bill's heart started to beat faster as more and more gold coins appeared glisten in the sea muck. He looked around for Corby but saw no sign of him. Bill collected the coins putting them into a small cloth pouch. He drove a stake with a red flag on it into the mud to make the spot.

Indian reeled in the fishing rods he had put out that morning it was most likely a sham incase other boats came by they would seem to be legitimately fishing. It had gotten rough over the course of an hour and a half and some big swells were rocking the energy by now. He saw that he had manage to hook a good size snapper on number two rod but he remove the hook and throw it back into the sea. It swam away rapidly as it hit the water. Indian made his way to the wheel house where bill's cell phone had been ringing like crazy. But before he could answer it James hurler voice came over the single side band radio. Energy energy captain bill you out there over. Bad weather coming repeat bad weather coming. Indian picked up the receiver, the captain is unavailable at the moment code red message received will notify the captain over and out.

Corby explored the wreck he was in what he though was the captain's cabin and saw some art fax. He shined the flash light into a dark area dived over to it. There was an iron draw turned over on its side he push his hand in and felt around for anything. Seconds later he screamed as blood filled his vision he no longer felt his hand it was gone. The spear gun hit the wreck's bottom and a Congo reel swam away fast with a hand in its mouth. The flash light in Corby's another hand dropped his heart was beating fast and he was losing a lot of blood.

It was hard not to panic but Corby was an experience diver what seemed like minutes was only 20 seconds later was when bill saw him in distress coming out of the wreck. Bill tied the string from the dive bag around the lower part of the arm. And headed to day light they were on the surface minutes later any faster would have blown apart their lungs.

Bill pull off his mask and shouted for help a trail of blood surrounded them.

The boat was a good ways off Indian saw them and lift anchor then maneuver the ship to their rescue.

Once on deck Indian brought the first aid kit bill gave Corby an injections of morphine. He had lost a lot of blood and was unconscious bill tighten the sting to minimize the hemorrhwging. Bill throw coffee onto the wound then wrapped it in bandage. They carried Corby inside and laid him down on the bed. As soon as he stops bleeding I can stich him up bill told Indian I can't give him any more morphine right now that might kill him. Bill started swearing I told the man musting wonder off but he wouldn't listen to me. It's down their, I had my mouth right on it look at these coins he said pulling the dive bag from his side.

James called said Indian bad weather headed this way.

Dam it said bill if we miss this opportunity now we want get another chance.

Indian stood at the compressor he filled two tanks with oxygen, he switched on the wench on the back deck and hooked a mesh bag on to a cable and eased it down into the ocean.

With bill exhausted Indian geared up for the death mission.

Down there well and scented up with all that blood said bill. Indian managed a smile put a knife between his teeth and pitched into the ocean. He pulled his gaggles down over his face just a second before he hit the water. Underneath was still milky with blood he pasted the cable line on the way down moving faster than usual it was not until he was almost half way down before he started to breath through the venter later on the dive tank. Indian saw the code of arms on the bow of the wreck as he passed by it. He headed towards the red flag of in the sea floor of in the distance. In the whirl of excitement he remain cam there were a lot of things to consider and the odds were stack against them. He took the small vacuum from the dive tray that was attached to the cable line.

More gold coins surfaced when the man clear the area, then he notice something was embedded into the muck. It was the treasure chest full of moss and there was a huge ancient pad lock on it, that hadn't rust away yet. He tried twisting it around but it didn't budge.

It took a while but he eventually clear away sand from around it completely and got the net under and around it. Nudge tight into the shape of ball. Then jerk the cable several times to signal. Bill read the message when he saw the cable jumping and clicked on the wench it began to roll. The chest rise slowly it was heavy on the cable Indian hovered over it about ten feet.

The thing was almost twenty feet long it came out of no ware its mouth was already open as it grabbed for the divers head. Missing it only by a few inches, dew to Indian's quick reflex he turned and with precision drove the eight inch digger into the creature's eye where it remained. The shark swam of swiftly into another direction the whole ordeal found the diver on the sea floor he was on his hands and knees.Another shark was above him it was a female and more aggressive she circled him.

He saw no way out it was a hell of a way to go, then he began to recite psalms 91 in his head. His hands were buried in the sand when he felt something it was a silver bracelet he squeezed it tight in his left fist. The shark was on his final round for some reason Indian felt invincible now it was the last chance to beat death.

He swam fast towards the surface took of the tank from his back and removed the mouth piece. Opened the value fully letting the pressure from the tank propel him even faster for a moment the shark was at his feet.

The shark grabbed at Indian's legs but Indian slide the tank into the shark's mouth as its jaws closed it bit the value. Air when in all directions the diver saw bubbles and foam below him. He swam for his life which was far above him twisting his body and kicking feet hard as he went up.

The tanks didn't explode but they gave the shark a good scare and broke off some of its teeths in the process. He descended slowly down to the sea floor then swam away.

Four minutes later Indian reached the surface blowing and gasping for air he made his way to the boat floating.

What kept you so long bill shouted from the back deck of the energy.

Two gypsy girls didn't want me to leave said Indian.

Police were questioning a man by the name of king rasp. The leader of the Rastafarian foundation of Cayman Island. He was brought in of the streets without bowings knowledge. Where were you four days ago when the two banks were robbed.

I don't remember some way bout with my woman not robbing banks said kingdon. Ummh and am sure she can verified that and give you a nice alibi right said detective Philips.

You remember were you was on February 18 when those boys from east end went missing. Kingdon didn't answer only a smarck came over his face. Rasta man Na ga a thing to do with the crime on the street we run a peaceful organization. The girl that disappeared the other day you know her ask Philips. She from the neighborhood yah, that bad wha happen to her the police should do their job and find her said king. You said something happen to her what asked Phillip. They can find her that wha happen said kingdon. Man look yah Rasta Na in no game thing Babylon with trick questions. What about this book and letters your foundation writing remarked Philips. I don't know wha you talking bout replied the Rastafarian leader. We know the letters are coming from your part of town said Philips. All kinds of people staying in the ghetto now foreigners and thing giving Rasta bad name claim kingdon.

The letters loaded with Rasta man philosophy said the detective. Putting a copy down in front of king. Oh these the letter you talking bout I see them already they all over the place for true them little letters thy joke. Look yah star Rasta Na in no discord business.

Bucking ham palace isn't taking it funny this the kind of shit that starts revolutions we got 13 of those now with that same kind of hatred. We're calling it a campaign. Phillip looked him the eyes. The Rasta man was drug up on something what you so nervous about he ask.

Kingdon replied smiling, 13 you say look like someone casing a spell.

Read psalms 109 every day boss man and no harm will come upon you said salassi the most high. I don't believe in any of that voodoo shit or salassi I have my protection right here said the cop referring to his Gluck 9. Tapping it with his four fingers under his arm.

Rasta na tell fairy tale star these days black people na give no trouble it the brown man running things the Rasta commented.

Look king you sold weed to an undercover police more than once that's why we brought you in. we can arrest you on that alone, you seem like a down to earth person tell us what you know and we can work something out with the charges. Kingdon was quite for a while he seemed nervous again he was sweating in the air condition room.

What about that Indian friend of yours, there's a lot of Indians and gyptsy scattered all over central these days think any of them responsible for what's going on. No said kingdon. How can you be so sure? Jah people don't do those things insisted the Rastafarian.

Phillips was beginning to get angry, don't give me no foolishness man things hard some of them would put salassi I aside and do what they have to do to survive. And use this Rasta thing for cover up even you is a suspect that's the second reason I hull your ass down here for today.

We at peace with the regime these days, it been that way for a while not like 20 30 years ago when the Rasta movement was struggling here in Cayman. The boys(police) let us be with our merchandise for personal use live and let live kindna of thing you know that MR detective. All that shit going to soon stop too, see what happening on the streets through us being nice replied the Philips. What are the gypstys up to he asked in the seam breath? What you mean ask kingdon. We know what's going on magic is part of their culture people pay them to smoke cigar and work obeah. I hear they can put a bull frog in your belly is that true and the women don't wear any draws neither. Hell if you even look one of those gyptsy in the eye you get bad luck they say or when you grind one of those women you never leave her.

They good people still said kingdon interrupting, that's just how they stay sam. We keep on one another good side up in the ghetto we stay out of each other's business too no out siders f--- with us cause they done know wha time it is.

The door swung open and babeth rush in a police woman in uniform stood behind her. I tell you no one is allowed in here ma'am the officer took her by the arm but babeth pulled away.

Its ok were just about done here. Babeth walked over and stood next to the chair where kingdon sat. Philips could see she was a gypst. What about you he ask you know anything about these letters? Babeth eyes rolled up into her head then closed she chanted for a few seconds then her eyes opened wide. She hugged kingdon around the neck crouch down and whisper into his ear. My gypsy girl say a dead man is writing the letter.

That's very funny said detective Philips.

But he didn't know what she meant.

The energy cut through big seas at almost full trolled headed for land. She rock and swayed from side to side things were falling out of the locker. The men had managed to slow down Corby's bleeding. He was coming in and out of consions, after the wound had been clean with peroxide the captain retied it and wrapped it up with white sheet from the linen closet.

That will have to do for now he said hurrying back to the wheel house to relieve the rope that held the wheel on course.

That was the biggest Congo reel I ever saw in my life, he was the size of an alligator said bill to Indian. I got a glimpse of him swimming away after he had done his damage. Taking the radio in his hand he said out loud the situation has change I repeat unforeseen boat trouble you will have to meet me by the bluff in one hour. He spoke to James hurlur on the other end of the radio. That was all he said over the air communicating in code langue apparently SITUATION CHANGE translated to bring doctor.

Bill hang up the radio we got her Indian he said we finally got her we rich who laughing now ah. Look at this coin one of these must be worth a hundred thousand easy.

This bracelet I found I think it belonged to one of those gypsts said Indian.

You may be right with that said bill we're rich Indian we done it.

The text came to bill cell phone a few minutes later. After reading it bill ask.

How well do you know kingdon?

All my life said Indian why what's wrong.

That was marisah, that detective what's his name pit bull arrested him a little while ago. They think he might be behind all this crime going on.

You could be friends with someone all your life and never really know them.

That's true said Indian, but king Na no criminal I can bet my life on it. He Na the only one I guess that they suspect. You right with that said bill all like how he got dread locks. That cop Patrick bowing looking a metal and a pay raise before he retires claimed Indian.

He looks like a pit bull too that name suits him said bill, the men laugh.

Honest negotiations had fail to retrieve the sugar baby stones. So mat o-Bryon would take the next step. The private eye continued to watch them and sometimes it was not only Sullivan that were up in those swamps. Mat nor Sullivan knew of each other presents at time the two were only yards from one another.

Mat o-Bryon had even dress up like a woman and talked face to face with bill Patterson about buying the stones. Now he and Adolfo had moved on to plan B.

There was a storm brewing people were busy whizzy. The sky was gray and there was a light drizzle rain falling.

Aliza stepped out of the super market with two grocery bags in her hand a man bump into her poking her skin with a syringe like uperatess.

It was loaded with nerve agent she never felt a thing.

By the time she reach her car she was dizzy and near pass out a man help her into the passenger seat of her own car. He calmly walk around to the driver side and then drove away. With Aliza next to him fast asleep. He jerk the brown ruby stone from off her neck.

The car was vandalized left in a dike road near the Indian man's home as a red hearing.

When she awoke hours later she found herself hog tied with nylon rope around her wrist and ankle.

Finally you awake said a voice I though I may have giving you an over dose. The room was dark except for the fading sun light that shine through a small window. She could barely make out the face of a smooth shave straight hair man. Who are you said Aliza broken voice.

Am a friend of your father and fiancé we are going have a nice time together?

Go to hell you frigging pervert yelled the girl.

It was raining cats and dogs by the time the energy pulled into the small cove at Pedro castle. The lightning and thunder had stop it was dark for four o clock in the evening the weather was terrible.

Indian still in his dive trunk jump onto land and tied the ship to a post the engine shut off. Mr. James harlur awaited them in a hummer he wasn't alone an elderly gentleman accompanied him.

He in the cabin down below bill told them. After antibiotics, and a little more morphine the black market doctor stitched the wrist closed 30 minutes later bill poured him a tall glass of whiskey. He will sleep for a day or so than start to come around he's one lucky son o gun I tell you that said the doctor. Going to need an I.V pack to help him recover I'll see what I can do in that regard of course. The administration is watching us heavy these days. Absolutely not a word to any one said James to the doctor. Of course not James what do you think I am? The doctor had lost his license in a mal practice case a few years back James knew him well. They were by the reef by volcano island spear fishing diving lobsters and conchs when one of those barracudas a big one attacked him and took his hand off said bill.

If you say so not any of my business my lips are seal said the doctor. As he put the roll of money in his pocket.

A small Cessna air craft flow over Cuba.

It had been in and out of the communize country air space numerous times. And one too many times I might add over the years.

Inside the were two Cuban Americans who hated Castro's regime with a passion. The plane dipped down and up just 30 feet from the ground over a little town in Havana, barely clearing building house tops and trees. One man pull a lever in the cockpit that was connected to a special hatch underneath the plane releasing left lets and fliers of a somewhat religious and revolutionary nature and loaded with slogans.

God is god to all who accepts him free my people fiddle Castro, were written on it in bold letters.

The plane pulled up sharply seconds before running into a mountain.

Cuba was still a strong alliance with the Soviet Union and Castro felt that the United Nations was behind the campaign that these heroes were undertaken. Cuba had threaten to shoot them down and the military didn't need to send a fighter jet up to do it or to waste fuel.

They had missile launchers that could easily reach three miles into the sky. If the plane pushed it's luck Cuba would blow them up and tell the world about it.

The chest was made from the heart wood of a cherry tree.

You would have never think that wood could last that long said bill to Indian and James who was back by now from leaving the doctor home. It was two feet long by twelve inches high a cordless grinder made little work of the pad lock. The gold coins were from the Mexican revolution they were other precious jewelry saphire and diamonds no doubt spoils of wars. There was dead silent as the three men looked in astonishment and disbelief. No way of knowing how much its wroth yet said bill but just a guess we don't have to worry about the bills for the rest of our lives They laughed. I'll put the next part of the plan into action tomorrow said James. Your share is safe in my hands nobody can double cross no body if one of us go down we all go down remember we committed to each other. Rather than every man get his cut and go their separate ways. We going keep the treasure together until we get the cash just like how we talked about. This thing will happen nice and smooth not bringing a whole lot of attention to any of us. This weather coming in from the southeast I can beat it going north all the reports say it will become a small hurricane, but I think it will break up over Jamaica and give us plenty rain.

The three men drank late into the night. Corby awoke terrified but managed to calm back down afterwards when he saw the treasure.

And had a few drinks and a couple puffs later he drop back to sleep.

They were possessed by some kind of evil spirit said Indian talking about the two tiger sharks that almost got him. It was 1AM when bill and James put the ice box into the hummer they had repack the treasure into it. There were other misilenious stuff in it to manipulate the radar screen and help them get cross customs. James would also carry a few buckets of pig tails and salt beef and a suit case full of bread fruits. There was no problem taking them into Florida the custom officer would be so amused he would make him walk right on by.

The next time I talk to you it will be to come and pick up the paper if you know what I mean. In the meantime hold on to this it all I could get my hands on for now it should keep you until I get back. James handed bill a stack of money thicker than a pocket dictionary.

I went cross Corby house told his wife a lie gave her something for the both of them. He's a good boy take care of him was the last thing he said driving away.

The galley seats were cushioned and comfortable aboard the energy where bill and Indian sat. It was 16 thousand dollars James had handed him, Bill gave half to Indian.

Am going to have to take her around in this weather this thing aint going to easy up right now. If a hurricane coming the best place for my baby is up in that sound said bill.

Repeated phone call went to Aliza cell with no answer Indian had been calling from the time he was out to sea.

I can't get Aliza said Indian, she always picks ups I got a bad feeling Mr. bill.

It was 5AM the men never slept they chatted until dawn. Bill took up the phone Mariah say Aliza never came home last night Indian.

An hour later a phone call to Indian confirm what he didn't want to hear. I got her said the voice over the line I'll accept the stones for her life your place 24hours don't try anything funny.

September 9th 2004 it was 5AM when the Cessna 200 took off from owning Roberts international. The storm was behind James and the south east wind carried him and the treasure turbulence free in the sky. The flight would take him two and a half hours crossing over Guantanamo bay then to a small airport in Miami.

The Cessna had been flying around dropping literature all morning. A soldier from a Cuban military base smoked an unfiltered camel cigarette as he watch it. Minutes later a man sitting behind a rocket launcher fired missing the small plane by inches. The Sargent slap the soldier in the back of the head in disappointment and said some curse word in Cuban Spanish. Then the explosion and an object drops from the sky into the deep blue. May Day May Day said the Cuban American pilot flying away.

Bill spoke to the two men in low and dishearten voice. James plane disappeared of the radar over Cuba this morning. A pilot reported an explosion just outside of Cuba and saw a small airplane go down. The US coast guard search the area but only found some burnt remain of the Cessna, nothing else Cuba denied any knowledge of the matter. Corby shook his head Indian face was in pain and there was signs of eye water flowing.

It wasn't meant to be I never told you all about the same dream I had twice about a gypsy woman. She told me we were sticking our noses were it didn't belong now I know what she meant said bill.

Dam her said Corby dam her.

Later that same night in an abandon parking lot.

Phillip's thinks that dread locks kid is guilty as hell he told me he could see that he was hiding something.

We have to put a stop to Delroy.

But he o us money.

We may never recover it he's insignificant now.

Am tracking him down from all corners said Sullivan to another man, I put the word out on the street that it was him who executed the six gang leaders just like you told me to do boss.

Good so now he's got gangsters to watch out for too, he would last too long now trust me.

We can't let this screw up interfere with the rest of our business said the other man. One way or another he and the Indian goes down for everything.

Delroy did his girlfriend because she had something to do with our money no doubt.

We'll pin the news reporter and the rest of the disappearances that we did on them too.

Yeah replied Sullivan that north sound has a lot mystery those sharks get rid of the problem quick after the doctor takes out what he wants.

What about the Heathrow mess asked the man.

We got paid for it before it left said Sullivan the sheik upset but he never lost any money. The boys in England made the mistake not us.

We're going to have to keep a shadow over Scott land yard to know what's going on said the other man.

Just before I came to meet you I notice the schooner coming in.

We got bill, marisah and Aliza cell phone tap but apparently the Indian doesn't have a cell. He's old school against his religion or something.

Sounds like the girl is missing since last night no call from her cell in the last two days.

Look like they starting to clean up they're good.

I have a gut feeling a big pay day is coming for someone they could have hide the money from the bank job aboard that boat.

They had to have gotten outside help to pull of that job. No way they done that alone. Said the man.

You go there and surprise them and take the money.

Ok boss said Sullivan.

The man's cell phone rang yeah what it is, a minute later he said to Sullivan our plane just cash on the bluff near the sheik's property.

The sheik had just been awoken out of his sleep with a phone call. About a drug plane crashing on the bluff at volcano island. Two of his best men were gone feared dead and his business was falling apart as the result.

He didn't know what would happen but he would claim innocent in everything. He would have to throw some more money at the problem buy some more friends that could protect him and save his own skin.

He spoke to the British prime minister over the phone.

Am not involve in any of this he said.

I believe you came back the reply on the other end.

PART THREE

It had been over six months now since the anti-coruption agent didn't received any thing in the mail.three months ago his boss had told him the department was going through some difficult times. Hang in there money is on the way.

It going to be a total rehaul as far as I can tell he said the communize party will remain in power another couple of terms. Even the secret service and MI6 are being shaffle around.

The communize party created MI6 about a hundred years ago so it would be in their best intress to make it the only agentcy in the whole british empire. The funds for the anti-coruption agentcy has been coming from the MI6 department for the last year.

Their cutting loose all the agents from over seas, they no longer want us in this business. Bermuda, Turks and caious, monsarack, British virgin islands they all gone. If they get rid of us the world won't be a nice place. I haven't gotten the word on you yet CAY1.

Their snooping around into A.C.A files we may have a mole or two in this department working for them there're leaks all over.

They may have gotten access to your report from 96 CAY1 MI6 and the communize party knowns who you are.

Be careful was the last thing lord nelson told him only three weeks ago now he was dead murdered.

It was October 1996 weeks before the Cayman Islands national election.

An Indian man with his hair all stuffed into a Tamm walked into the office of the complaint commissioner.

I would like to speak to the commissioner please he said to the secretary.

Do you have an appointment she asked?

No, said the man.

Am afraid he can only see you if you have an appointment.

Well am here now insisted the man.

The commissioner can't see you today said the secretary.

You haven't ask him said the Indian man. Look ma'am can you please tell the commissioner it is in his best in tress that he talk to me today. Tell him it's a matter of life and death.

And who may I say wants to see him ask the secretary.

My name isn't important the man said.

The secretary paired her lips together and there was a look of confusion on her face she walk away.

Excuse me sir she said with an educated voice entering the room.

Yes what is it said the English accent.

Am sorry sir but there's a very determine young man here insisting on seeing you, he doesn't have an appointment sir.

Umm a local chap I supposed said the commissioner.

Yes sir seems aggressive.

Send him in let me hear what he has to say.

Have the guard pat him down before you let him through.

It was a decent size office with a book shelve and a wooden desk two chairs were on the opposite end in front of it.

The commissioner stood with his back to the door a book was in his hand he pointed to a chair when the Indian looking fellow come in.

Have a seat what can I do for you today he said with his back still facing the Indian.

Am Ezekiel.

That's ok son you don't need to tell me your name I already know who you are.

Yes sir I come to tell you about a murder.

The commissioner turn around and sat, looking the Indian eye to eye.

He was an older man his hair was black with high light of grays slightly balding. He wore black frame glasses but they where not big on his face.

And his baby chin made his whole face look muscular and tone especially with the thin mouth stash.

A murder he said by whom.

Sparks and doughy said the Indian.

Am listening go head said the commissioner relaxing in his chair.

I have proof to everything that am telling you sir said Indian reaching into his back pack and pulling out a piece of paper, he handed it to the complaint commissioner.

Your malicah son aren't you said the complaint commissioner while looking over the letter.

That's right said Indian my father worked for those crooks.

But he isn't dead right son.

Might as well be he cripple up stationary to a wheel chair waiting to die. He even worst now two months ago he was admitted to the hospital with numerous complications. The doctor say they all related to the fall he suffered two years back. His body is shutting down completely the nervous system is going crazy. The pain in his body never stops repertory problems, muscle spasms, pinch nerve, the fusion Sergey done to his back didn't help. It is unbearable for any human being I sit hopelessly next to his bed side each night listening to him grune.

Doctor says he taking pain killer like candy there not doing him any good, his body is already amound to them. He's adicted to morphine according to the doctor he only got a week or two left. Then his system will break down rapidly and he's a flat liner.

Am sorry to hear that son.

They hated my old man and made this happen to him cause he had something on em.

The paper I gave you is what sparks and doughy construction force all 500 of their workers to sign. Stating that they agree to work without pension or health insurance or overtime pay.

They even made them wave their rights to work for less than minimum wage and no workers compensation.

A trade man in their company was only getting five dollars an hour.

You say they force them said the commissioner.

Yes sir that's right sign it or find another job they told them. I done my homework sir and any document of this kind is against the Cayman Islands labor law.

The complaint commissioner was impress. Where did you get this letter from he asked.

Dad was a regular lover boy he and the secretary had something going on he romance her into getting a copy of it illegally.

The company keep them in the file locker in the basement of their office building.

It was drafted by one of their fancy lawyers Chas orange.

Is that right said the complaint commissioner de Chas orange.

Yes sir, the same one running in this election people say he going get in too.

His name doesn't appear anywhere on the document son so that is speculation and hear say.

I know that mister but he represents the company, if you look carefully you'll see a small signature next to a not so popular notary republic at the time.

They protected themselves from any liabilities in case they were being sewed by any one.

Yes I see it answered the commissioner looking through a magnifying glass.

The notary republic is an elderly man now I talked to him at the retirement home here in town. Admits he took a bribe from Mr. Orange himself. He was trimberling as he told me the story says he denied everything in the court of law if it ever comes to it. Would claim someone forged his signature. Sparks and doughy weren't the only company doing that kindna of thing back then he told me but they were the biggest of the bunch.

And the secretary ask the commissioner.

She was upset when my old man break up with her he told her my mother had found out about them.

Dad had told her he had no ties no children and all that, lone lies.

She was mad so she rat him out to the higher up's at sparks and doughy.

They could have fired him without reason or pay if they wanted to all that was stated in the document they made them sign.

Instead they protended like they knew nothing and plan his death.

My old man daddy was going to blow them wide open with their corruption.

He was about to take the papers to the head of the employment relations and the human rights board.

Dad was working with a cop they call pit bull I don't know his real name or anything about him yet am still investigating him.

But they got to the old man first and took him out.

Can I get you a soda asked the commissioner?

No, I don't drink sodas sir.

Juice, milk, alcohol or maybe some water am not going to prison you if that's what your afraid of said the commissioner with a smile.

A juice would be fine sir said Indian.

He push a button on an instrument on his desk and said, milly dear would you please fetch us two glasses of cran berry juice from the kitchen. Right away sir came the reply.

Indian glanced all around the room he wasn't sure if he had hang himself or not. His caymannaki philoshy had showed him their was little justice in the world and don't trust the government.

Indian had a smirk on his face.

There was silent for a while, the commissioner walked up and down the room like he was considering something.

The juice arrived, Indian took a big gulped. And started to speak again.

I going to deal with this my own way sir my father Na going die in vain.

I know you don't trust anyone Ezekiel which is good sometimes especially in my line of work. But don't do anything foolish son you must learn to control your anger.

I just want you to know I Na an informant for the law, it Na right wha these people doing sir.

Of course not continue tell me the rest.

If you know malicah Howett then you know he didn't go to a battle with just one knife.

It's the old caymanaki secret he said passing the commissioner another piece of paper this time it was a folded up newspaper ad.

He also gave him a photo copy that was in his lap of a cheque.

That's an ad gazette talking about the new high school that sparks and doughy won the contract to build for 25 million dollars. Here's another copy of the real cheque said Indian digging into his bag of tricks once again. This one was also obtained by the same secretary my father's lover. Its dated one day before the newspaper article a 33 million dollar contract sign seal and deliver.

Why those bastards said the complaint commissioner from behind his desk. Looking at the name on the cheque I remember him Hendricks Hopkins. H.H they use to call him the then leader of the communize party he's dead now. They pocketed 8 million dollars the communize party owns sparks and doughy.

They stole from the people and the crown said Indian that first class corruption.

This is bigger than we can ever imagine said the commissioner up of his seat talking from across the room. He was speaking openly by now with Indian, this kind of thing doesn't happen without someone in the British Empire knowing.

And with the illegal documents they made their workers sign they save at least another million dollars by, bi-passing the labor laws.

There's mores said Indian flip over the page sir.

What's this said the commissioner.

It shows two other companies had a better bid by about 2 million less than 25 million dollars said Indian.

The new high school job went out for tender but it was just a sham the government of the day rewarded the contract to their biggest political supporters. Some of the communize party members were shareholders of the company sir like you say.

Of course it all falls into place said the commissioner.

Sparks and doughy then sub-contracted sections of the work to other communize party supporters down the ladder.

One two people got work their but the bulk of it was political connections.

Those outside the ring were given work to see if they could be swayed into becoming communize voters.

Some of them become communize party members too sir I know that for a face I come from the streets. You see they needed the employment.

Indian reached into his back pack again.

How much more you got in that thing ask the commissioner.

This is all now said Indian revealing another paper this isn't a copy it the original fax. Malicah stole it from the office of sparks and doughy. With the help of the secretary.

They wanted my father dead badly. Sparks and doughy tender should have never been considered in the first place. Because they submitted it five days after the tendering dead line. The fax shows the date and time the bid went in. Where's the girl now the secretary asked the commissioner.

She was smart but got addicted to med. Not last year but the year before I think it was, when they found her? According to the pathologist report I read in the papers she over dose on pills and alcohol. Of course she did said the commissioner. I know what went on they killed her. Dad was so discouraged and confused mostly for his family to see suffering he was beaten and could no longer go on. I found all these papers up in the attic in one of his suit cases. He didn't want me to get mix up in any of this he told me.

Where do you work Ezekiel asked the complaint commissioner.

Right now am currently unemployed at the moment sir.

That's what I thought, that a big fish you got there son too big to pull in if and when justice come it will be a long time.

There's a lot of players involved in that story.no dough I believe you the evident speaks for itself. It's very clear to me that the British politicians got their feet in this mud also.

It's a bloody mind field is what it is you step in the wrong place and boom it's all over.

You mean like organized crime sir.

Call it what you like am afraid your life is over son, when you go out that door things will never be the same for you.

You're a mark man just like your father maybe even more than he was.

It already started I heard about your encounter the other day up at sparks and doughy office.

Chas orange called in and told me about the bomb threat you made. Said there was a mad man in the place.

The son of malicah Howett the man who had falling of the building a few years ago.

Said that he was cursing and claiming to blow the place up.

Indian kept silent and listen with amazement and astonishment.

They black listed you ever since you got involved in this case and mixed up in the political game.

You're by partisan I suspect a none voter don't support any of the political parties.

Yes sir that's right.

That's what I thought politics is a dangerous thing especially for political activist like yourself.

You'll never work again in life not on this island maybe nowhere on the face of the earth. It the same crap all over the world. You will always face opposition because of these people. And it will come from both sides of the political arena. The wicked is a powerful force and they all inter link these days. Sparks and doughy have lawyers working right here in this office.

I must say however I admirer the piece of work you just shown me.

I was truly educated not surprised mind you but educated.

What would you say if I ask you to come and work for me?

This office thing aint for me sir thanks said Indian.

I don't mean here in the office out in the field said the commissioner.

What kind of work.

As an agent.

You mean like a spy said Indian.

You'll be an anti-corruption agent A.C.A strictly under cover you'll only talk to me that's it no one else.

The room was quite for a while, the man behind the desk took his square frame glasses off. Then walked over to the book shelve and pulled some books to one side. A video camera was built into the wall behind it. He pressed eject and the compartment that held the video tape opened up. He removed it and dropped it to the red carpet floor and smashed it with the heel of his shoe. Then picked it up went to the bath room and flashed it down the toilet.

All conversations in this room are recorded he said from the bathroom door in his office. In case anyone in London needs it for future references.

That's the only tape of what was said here today only a written report will be keep on file for the agency.

You and I never spoke you never came here this morning. I make sure that the secretary and the other confuse you with someone else.

When you leave this office you'll go up onto the roof and through a window there. And then take the fire escape ladder all the way down to the ground floor you're not afraid of heights are you.

No sir.

Good, it leads to an abundant alley between two buildings.

If you except the job you will go on living your life as normal. I already know every thing about you.

An envelope will be in the mail every three months discized as treavel brochers and junk mail with a special stamp on them.

Inside will be cayman currency cash that will be your pay,no one will know it's from the anti-corruption agency.

I,ll give you covert assignments every now and then.

You want be cop you're a agent you wont arrest no one it may blow you cover. You,ll only report what is nessary about corruption,you don't get a gun issued to you by this agentcy. But you have the right to defend yourself if face with danger in other words you have a license to kill.

All details of any case or criminal act related to corruption will be reported to me. And I,ll call in the local police to make an arrest for us.

Only a few people in England know we exsist,we don't share intelligent with no other countries. your to tell no one not even your mother. You will not work with any other A.C.A and you will be unawear of each other.

I know you know a little karate but we will teach you more and you will become a expert in self-defence.

And you will learn every thing you need to know about computers.

Once you become an anti-corruption agent you will be one for the rest of your life. There's no out of this organization only by death just like the mafia, only where're the good guys.

The agency will always protect you.

You will be given a number of pass ports from difference countries around the world. Including Cuba, Russia, Korea, and china.

We will teach you the language of all the counties you're given a pass port to.

You'll be the only A.C.A in Cayman just so you know and will be the youngest ever in the bureau.

Do you have any questions he asked Indian?

Am I MI6?

Absolutely not A.C.A is a notch above those, we, re in a different category all together.

Those guys are mostly professional assassins their the killers in the family.

Their service maybe needed from time to time if the A.C.A has no choice be to eliminate a subject.

So what will it be you want the job?

Why not said Indian.

That's a yes is it not, welcome aboard young man. My name is lord nelson.

From now on we only communicate by this special phone he handed him a simple looking cell phone. You're to delete my number every time we speak. Even though it can't be tap or damage it equipped with anti-blocking device. There's a beacon implanted into it so I'll know you location at all time.

Double O-seven has one just like it.

You mean that guy is real said Indian.

Of course he's real I trained him myself.

CAY1 is you file number.

Code name agent black ball.

This is your first assignment you specialize in construction I understand.

Yes boss said Indian.

You catch on fast CAY1 I like that looks like I made a good decision about you.

How did you know that I would accept the job sir you have my first assignment ready.

The short story on that is the British Empire knowns every one of their citizens on a first hand bases. From the time they are born it takes a special breed to become a British agent and their selected weather they accept the job or not.

This is right up your alley said lord nelson handing Indian a sheet of paper with the name Thomas spring.

Over the years more trust was developed between lord nelson and agent black ball.

There was a new crime fighter on the streets of Cayman and many white collar criminals went to jail. Preacher's doctors business men all brought down by an unknown force.

The 1996 elections brought with it surprises and the communize party lost the elections.

After the scandal broke more documents surfaced mysteriously proving that spark and doughy construction. A company owned by the communize party of Cayman opened life insurance on their workers without the workers knowledge.

Some died or no foul play was suspected and money collected.

Likewise homes were insured as well by them and would burn down due to unknown causes faulty electrical etc. and lightning strikes when there was none. Right wing Politian like chase orange remain a back bencher in agony. And had been exposed and shame upon. He had lost money after the racket came to light. And would do whatever he had to do get back at those responsible. After he found out who they were. By 2000 things had change. Again the people had forgiven the communize party. Cayman need them back. Chase orange became premier of the country and in charge of the financial portfolio. By then Lord Nelson was relocated, back to the central intelligent building in down town London. He continued his post at the anti-corruption-agency looking into financial crimes money laundering and official corruption and other intelligent matters, concerting overseas territories and the kingdom. But the communize party looked over his shoulder.

Two days later at a condominium complex in seven mile beach an important message from the M.I.6 headquarters came over an agent's cell phone. It's time to execute plan. The agent smiled.

The Indian had said his last pray. Today was the day weather he lived or die he had no choice, but to fight. Everything was set and he was ready as he'll ever be. He had been alone in his soul a long time he was angry and disappointed that it would end this way. The system had turned him into this monster that would never be teem. All his hurt had been used up. Tears were no more easy flowing. He had seen his family and people suffer for too long from lack of basic needs. They had done this to him, they had black ball him for the truth that he had told. And now Aliza was involved. And might die too today, why it has to be this way he ask god for the final time. You are my only freedom god remove this curse. Undo what man has done to me dear creator he reasoned. This life had been hard over the years living from day to day. I don't care if I die now am already dead. Dear father god am nothing to question you but let her live. The moon was changing into the waning phase time to banish. He put on his apathy war paint on the face and sharpen and replaced his weapons. Booby traps were set up all over the property. He had come across some explosives and would use them in a heartbeat. No one knew how it would end. They had force my hand into this he said and compelled me there was no other way out. I went up against the system and lost. So it doesn't matter what happens. I had gotten myself into this mess he said to his own self. And now it time to end it. The butcher and the P.I. would die. Aliza and mom would be alright. They would miss me but life goes on. As for the children they'll understand someday. My children would be fatherless and my wife a widow. But my satisfaction would be from the grave that my enemies were exposed and some of them dead. I'm a good guy he said, looking into his mind. But, sometimes you have to give the people a taste of their own medicine. Being good don't mean nothing among the heathens. You see he was a vampire slayer, I kill demons cut them open and ripped there hearts out. They were all useless. I may not even have to get my hands dirty the traps should take care of the two of them nice and sweet. If not nobody may get out of this thing alive. There was no escape plan. He had to get them before they got him. If I dead here today he said I go make sure these maggots go down too. All the missopportunities my enemies prevented me from getting. I will die a poor dog and this Treasure that I never found is what kill me. All was in the hands of the greater man now. The Indian droved some long nails into a piece of lumber and covered it with leaves and grass.

The butcher slash Italian cook, cocked back a 45 automatic before he stepped out of the car. He held it in his hand. The Indian towed a small traveling bag in front of the man. There's your money I don't want any trouble with you. Take it and leave. He went over and opened the bag it was all good. He turned and walked away. Then the board with nails penetrated unto the center of his foot he hallowed from pain, and dropped on his knees you darn back stabbing Garifuna aborigine was the last thing he said shooting off a few rounds before the Indian jumped into the air and came down with an axe on his head splitting his face wide open.

It was raining all morning and the water had washed away the blood from the last murder scene, by the time Matt o-Bryon came to the Indian camp. He held her with one hand by her hair, She was still gadded and hands tied at the back she looked beaten up frighten, not far away was a

S.U.V. parked on the side of the road officer and marine police Sullivan saw a second car drive into the location. Something was going down big money was being exchanged and pasted around. He would make sure we get his share of the action. Soon, he thought. I'll go in and take them out and walk away with the cash.

The Indian shouted to the PI, let the girl go Matt. I know who you are this with me and you not her. You got something that belongs to me Ezekiel hand it over then she goes free. Where is it? Matt looked around but saw no one. This is about me and only me, and the treasure I know what you and the old man been doing up in this swamp. Your treasure hunters and you guys got lucky. But you should be more careful. There's a lot of Pirates out there. now I want it all not only the stones. Show yourself he said swinging his head around in the marsion forest looking unto trees and whatever else. The Indian appeared in the back of them. Matt spanned round. Let the girl go Matt what you come for is right over there. What you think am foolish enough to fall for that, go get it and bring it over here. He said motioning with the gun. The Indian open the duffle bag matt saw some gold coin and the brown stones he thought he was looking for. The darkness of the evening in the mangroves played games with his eyes. I knew it was you who did those bank job said the PI looking at the stacks of cash. Mostly news paper under neat some cash around it. He didn't check it in detail. It was all good. It wasn't a big treasure matt only the stone and some small art fax a million in cash and another 10 for the sugar babies you still come out on top O-Bryon. matt took one of the stone and held it up into what little light come through the leaves. There fake, what you think am stupid. You Mayan bastard. Matt raised his hand to shoot, Aliza pushed him hard with her body the bullets went into a tree. The Indian disappeared Aliza ran off, but fell down. Matt pointed the gun at her. She would die. The Indian reached down in the dirt and that same second a bow was pulled back to it capacity and two arrows sailed in the wind. One going into Matt's right wrist he dropped the gun. The other into his shoulder. The Indian could have finished him but he didn't just yet. The gun lay in the mud. Aliza was gone not to be found by Matt. He broke the arrows off and pulled them through the wound. Matt stood up fully. The Indian stood right in front of him face all painted. The blood dripped from a flash wound on the Indian mid side the butcher almost got him but nearly doesn't count old boy. He tossed the bow and arrows away and threw a knife at Matt's feet that what I talking about manor a mano said Matt a Marshall Arts expert himself. He took off his shirt vigorously revealing his small bird chest. Matt rushed the Indian with the knife in his hand. But it was over quick. The Indian flipped a couple times cutting Matt up with a blade of a big knife. Matt was on the ground he found the gun, before he could squeeze the trigger and shoot the Indian pitched the knife into his chest plate stopping his heart immediately. He died with his mouth and eyes open. Aliza had freed herself from the ties she ran over and kissed then hugged her man. She stocked a wild flower into Indians wound, tore a piece of her blouse and wrap it around him.

Sullivan saw the third car droved into the dirt road, where the Indian was at. No one was expecting it. It was a rental with an uncle white man in it, Sullivan followed a minute later. It was raining a heavy down pour by now. He pulled in and stopped behind the rental car. They were no other vehicles around or anyone. He looked the site over. An image in black moved around the outside of the shack then went into the bushes out back. Sullivan got into a yellow Government Issue rain coat and took out his M-16 from the trunk. He wasn't going to play around whoever was at the bad lucked end of the gun was history. A hurricane coming men I got to get home to my family he said out loud. As he slammed the car trunk he was under fire from a big sounding gun. It made a one foot diameter hole in the side body of the car. It came from the bushes Sullivan noticed he smiled he liked the shit. He fired back towards the woods and ran for cover in the house that was being constructed. Look like I run into an f----- ambush he said over the police walki talki.

An hour or so had past the gun fire died down Sullivan worked himself sneaking into the bushes. The button wood swamp held the scent of blood despite the rain. The MI6 agent search around looking for any type of life form at this point preferably Indian and Sullivan. He would kill every last one of them. The swamp wasn't his style but he could adapt to it remained him of a mission he had done in Cambodia. Where was this dam creole Indian he thought but Indian was nowhere to be seen. The MI6 shot at something he saw in the mangrove roots. Sullivan heard the shots he was starting to wonder where everyone was. Who had gotten killed this time maybe the Indian that would be good, the payoff always goes bad. Sullivan moved slowly but at that very same time the earth made a cracking sound.

A huge log dropped from a tree the tree sprang up tighten a lope on a rope catching the cop in seconds. He was upside down six feet from the ground hanging from one leg. The MI6 agent walked towards that direction after hearing something he came face to face with Sullivan. Who the hell you is what you doing in this bush yelled Sullivan. A big gun was against his forehead. But there was no reply. Am a cop said Sullivan you looking for that Indian too me and you may be on the same side. The boss said MI6 guys probably helping us out on this one that Indian is a big time murderer.

That shitting Caribe Indian got booby traps sat up all over the place, what you waiting on get me down from here old boy we can kill him together.

I don't take orders from you said the MI6 agent the one with rings on his toes and fingers. The MI6 cover was jeopardized he wanted to blow Sullivan away right there and then. You lucky I don't kill you he said to Sullivan. Men wha you talking about we can get that Indian more easier they two of we. He's already dead the body is over there. And the money asked Sullivan. Your guess is as good as mind replied the MI6 agent. Not part of my manifesto I wanted to kill him slowly but someone got to him before me.

Men wha you talking bout we needs to find that money, you sure that's him over there said Sullivan. Who head was beginning hurt from being upside down the blood was filling his head. His face was a reddish purple.

He was too close before the men saw it out of nowhere appeared the large caimana crockadale it looked hunger and angry. The MI6 agent fired shots but it moved swiftly in the darkness of the woods. The agent backed himself right into another trap the Indian had left for some one. Coconut branches that had been place on the ground nicely broke way and the MI6 fell backwards into a hole with sharpen stakes that were pointed up. Before he realized what happen he was dying slowly painfully. And would soon be supper for a crockadile. Sullivan rocked and swing from the rope trying to reach his gun, but his fingers came short of grabbing it every time. He shouted and curse at the creature but Sullivan was unable to help himself. He was easy picking for the reptile.

It was not until September 10 before people took the hurricane warning seriously but by then it was too late. Hurricane Ivan was just hours away there was little time for some people to prepare, and was caught off guard. It was only a category one most people thought and they would ride it out in those old style Caymanian cottages. September 11 2004 6PM a curfew had been issued by the Cayman island government the streets were evacuated and Cayman was ready as it would ever be. In a few hours seas from the south would meet those from the north.

The little shack in the swamp had been shaken to pieces the roof was gone and parts of the walls. The place was half standing. A burst of water shot through the ground from the hole that the Indian had been digging. That is when it became a reality and the myth a true tail.

September 12 the worst of it was over the wind had died down a lot by evening but there were still some big swells out to sea. Bill Paterson schooner the energy was gone washed away by Ivan presumably. They had been no exact death toll yet but the authorities would hope for the best. Nowhere on Grand Cayman had escape the Ivan's wrath debris was all over. A hotel near the beach was whipped of its foundation and completely destroyed. Rescue teams found some of them too late they themselves were being put in danger. By reason that many people could not be help during the ordeal. The United States coast guard had reported rescuing a couple in a sail boat of the Florida Keys after a distress call came in. They had just made it out of Cayman in the nick of time.

It was September 13th the rotting bodies of a man and a woman were found at a little cottage in frank sound. Apparently they had disregarded the hurricane warning and evaded the mandatory evacuation. The National Guard had went to door to door before the hurricane moving resident out of these vulnerable areas. But no one was found at this particular address during that process. The bodies were unidentifiable said the police report there was substantial trama to the bodies accustom to hurricane injuries. A tree had fallen on the home and faces of the bodies were unrecognizable. Some kind of animal had been eaten them said Patrick Bowing to a bunch of other men investigating the scene. Philips removed a water proof pouch from one of the victims side here are their pass ports and ID. It them said bowing after looking the documents their family reported them missing on the 11th. There the same high and make as Ezekiel and Aliza take their finger prints and run them said Bowing to the CSI personnel. They've found Aliza car said Philips to Bowing after talking with an officer with blue jump suit on. Where asked Bowing. Half mile down the road partly under water. The police men walked around the site the block structure that was being constructed was still standing.

The wench was attached to a chain around the lintel in the building the rope was still dangling. Other garden tools where scattered over the place. Look like they were trying to secure themselves poor kids said Philips after seeing the objects, his woman was pregnant too. They had little change up in this bush said Bowing. We don't know if they got eaten alive or if they were already dead. I wouldn't wish this kindna thing on my worse enemy replied Philips. He got what he deserved he was a criminal remember committed Bowing.

It looked like it was only 30 feet deep but the sea water hid its true dept. The flooding probably caused it to reach sea level said bowing looking down into the bottomless hole. Where two men dig and had dreams of finding buried treasure just days and weeks before. Ivan must have uprooted and crack the core he continued speaking, you have to know what you're doing to build a house in these swamps. No one knew it would get this bad we were only expecting a category two until this thing hit us. It increased strength overnight this hurricane had title waves and tornadoes. If this had happen during a high tide we wouldn't be here now none of us. Patrick Bowing had become a hurricane expert overnight. Bowing went back into the house he was searching like a mad man for money or the book if indeed it did exists or survived through the hurricane. He came up empty handed. Get rid of these bodies ordered Bowing, far as we concern we never found anything here today. Sullivan might be dead too we've not heard anything from him yet said Philips. The last thing he told me was that he was on his way home to his family.

Lower valley was the safes place on the island when it came to the hurricane. And the Indian reservation's suffered minimum damage Indians mother and the rest of his people were safe and sound. She had heard the news of the death of her son refused to believe it refused to mourn. They had also been a remembrance service for Aliza and Ezekiel. All the boys were there along with the Patterson's kingdon said a few words.

Months had gone by tarpaulins could still be seen on house tops, generators were blaring and being overrun. Old and damaged building were being demolished hurricane debris was still being cleared away. Private buildings and institutions, churches, and rich people homes were among the first things being rebuilt. It was still the after math conditions of Ivan and old habits die hard however. Looters plague the streets and robberies went on like before with no serious suspects arrested.

A dreadlocks man pulled a ski mask over his head. And went into a liquor store. But things got ugly the man behind the counter pull out a gun to protect himself from being robbed. Shots rang out hitting the store keeper in the arm. Within minutes Bowing and Philips were on the scene. Come out with your hands up Bowing shouted through a bull horn we got you surrounded. There was a silent then two men came out side, the one with the ski mask had a gun to the Chinese man head. Drop the gun you'll never get away with it said Bowing. The crook looked around there was about ten guns pointed at him. He throw the gun to the asphalt and put his hands up in the air. Patrick Bowing smiled dead man tell no tail were the words that ran through his mind as he pulled the trigger it blew the criminal back about ten feet. Phillips looked at bowing but said nothing. The detectives removed the mask from the dead man it was Delroy Jenkins. We been looking for you said Bowing.

September 2005 Aliza's benefits and insurance at A.I.G listed the Patterson's as beneficiaries. Indian's life insurance when to his mother. Their property in frank sound would be shared between the Patterson's and Indian's mother. Mr. Patterson himself well he had finally won the lotto was the word on the street. The nighten gale house had been expanded. The Cayman Islands government had hired social workers to be employed there. Bill bought a piece of land up to windard in frank sound away from the orphanage and built a house there for his family.

With the money he won from the Miami lotto he was an instant millionaire. He finished the concrete home and developed the land in frank sound. Someone was coming to look at it today life was good after all. The nightingale boy's football team had finally won the championships this year. Last year the hurricane had brought the league to a halt. Indian and Aliza had helped the island to be a better place the would remain heroes in the dark. The will of god had been for filled and he had it his way.

4 AM man ran along the seven mile beach bare footed in the boggy

sand. He ran for two hours before stopping and checking his watch. Later that day he would meet with someone at a new neighborhood in frank sound. Just a year earlier that whole area was swamp. And two men dig for gold and their lifes became a hard luck story. But they had learn that Gods blessing was the true treasures of life.

Epilogue

As the 2005 vehicle drove into the neighborhood the Patterson's knew who it were they had been expecting them. The road in the development had been paved and water lines and power poles put in, the sign at the entrance read CAY1 Drive. They looked a year older than the last time they had saw one another. Their pass port showed they were Americans in their upper 30, s. The couple had inherited billions of dollars from the girl's ancestors.

Bill had met them a year ago in Switzerland weeks after the hurricane and after winning the lotto. They had the same characteristics as Indian and Aliza. If you ask bill Patterson he would have tell you they were the same people, But that it was a secret. The woman worn a gold chain with a big stone as a pendent around her neck.

There was a silver bracelet on the man's wrist that he would tell his friends that he fought two gypsys for. Each held an infant in their arms as they got out of the minivan. Aliza kissed marisah on the cheek as she was standing by the door way. The beers and the wine is in the trunk said Indian. Came right in guys kindon is almost done with the grilling out back said bill in a cheerful voice.

The video tape show up at the secret service headquarters office in Downing Street. No one knew who sent in the information. It showed clearly Sullivan and Bowing loading a pallet of cocaine into a warehouse at the airport. There was even more evident with the two men in an abandon parking lot. Talking and admitting to drug dealing, killing, racketeering, and extortion. His own partner Harry Phillips had thrown the cuffs on him after orders from the commissioner of police. They carried Bowing out on British Airways in shackles guarded by four military police he would never see the light of day again. Operation big fish carried out by British fines cased a big net. And politicians business men and big shots were interrogated, water board and torture to the point of near death.

Tell us how you found it Indian tell us how you found the treasure said the boys out on the patio they were pulling an all nighter. I heard the chess was the size of that car you got out there. Nothing happens before it time said Indian and he began to tell the tail.

It was the peck of the hurricane season October 1999. It was raining heavy that day Indian was up in his land in frank sound. Taking measurement and considering where on the site he would put his dream house. Only a couple of months earlier I had paid off the back tax and brought them up to date said Indian. The tax was more than what the land valued at that time. This was family land and I wasn't going to lose it beside that I love this place.

Indian put the half lit joint in the ash tray he had a enough for now. Yeah he said I was alone up this bush I remember good there was a full moon and she was already high at 4 in the evening. The rain picked up from a drizzle to a down pour Indian found shelter under a tree. His feet and shoes had been wet all afternoon. I was drinking white rum to chase way bad spirit while I was in this swamp by myself. Sat there on a bucket still getting wet talking to myself cursing the Babylon system. Jah had left the devil alone little bit to temp the good people I said. I was angry my enemies were getting bigger I told myself. I had lost a contract to build a house to an expatt. Flat down on my luck and I had a knot in my stomach I was so hungry. That was the story of my life. But I wouldn't accept it and would do whatever it took to make a better life for me and Aliza. I wasn't willing to steal or kill but tell you the truth I was thinking about it. Mama and daddy both needed help and I could not do anything for them as a big man and a son. I removed my shoes and wet socks and took a drink of rum. I shouted out loud looking up into the heavens Jah show the way. My voice was full of tears and discouragement my head come down and focused on the running water. That was accumulating under that back mangrove tree you see out there. Everyone knew which tree he was talking about. There were some button wood trees there too around it I was chopping out that area that day. The machete was just bouncing off them they were so hard. My vision was kindda blur but I saw a reflection under the clear water. The whole land was flooded with about one foot of water by now. It had been raining of and on for days. I pushed my hand into the water were I saw the reflection and felt something.

The next day Indian took the brownish stone to bill Patterson. So the myth might be true about that place said bill. Only one way to know for sure start digging. Bill had contacts and the plan was if they ever get lucky with any treasure. The schooner would be loaded up and they would smuggle it out of the country. Most people thinks that old schooner out there in the sound is condemned but that baby is reliable. Once we reach United States we can then get it into Europe then Switzerland. It will take time and patience Indian, we might spend years and never find nothing.

Aliza's grandmother died in the early 90, S her property was turned over to Aliza and her fiancé. It was a peace of swamp land on the eastern part of the island in frank sound to be exact. Aliza's mother had long ago passed away and she was the last living survivor of the Drakes family. And had been raised by the Patterson's.

Aliza changed her surname from Drakes to Blake's officially when she became an American citizen.

During the turn of the century the communize government of Cayman confiscated thousands of acres of land from native Caymanians. Indians, colored, and blacks were in prisoned after refusing to leave their land those who retaliated were simply killed. It wasn't until 1970 when the British government forward a petition to Cayman parliament. Stating that all those families who suffered in the land revolution to rightfully reclaim their property. With this said there were still taxes to be brought up to date. And plots and blocks of land sold under that crisis were consider a lost. Certain areas especially in George Town however remained in the custody of the Cayman island government. And emanate domain laws were being pasted.

The particular piece of land that Aliza inherited had always belonged to the Drakes family for about three hundred years to be precise. Going as far back as sir Francis Drakes himself. With all the red tape Ezekiel and Aliza would have to practically buy the land back from the Cayman island government.

1584 sir Francis Drakes was headed back to Manchester England from Porto cabelo panama. It was a long campaign supported by the then world power England. Two of his ships would Ronda vow on the north side of Cuba to meet a third ship. So that the three could journey back to England together two of them carried gold and rubies. From panama pocessions that now belonged to the king of England. They feared pirates so the third was a gun ship as a back up. The seven day trip took Sir Francis fifth teen days on the count of bad weather. The eventually took a detour and sought refuge at the island of las Tortuga it was an unexpected stop. The men feared their life on the count of the island was home to known renegades and pirates. Although they lived in hiding and scattered over the island close to natural water supply and the coast line. There was also a large population of Indians living on the east side of the island and on a rocky mountain out in the sea. That the Indians call the island of the gods which became known as Volcano Island. The Indians welcome Sir Francis and his men and one night around a camp fire and peace pipe. The old Indian chief told Sir Francis drakes that his people were there since creation. One of my ancestors had a dream one night the gods told him to run to the caves in the high mountains of Volcano Island. Where the people would be safe from the great flood. When they were all there the gods sealed the caves with a rock said the Indian chief. There was enough air to breathe and live while the flood waters subside. A small fresh water lake ran through the cave and they ate berries and other fruits we had gathered before the flood. And we ate fresh water fish from the lake and lived contented while the world was under water. Generations and generations of Caymanaki Indians had told the tale of the great flood thereafter.

During this short time they had already been numerous attempts by pirates to kill and steal the gold from Sir Francis and his men. I wish to hide this treasure on this island, and I give you some for you and your people said sir Francis Drakes to the Indian chief. I need no gold or rubies they bring miss fortune to my people said the chief. But I see in many seasons from now my people will be lacking and in need. The Indian chief had a vision days before that a white man would visit him. And the gods

234

had showed him his grandchildren in him. There was a spiritual bond between the two men. And the Indian chief gave sir Francis Drakes his oldest and most beautiful daughter to have as a wife.

Five years later an Indian woman stood on the bay of the island of the gods holding twins in her arms. Looking out upon the horizon she saw a man in a dory paddling towards shore it was sir Francis Drakes. This was now his new life as he was supposed to have died three months earlier from a bad dose of food poisoning. In panama and was buried at sea just of the coast of Porto cobelo with a chess of gold. Over looking two mountain pecks on the horizon as the legend was told. According to his secretary an officer of the law who swore on record and in his log book to the fact. Treasure hunters searched for that location and dove for that gold up to this day.

Decades went by sir Francis Drakes was an old man but happy in hiding his former life history. And his family back in England taken care of. The Tortugas remained still pretty much remote and Francis Drakes would keep up with the outside world. By way of hearing news from passing ships even though he and the Indians continued to live in seclusion. However spanards still practically dominated the Caribbean and Central America.

By 1670 a treaty surfaced warning outlaws and people who did not belong on the island of las Tortugas to leave. The two other smaller las Tortuga islands were already inhabited with civilized slaves, slave masters, fisher men and common people. With pirate-tisum dying they become more desperate and bold. During these times there were still uprising between them and the Indian and Britain.

Some of them died and some of us died said Ezekiel, Indians became slaves and new comers became Indians. The Caribbean was becoming more civilized like Europe, the orients, and the Americas. All types of people were living amongst each other it was somewhat a golden era for the Caribbean. Pirates came unto land at that time and changed their clothes and hid their attitudes. And settlers began to live in harmony under this dream. Sir Francis Drakes was long gone by now but not for gotten, the gold still in the Indians possession. They had even manage to pile some more on top of it the treasure was moved around from time to time, folk tale pirate story and so call myth brought people looking for it. The Indians still owned the islands of the gods and new comers kept away from there didn't go near it. With the Indian tribe expanding some of them settled on the east end of Grand Cayman.

In the 1900s the British government prohibited living on Volcano Island. It was some time during that period one night six canoes paddled by caymanaki Indians entered a small bite in frank sound. With some valuable merchandize and unloaded it on a piece of land belonging to sir Francis Drakes distant grandchildren. Where it remained under the ground somewhere until 2004. After a big hurricane and the rightful owners claimed it. An old Indian catacomb burst and reopened a water vein, a water spout shot out of the ground. Pushing gold and silver coins into the air some landing on the porch of the little cottage nearby. It took the man and woman two days working around the clock to remove the chess from the hole. And clean the site of any evidence they finally got it aboard a schooner that was tied up in the bite.

It's not sure where the two dead bodies came from the cemetery nearby or they had been casualties of Ivan's destruction. The Cayman island finger print data base was manipulated. And when the finger prints of the two dead people were ran through the system it showed they belonged to a one Ezekiel Howett and Aliza Blakes. Then indian and Aliza made their escape three days later they were in Miami harbor safe and sound. Ivan went before them swinging into the gulf of mexico more to the south east tip of the united states hitting texas. The couple on board the schooner were both American citizens and was welcomed home.

January 17th 2006 It was 2AM when indian,s cel phone rang a strange area code appeared. I I have a new assignment for you said a woman,s voice with a british actcent.

The end

CPSIA information can be obtained
at www.ICGtesting.com
Printed in the USA
JSHW031032020223
37129JS00010B/342

9 781956 876451